PRAISE FOR THE AUTHOR

"He has a gift for dialogue."

ew York Times

"Really special."

-Denver Post

"A crime fiction rara avis."

—*Los Angeles Times*

"One of the best writers in the mystery field today."

—*Publishers Weekly* (starred)

"Ebullient and irresistible."

—*Kirkus Reviews* (starred)

"Complex and genuinely suspenseful."

—*Boston Globe*

"Credible and deeply touching. Russell has us in the palm of his hands."

—*Chicago Tribune*

"He is enlightening as well as entertaining."

—*St. Petersburg Times*

"Enormously enjoyable."

—*Ellery Queen's Mystery Magazine*

"Russell is spectacular."

—*San Diego Union-Tribune*

"This work by Russell has it all."

—*Library Journal*

"Grade: A. Russell has written a story to satisfy even the most hard-core thrill junkie."

—*Rocky Mountain News*

THE HOMECOMING

OTHER TITLES BY ALAN RUSSELL

The Gideon and Sirius Novels

Burning Man

Guardians Of The Night

Lost Dog

Stand-Alone Novels

No Sign Of Murder

The Forest Prime Evil

The Hotel Detective

The Fat Innkeeper

Multiple Wounds

Shame

Exposure

Political Suicide

St. Nick

A Cold War

THE HOMECOMING

ALAN RUSSELL

THOMAS & MERCER

Published by Thomas & Mercer, Seattle

www.apub.com

ISBN-13: 9781477820087
ISBN-10: 1477820086

Cover design by Cyanotype Book Architects

Printed in the United States of America

To my three children: Luke, Hart, and Brooke.
Great kids all.

CHAPTER ONE

"Don't get too near the fire, Stella."

It wasn't the first warning Eleanor Pierce had given to her seven-year-old daughter, and it likely wouldn't be the last.

"All right," Stella said, but she didn't stop dancing around the fire pit. Stella was of an age where she appeared to be mostly hair and eyes. A pixie, her father called her. Her blue eyes seemed to dance as much as her thin limbs. She had Eleanor's hair, but blonder. Southern California always produces a bumper crop of blondes.

"For how many thousands of years do you think parents have been warning their kids about not getting too near the fire?" asked Duncan Pierce.

The other adults offered knowing nods. All four couples had children scattered around the beach. Six-month-old Kenny Hart was in the arms of his mother, Arlene; the three Stewart children were throwing a Frisbee; best friends Michael Pierce and Luke Hart were digging to China, while Ricky Wertz was more interested in hermit crabs; the other two Wertz children were playing surf tag, seeing which could stand his ground the longest without being tagged by a wave.

There were ten children in all, including Stella, who was dancing with the fire. Every so often one of the parents did a head count. They had the beach mostly to themselves. Their get-together had saved them from having to scramble for babysitters and struggle for restaurant reservations.

The weather was in the low sixties. All the adults had on sweaters or light coats. The children were wearing short sleeves and bathing suits, resisting any and all efforts by their parents to further clothe them.

"Valentine's Day," said Rusty Wertz. "It seems like only yesterday it was wine, women, and song. Now it's beer, the old lady, and whatever's on the radio."

His wife, Dina, smacked him on his backside. "After fifteen years of marriage," she said, "you'd think he would be better trained."

"The threat of being struck again notwithstanding," said Rusty, "did I neglect to say that I wouldn't change a thing?"

This time the couple kissed. The men made disparaging noises, while the women all went, "Ahhh."

Eleanor looked at her watch. It might be Valentine's Day, but it was still a school night. "Duncan, maybe we ought to call in the troops."

"Good luck," said Randall Hart. "Did you bring a lasso?"

"I have a secret weapon." Duncan cupped his hands around his mouth and shouted, "Who wants s'mores?"

The children had been remarkably deaf up until that time. Now they all came running. Each clamored to be first.

"I have enough skewers for everyone," said Duncan. "The skewers are not to be used as swords. Do not attempt to poke out the eye of your brother, sister, or friend."

His words didn't seem to be much of a deterrent, but he added, "And if I see any horseplay with these things, I'll confiscate them and you won't have any s'mores."

That was the deterrent.

Each of the children picked up a skewer and started impaling marshmallows. The fire ring was large enough for all of them to have a spot.

"Flame on!" yelled Michael Pierce, brandishing a ball of flame—his marshmallow—proudly in the air.

At eleven, Michael was three and a half years older than Stella. Usually she heeded his opinion, but here she felt his s'mores-making technique was all wrong.

"Your marshmallow is burned," she said.

"That's how it tastes best," said Michael.

"No, it doesn't."

"Yes, it does."

He took a big bite of his blackened marshmallow and said, "Perfect!"

Stella looked askance at her brother and went ahead with her own careful preparations. In the time it took her to make her one s'more, Michael ate three, announcing the immolation of each marshmallow with the shout, "Flame on!" Luke Hart copied Michael's marshmallow-flambé technique and echoed his cry, but even that didn't hurry Stella.

Eleanor watched the goings-on and hid her smile. Stella was secretly—or not so secretly—sweet on Luke, but she liked to do things her own way. "You can't hurry perfection, can you, sweetie?" she asked.

Stella looked up from the serious business of marshmallow cooking and gave her mother a fairy-bright smile.

"Pyromania and sweets," said Dave Stewart to his wife, waving his flaming marshmallow. "What an unbeatable combination."

When everyone was full of s'mores, the beach chairs were dragged closer to the warmth of the fire. The younger children found laps to settle into, while the older kids quieted down, mesmerized by the flames. The sun had sunk into the ocean an hour earlier, and there was little in the way of a moon, just a sliver of feeble light. It felt almost as if they were on an island.

"This reminds me of going to camp when I was a kid," Dina said, voice low and almost reverent. "We'd sit around the campfire telling ghost stories."

"I know lots of ghost stories," said Michael.

"You do not," said a skeptical Stella.

"He does so," said Luke, defending his best friend's honor.

Michael rose to Stella's challenge: "Once upon a time there was this ghost named Gory George."

According to Michael, Gory George was a ghost with horrible green eyes and a large, bloody mouth with dagger-sharp fangs. For unspecified reasons, Gory George hunted down a boy named Tom. None of the parents mentioned that George sounded more like a ghoul than a ghost. Whatever his supernatural genus, George was a persistent creature, pursuing Tom over hill and dale, across the sea, and then around the globe.

"And then George finally caught up with Tom," Michael said. "There was no place for Tom to go. Step-by-step, Gory George came forward. His breath was horrible, and he had this awful B.O. His mouth was open, and blood dripped everywhere. He lifted his arm in the air, and these razor-sharp claws popped out. Then he slashed downward . . ."

Michael's voice cracked. It wasn't puberty, but his transition from intensity to frivolity. "And George said, 'Tag, you're it.'"

Most of the adults expected the punch line, but applauded anyway. Then the children clamored for a *real* ghost story. Eyes turned expectantly to Candy Stewart. As an undergrad, Candy had majored in dramatic arts. Nowadays she used those thespian talents as a storyteller in classrooms and libraries.

Candy acknowledged the waiting eyes with a smile. She collected her thoughts by looking into the fire, and seemed to draw her inspiration from the flames.

"This isn't your usual ghost story," said Candy. "I heard this tale from my cousin Jean, who says every word of it is true and that she personally knows the family I am going to tell you about. Among my kin, Jean's word is considered gold."

Candy paused for a long moment. The dramatic effect worked. All her listeners leaned closer, taking a deep breath and holding it, waiting for her to begin.

"There was a terrible fire," Candy began. "Not a fire like the one warming us, but a raging inferno of hate. The fire sprang to life in a two-story home. One moment there was a spark, and the next the flames were everywhere.

"This was a fire with a hunger to burn. It swept through the house, its flames so hot it made the glass windows weep, melting the panes down to nothing. The fire turned the night sky into a Halloween nightmare, sending off colors of orange and red and black."

Candy's hands moved upward, painting the conflagration.

"Will and Sue Berry woke up with their room in flames. The fire was everywhere. There was no time for them to think. They had to react or die. With flames already reaching for them, they jumped out the window. But as soon as they were outside, they started screaming for their seven-year-old boy, Jason. They tried to reenter the house to rescue their son, but were driven back by the heat. It was as if the fire physically fought them off. They were frantic to save their boy, but helpless against the flames."

With her hands, Candy showed their struggles and how the flames forcefully rebuffed the couple.

"They knew Jason couldn't survive such an inferno, but still prayed that he somehow would. Their cries of pain merged with the sounds of approaching sirens, but the firefighters arrived too late. The flames had eaten everything.

"Neighbors tried to lead the couple off, but they wouldn't leave. They wept and wept. Some of their tears fell on hot embers, causing steam to rise and producing a hissing that sounded like small, evil laughter.

"Weeks, months, and then years passed. Will and Sue tried to put their lives back together. They rebuilt their house, but it was a silent dwelling, empty of life. Jason's death haunted them. How could they have escaped the fire while leaving their son to perish? The knowledge that they surely would have died attempting a rescue was no consolation. Nothing could make them feel better, nothing at all.

"The fire had not only taken their son; it had taken most of the mementos of his existence. Almost all tangible reminders of Jason were gone, including their favorite pictures that had been displayed throughout their home.

"'A family picture of us standing with Jason,' Sue lamented. 'Why couldn't we have been left with at least that?'

"Will held her in his arms and they wept together, but it didn't ease their relentless pain. With so few earthly reminders of Jason, it was almost as if he had never existed.

"Their loss drove the couple apart. They decided to split up. And that's when Jason came back to them, but not as flesh and blood. A spectral figure materialized in their bedroom.

"'I can't stay,' he told them.

"Sue and Will both started weeping. They tried to hug their son, one from each side, and somehow ended up in each other's arms.

"'Hurry!' Jason said. 'Take a picture of all of us!'

"Will grabbed his phone and set the camera's timer. Then he and Sue huddled around the ghostly figure that was their son. The phone camera flashed, and the shot was taken.

"'Now you have your picture, Mother,' said Jason, 'even though it wasn't necessary. I've always been in your heart. You needed to look no further than there.'

"Their boy, looking radiant and beautiful, smiled at his parents one last time. And then he told them that he would always love them, and said good-bye.

"For a long time Will and Sue held off looking at the picture, telling each other that Jason's visitation was all they needed. To each other they repeated, 'Love isn't something you need to capture in a picture. It just is.' And they believed that. But the truth is, they were afraid to look. They wondered if Jason's return was something they had deluded themselves into imagining.

"Finally, they decided they had to look. Will went and got his phone. 'The shot might not have turned out,' he warned. 'You know how tricky the timer function is. And maybe it didn't autofocus.'

"'The room was *dark*,' agreed Sue, 'maybe too dark to get the picture.'

"With trembling fingers, they looked at the photo. Standing between them was a pale but smiling Jason. And they also saw the time stamp with the picture, a date three years after Jason's death."

In the silence that followed Candy's ghost story, a piece of firewood suddenly crackled loudly, sending sparks up. And people. Both children and adults jumped, and then laughed uneasily at themselves.

"That's a rather intense story, Candy," said Rusty. "And I have the underwear to prove it."

Comic relief prevailed. The adults laughed long and hard, overdoing it a bit.

"It reminded me of one of the *real* Grimm's Fairy Tales," said Duncan. "Before they became childproof, people were dying right and left in all sorts of horrible ways."

"Well, just think of the story of 'Hansel and Gretel,'" said Arlene Hart. She was a social worker and viewed the world through that vocational lens. "In a very few pages we read about child abandonment, the occult, cannibalism, and murder."

"And it's not like children's rhymes are innocent," said Eleanor. "'Ring Around the Rosie' is a rhyme about the bubonic plague and everyone dying."

"Children's songs aren't any better," said Dina. "Everyone thinks 'Alouette' is this little French song that children sing, but what it's about is the desire to catch a songbird, pluck its feathers, dismember it bit by bit, and eat it."

"Alouette, gentille alouette, alouette, je te plumerai," sang Rusty.

The children smiled at hearing a familiar song.

"Rusty," warned Dina.

Her "shut up" was implicit, so he replied, "Yes, dear."

"When I was a kid," said Duncan, "I remember being scared to death of those ghosts in *A Christmas Carol.* Marley and his chains had me hiding my head behind a pillow. And the ghost of Christmas Future—forget it. I always had to leave the room."

"A not-so-subtle ghost of the present offers similarly scary news," said Eleanor. "It's a school night, and the kids need their sleep."

All the mothers voiced seconds of that motion. Even the children didn't seem inclined to argue. Most of them looked sleepy, with the exception of Stella. Her attention was on the embers floating up into the sky.

In his best Tiny Tim voice, Duncan said, "Well, then, Happy Valentine's Day, all, and God bless us every one."

CHAPTER TWO

A so-called simple family trip to the beach, Duncan often complained, was like a major military campaign. But now their car was packed, and they were finally on their way home. Luckily home wasn't far away, especially since Michael had decided to sing "One Hundred Bottles of Beer on the Wall."

Stella made herself heard over her brother's singing. "Do you think we could see that picture of Jason?" she asked.

It took a moment for Eleanor to figure out what Stella was asking. "It was only a story, sweetie," she said.

"But Aunt Candy said her cousin told her the story and that she knew the family."

One-upping a younger sister was even better than singing an obnoxious song. Michael stopped singing and said, "She probably doesn't even have a cousin Jean."

"Your aunt Candy is a storyteller," said Eleanor. "Sometimes that gives her what's called literary license."

"Jason was seven, like me."

"Jason was goofy, like you," said Michael.

"That's enough, Michael," said Duncan.

Eleanor turned to her husband. "I really didn't think that was an appropriate story, did you?"

Duncan shrugged. "It seemed okay to me."

"There were a lot of young, impressionable ears there."

"Well, like everyone was saying, some of the best kids' stories aren't all fun and games."

"Would you miss me as much as Jason's parents missed him?" asked Stella.

"See?" Eleanor said to Duncan before turning to their daughter. "We would miss you more than anything in the world."

"I wouldn't miss you," said Michael.

"Michael," warned his father.

"We really should have a fire safety plan for our house," said Eleanor, "complete with drills."

"I should probably get some extinguishers," said Duncan.

"Did Jason go to heaven?" asked Stella.

"Jason's not real," said Michael.

"Aunt Candy said it was a true story."

"In that case, my story was true, too," said Michael. He reached over and tapped Stella's head. "Tag, you're it."

Stella hit him in return.

In the same tone and at the same time, both adults said, "Keep your hands to yourselves."

Eleanor stared down each child, making sure they obeyed.

"Mom?" asked Stella. "Do you think Jason's happy now?"

Eleanor smiled at her daughter. It wouldn't surprise her if Stella ended up being a doctor or a vet. She always wanted to tend to the hurt or needy. If Stella had her way, they would have adopted every dog or cat in San Diego County looking for a home.

"Honey, I don't think Jason really exists. He's like Winnie the Pooh or Mr. Toad."

"Or Casper," Stella offered.

"That's right."

"Because Casper's a ghost."

"There are no such things as ghosts," Michael said.

Stella wasn't about to concede. "Then what about Jason?"

◆ ◆ ◆

The Pierces' Del Mar home was a little more than a mile from the beach. They never would have been able to afford the property if Duncan's parents hadn't previously owned it. There was nothing fancy about it save for its proximity to the Pacific. Still, it was a comfortable home in an upscale neighborhood.

"Take off your shoes," Eleanor told her children. "And brush off your arms and legs. This time let's try not to bring the entire beach into the house."

Under her watchful eyes, both children did as she asked. "Okay, now go brush your teeth. I'm sure they're full of chocolate and marshmallows."

"I had seven s'mores," said Michael. "Flame on!"

"It's too late for a shower," Eleanor said. "But tomorrow morning I want each of you to take one."

While Duncan unpacked the car, Eleanor put the children to bed. Michael didn't let her fuss with him too much, reluctantly presenting a cheek for her to kiss. He was getting to an age where he liked to think he was grown up. But Stella enjoyed letting Eleanor sit on the bed and brush her hair. When she finished, she leaned down and kissed Stella's forehead.

"Do you want me to close your curtains?" she asked.

Stella shook her head. She liked to fall asleep looking out her window at the night sky. When she started singing one of her favorite rhymes, Eleanor joined in.

> "Twinkle, twinkle, little star,
> How I wonder what you are!
> Up above the world so high,
> Like a diamond in the sky."

One verse wasn't enough for Stella. The last lines of the poem seemed to be her favorite, even though Eleanor thought the words were a bit strange. Still, she sang with her daughter:

> "As your bright and tiny spark,
> Lights the traveler in the dark,
> Though I know not what you are,
> Twinkle, twinkle, little star."

Duncan entered the room just in time to join them in singing "Twinkle, Twinkle, Little Star." Then he leaned over and kissed his daughter.

"Daddy!" said Stella. "Are you going to read to me?"

Reading a story was the nightly treat for both of them, but that was not about to sway Eleanor, who was already shaking her head.

"Not tonight," she said. "It's too late."

"Just a few pages," said Stella.

"Your mom's right," said Duncan. "Tomorrow night I'll read twice as long. If I remember correctly, Harriet and Sport were in the middle of their spying."

Stella smiled, and her father kissed her on the forehead. "See you later, Alligator," he said.

"In a while, Crocodile."

Her parents closed the door as they left. Even though it was late, Stella didn't feel sleepy. She listened to the murmur of their voices outside the door.

The stars were bright. They looked so close she almost felt like reaching out to them. She saw something else in the night sky, too. It was lit up, but it didn't look exactly like a star. Stella climbed out of bed to take a closer look.

◆ ◆ ◆

Michael surreptitiously slipped in one earbud, then pressed that ear to the pillow. The week before, his mother had caught him listening to music late and had threatened to confiscate his phone. From under the covers he thumbed through his playlist, and then settled on a Coldplay song.

This time, Michael thought, he wasn't going to make the mistake of alerting his mother through his singing. Still, he couldn't help humming along to "Hymn for the Weekend."

◆ ◆ ◆

"Hey," Duncan said, reaching across their bed and placing his arm around Eleanor's waist.

"As I tell my schoolchildren, hay is for horses."

"Hey, Valentine."

She felt the heat of his unsaid communication, and drew close to him.

CHAPTER THREE

At a quarter after six, Eleanor yelled for the kids to get up and washed. A few minutes later she heard the shower running.

She went downstairs, made the children's lunches, and put out cereal and toast. Michael was the first one downstairs. Usually he was the last.

"Where's your sister?" she asked.

Between mouthfuls of toast, he said, "Don't know."

Eleanor yelled, "Hurry up, Stella."

There was no response.

"Stella?"

She's probably in the bathroom, thought Eleanor, but she went up the stairs to see for herself. She had a long-term subbing job, but luckily the elementary school was close to home. Still, she needed to be on her way, and this time her voice meant business: "Stella?"

No answer again.

The shower wasn't running. Could she still be sleeping? Eleanor opened the door to her room. Stella wasn't in bed.

The room was still. Eleanor tried to ignore the sensation that came over her. Stella's bed didn't even look slept in. The covers weren't tossed all around, as they usually were.

She shouted toward the room next door: "Duncan? Is Stella with you?"

From their room Eleanor heard him call, "No."

Maybe she was out walking the dog. Sometimes when Stella was the first up, she did that. Eleanor hurried down the stairs and saw Copper sleeping on the sofa, where he knew he shouldn't be. Eleanor didn't even pause to discipline him.

"Stella!"

This time she couldn't keep the alarm out of her voice. Michael stopped eating; his cereal spoon was suspended in air.

"Michael, help me find your sister. Check the garage, and if she's not there, go outside and look around for her."

Both of them started calling. Their cries brought a half-shaved Duncan down the stairs. Their eyes met, and he could see how scared Eleanor looked.

Duncan said, "She's probably walking the dog."

Eleanor shook her head. "Copper is in the family room."

"Did you check the backyard?"

"Not yet."

"You do the once-over upstairs, and I'll look out back."

She ran upstairs again and checked everywhere. Duncan was waiting for her downstairs. Both shook their heads.

"It's possible," said Eleanor, "that she got up early this morning and went over to Patty's or Jessica's."

Both girls lived on their block. Stella had never done such a thing before, but parenting brought daily surprises.

The front door opened, and Eleanor drew in a quick breath of hope, but Michael entered without his sister. "I didn't see her," he said.

"You call Patty and Jessica," Duncan said to Eleanor. "I'll drive over to the park and check the playground."

"What do you want me to do?" asked Michael.

For a moment Eleanor considered asking him to look on one of the side streets, but she reconsidered. "Stay close to me."

She grabbed her cell phone and made calls. Neither of Stella's friends nor their parents had seen her. It took all of Eleanor's restraint not to panic. Her throat felt as if a noose had been tightened around it.

"Did you see Stella this morning, Michael?" she asked. Her voice was high pitched; it didn't even sound like her.

"No."

"Let's go to the neighbors'," she said. "You know how Stella likes to visit with people on the block."

They knocked on Meg Downing's door first. Eleanor rapped hard. "Come on, come on," she said.

But Mrs. Downing was in her late seventies, and not about to be rushed. She was a widow, and cautious, pushing back the curtains to see who was standing there.

"It's Eleanor Pierce, Meg. Is Stella with you?"

The door opened. Mrs. Downing was holding her robe to her throat. "Stella? Why, no."

"Have you seen her this morning?"

"No . . ."

Mrs. Downing didn't get the chance to say anything else. Eleanor grabbed Michael's hand and hurried off without so much as an apology for intruding.

They went to the Howells', their neighbors on the other side. Stella was a social girl, always greeting everyone she saw. Duncan had dubbed her "the town crier." Someone might have invited her in for cocoa.

But the Howells hadn't seen Stella. And neither had the Wongs, the Baumgartners, the Crandalls, or the Harts. With each failure, Eleanor grew more panicked. She ran from door to door, screaming out Stella's name. People came out of their houses to see what the commotion was about.

A familiar car pulled up to the curb, but Eleanor saw that her husband was alone.

"Oh, God," she said. "No one's seen her. No one."

"I'll call the police," Duncan said.

CHAPTER FOUR

When he saw the name on his phone's screen, Detective Orson Cheever's stomach started doing flip-flops. Homicide Team IV was third up in the rotation. Lieutenant Martin Ramirez's early-morning phone call could mean only one thing.

"We got a critical missing on a little girl," said Ramirez.

"Critical missing" was cop talk for a situation requiring immediate attention. Cheever hated the missing-kid calls more than anything. He dressed while Ramirez talked. Other cops would have grabbed a notepad, but not Cheever. On the force his memory was legendary. If his recall wasn't eidetic, it was close to it.

Using his shoulder to prop the phone next to his ear, Cheever put on khaki slacks, an oxford shirt, and a blue blazer. It was likely he'd be wearing the same clothes for the next twenty-four hours or more.

Ramirez and Cheever had been part of the same police-academy class more than twenty years before. As Ramirez had advanced through the ranks, Cheever had been content to remain a detective working homicide, refusing all promotions. That hadn't stopped Ramirez from appointing Cheever and Homicide Team IV as the department's RAMP (Retrieval of Abducted and Missing Persons) team. In his day Ramirez had been a pretty good cop, but he'd never been even half as good as Cheever. No one was.

The more Ramirez talked, the less Cheever liked the sound of the case. Seven-year-old Stella Pierce had gone missing sometime during the night. Cheever thought of his daughter, Diane. She had been a few months shy of six when she'd died of leukemia. Missing or hurting little kids got to him like nothing else.

"I already called the Falcon," said Ramirez. The "Falcon" was Sergeant Dean Falconi, who headed up Homicide Team IV. "He put out the call to the rest of the team. I told him I'd be conferring with you."

The Falcon would be the public face of the investigation, handling the logistics and managing his investigators. Cheever would be the lead detective.

"I'll call you when I know more," said Cheever.

◆ ◆ ◆

Judging from the flashing **Missing Child** signage Cheever saw as he drove south on Interstate 5, the early-warning system was already operational, with the public being asked to stay on the lookout for Stella Pierce. An alarm had been sent to Cheever's cell phone, as well as about half a million others, offering up a description of the little girl. There was also a media blitz under way, with messages going out over the airwaves. The hope was that in the face of such a concerted public onslaught, the kidnapper would release the child unharmed. The Amber Alert meant that the Tijuana border crossing into Mexico had been notified, as well as the Border Patrol checkpoints along Interstates 5 and 8.

The morning commute was stop-and-go, but Cheever still managed to drive from Leucadia to Del Mar in less than fifteen minutes. As he neared the Pierce home, he became aware of a helicopter flying overhead. If the kid didn't turn up soon, the Falcon would put everything in the sky he could.

The street where the Pierces lived was already closed to traffic. The San Diego Police Department was in the process of setting up checkpoints in the surrounding blocks. No one was going to get in or out of the area without being questioned.

A familiar face flagged Cheever down, and he lowered his window to talk to Cory Lincoln, the youngest detective on Homicide Team IV. Everyone on the team called Lincoln "the Kid."

"The Falcon has me covering this corner until a uniform relieves me," he said. "That'll teach me to be first to the scene."

"Mother Maria and the Walrus aren't here yet?"

"Mother Maria" was the nickname for Jacoba Diaz; "the Walrus" was Will Hayes. They were the other two members of the team.

The Kid shook his head.

"As soon as you're relieved, I want you to go door-to-door and start conducting searches of every home on the street. You'll need to look at every space; and that means car trunks, abandoned chests, ditches, gardening sheds, crawl spaces, and refrigerators. Check all swimming pools as well."

"I looked at a map of the area," said the Kid. "There are a lot of canyons around here. Who's working those?"

"The neighborhood abuts the Torrey Pines Reserve Extension. I'll be calling the park rangers and asking for their help searching through the reserve."

"They're going to be stretched thin," he said.

"I've got the marines coming," said Cheever.

The Kid wasn't sure if Cheever was kidding or not. As it turned out, he wasn't. Not even an hour later, a platoon of marines, trained in search and rescue, arrived from Camp Pendleton in Oceanside and joined the search.

CHAPTER FIVE

They used the Falcon's Yukon as the command post. Inside the vehicle, away from prying ears, Cheever conferred with his sergeant. Falconi sat in the driver's seat. He was a big man and filled much of the cabin's space.

The search warrant had just come through—a precautionary move in case a family member was involved in the child's disappearance.

"Prior to our getting the warrant," said Falconi, "the family asked me to search the house. I did a quick run-through, but didn't see anything."

"Where are the parents now?" asked Cheever.

"I asked them to stay next door while their house was being processed. I figured you'd rather talk to them there than at the station."

The two men worked out the early logistics of the investigation, deciding who from the team would be case agent, who would have charge over the neighborhood search, and who would do record checking. There was a series of protocols to be followed, and the two cops made sure all their bases were covered. If the child wasn't found in the next two hours, an additional series of protocols would demand their attention.

The windows of the Yukon were fogged up by the time the men finished talking. As Cheever moved to leave the car, the Falcon said, "It wasn't the parents."

Cheever turned his head and looked at Falconi. "No?"

"You'll see," said the sergeant. "This is the kind of family Norman Rockwell would have painted. They're throwback. They could have stepped out of one of those black-and-white sitcoms from the fifties."

"Then this is a rude wake-up call from the twenty-first century."

◆ ◆ ◆

Cheever conducted a thorough, but speedy, search of the Pierce house. Judging by the family pictures on display, the Falcon's Rockwell remark seemed spot-on. The Pierces were a handsome nuclear family, with two parents and two kids and an obligatory dog. The towheaded daughter—the missing Stella—had a big smile for a little girl. Once upon a time Cheever had had pictures of Diane similarly displayed.

When he finished with the house, forensics began processing the scene. As he made his way next door, he wiped his hands on his pants and took a few deep breaths. The Pierce family would be crazy with worry. Until they found out what happened to their daughter, he would be their support system and their point man.

Cheever only got one knock in before the door opened. An older woman greeted him. Standing behind her were three anxious faces: ones Cheever recognized from the pictures he'd seen, though in those poses they'd been smiling and relaxed.

"I'm Detective Cheever," he announced. "I'm the lead detective on this case."

Even before Cheever was shown into the house, Eleanor Pierce asked about her daughter: "Have you found Stella?"

"No," said Cheever.

Everyone seemed to deflate in front of his eyes.

◆ ◆ ◆

In the privacy of Mrs. Downing's den, Cheever began the family interviews, starting with Duncan Pierce. Behind closed doors the man's granite veneer broke; he no longer had to be strong for his family. As Duncan choked up and his tears fell, Cheever surreptitiously observed him. He would have bet the farm he wasn't seeing alligator tears.

"Take some breaths," Cheever advised. "You okay to answer a few questions?"

Duncan nodded, and Cheever said, "Last night did you check and see if the house was locked up?"

"I think it was," said Duncan, even though his face showed his uncertainty. "I remember making sure the front and back doors were locked, but I can't swear I checked all the windows."

"If you had to guess whether you did or didn't check them, what would you say?"

"I'd say that I did. Usually I just do it on autopilot."

Cheever nodded. He hadn't seen any sign of forced entry, but the locks could have easily been picked.

"We don't have much in the way of valuables," said Duncan. "And with all three bedrooms on the second floor, I never thought I had to worry about an intruder."

"Do you remember your dog barking last night?"

Cheever had encountered the enthusiastic young golden retriever in the Pierces' backyard.

Duncan shook his head. "Copper isn't much of a watchdog. The family joke is that a burglar would be in more danger of being licked than being bitten. We thought that was a good thing, especially with all of Michael's and Stella's friends coming and going."

"Was the dog inside the house last night?"

Duncan nodded.

Cheever continued with his series of questions. He would be asking most of the same questions of all the family members. The detective was looking for any deviation in what they had to say. At the same time he was already convinced he was spinning his wheels.

Still, experience had taught him to listen carefully when an interview was concluding. That's when people usually offered up what was really on their minds.

"I didn't read to Stella last night," said Duncan. "I usually read to her." Tearing up, he added, "I wish I had."

◆ ◆ ◆

Unlike her husband, Eleanor Pierce didn't try and hide how distraught she was. Seeing her pain reminded Cheever of how his ex-wife, Karen, had looked while trying to cope with the illness of their daughter. Her desperation had bordered on madness. That's what happens when you're overwhelmed by worry and grief. In retrospect, Karen had been more honest about her feelings than he had. And after Diane's death, his emotional distance had done in their marriage.

Cheever wished he could tell Eleanor Pierce that everything would be all right, but he was afraid she would read the lie in his face. He knew only too well how things didn't always turn out all right. It was his job to be steady and reassuring. The family needed a shoulder to lean on, and he could be that.

"After going to bed," he asked, "do you remember hearing anything unusual during the night?"

In any investigation you look for lies or inconsistencies. So far no red flags had turned up. Eleanor shook her head, but then she averted her eyes.

"Last night Duncan closed our door to the hallway. It's usually open. If there were noises, I doubt we would have been able to hear them."

"Why did he close the door?"

She hesitated a moment. "We were intimate." With trembling lips she added, "It was Valentine's Day," as if she felt the need to justify their need for privacy.

"What time did you fall asleep?" Cheever asked.

"It was about ten thirty. Right after—after—we both dropped off. Usually I make a point of reopening our door. But I fell asleep."

There was no forgiveness in her admission. Eleanor Pierce was blaming herself.

"We don't know what happened to your daughter," said Cheever. "But nothing you've said puts you at fault."

She shook her head. "I should have reopened the door."

As her tears fell, Cheever traveled back through time and saw Karen's anguished face.

"I never heard anything," Eleanor said.

◆ ◆ ◆

Michael Pierce's room was on the other side of Stella's. Like his parents, he hadn't heard anything; like his parents, he also had a tearful admission.

"Last night I was listening to music." Speaking so softly so as to barely be heard, he added, "I'm not supposed to do that."

"How late were you up?" Cheever asked.

The eleven-year-old boy shook his head. "I'm not sure. I guess it was around ten. I fell asleep with headphones on."

"So you didn't hear anything other than your music?"

Michael nodded, then roughly wiped away tears.

"I used to listen to music when I was your age," Cheever said. "My parents didn't allow it either, so I always had to sneak my radio into bed."

"I listen to music on my cell phone," Michael said.

Cheever knew better than to ask the boy his favorite bands or music. He was about twenty years behind the times, and he knew it.

Instead, he said, "I understand your family was at the beach last night."

Michael nodded.

"What was your sister doing most of the time?"

"She was playing with all the kids."

"Did anything unusual happen?"

The question made the boy think, but finally he shook his head. "No."

"Did you notice Stella talking to any strangers?"

Michael offered another shake of his head.

No stranger danger, thought Cheever. No anything.

CHAPTER SIX

Normally, Luke Hart would have been ecstatic about getting a day off from school, but there was nothing good about getting this day off. His mother had kept him home after learning that Stella had disappeared. In the three years since Luke had moved into the neighborhood, he and Michael Pierce had become inseparable. Michael was a year and a half older and acted like the older brother he didn't have. Because the two boys were always together, Luke saw a lot of Michael's sister, Stella.

She wasn't a bad kid, really, except she always wanted to hang out with them. Sometimes it was fun to have her around, though. She was almost as fast as the boys on a bicycle, and could skate better than either of them. And unlike other kids, Stella never whined or cried much. She didn't snitch either. There were a few times when Luke and Michael would have gotten into some pretty hot water if Stella had squealed, but she never did. Stella was always bringing him things, too, like cookies or juice boxes. During the summer, she'd operated a lemonade stand and given him free glasses. Michael teased her, saying she had a crush on Luke. Instead of denying it, Stella had said Michael liked a girl named Tracy, which put him on the defensive. For a youngster, Stella was pretty smart.

Michael was right about her liking him, though. Just yesterday, his mom had brought him a big manila envelope that had been left on their porch with his name on it. Inside the envelope was a handmade valentine. Lots of effort had gone into its making. Rose petals and beads had been formed into a huge red heart. In big, if uncertain, letters, a secret admirer had written, I LOVE YOU LUKE HART.

Stella hadn't signed it, but he knew her block printing. And there was another giveaway: Stella always called him by his full name. To everyone else, he was just Luke. But to Stella he was Lukehart, like it was one word. Michael had once said, "Why do you call him Luke Hart? Why don't you just call him Luke? That would be like him calling you Stella Pierce instead of Stella." With the kind of dignity you wouldn't expect from someone her age, Stella had replied, "His name is Luke Hart, isn't it?"

For a little kid, Stella was something.

He hadn't told Michael, or anyone, about the valentine. Usually he tossed out things like that, but Luke had deposited it in his desk drawer. He had even secretly pulled it out a few times to admire it. Everything had been cut out and pasted very carefully. There were even ornate designs along the borders.

Labor of love, thought Luke. It was an expression he heard his mom use sometimes. Now he understood what she meant. It must have taken Stella days to make the valentine. She would have done it secretly, knowing Michael would tease her unmercifully if he found out what she was doing.

Now that Stella was missing, the valentine made Luke feel funny. It sort of hurt thinking about it. He had considered showing it to his parents or the police, but hadn't felt quite right about violating Stella's secret.

Luke wondered where she was. The whole world seemed to be wondering the same thing. He and Michael had spent most of the day leading the police to all their secret spots, places to which Stella had tagged along with them. The police spent a lot of time at the flood channel, pulling out big flashlights and going real far into the storm drain. At the Torrey Pines Reserve, the police picked up some candy wrappers from their "cave," which was really nothing more than a recessed rock overhang, but they didn't seem to think that Stella had left the wrappers there. The boys even showed the police the spot where they played "alligator" near the railroad tracks. That's what they called it, because not much more than their eyes showed aboveground as they waited for a train to come along. They put pennies on the tracks and hunkered down near the rails, close enough so that when the train raced by, the ground beneath them shook and they could feel its heat. The hot air always whipped at them, and their senses were overwhelmed by the noise and the clacking of the rails. From experience, they knew that pennies flattened best. Dimes worked, and so did quarters, but not nickels. For whatever reason, the train wheels picked up nickels and carried them along.

Stella was always fascinated by the way in which nickels hitchhiked a ride. She thought there must be something special about them. When they went to the tracks, she always brought along a nickel. Michael thought what she did was stupid. Instead of getting a trophy, she just lost a nickel, but Stella didn't see it that way. For her, the nickel went on a trip. She always wondered how far it traveled.

One moment it was there, and the next it disappeared.

Sort of like Stella.

When Luke and Michael ran out of places to show to the police, they returned to a neighborhood very different from one they had ever known. It was almost like an invasion was going on. There was activity everywhere. Uniformed marines jogged up and down the streets. Lifeguards had moved inland from the surf and were using ATVs, binoculars, and walkie-talkies to help in the search. The Border Patrol wasn't looking for undocumented workers, but a little girl. Helicopters and planes flew low over the houses, and a bloodhound team kept sniffing its way around the area.

Luke wanted to join in the search, like a lot of his neighbors were doing, but his mom wouldn't let him go out without his father. His dad planned on coming home early, though. Then he and Michael and his father would go out and find Stella, and he'd thank her for the valentine. He wouldn't care what anyone else thought.

In the meantime, his mom seemed intent on hugging him as much as she could.

CHAPTER SEVEN

Cheever paused for a moment from his call making to observe the setting sun. The day might be over, but he and his team would continue plodding even if the investigation seemed to be going nowhere. There were officers reviewing CCTV footage from the area. They were hoping to pick up *something*—be it a vehicle, or an individual, or even a glimpse of Stella slipping out of her house. So far they had nothing.

Incoming and outgoing calls on the Pierces' house phone and on their cell phones were being monitored, but there had been no ransom calls, and nothing to indicate Stella had been kidnapped.

From inside Duncan's home office, Cheever called another one of Stella's classmates. He identified himself to the mother, but didn't need to say much. Everyone knew about Stella. The woman got her daughter on the line.

"Hi," he said, "this is Detective Cheever."

◆ ◆ ◆

Eleanor Pierce froze in the hallway. Cheever had asked the family to think back on anything out of the ordinary that might have happened of late, and she'd remembered Candy Stewart's ghost story. She had come to tell him about it but heard him talking on the phone. Judging from the detective's high-pitched and overly friendly tone, she suspected he was talking to a child.

"And that's the last time you saw Stella, Caitlin?"

Caitlin Richey, thought Eleanor; she was Stella's classmate.

"And has she seemed sad lately? Has she said anything about being unhappy?"

Eleanor felt the heat rise in her cheeks. It was silly for her to be offended by the detective's questions, but she was. Wasn't she a good mother? But today she felt so—negligent. She knew it was easy to second-guess everything that she had done the night before, because she was doing a good enough job of that herself. All day she had been questioned, and it seemed to her that everyone was judging her to be an unfit mother. If she had been more conscientious, the questioning looks seemed to say, nothing like this would have befallen her daughter.

"Have you noticed anyone approaching Stella recently, someone besides a member of her family? Maybe an adult you don't know? I want you to think about that . . ."

Eleanor stopped listening. The detective had asked her the same kinds of questions, though not in the sugarcoated voice he was using now. She listened while he finished his conversation with Caitlin.

Cheever must have been alerted by her shadow. When he stepped out into the open, Eleanor didn't even try and pretend that she hadn't been eavesdropping. His eyes took a read of hers; she hoped she didn't look as lost as she felt.

"I came over to tell you a ghost story I heard at last night's beach gathering," she said, "but while I was standing here, I decided it's probably nothing."

"Tell me about it," said Cheever.

Eleanor told him the story of Jason's death in the fire, and his brief return, and how the boy had posed for his final picture.

"The story seemed to make an impression upon Stella," she said. "She talked about it all the way home. Stella even asked us whether we would miss her if she died, and I told her we would miss her more than anything in the world."

Silently, tears dropped down her face.

"The ghost story is likely only a coincidence," Cheever said, his words as soft as the hand he put on her shoulder.

Of course it was, thought Eleanor.

"There's nothing more difficult than waiting," he said. "I know. I lost my only child, a little girl, to leukemia. As awful as the disease was, what made it worse was that purgatory of waiting. You want to go punch brick walls, but instead you're forced to sit and wait. You want to scream, but you're forced to whisper."

Eleanor decided not to correct him. She wasn't in purgatory; she was in hell.

"Did you and Mary Beth finish up Stella's Facebook page?" he asked.

Eleanor nodded. Mary Beth Carey was an SDPD criminalist who was especially good with computers. "It's up and running."

"I'd like to see it," he said.

The detective followed Eleanor to the living room, where she brought up the Facebook page. Beneath a picture of Stella were the words HELP US FIND STELLA! There was a physical description of Stella and contact information, along with pictures of her.

"Until today I never realized how many children go missing in California," said Eleanor. "Mary Beth told me there are almost a hundred thousand of them every year."

She wasn't even sure she'd voiced her thoughts aloud until the detective answered.

"It's a quiet epidemic," said Cheever, "probably because the vast majority of the kids who go missing are runaways."

She nodded. Mary Beth had said the same thing. Eleanor felt the need to make one thing clear, though: "My daughter did not run away."

"I know that," said Cheever.

Her cell phone began ringing, causing her hands to shake. She was scared of what she might hear. In the next room the techs were suddenly on alert, ready to listen in on the call if necessary. Their anticipation was short-lived. Arlene Hart was on the line.

"I know you told me earlier that you didn't need anything but my prayers," said Arlene, "but I'm bringing over a pot roast. I also have a coffee cake for the morning."

"You don't . . ."

"I do. I'll be over in five minutes."

Tears welled up in Eleanor's eyes. It was awful feeling so helpless.

"There's a pot roast on the way," she said. "It's likely to go to waste unless you and your team eat it."

"What about your family?"

"I might be able to get Michael and Duncan to take a plate," she said, but she didn't sound hopeful.

◆ ◆ ◆

As six o'clock rolled around, the activity level inside and outside the Pierce home became noticeably less frenetic. The detectives from Homicide Team IV were still working the case, but there were fewer uniforms. A few search-and-rescue teams were still looking for Stella, but most had conceded to the darkness. Still, dozens of officers were going door-to-door talking with residents they had been unable to interview earlier in the day. Every stone was being turned over.

Cheever found Eleanor and Duncan Pierce in the living room. Both looked up when he walked in, but they could tell by the expression on his face that he didn't have any news for them.

"I have some photos I'd like the two of you to look at."

He registered their nods of agreement and sat down facing them. Neither Eleanor nor Duncan inquired as to what kind of photos they'd be seeing, and Cheever didn't tell them. Earlier in the day he had asked for the booking photos of all convicted sex offenders in the area. He had also asked for a wide array of noncriminal pictures—men and women who had never been arrested.

As Cheever arranged his photos, he heard one of the search parties calling out Stella's name. It was a desperate game of Marco Polo, thought Cheever, with no Polo.

Light penetrated the closed curtains into the darkening living room. A news team was preparing to do a live spot from the Pierce front yard. Duncan had already appeared in a number of interviews. In a few of the broadcasts, Eleanor had stood by his side, but had not trusted herself to speak.

Cheever watched as Eleanor raised her head to a woman's voice crying: "Stella!" But it proved to be just another false alarm. The woman kept calling Stella's name, and Eleanor kept trying not to flinch.

"Most of the pictures you are about to see are not of criminals," Cheever said. "They're just everyday people. But there are also pictures of individuals booked for crimes."

Cheever didn't tell them the booking photos were of registered sex offenders living nearby. Law-abiding citizens were always surprised by the numbers.

"I think the best way to do this is for me to hold up a picture and allow you enough time to study it. When you're finished, I want you to look away. Think about that face you saw. Does it set off any memory alarms? Maybe you'll feel some inkling of recognition. Don't worry about a name or a context. Given any possible glimmer of recognition, I want you to flag that photo for me. Are you ready to give it a go?"

They both nodded. Cheever showed them the first picture. Eleanor and Duncan studied it and then looked away. The face didn't look familiar to either one of them.

They went to the next shot, and the next. Eleanor was glad she didn't know who was guilty and who wasn't. Was this man a monster? Did he target innocent children?

The Pierces kept looking at faces. Dozens of pictures, but no face caused bells to ring.

The detective lifted up a new photo. Even though it was just a picture, Eleanor could feel the man's eyes bore into her. They were cold and unforgiving, and what was worse, they were somehow familiar. Neither of the Pierces turned their heads. Both kept staring at the picture. It was Duncan who found his voice first.

"I think I've seen him before," he said, and then his voice grew louder. "Yes, I've definitely seen him before."

CHAPTER EIGHT

"I know that guy from somewhere."

Duncan was concentrating so hard his face was set in a grimace, and he clenched and unclenched his hands. He cleared his throat twice, then let out some pent-up air. "Maybe he's just a look-alike."

"No," said Eleanor. "I've seen him, too."

They reached for each other's hands.

Their suspect wasn't smiling, but still managed to exude smugness. He had long, slicked-back, dark-brown hair, and his pupils appeared as black pinpoints. There was something in his appearance that made him look like a snake that had just eaten.

"Where do we know him from?" asked Duncan.

Eleanor bit her lip and shook her head.

"Just relax," said Cheever. "It will come to you in time, especially if you're not pressing."

"Is he a criminal?" asked Duncan.

"I think it's better to not say," said Cheever.

"Maybe he just looks like a lawyer I know," said Duncan.

Eleanor was lost in the picture. She had this feeling of being caught in a spiderweb and not being able to break free. The man's eyes had her tangled up. She remembered those eyes.

"Pizza delivery," she said.

The man had been at their house at least twice during the past month. The last time there was something disquieting about the way he never met her eyes, even when she paid him. His attention had been behind her, where Stella was playing.

"That's it," said Duncan, slapping the table. "He's delivered pizza here."

"Suddenly I'm in the mood for pizza," said Cheever.

◆ ◆ ◆

When Cheever heard the summons of the doorbell, he yelled, "Coming." He was in a home one street over from the Pierce residence. It was a miracle they'd set up the sting as fast as they had, but every moment was potentially critical.

Cheever didn't open the door right away, but instead took a moment to survey the man through the peephole. Guy Wilkerson looked like a cleaned-up version of his booking photo. He had short hair and was clean shaven; he was wearing a polo shirt, dress slacks, and loafers. Dress for success, Cheever wondered, or dress to molest? There was nothing in his outward appearance that would make people think Guy might be a threat.

Both his hands were on the pizza box. That would make it harder for him to reach for a weapon. Cheever looked past Wilkerson to a car parked in the shadows. He waited for, and then saw, a flash of light from inside the car. That was the confirmation he wanted.

Cheever opened the door.

"Large pepperoni and mushroom?" asked Guy.

"Sounds right."

"Nineteen dollars."

Cheever reached for his wallet. "Been busy tonight?"

"So-so," said Wilkerson.

"It's been crazy around here. Bloodhounds, helicopters with spotlights, search-and-rescue teams. Everybody's been thinking about those poor people."

"That's nineteen," repeated Wilkerson.

Cheever started thumbing through his wallet. "Hey," he said, "I was just thinking, those people could use this pizza more than me. Would you mind taking it over to their house?"

"I don't know . . ."

"How about I give you thirty bucks, and you keep the change?"

Wilkerson debated for a moment before saying, "All right."

"You got their name and address?" asked Cheever.

"Pierce," said Guy. "Fourteen twenty Ranchero Way."

"Good memory," said Cheever. "You didn't even have to think about it."

Wilkerson's eyes narrowed, and he hesitated before responding. "The address has been all over the news," he said.

Cheever shook his head. "For once, the media's been responsible. They haven't released the street name. They've only given out the general area."

He displayed his wallet badge. "I'm Detective Cheever of the San Diego Police Department, and I'd like to ask you some questions, Mr. Wilkerson."

The suspect rolled his eyes and sighed, acting as if he was being unjustly persecuted, but in the midst of his posing, he suddenly hurled the pizza box at Cheever and sprinted toward his car. He was fast, but hidden officers with drawn guns revealed themselves and started shouting.

"Halt! Stop! Down! On the ground! Don't move!"

Wilkerson reluctantly dropped to his knees and raised his hands. He complied carefully; it appeared he didn't want to dirty his clothes. Cheever came up from behind, cuffing him first and then patting him down for weapons. He found a hunting knife strapped to the guy's calf and a sharpened screwdriver in his pants pocket. The detective's discoveries didn't seem to bother Wilkerson as much as Cheever's greasy hands.

"Parole violations, Guy," said Cheever. "Not to mention assaulting an officer with a deadly weapon."

"I threw a pizza. I didn't shoot you."

Half the pizza had escaped the tossed box. Cheever peeled some cheese away from his face. "When you burned me, you burned yourself, Guy." He scraped some of the pizza from his blue blazer and sampled it.

"Good pizza, though. Maybe I can take that into consideration, and we can work out some kind of deal."

Wilkerson was already shaking his head. "No deal. Don't even try. I want to talk with my lawyer. I'm not going to say a word without him present."

Cheever nodded. He wiped his coat, clearing it of tomato sauce. "Okay, since you're so anxious to lawyer up, we'd best get moving. Let me give you a hand up."

Wilkerson recoiled from Cheever's red and greasy hands. "No," he said. "Keep your slimy hands off me."

"Oh, jeez," said Cheever, "I didn't notice. Would you look at that? I'm afraid my handprints are all over you. What a shame that you'll have to do your walk of shame for those TV people. They're going to think you're some kind of slob, Guy. What was that word you used? Slimy—that's it. They'll probably call you Slimy. It's funny how names like that can stick with you forever."

"Let me clean up."

"Can't, Slimy. You're a flight risk."

"I want to talk to my lawyer now."

Cheever sniffed the air, then wrinkled his nose. "He might not want to talk to you. What's that I smell? Oregano? Garlic?"

"Yeah," said one of the uniforms. "He's a regular Chef Boy-are-me."

"Guy Wilkerson," said Cheever, "you are under arrest. You have the right to remain silent. Anything you say can and will be used against you in a court of law. You have the right to speak to an attorney, and to have an attorney present during any questioning. If you cannot afford a lawyer, one will be provided for you at government expense. Do you understand these rights as I have explained them?"

"Yes. I want a lawyer. I'll be suing for entrapment, battery, and false arrest, just for starters."

"And don't forget I stiffed you on the pizza delivery and your tip, Slimy," said Cheever.

CHAPTER NINE

The clock was running. It had been an all-nighter for Cheever. He took in the view from the downtown office building, looking out to the blue expanse of San Diego Bay. Who said crime didn't pay? The criminal defense firm of Spiegel, Brass, and Towers seemed to be doing quite well.

Barry "BB" Brass entered the conference room carrying a large mug of coffee. "Java, Detective?" he asked. "You're carrying some heavy bags under your eyes."

"I'll call a bellman," said Cheever, shaking his head at the offer. His stomach couldn't take any more coffee.

The two men knew each other from other cases. Their relationship was amicable enough, given that each always wanted the opposite of the other. The lawyer wasn't even in his chair before Cheever started pressing him.

"Here's what we got, Counselor," said Cheever. "Your client was found with a sock monkey in his apartment. That same doll was positively identified by the Pierce family as belonging to their daughter, Stella."

"How are they sure it's *her* sock monkey?"

"Mr. Sparkles—that's his name—has some telltale characteristics. He only has half a tail. There's also a large and permanent grape-jelly stain on his chest. The doll missing from the Pierce home, the same doll found in your client's apartment, fits that description perfectly."

BB scratched his beard, doing his best to look unimpressed. "What else do you have?"

"It's clear your client has more than a passing interest in Stella Pierce."

"And you know this how?"

"He made the mistake of not erasing the memory cards in his cameras. Lo and behold, that's where we found Stella. And guess where most of those shots were taken? Your client was in the vicinity of Sunrise Elementary, Stella's school. Being that close to a school is another parole violation."

"My client is an amateur photographer."

"No," said Cheever, "he's an immature photographer. His subject matter is children under the age of twelve. And speaking of underage, we found your client's child porn in his apartment, stashed in the hollow of a door. That illegal filth will get him at least ten years."

BB pretended he was covering a yawn. "As you know, we will be challenging the validity of your search."

"There's a lot more you're going to have to challenge. We're digging into his tutoring business."

Pizza delivery wasn't the only way Wilkerson got near children. He'd been working as a tutor.

"If you'd like," the lawyer said, "I can provide you with testimonials saying what a wonderful tutor my client is."

"I know two sets of parents who won't be writing one," said Cheever. "Those are the parents of children, a boy and a girl, who have come forth and told us that Wilkerson was working on more than books with them."

"What you're saying is news to me. And since I don't hear you detailing specifics, my guess is that you're alleging peccadillo rather than major sin."

"What I'm talking is substantial jail time, BB. The only way we're going to go light on these charges is if your client offers us information that secures the return of Stella Pierce."

"Are you offering us a deal?"

Cheever nodded. "If Stella is alive and unharmed, we'll waive everything but the kidnapping."

"Maybe you should go into the car-financing business, Detective. When they waive the first month's car payment, they don't mention the fifty-nine to follow. Basically you want me to go to my client and say, 'I got a great deal for you. In forty years you'll be out.'"

"That's not how I would sell it. I would tell Wilkerson we're giving him the opportunity to be alive in forty years. If he doesn't come clean now, you tell him that he's looking at a date with some toxic chemicals."

"I'll tell him."

"We'll need an answer by noon. The offer will be off the table after that."

Cheever followed the lawyer's lead and stood up. He tried to hide his exhaustion, but couldn't. He had taken a half-hour catnap at three in the morning. That would likely be all the sleep he would see today.

"May I speak off the record, Detective?"

"Sure," said Cheever. "This will be just between us."

"I have a daughter of my own," said BB. "She's only a year older than that girl. So believe me when I say I know the hell that family must be going through."

BB looked at his hairy hands. "I talked to my client a short time ago. I assumed you would be coming in with an offer, so I tried priming his pump. He told me he didn't take the girl and said he knows nothing about her abduction. He admitted seeing her around, but said that is as far as it went. Most importantly, he says he doesn't know where she is. I tried, Detective, I really tried."

"Try again," said Cheever. "Stella's life might be in your hands."

CHAPTER TEN

Even before Cheever opened his mouth, Duncan Pierce knew the news was bad. It was written all over the detective's slumped shoulders and gray, unsmiling face. Duncan wanted to cover his ears, but instead he put his arm around Eleanor.

Cheever shook his head. "He's not budging from his story."

Duncan started swearing, spitting out every profane word he knew. He stopped only when Eleanor began weeping.

"How does the asshole explain having Mr. Sparkles in his possession?" Duncan asked.

"Wilkerson claims he picked the doll up from the sidewalk three nights ago," said Cheever. "He said he was doing a pizza delivery at your next-door neighbor's house when he swiped it. We confirmed he did the delivery. Is he right about the doll going missing at that time?"

"He planned this," said Duncan. "He took Mr. Sparkles as an alibi to confuse the time line."

"You might be right. But I need to know if that's when the doll went missing."

Eleanor nodded while Duncan fumed.

"The point is, this SOB stole Stella's doll. Maybe he used it to entice her. Who gives a shit when he took it?"

"We're looking for holes in his story, Mr. Pierce."

"The man's a convicted sex offender. You've got children in this town who say he molested them. You found pictures showing he was stalking Stella. Isn't that enough?"

Duncan started pacing furiously around the room. This wasn't right. None of this was right. The pervert could have locked her up somewhere. She could be gagged and bound at the bottom of some pit or hellhole. While they did nothing, she could be choking on her own vomit or dying of thirst.

"I want to talk to him," said Duncan. "Give me two minutes alone with him."

"I wish it was that easy. You're a lawyer. You know he has his rights."

"What about Stella's right to grow up, and her right to be a child, and her right to be our little girl?"

Duncan's words grew weaker and weaker until they faded out. His chin was trembling. He hated being reduced to this. He detested having to look weak. Their hopes had been raised when the animal was arrested, but now it was all turning bad.

"Has he concocted some Valentine's Day alibi?" said Duncan.

Cheever shook his head. "He wasn't working his pizza-delivery job on Valentine's Day, but he did have three separate hour-long tutoring sessions. Wilkerson finished with his last student at eight o'clock. We confirmed that. After that, he said he watched TV."

Duncan wondered whether the bastard had been waiting in their house when they arrived home from the beach.

"Maybe he had an accomplice in all of this," Duncan said. "That could explain why you didn't find more evidence in his apartment connecting him with Stella's abduction."

"From all accounts, the suspect is a lone wolf," said Cheever. "At his former workplace, he kept to himself. If he does have any friends, they never came around his apartment."

"What about some sicko he met in prison? Maybe he's working with one of them."

"We have a whole team investigating his past. We're looking at everything."

"What can I do? I'm going stir-crazy just sitting here."

Duncan couldn't keep the desperation out of his voice. Lately it seemed as if he and Eleanor spent all their time pacing. They shuffled from room to room. Neither of them could sleep or eat. Their whole world had been turned topsy-turvy.

"You need to keep working with the media," Cheever said. "The more publicity we get, the better the chances are someone might remember seeing something. And," he added, "it couldn't hurt to pray."

CHAPTER ELEVEN

Duncan left the praying to his wife. The media *he* handled. Even as others gave up hope, he continued to advocate for his missing daughter. He appeared on local and national shows, prompting leads to come in from around the country. Cheever and his team prioritized the leads from most to least likely. Stella was said to have been seen with a band of gypsies; she had been sold overseas to a child prostitution ring; she was with a family that had lost their own child; a rich child molester was holding her in his mansion. Cheever made sure they ran down every tip, no matter how unlikely.

Days passed into weeks, but Duncan refused to give up. His efforts were a way of keeping Stella alive. Over time he broadened his message by targeting a penal system that "coddled" the likes of Guy Wilkerson. Duncan began to lobby for "Stella's Bill," a piece of legislation that would take "Megan's Law" a step further. Megan Kanka had been Stella's age when she met a tragic death at the hands of a convicted child molester who had moved into her family's New Jersey neighborhood. Megan's parents successfully lobbied to have information about high-risk sex offenders made available to the public.

"In the state of California, there are more than sixty thousand convicted child molesters and rapists," Duncan said during one of his interviews. "Our citizens should be able to easily access the Sex Offender Database by phone or by computer, and know where these criminals are at all times. Even after parole, these criminals need to be constantly monitored. We should have the right to make our neighborhoods safe."

Nothing could fill the void of Stella's absence, but having a cause filled Duncan's days. By displaying his pain in public, by trying to make something positive come out of something terrible, Duncan coped.

Eleanor admired her husband's passion. She wished she could go out and beat the drums as he did, but that wasn't her way. Her suffering was done in silence. Stella's absence was her own black hole. It threatened to swallow her, drown her in darkness. She felt as if she was on the edge of falling into a chasm. What was hardest was the uncertainty of whether Stella was alive or dead.

◆ ◆ ◆

Cheever walked up the path to the Pierce home. The curtains were half-closed, reminding him of a flag flying at half-mast. Ostensibly he was there to talk about developments in the case. In truth, Duncan had asked him to stop by and see his wife. Eleanor was meeting with a counselor, but neither those sessions nor her newly prescribed antidepressants appeared to be helping.

The Pierce home was now equipped with an alarm system, but Duncan said even that didn't make Eleanor feel safe. Bars were in the process of being installed on the windows, and security fencing was going up around the perimeter of the property. To Cheever's thinking, it was a bit like closing the barn door after all the animals were loose. Eleanor was becoming a prisoner in her own house. Duncan said his wife now insisted that Michael sleep in their room, but even that didn't stop her from getting up four and five times a night to check on him. She no longer let him walk to and from school with friends. Every day she picked him up.

Cheever rang the doorbell.

Eleanor was slow to answer the door. From the sounds of it, she was still getting used to deactivating the alarm system. Every time Cheever saw her, she was a little paler and more drawn. He could understand her husband's concern: she was turning into a ghost in front of their eyes.

Still, she hadn't given up hope. He saw it there in her inquiring eyes. Cheever shook his head. "No news to report, Mrs. Pierce. The migrant-worker story didn't pan out."

Someone had called in a tip saying a white girl was living in a small migrant camp on the outskirts of a canyon in Encinitas. They had found a girl living in the camp, but she was a light-skinned Mexican national.

"How is it possible Stella just disappeared, Detective?"

Cheever tried to hide his own frustration. Since taking on the case, he hadn't slept more than four hours on any night. He hadn't felt so helpless since Diane's illness.

"I don't know."

What he didn't say was that San Diego County was larger in area than some states, with no shortage of remote outlying regions. A body could be buried in the Anza Borrego Desert or the woods of Julian, and never be found.

"Should I assume she's dead?"

"Everyone thought Jaycee Dugard was dead," Cheever said. "And no one was holding out much hope for Shawn Hornbeck, but he was found six years after his abduction. I haven't given up hope. That's why we're still working every angle."

"My husband says he will make it his life's mission to see that Wilkerson never gets out of prison."

Cheever nodded. Usually he knew in his gut that a suspect was guilty, but not this time. The most serious charge they had on Wilkerson was his alleged fondling of two of the students he was tutoring. Even so, children sometimes lost it on the witness stand, and Wilkerson's conviction wouldn't be a slam dunk.

"I hardly see Duncan anymore," Eleanor said. "He's been talking with the DA so much I think he should become a prosecutor. This morning he's doing a radio interview, and this afternoon he'll be speaking at a luncheon."

"We're grateful for all his efforts."

"It's Duncan's way of coping."

What's yours? Cheever wanted to ask.

"Is the hotline generating any more tips?" Eleanor asked.

"Calls have slowed," he admitted. "But we're still following up on everything we get, even the crazies."

"Are there lots of those?"

Cheever nodded. "I think people want to help. They want to believe. To try and get our attention, they often say they're psychics. As you might expect, they're invariably short on specifics."

"Aren't there psychics who help the police?"

Cheever wished he hadn't brought up the subject. "For every supposed hit, there are probably a hundred failures. There was a book that tracked the successes and failures of so-called psychic detectives. On the whole, their record isn't very impressive."

"That's been your experience?"

It would have been easier to just nod, but he couldn't quite do that. "I've been on the force a long time and seen my share of crackpots. Hundreds of self-proclaimed psychics have come forward to help, but I only know one who ever has."

Eleanor suddenly perked up. Her eyes had been distracted, but suddenly took on a laser focus as she waited for him to continue.

He held up a hand to forestall her hope. "Linda hasn't helped every time, mind you. On more than a few occasions, she's struck out. But she was a big help on two cases I worked. In the first one, we suspected the husband had buried his wife somewhere in the vicinity of their house. The bloodhounds came up empty, and I was dubious she'd do better, to say the least. I brought her a topographical map of the area in question, an area of about five square miles. And lo and behold, Linda marks an X on the map, and that's where we found the buried wife."

Cheever realized he was making an X with his index finger, and brought his hand down to his side. It wouldn't do to make more of this than necessary. "In the other case, we had the body, but not the murder weapon. Linda described her impression of where the gun was, saying it was hidden under a large, gray boulder. She wasn't exactly sure where that boulder was. I figured that was just another fuzzy description that psychics are famous for giving. But when I went back to the scene of the homicide, I noticed an outcropping of rocks on a not-too-distant hillside. I tromped up there and found this huge, gray boulder. I really had to put my back into that rock to move it, and the whole time I was working it, I remember feeling stupid, but when it finally budged, there was the gun."

"I want to talk with her," said Eleanor.

◆ ◆ ◆

Linda Fabian didn't look like the kind of psychics featured on television shows. There was nothing exotic about her. She was in her midfifties, and her mop of hair was in need of a new dye job. She was heavy, but seemed comfortable in her heft. She didn't read palms or tea leaves or tarot cards, and she had a day job as a real estate agent. Her "impressions" were something that had been with her since childhood. There was no rhyme or reason to what she sensed. Linda didn't look her gift source in the mouth. It just was.

She didn't ask for, and wasn't willing to take, any compensation from Eleanor. Receiving money might taint her vision.

"I'd like to see Stella's room," Linda said.

She was led upstairs. Without being told, Cheever and Eleanor stopped talking and stayed outside the room. Linda walked around, taking in her impressions. She paused at the bookshelf, then reached for one particular book: *Charlotte's Web.*

"Her favorite book," Linda said.

She wasn't asking a question, just stating her finding as fact. Eleanor nodded anyway.

Linda's double chin started vibrating. It was like she was being pulled somewhere. She went over to the window and peered out into the distance.

"She loved looking at stars," said Linda.

Though it was midafternoon, the room seemed to darken. It was almost like Linda was seeing Stella's stars in the sky.

She walked over to the nightstand and opened its drawer. She thumbed through the items. The "P" drawer was what Cheever called it—pencils, pens, pad, papers, and pictures.

"She took a picture with her," Linda said. "There was a house. And people. It was very green." She shook her head. "Not a house. More like a cabin, with big trees around it."

Eleanor appeared confused until a look of realization came over her face. "Last summer we took a family vacation to Big Sur. We all stayed in a cabin. Stella had a copy of that picture. She told me she wanted a frame for it."

She hurried over to the drawer, pulled out the other pictures, and flipped through them. "It's not here," she said.

But Linda wasn't listening. She was back at the window, looking out. She was still, but her pose reminded Cheever of one of those dogs who point. There was a lot going on inside her, turbulence of all sorts masked by tensed flesh.

"She's alive," Linda said.

Eleanor gasped, half sob and half glee, but Linda only looked puzzled. Her eyes were scanning the sky.

"I've never experienced anything like this. It's like she's here, but not here. I know that doesn't make any sense."

She closed her eyes. She looked like a person straining to hear.

"She's alive," Linda said again, this time with even more certainty, "but she's far away, far, far away."

She shook her head a few times, as if not understanding.

"Far away," she whispered.

SEVEN YEARS LATER

CHAPTER TWELVE

Luke put a hand on Michael's shoulder. "You don't have to do this," he said.

They were standing atop a bluff known as Dead Man's Cliff, overlooking La Jolla Cove. The cliff was well named. People had died while attempting the hundred-foot jump down into the Pacific Ocean.

Most locals referred to the spot below them as the Clam. It had gotten its name because of the way two of the edges of the cliff stuck out over the water and resembled a stony clamshell. It wasn't only the jumping spots that had names; you didn't want to land in an area known as the Washing Machine, which typically demanded its pound of flesh or more.

For more than twenty years, it had been illegal to jump anywhere on the cliffs. NO TRESPASSING signs threatening hefty fines and arrests attempted to discourage the daredevils, and during the summer there were frequent lifeguard patrols. In February, though, the lifeguard presence was minimal. Still, to survive a leap, the conditions needed to be right. There were only a handful of days in every calendar year when the tide was seven feet or greater and the swell was gentle enough that you didn't have to be afraid of smashing into the rocks. Even then, land the wrong way, with a face-plant into the water, and you risked the possibility of blacking out.

Michael took off his street clothes. His swimming shorts were underneath his jeans. He put on a rash guard, booties, and wet-suit gloves.

"There's too much bird crap on the rocks," said Luke, surveying the area. "You won't be able to get a running leap. You'll slip and break your neck even before you have a chance to jump."

Michael didn't respond; his attention was on the blue ocean expanse.

"In your heart you know this is stupid, bro," said Luke. "Don't you get enough thrills doing your wild-blue-yonder thing?"

Luke was the hard-core surfer; Michael's passion was the air. Despite his mother's objections, Michael had gotten his single-engine private pilot's license at the age of sixteen. He loved nothing more than being airborne. When he was up in the air, he was free of his mother's smothering and all the crap that had come with his sister's disappearance.

"I've never been a fan of gravity," said Michael.

"Duh," said Luke. "And you wouldn't want your whole future messed up, would you? What would the big brass at the Air Force Academy say if they heard about this jump of yours?"

"They'd probably say I'm perfect to fly a Viper."

Luke snorted. "Yeah, right. I'm pretty sure they only want someone levelheaded at the controls of a jet that costs millions of dollars."

"Even so, I can't disappoint the Y-Girls," Michael said. "They're waiting for a show."

"Screw them," said Luke.

The Y-Girls were the in-group at Torrey Pines Academy. The queen bee was Tiffany, who was usually flanked by Courtney and Kimberly. In lockstep just behind them, you could usually find Sherry, Cassidy, Emily, and Brittany. Since the seven of them had names that ended in *y*, they referred to their group as the Y-Girls. Nonmembers liked to call them the "Yes Girls."

"I told Courtney I was going to do it," said Michael, "and she told the rest of them."

Michael and Courtney were a sometimes couple. "So?" said Luke. "Tell her you changed your mind."

"Everybody's waiting for a show. Besides, don't I always say it's better to live fast, die young, and leave a good-looking corpse?"

"You say a lot of stupid things. That doesn't mean you really believe them. In four months you're supposed to be reporting to Colorado Springs."

Michael didn't comment. He was still looking at the ocean. Luke wanted to get him to look elsewhere.

"Maybe you're just doing this to make your mother happy," said Luke. "Is that it? If you hurt yourself you can change your mind about the Air Force Academy and go to UC San Diego. Isn't that where she wants you to go?"

Not hiding the annoyance in his voice, Michael said, "Like I've been telling you for years, as soon as I graduate, I am getting the hell out of Dodge."

"Listen," Luke said, "I didn't want to be a party pooper, so I came along, but right now I got to tell you that I'm feeling real sick. I mean my stomach is doing flip-flops, and I wouldn't be surprised if I started hurling chunks. And since you're my ride, I kind of need you to take me home right now. I'm like ready to get into bed and hibernate."

Michael finally looked away from the water. Luke was holding his stomach and had adopted a pained expression. When Michael took an involuntary step back, Luke found himself breathing a little easier. It was a good start. Michael opened his mouth to reply, but was interrupted by the sound of girls cheering from below them.

"If you got the game, we got the cheer!"

Those damn Y-Girls, thought Luke. Their timing couldn't have been worse. They had positioned themselves on the rocks below so as to better see and record Michael's leap of faith.

"No fear," they chanted, "more cheer. No fear, more cheer!"

Luke could see Michael's expression change.

"They're like Sirens," said Luke. "All they're doing is calling you down to the rocks."

Luke's English class was reading *The Odyssey*, which is how he knew about Sirens. But his argument didn't seem as convincing to Michael as the Y-Girls' cheering.

"Go, Michael!" yelled Courtney.

"Misters before sisters," pleaded Luke.

Michael shook his head. "The ocean's calling for me."

"That's not the ocean. It's a bunch of sea lions and seagulls. Nothing is calling for you. I know that because I'm right here, and I'm talking to you."

Michael didn't seem to hear a word Luke was saying. His friend's eyes were on the ocean again. He wasn't even hearing the Y-Girls, who had started another inane cheer.

"I'll tell everyone your dad called me," said Luke. "I'll say someone tipped him off. I'll swear he told me that if anything happened to you, I would be prosecuted."

"That sounds like law-and-order Congressman Pierce," Michael said, not hiding his derision.

"Yes, it does," said Luke. "Everyone will believe it."

"But it will be a lie," said Michael. "And I'm kind of tired of living a lie. That's what my life has been since—well, you know."

In his head Luke heard Mrs. Pierce's words: "Promise me you'll watch out for Michael."

Luke had only been a kid when she'd extracted that promise from him. It wasn't fair. He was more than a year younger than Michael, but Mrs. Pierce had still made Luke his keeper. For all these years, Luke had been looking out for Michael. And now he had to stop him from going over the cliff.

"You're lucky to have two parents who love you like they do," he said.

"Stella has been gone for seven years, but they're still not over it. None of us are."

"Your sister's disappearance was a tragedy," said Luke. "But isn't one tragedy in your family enough?"

It was too late, though. Michael's berserker had come out. That's what Luke called it when his friend acted without regard for his own well-being. Stella's disappearance had resulted in Mr. and Mrs. Pierce trying to keep him on a short leash. The berserker came out when Michael's wild child rebelled against being bottled up for too long.

Michael began taking fast breaths, getting psyched for the big leap.

If Luke could wrestle him down, he might get him to listen to reason. But Michael was a big, strong kid. Luke would need to blindside him. He crouched down, readying to hit him low, but an instant before he could make his move, Michael started his sprint across the rock. Luke tried to stop him anyway. He went horizontal, reaching for Michael's ankle, but he missed.

"No!" he yelled, but Michael didn't slow. Luke watched his best friend disappear over the edge of Dead Man's Cliff.

Luke got to his feet and ran until there was no more real estate. The Y-Girls were whooping it up sixty feet below. He scanned the blue water, waiting to see Michael's head emerge, but it didn't show itself.

"Where's Michael?" he screamed, his voice penetrating through the Y-Girls' cheering.

They stopped shouting and turned their attention to the ocean.

"We saw him jump in," Tiffany yelled.

Luke kept looking for his friend. Shit, he thought. What if Michael had passed out? What if the water was too shallow and he was now paralyzed?

He scanned the ocean one last time. Michael wasn't to be seen. The Y-Girls were acting all concerned now, screaming, "Michael! Michael!"

Without thinking about what he was doing, Luke backed up. It was important to get a good takeoff, he knew, because the last step was going to be a doozy. To clear the rocks below, he'd need to jump up and out.

He ran forward. He was wearing sneakers, jeans, a polo shirt, and a hoodie—not exactly dressed for the water. As he pushed off, he took notice of how blue the sky was. The big storm that had hit the day before seemed to have blown away all the clouds and fog, and left a sparkling horizon.

Too late, he thought about how he should be positioning himself and controlling his body. He tried to tuck his head close to his legs before he struck the water. It mostly worked; an onlooker would have thought he'd planned on doing a cannonball. His hard entry into the water drove him to the ocean's floor. He felt as if he'd been slapped by a giant, wet hand. The body blow left him reeling, but the cold water was antidote enough to clear his head and get him moving. He kicked off from the ocean floor and propelled upward. When he broke the water's surface, he started treading water and looking around.

Because there wasn't much of an ocean surge, visibility was good, but Michael wasn't to be seen. Treading water quickly became a struggle; Luke's jeans and clothing were weighing him down. He kicked off his sneakers, slipped out of his hoodie, loosened his belt, and pulled off his pants. He knew that surviving the jump was only the beginning. Most drowning deaths attributed to the Clam were a result of exhaustion. When the surge was strong, swimmers were thrown against the rocks. If you didn't have enough strength to escape the water's grip, you could die.

"Michael!" yelled Luke.

He turned in a circle while treading water, searching for any sign of movement or color. He saw a flash of bright orange in the kelp, but it was only a Garibaldi fish. There was no sign of his friend—nothing. But Michael had to be there somewhere. Luke tried to fight off his panic. The water temperature couldn't be much more than sixty degrees; neither of them was wearing a wet suit. He could already feel the ocean's cold grip squeezing his chest.

"Michael!" he called again.

From behind him he heard a gasp, and then the sound of a deep intake of air. Luke turned around. His feeling of overwhelming relief changed when he saw that Michael was laughing and looking all too pleased with himself.

"You fucking asshole!" Luke shouted. "We both could have died."

"I love you, too, brother. You shouldn't have come after me, but thanks for having my back."

Michael swam over and draped an arm across Luke's shoulder and neck. Despite wanting to remain angry, Luke found himself returning the hug. On the rocks above them, they could hear the Y-Girls cheering.

"What the hell were you doing underwater?" he asked.

"I was thinking," said Michael. "It was so peaceful and so beautiful, I almost didn't come up. Almost like being up in the air looking at a clear horizon. But then I heard you calling."

"How could you have heard me underwater?"

"I don't know, but I did. Either that, or it was a mermaid."

"You're fucking crazy."

"I'm not the one who jumped in the ocean with my clothes on."

"Speaking of which, you're going to owe me for lost clothing and shoes. Now let's get the hell out of here before we both start cramping up."

CHAPTER THIRTEEN

Eleanor sat next to the admiral and his wife, pretending to be absorbed by what the speaker was saying. She owed at least that much to her husband. Other congressmen's spouses worked in tandem with their partners. They gave speeches, performed all sorts of civic duties, and put out their last name to the constituency. Eleanor was the opposite of a politician's spouse; she was a recluse who rarely left her Del Mar home. This was Duncan's second term in the House of Representatives, and she not only hadn't moved to a Maryland suburb like so many spouses did; she rarely visited the Capitol itself. Eleanor claimed she didn't want to disrupt their son's life, but that was a convenient fiction. In the seven years since Stella had disappeared, she had remained afraid.

Even having to go somewhere innocuous like the grocery store provoked an anxiety attack. When she left the house, she felt like someone with a terrible physical deformity. People often stared at her. Some didn't want to get near her, as if her daughter's disappearance was contagious, while others were overly bold and went so far as to approach her with questions.

Duncan had somehow managed to make lemonade from hemlock, while Eleanor was still drinking the poison's dregs. Michael had been the only thing keeping her going. He was her reason for getting up every morning. But now Michael was ready to fly the nest—literally. In June he would be joining the other plebes at the Air Force Academy.

For years Duncan had been patient with her, but with Michael's planned departure, her husband had finally had enough. He told her they needed to put their house on the market, and she needed to join him in the DC area. For the sake of maintaining residency in their district, they would buy a condo in the area, but it didn't make sense to have homes on opposite sides of the country.

Her husband was a good man. In his own way, Eleanor knew he grieved as much as she did. But he had found ways to sublimate his pain.

Sublimate. Even thinking words like that bespoke too many years in therapy. And what good had it done her?

She looked at Duncan up on the podium and admired the way he had aged. There was now gray in his hair, but it made him look distinguished, giving him the appearance of someone seasoned, someone to trust. His constituency apparently agreed. In the last election, he had received almost 80 percent of the vote. The next time around, the other party was talking about not even fielding a candidate against him. His district was a lock. But it was possible he would be seeking out greener pastures. There were those trying to draft him to run for governor, and still others who wanted him to be California's next junior senator.

The crowd laughed at something Duncan said. A little late, Eleanor joined in the laughter, not wanting to be caught without a smile. It hadn't taken much effort on Duncan's part to tap into the good spirits of this crowd. Their loved ones were coming home.

For six months the aircraft carrier *Lewis and Clark* and its crew of almost five thousand had been on deployment. North Island's Naval Air Station in Coronado was now welcoming its own home. The US Navy Band had been playing Sousa and other upbeat tempos all morning. Balloons and colorful banners were everywhere. In one special pavilion, there were several dozen mothers holding newborns that their husbands had never seen. "Daddy's coming," they told their babies. "Daddy's going to be here soon."

Many of those waiting hadn't come empty-handed. There was an abundance of balloons, flowers, candy, and champagne. Colorful homemade signs screamed **I Love You** in all sorts of ways. The Navy League was making sure no one was going hungry—handing out doughnuts, pancakes, soft drinks, juice, and coffee.

Duncan waited for the laughter to stop. "I'll keep my comments brief today," he said, "not because I want to, but because I'm told the *Lewis and Clark* will be docking within the hour."

He let the cheers of the crowd subside before continuing.

"I'm not sure whether you are applauding the announced brevity of my remarks," he said, "or the imminent return of our heroes."

The crowd cheered again. They had set up the grandstand in the open area off the Pier and Quay Street. Across the Bay was the downtown San Diego skyline. In the distance, eyes were tracking the approaching aircraft carrier as it was brought in by tugs. It was hard to miss the vessel. The ship was longer than three football fields and dwarfed everything around it.

Duncan's face turned somber, and his body language grew serious, thoughtful. The crowd quieted, waiting on his words.

"I have a duty as a member of Congress to think about the path of our country. Trying to steer this huge ship called America is not an easy task. Everyone seems to have a different idea about the course we should be plotting, and there's never a shortage of those trying to make themselves heard. But I have found a way to mute the noise and quell the distractions. When I want to look forward, what I do is look back. On a day like today, I am especially mindful of the sacrifices of our forefathers, because the more things change, the more they remain the same."

He pointed in the direction of the aircraft carrier. "Those in that ship know all about the need for sacrifice, just as you who are waiting for your loved ones have had to sacrifice as well."

Amazing how he never looks at his notes, thought Eleanor. Over the years she had been pressed into speaking on several occasions, but what she really did was read from index cards. Duncan was so confident, so assured, in front of a crowd. It was hard to believe he was the same man who one of the partners in his firm had once labeled "hopeless" as a trial lawyer. Stella's loss had brought out a gift in him. His tireless work as a public servant was driven in large part by what had happened to his daughter.

"Our country," said Duncan, "was built on the foundation of those willing to sacrifice everything for the sake of freedom.

"There were fifty-six signers of the Declaration of Independence. Those individuals knew that by signing, it could be tantamount to a death warrant. Their lives certainly would have been simpler, and easier, without making public such a declaration. What they did was like waving a red flag at the enemy. These were men who, for the most part, were well-off. But they were willing to lose all. They declared that a hangman's noose was preferable to silken bonds. Above all things, they showed the world how much Americans value liberty."

He didn't pontificate. He spoke in an intimate manner, almost as if he were talking to friends.

"Then, as now, freedom exacts a price. Supreme Court Justice Felix Frankfurter once wrote, 'We have enjoyed so much freedom for so long that we are perhaps in danger of forgetting how much blood it cost to establish the Bill of Rights.' The service of your loved ones shows that we have not forgotten the price paid by our forefathers, and the price that each generation must pay anew. For half a year, your loved ones have been away protecting our country. How many times did you wish someone else could have taken up that burden?

"In his second inaugural address, Dwight D. Eisenhower said, 'History does not long entrust the care of freedom to the weak or the timid.' Because you, and those you love, have been willing to pay the heavy price that freedom exacts, our country has endured. My heartfelt gratitude goes out to those serving on the *Lewis and Clark*, and also to every one of you. May God bless you, your loved ones, and the United States of America."

His timing, as usual, was impeccable. It was almost as if the aircraft carrier was waiting for him to finish his speech. In the distance, the ship started blasting its horns, and the audience wildly responded to both the congressman and their loved ones who were finally coming home.

◆ ◆ ◆

Eleanor came to a stop at the entrance to their driveway. A **For Sale** sign was hanging from the security fencing. At the bottom of the sign were the words **By Appointment Only**. She wondered if that would dissuade the curious.

She punched in the security code, and the driveway gate slowly opened. The new owners would probably do away with all the bars, locks, and safety features, what the Realtor had referred to as "the penitentiary look." But their Realtor had never lost a daughter to an intruder.

From the car, Eleanor unlocked the mailbox and gathered the letters. Duncan's speech hadn't been the only thing to bring him back to California. Guy Wilkerson's parole hearing was scheduled for that afternoon.

Damn him to hell forever.

Five years ago, against her husband's wishes, Eleanor had visited Wilkerson at the California Men's Colony, a medium-security prison in San Luis Obispo. Just the act of remembering that meeting made Eleanor shudder. Even thinking about Wilkerson meant embracing the toxic.

Behind the glass partition, he smugly faced her, the little smile never leaving his face.

"I am here because of my daughter," she told him.

"No," he said, "I am here because of your daughter."

"What happened to her?" asked Eleanor.

"I have chewed on that question for quite some time," he said, his smirk growing. "It is a favorite bone of mine to pick."

"I need closure," she pleaded.

"We all need something. Getting it is another matter."

"If you know something—"

"Oh, I know lots of things. Let me tell you a few of the things I know."

She tried to not listen, but he furiously whispered his polluted thoughts, his words surging up from the sewer he called a mind. Eleanor pulled the phone away from her ear; it stung as if she had been the target of a swarm of hornets.

"What happened to my little girl?" she screamed.

Everyone within earshot stopped talking. Her scream brought one of the guards over to her.

"All you all right, ma'am?"

She took a deep breath. This was her chance to learn things, maybe her only chance. She nodded, offering a weak smile, and then put the phone back up to her ear.

"Do you know where she is?" asked Eleanor.

"I have thought about what might *have happened to her." Wilkerson was so careful to use that word* might. *It spared him from implicating himself.*

And then he started offering his suppositions to Eleanor. She tried interrupting him, tried asking him questions, but he kept talking until she dropped the phone and fled from his twisted imaginings.

Eleanor prayed they were just imaginings.

That was why Duncan was at the Parole Board hearing today. Because there had been little in the way of physical evidence to connect Wilkerson to the abduction of their daughter, he had only been convicted of fondling two minors and possession of child pornography, along with violating the terms of his parole. Duncan's presence might tip the scales toward keeping Wilkerson locked up.

Eleanor was supposed to accompany Duncan to the hearing, but she had bowed out, telling him her agoraphobia had been acting up. He'd believed her, of course. It was a condition she had suffered from ever since Stella had disappeared. What she hadn't told him was that there was an even more pressing reason for her absence. Duncan had put Stella's disappearance behind him. Eleanor was now about to do the same thing in the only way she knew how.

◆ ◆ ◆

The congressman's driver pulled the car up to the reserved parking space. Duncan checked his watch. Only two. Good. There was an hour before the hearing. He'd taken a commuter flight from Lindbergh Field to LAX that had gotten him in early, but he would put the time remaining to good use. His chief of staff had arranged for the media to be waiting.

This was Duncan's second appearance at a parole-consideration hearing. He expected much the same show he had witnessed two years before—Wilkerson's attorney trying to portray him as a model prisoner; the assistant DA insisting that his release would pose a threat to society.

The bad news, Duncan thought, was that because of overcrowded prisons, it was increasingly easier to get parole in the Golden State. California's nine-member parole board heard more than two thousand cases a year, and were under pressure to release nonviolent offenders. It was up to Duncan to show that Wilkerson wasn't nonviolent, and continued to be a threat.

Duncan was a law-and-order candidate, a badge he wore proudly. It was just a shame they hadn't been able to sentence Wilkerson to more jail time from the onset. He'd received thirteen years, but that included the possibility of parole after four years served.

If Duncan had his way, Wilkerson would serve every minute of his thirteen years. Duncan was still holding out hope that before Wilkerson's release date, they would somehow be able to link him to Stella's death. There was no statute of limitations for murder. Down the road he hoped Wilkerson would get the penalty he deserved—death. In the meantime, though, it was Duncan's job to make sure he continued to rot in prison.

The first reporter caught sight of him. "Congressman!"

I'll never forget you, Stella, he thought.

CHAPTER FOURTEEN

It hadn't been that long ago that Eleanor had walked fearlessly into unruly classrooms, like a ringmaster in control. Even before that, after graduating from college, she and two friends had ridden their bicycles across the country from coast to coast. Mountains hadn't stopped her, and thunderstorms hadn't slowed her. That was the person she once was.

She was tired of being a recluse. She hated the individual who had emerged after her daughter's disappearance. Losing Stella had brought on what felt like a terminal illness. There was no joy in her life. And she knew that she'd been a disappointment to Michael and Duncan. She hadn't even been able to bring herself to watch Michael play his high school football games. It wasn't only her fear of seeing him hurt. It was her overall fear.

Her family would be better without her—it was what she had been thinking for years. Now was the right time to act. Michael would leave for Colorado Springs and the Air Force Academy in June. Her son was already independent, and didn't hide the fact that she was an embarrassment to him. As for Duncan, he had a workload that was enough for two people.

If all went as planned, no one would ever suspect she'd killed herself. For weeks she had pretended to be increasingly upbeat, and earlier that day she had done some particularly good acting at the homecoming. Duncan had been pleased she'd joined him, and she'd been smiling and cordial with all the military families. She had kissed Duncan good-bye, and they had made plans for his congressional break.

Michael wouldn't suspect either. When they'd talked in the morning, she had asked when he'd be home. Every day she needed to be reassured by his ETA, and Michael knew to call if he would be late. He'd promised he'd be home by five, and she'd asked what he wanted for dinner. He'd decided on fried chicken and home fries.

It was almost two o'clock. That gave her three hours to die.

Eleanor made Copper's dinner, as she always did. That would look normal as well. She gave the family's golden retriever a hug. He was ten now, and his face was gray. The dog had been her constant companion all these years. One of the great things about dogs is that they are not judgmental. She left his emptied can and the bag of kibble out. It would be yet one more indication of her natural death.

During the past year, her shrink had prescribed her plenty of pills. She had studied up on the dosages, and knew what combination of pills and amounts would kill her. She was leaving nothing to chance.

Eleanor set out the dinner preparations. She lined up the seasoned flour, buttermilk, bread crumbs, and chicken, and put russet potatoes on the counter. Then she made a show of sorting the mail. She paused to study an envelope-size flyer. On one side it advertised a cellular-phone sale; on the other were the words HAVE YOU SEEN ME? She looked at the pictures, as she always did. One showed a little boy. Next to it was an age-progression picture. The boy, taken at age eight, had been missing for twenty-five years.

Somewhere, Eleanor knew, parents who loved that boy were still waiting for a phone call. Soon she would no longer have to relive the pain she felt every time there was a child-abduction case. She couldn't take any more pain. Her personal statute of limitations had run out.

If she was lucky, there would be an afterlife, and she would see her daughter there.

She poured herself a glass of water and took her first handful of pills.

◆ ◆ ◆

Eleanor lay down on the sofa. She wanted to look peaceful for Michael's sake. In forty-five minutes she'd take another handful of pills, and then in another forty-five minutes, she would finish the last batch. She doubted they'd perform an autopsy on her, but if they did, the medical examiner would discover that the pills had been taken over the course of more than two hours. They'd assume she was disoriented, that she had forgotten that she'd already taken her pills. It would look like an accidental overdose.

Already she could feel the pills' effect. The Ativan combined with Xanax had taken the edge off. She steadied her breathing, preparing for the big sleep.

But then a buzzing sounded. Someone was pressing down on the intercom at the front gate.

Go away, Eleanor thought.

As if the person was responding to her dismissal, the buzzing sounded again. This time it lasted longer, and sounded even more insistent than the first buzz.

Leave me in peace, she thought.

But whoever was out there wasn't yet deterred. They buzzed again. And now Copper joined in the discordant chorus. He was barking furiously. Normally he barely stirred, but something had gotten into him this time. He was racing around the house, running from room to room and sounding the alarm.

"No, Copper, no!" Eleanor yelled, but the old dog wouldn't listen.

He started scratching at the door, apparently frantic to get outside.

"Stop that!" said Eleanor.

Their normally obedient dog ignored her, continuing to bark and scratch.

Things weren't going as Eleanor had imagined. In her final hours she had envisioned the grayness finally turning to a black that she wouldn't be around to see. All this bedlam wasn't part of her plans. When the intercom finally stopped buzzing, she sighed in relief, but the respite didn't last for long. The intercom buzzed again.

"Dammit," she said.

She got up and walked over to one of the security-station monitors. There were CCTV cameras and alarms all around the home, and she narrowed in on the screen that showed a view of the front gate. A young woman was standing there. Probably because of the **For Sale** sign, thought Eleanor. The girl's garb looked a little off, or at least a little different from what girls seemed to be wearing these days. Maybe the girl herself was a little off.

Stay calm, she thought. It wouldn't do to get overwrought. She didn't want a rush of adrenaline slowing down her time frame.

Eleanor pressed the intercom button and asked, "May I help you?"

The girl looked startled by the sound of her voice. She turned around, searching for its source. Then she said a single word, but Eleanor was sure she'd misheard. Copper was still barking, which was making it hard to hear. And the girl wasn't facing the monitor or speaking into the microphone.

"I wasn't able to hear what you said," Eleanor told the girl. "You'll need to talk in the direction of the monitor."

The girl turned to face the screen and microphone. When she spoke again, the word was clear and unmistakable: "Mommy?"

This time Eleanor couldn't pretend she hadn't heard. Still, the word hit her like a blow to the stomach and took her breath away. When she was finally able to reply, her voice was raspy and devoid of any welcome: "You have the wrong house."

Instead of backing away from the gate, the young woman shook her head.

She's crazy, thought Eleanor. She's not right in the head. The security system was hardwired to the alarm company, and Eleanor's finger hovered over the panic button. The alarm would certainly send the girl scurrying away. It would also bring help. Guards would be dispatched, and the security company would call Eleanor to make sure everything was all right. When that happened, though, she wouldn't be able to follow through with her plan.

The girl didn't look like much of a threat anyway. She was craning her head around, as if orienting herself. For the first time, Eleanor got a good look at her. She was very pale, her skin almost translucent. The camera's wide-angle lens was better at showing the big picture than pulling up details, but Eleanor could see the girl's blue veins standing out on her see-through skin.

Her hair was almost a white blonde, a color usually seen only on young children. She wasn't wearing makeup, but instead of looking washed out, the girl's extreme paleness gave her an almost ethereal glow.

Again, she moved her mouth closer to the intercom. This time there was no mistaking her words.

"Mom," the girl said, "I've come home."

A current ran through Eleanor's body. With so many of her emotions vying, it felt as if her insides were short-circuiting. Seven years of scar tissue threatened to rip away. To survive this long, she had accepted disappointment as a way of life. She was prepared to kill herself, but she wasn't prepared for one more letdown.

And yet the worst letdown of all had been saved for last. This was someone's idea of a cruel, terrible hoax.

A single sob escaped her. Her agony played out over the intercom, but still the hateful girl didn't have the decency to leave.

"Go away!" shouted Eleanor. "Leave!"

The girl was clearly mentally ill. She was standing there with her mouth open, looking as if she was the one who was about to cry.

"I'm calling the police," Eleanor said.

The girl didn't move, save to look into the camera. Seven long years melted away. Those were Stella's eyes. Oh, God, it couldn't really be true, could it? Was this her little girl?

"Stella," Eleanor gasped.

She ran for the front door, where Copper was scratching. When she flung the door open, the dog streaked for the fence, crying out joyful noises with every step. Eleanor followed right behind, shouting, "Stella, Stella, Stella!"

As she ran, she prayed. Please don't be like before, she thought. Please. Please. There had been times, especially early on, when Eleanor was sure she had heard her daughter's voice calling to her from outside. Time and again she had run out the door, screaming her name, but there had never been an answer.

Until this time.

She ran down the front pathway, and she saw, standing at the gate, the girl she had never thought she would see again. Whenever Stella had been happy as a little girl, she'd shown her joy through what the family called *jazz hands*. Her fingers would go up and down. They were doing that now while Stella hugged a joyful Copper, who had managed to vault up and over the fencing. Eleanor had half a mind to jump over the fence herself. The sleepiness that had come with taking the meds had vanished. Now she was Whitman's body electric. She tried to cry out, but speech melted from her. She could only make trumpetlike sounds, high-pitched, unintelligible, but joyous.

The fence stood between them. Eleanor desperately tapped out the code to the security gate while tears ran down her face. And then the gate opened, and Stella was there waiting for her.

Eleanor threw her arms around her daughter. Her little girl was now a young woman as tall as she was. Eleanor reached her hands to

Stella's face and felt her flesh. She was real. She was beautiful. She was her daughter.

There were so many things she wanted to say, but she lacked the vocabulary for what she was feeling. She had lived in darkness, and the sudden light was blinding. Her joy was so intense she was almost afraid of floating away. That was how light she felt. She wanted to sing out as only the angels could, but instead she held her baby close, stroking her, looking at her, absorbing her presence.

"I missed you, Mommy."

Something had to come out, or Eleanor was going to shatter. "Stella." She announced the name like it was a word in a language she didn't know. It was said in wonderment, in bewilderment, in ecstasy, in awe.

"I know, Mom."

Eleanor's screams had alerted Meg Downing, bringing the elderly woman out to her stoop. Mrs. Downing was squinting at the two of them, trying to make out what was occurring. Even with her thick glasses, she had trouble seeing.

"Is everything all right, Eleanor?" she called.

Stella answered for her mother: "Hello, Mrs. Downing."

The old woman squinted a little more. "Who's that?"

"It's Stella."

Age hadn't dimmed Mrs. Downing's faculties. "Stella?" she said incredulously.

"I've returned, Mrs. Downing."

The old woman hobbled down the path, while Eleanor continued hugging her daughter. When Mrs. Downing was close enough, she reached out a hand.

"She who was dead," Mrs. Downing said, "is alive again. She who was lost is found."

Her wrinkled hand touched Stella's hair where Eleanor's tears hadn't yet soaked it.

"And now I feel the nourishment of the Holy Spirit," said the old woman. "It's a miracle. It's a miracle."

◆ ◆ ◆

Duncan felt his phone vibrate. The hearing was just about to begin, and the bailiff had already cautioned everyone about turning off their phones and electronic devices. He surreptitiously checked the display and saw that Eleanor had texted.

Call home!

Excusing himself, he rose from his chair. In the hallway he called up his contacts and hit the home phone number. Eleanor answered on the first ring.

His wife was clearly hysterical. She was shouting and talking and laughing and crying all at once. Her words were gibberish. "Stella was at the gate she's beautiful no warning just out of the blue and I still can't believe it it's just beyond incredible and wonderful and I'm still having trouble taking it in . . ."

"Eleanor," Duncan said, "slow down. I can't understand a thing you're saying."

The hearing had probably put her over the edge. His wife had started to decompensate years ago. Her mental state had worsened after she'd visited Guy Wilkerson in prison. She had come back damaged. That's what animals like Wilkerson did. Their actions pulled apart families and tore at the fabric of society.

"Stella," his wife managed to get out, "is here. She's sitting next to me."

Oh, God, Duncan thought. He had been afraid of this. After seven years you would have thought Eleanor might have learned how to cope. But she'd grown worse, if anything. She usually went into a funk several days before Valentine's Day, and didn't emerge until a few days after, but she had never actively hallucinated until now.

"I'm going to call the doctor, Eleanor," he said. "You've been under a severe strain—"

"I know it sounds too incredible! I wouldn't believe it either. It's a miracle. But it's true!"

"The hearing is about to start—"

"Forget the hearing, Duncan. Your daughter is here."

His frustration erupted. "Get a grip on yourself, Eleanor. Stella is not there."

Duncan looked around, realizing too late that he was all but shouting. Luckily, there weren't many people around. But his outburst had drawn the attention of Barry Brass. Wilkerson's lawyer was on a call of his own that seemed to have all of his attention. "You're kidding," Duncan heard him say.

"Our daughter is sitting right next to me," said Eleanor. "She's alive. She's beautiful. She looks more like your pixie than ever. Of course she's taller. She's willowy . . ."

"Stop it."

"Talk with her, Duncan."

The phone apparently changed hands, and then another voice came on the line: "Hello, Daddy."

Could it be Eleanor speaking in a higher voice? Could she have completely and utterly snapped?

"Daddy?"

But no, that wasn't Eleanor's voice. Someone was pulling a heartless deception, preying on an extremely vulnerable woman who was blinded by her desire to be united with her daughter.

"I'm here."

"You sound like you're mad at me, Daddy."

"Let me talk with my wife."

He heard the phone being handed back to Eleanor. "Do you see?" she said.

"Someone's posing as Stella," he said. "I don't know what her game is, but I'm going to find out, and she is going to be punished."

"If you were here, you would see—"

"I'm not there, Eleanor. I'm here at Wilkerson's parole hearing. It's time to remember where you are as well. Have you even thought to question that girl?"

"No. I've just been soaking in the experience of having her with me again. She's our daughter, Duncan. Don't you think I would know my daughter?"

He didn't answer; she wouldn't want to hear what he really thought. Springing this girl on his wife was like throwing a lifeline to a drowning person. Of course she had grabbed at her—at it.

"Are you being threatened by this individual, Eleanor? Are you in any danger? Just answer yes or no."

"No. She's our daughter, Duncan. Please, please, believe me."

Duncan wasn't going to argue. His wife apparently preferred her delusion to reality. "I want you to leave the security gate and the front door unlocked. Do that without bringing any attention to yourself."

"Why?"

"Because when we finish talking, I'm calling the police."

"But I've never been better, Duncan, never in my whole life. Dare I say the word? I will. It's a miracle."

"I don't believe in miracles."

"You will."

"I'm coming home, Eleanor. I'll get there as soon as I can."

◆ ◆ ◆

Duncan was lucky there'd been a seat open on the commuter flight to Lindbergh Field. Now he was speeding along Interstate 5. His rental car smelled of smoke. Or maybe, thought Duncan, the smoke was just coming out of his ears. He had wanted to believe that Eleanor was finally turning the corner. Earlier that morning she'd comported herself perfectly around all the military brass and their wives. He had deluded himself, of course. Losing Stella had cut Eleanor off at the knees. And maybe above the neck. As much as she had tried to get on with her life, nothing worked. Not therapy, electroshock, meditation, drugs, or special diets. Not anything. He had told her they needed to sell the house. In that way he hoped she could leave the bad memories behind. Finally she had agreed to put the house on the market and come live with him in Washington, DC.

And now this.

For seven years Eleanor had been an absentee wife. Even before the geography of his job separated them, their love life had ceased to exist. There was a time when Duncan had been the envy of all his friends. Even with two kids, he and Eleanor had still been like honeymooners. But after Stella disappeared, everything changed. Eleanor was consumed by guilt. There was part of her that believed closing the door for privacy had resulted in Stella's being taken from them. To Eleanor's thinking, they had failed their daughter, putting pleasure in front of duty.

There were times when he'd considered divorce. At one time that would have been political suicide, but no longer. Even conservative icons divorced and remarried these days, and still preached family values. But that wasn't what Duncan wanted to do. He had hoped that his and Eleanor's living together would help them return to normality.

But now this. If it didn't hurt so much, he would laugh.

He tried calling home again. The line was still busy.

Being a congressman had its perks. As soon as he'd gotten off the phone with Eleanor, he had called SDPD's chief of police. She had personally assured him that her officers would try and quietly take the intruder away. Duncan was hoping to keep the story from the media. He didn't need that craziness.

The girl posing as his daughter had a hell of a nerve trying to pass herself off as Stella. He wasn't sure which posed more of a threat to his wife: a criminal or a crazy. It would certainly be easier to forgive the impostor if she was deluded, as long as she wasn't violent. But this faker had better not have tried to scam Eleanor out of money. If she had, he would make sure she paid big-time for causing Eleanor to suffer. It was hard to imagine a crueler deception.

He exited the freeway, turning west on Del Mar Heights Road. From atop the hill, he caught sight of the Pacific Ocean. Before their tragedy, he and Eleanor had walked almost every night along the sand.

It's been seven years, thought Duncan, since I walked on the beach.

He continued west, then turned onto a residential road. The area around his home was generally very quiet, its border the eastern expanse of the Torrey Pines Reserve Extension. But today something had upset the hive. Ahead, he could see the clustered media vans. The cameras had brought out spectators, and both sides of the street were lined with cars.

Déjà vu. Seven years before he had seen the same sights.

Duncan pushed on the accelerator, but didn't get very far. The police had set up a barricade a block from his house. An irate cop tried to wave him away.

"I live on this street," said Duncan. "What's happened?"

The cop didn't answer his question. "In order for you to pass, I'll need a picture ID with your address on it."

Duncan pulled out his wallet. "Is my wife all right?" he asked. "I'm Duncan Pierce."

He handed over his congressional ID, and the cop did a double take. He was young, couldn't have been more than twenty-five, but already had a world-weary face. His attitude changed immediately.

"Sorry, sir," he said, handing back Duncan's ID. "People have been coming up with all sorts of stories to try and get by. As far as I know, sir, your wife is fine."

As he moved the barricade aside, the officer asked, "Is it true about your daughter, sir? Has she come back?"

Duncan offered a noncommittal smile. But what he was thinking was, shit, shit, shit. Eleanor must have let the cat out of the bag. It sounded like she'd gone public with her delusion.

This was going to look bad, thought Duncan. Eleanor had been set up by the impostor. Maybe his political enemies had decided to discredit him with a Trojan horse. Duncan was known as a comer in the party, a man on the way up. But in order to be listened to, he had to be credible. If his wife was making herself a national laughingstock, there would be plenty of guilt by association.

As he neared his home, he could see that he would have to traverse a media gauntlet. The vultures were all lined up in front of the house. For once, Eleanor's security fencing served a good purpose—keeping them off the property. It still wouldn't look good on TV, though. Their house would look more like a prison than a residence. All it needed was a watchtower and a revolving spotlight.

Two police cars were parked on the street. Duncan wondered if the officers had already arrested the intruder. He managed to drive up to the gatepost before the media noticed him. As he tapped out the security code, cameras and reporters with microphones rushed him. Duncan smiled and waved. The first rule of politics: never let them see you sweat.

"Congressman! We need a comment!"

"Representative Pierce, is it true your daughter is inside?"

"Congressman, have you talked with Stella yet?"

"Congressman! Have the police confirmed your daughter's identity?"

At least a dozen voices vied to be heard. Duncan's smile became a little more forced.

If only the damn gate wasn't taking so long to open. There were so many arms with microphones aimed his way that he felt as if he were being confronted by a giant, writhing octopus.

"Please excuse me," he said, inching the car forward.

The arms moved along with him.

"After I get some answers, I'll return and fill you in on what I've learned," he promised.

The arms reluctantly pulled back, and Duncan was able to pull in to the safety of his driveway. With the cameras no longer trained on him, he dropped his smile. His stomach was knotted up, and his head throbbed. He was angry that the police hadn't just quietly arrested the intruder, and upset at Eleanor for putting him in this spot. But most of his ire was reserved for the trespasser.

She was probably just another troublemaker looking for her fifteen minutes of fame. In-your-face tactics were becoming ever more common by groups demanding one political action or another. If it wasn't pies being thrown, it was manure being dumped, or backsides being exposed. The tactic didn't matter, as long as their agenda was publicized. The intruder would probably have some prepared speech about saving the banana slugs.

The front door opened when he was only halfway up the walkway. He could make out Eleanor. Next to her was the girl, but she was obscured by the shadows. Where were the police, and why hadn't she been arrested?

But as Duncan came closer, he fought off a sudden weakness in his legs. No wonder Eleanor was confused. The young woman in the doorway did bear a striking resemblance to their daughter. Last year the National Center for Missing & Exploited Children had done an age-progression photo of Stella. This young woman looked amazingly like their extrapolation, with the exception of her hair, which had been pictured as sandy blonde. This girl's hair was the same pale blonde as Stella's on the day she disappeared.

"Daddy!"

The girl met him at the door, throwing her arms around him. Without thinking, Duncan responded, returning her hug. Then he remembered himself, and also remembered the probing eyes of the media. At least the only shot they'd get would be his back. Duncan closed the door behind him, then dropped his arms to his sides. That didn't stop the girl from continuing to hold on to him tightly.

"I'm so happy to see you, Daddy," she said. Then she whispered for his ears only: "All these years I could hear your voice in my head talking about Curious George and Stuart Little and Mr. Toad. Remember how we laughed about Mr. Toad and his driving?"

Duncan's jaw was trembling. It would be hard for someone posing as his daughter to know how the two of them had laughed at silly Mr. Toad. He looked at his wife. Eleanor was nodding at him and laughing through her tears. His eyes dropped back to the girl, who was still hugging him. He wanted to reach down and lift her, wanted to wrap her in a bear hug, but he fought the impulse. She couldn't be Stella. It was impossible. By sheer force of will he ignored her clinging presence, taking notice instead of two uniformed policemen standing in the hallway. They were doing their best to pretend they weren't watching what was going on.

Duncan questioned them with his eyes, and the short, swarthy man spoke first: "I'm Officer Ruiz, Congressman."

The man with the football-player build said, "Officer Jensen."

"I talked with the chief of police earlier this afternoon," Duncan said.

The officers understood his reference, and with it his unspoken question: Why hadn't they arrested the intruder?

"We were going to take this young woman in for questioning," Officer Ruiz explained, "but your wife strongly objected."

"After seven years, Duncan," Eleanor said, "I wasn't going to let our daughter go anywhere."

"We had fingerprints on file from when your daughter went missing," said Jensen. "We fingerprinted the young woman, scanned the results, and then sent them into the lab. They compared the prints and just now called back with the results."

His wife was crying again. And laughing. Even the officers were smiling through their own misty eyes. But Duncan needed to hear the words.

"And what in God's name did the department tell you?"

"Sorry," said Jensen. "The fingerprints are a perfect match. Of course we'll do a DNA test as well. Your daughter's former pediatrician will be making a house call today and will be taking DNA swabs, but everything we have so far says this is your daughter, Stella."

Duncan didn't know quite how to react. He had been sure this moment would never happen. For seven years he had steeled himself against any hope. But now he had no defenses. All the dams he had erected were swept away.

He threw his arms around Stella. It had been years since Duncan had last cried. His eyes had watered up a few times over certain movies, and there were a few sentimental occasions when he'd wiped away a tear or two, but not since Stella's disappearance had he lost it.

But now the sobs wouldn't stop. He held on to his little girl for dear life. The harder he tried to suppress his emotions, the more sobs racked his chest. He cried until he was weak and his abdomen hurt as if he'd been punched by a heavyweight. But the pain didn't matter. Nothing mattered.

His daughter was back.

CHAPTER FIFTEEN

"Shit!" said Dr. Benjamin Froke.

When had those flashing lights appeared behind him? The last thing he needed was another ticket, especially after pleading guilty to reckless driving the month before. He'd been lucky to get off that easy. The Breathalyzer hadn't shown what blood work would have.

He pulled his Lexus over to the side of the road. Everyone assumed he owned the car; Froke didn't advertise that it was a lease. Every month he had to come up with three grand to pay his med-school nut. It was like owing a loan shark. That didn't leave much, despite the MD after his name.

Froke glanced in his rearview mirror. He'd been pulled over by an unmarked car. The driver—a detective, Froke supposed—was wearing a gray suit. He had on polarized Oakley Half Jackets, the kind that hid the eyes. Next to him was a man who could have been his twin. He was wearing the same dark suit and shades. In fact, both men reminded Froke of the villains in those *Matrix* movies.

As they approached his car, Froke could just make out a slight bulge in the driver's tailored suit, which indicated he was carrying a gun. But instead of walking up to Froke's window, the driver made a side approach, came up to the passenger window, and rapped on the glass. Froke rolled down that window. The man gestured with a downward stroke of his index finger for Froke to unlock the door; a moment later he did. Without asking, the man took a seat next to him.

"I wasn't speeding," said Froke, even though he was well aware that he had been.

"I wish you hadn't started our relationship with a lie," said the man.

Froke frowned.

"You have been a bad boy, Dr. Froke." The man passed over a folder. "I don't think the state medical board would take kindly to all those fake prescriptions you've been writing for yourself."

Froke began thumbing through the photocopies in the file but had to stop when his hands started trembling. "Who are you?" he asked.

"Call me Scarecrow," said the man.

"Are you a cop?"

"I'm an agent."

"I'd like to see some identification."

"You're holding my identification. With one call I could have your license to practice medicine suspended, and you arrested."

"What do you want?"

"In the next hour or two, someone will contact your office asking if you can meet with a new patient, the daughter of Congressman Duncan Pierce. You will agree to do so."

Scarecrow handed Froke a manila envelope. "Before meeting with this patient, you will study the contents of this envelope. When you meet with her, you will ask the questions we have suggested and follow the script we have provided. Afterward you will meet with her family. We have bullet-pointed what you need to stress with them. You will also emphasize this patient's need for intensive therapy that will involve at least three sessions with you per week. To make it easy on the parents, you will agree to initially meet at their house before transitioning to your office for the suggested three-times-weekly sessions."

"I don't make house calls," said Froke.

"As of today you do."

"Who do you think—?"

Froke's protestation was cut short when the man said, "I *think* if you don't want your life as you know it to end on a tragic turn, then you had better do as you are told. We both know what a very bad boy you have been, Dr. Froke."

With absolute certainty, Froke knew that this man and whomever he represented had him dead to rights. The shrink's body betrayed him; every one of his sweat glands seemed to kick in at once. The pores of his face opened up and all but wept.

"I can *see*," said Scarecrow, "that at this moment you're only thinking of the downside of our relationship. But there is an upside."

Scarecrow reached inside his coat pocket. Froke thought he was reaching for his gun, but instead he pulled out bundles of hundred-dollar bills.

"As a token of our goodwill," said Scarecrow, "I'm giving you twenty-five thousand dollars. If you follow our protocols, if you do exactly as I say, we will continue to regularly reward you in similar increments."

The bundles piled up in Froke's lap like manna from heaven.

Scarecrow pulled out a cell phone and handed it to him. "Keep this phone on your person at all times," he said. "If it rings, I will be the caller. No one else is to be present when you take the call."

"What if I need to get in touch with you?" asked Froke.

"Press the number one and then hit the pound key," said Scarecrow. "That will activate a prerecorded number. I will be the one who answers. But don't bother me unless it's an emergency. Is that understood?"

At Dr. Froke's nod, Scarecrow took leave of the car.

CHAPTER SIXTEEN

Cheever pulled his unmarked vehicle over to the side of the road. In any individual's life, there are a few special moments you return to time and again. Cheever had a feeling this would be one of those moments.

"Can you repeat that?" he asked.

Sergeant Falconi was usually unflappable, but even he couldn't hide his excitement as he relayed the news.

"Thanks," said Cheever, not sure he could have managed more than a monosyllabic answer.

"I'm betting your next stop will be their house," said the sergeant.

"Yes," said Cheever, another solitary syllable.

"Good luck, then," said Falconi, and clicked off.

Cheever distrusted his emotions, as did most men of his generation, but he couldn't stop the tears from pouring down his face. Stella Pierce was home? It's rare that someone goes missing for years and then turns up. Usually what turned up were remains. Cheever had always hoped the girl might return, but had never truly expected this day would come.

He had never given up on the investigation, though, and could still quote the casebook by heart. There wasn't a report he hadn't memorized. He could tell you the name of every neighbor not only on the Pierces' street, but on all the nearby streets. Stella Pierce's disappearance had been the greatest mystery of his life.

Not a week had gone by over the past seven years that the detective hadn't talked to Eleanor, Duncan, or Michael. He kept them up-to-date on every lead he worked. They knew Cheever had put thousands of miles on his car investigating Stella sightings, and also knew he had done most of this work on his days off.

What they didn't know was that almost every night, Cheever had fallen to sleep thinking about Stella and what he might have missed. He'd been divorced and not dating for many of the years spanning Stella's disappearance, but during the past year he had entered into a relationship with a shrink, Dr. Rachel Stern. Cheever had never tried to hide from Rachel his obsession over the case. To the contrary, he'd talked about it with her, asking for her input.

The one that had gotten away had consumed him, but finally he was going to get answers.

Cheever wiped his eyes dry, then set out for Del Mar.

◆ ◆ ◆

Ten minutes into his drive, Cheever's cell phone rang. His car's display told him that Duncan Pierce was calling. "Accept call," he said.

"I tried to get you at your desk," the congressman said, "but you weren't there, so I asked Sergeant Falconi to call you with the news."

"He did."

"I hope you're on your way here."

"I am."

"I have a bottle of champagne I've been waiting to pop open for a long time," said the congressman. "I want you to have the first glass."

"In ten minutes you'll be able to start pouring."

◆ ◆ ◆

Cheever hadn't counted on the media phalanx, so he was three minutes later than promised. Seven years ago he'd hated the way the media watched his team's every move. The fishbowl existence had made a difficult case feel like an impossible case.

A *Union-Tribune* reporter who had spent time working the crime beat recognized the detective and peppered him with some questions, but Cheever merely waved and yelled, "Good afternoon!" The cop's friendliness took the reporter aback; Cheever's intensity usually made for more glowers than smiles.

Of course Cheever knew his job was far from finished. In some ways it was just beginning. There were seven years of loose ends to tie up, but at least this was no longer a missing child case. Now he'd finally learn the details of Stella's disappearance.

The congressman met him at the door, and the two men hugged. Behind closed doors there was more hugging. Duncan pressed a flute of champagne into Cheever's hand, and the two men clinked glasses.

"To happily ever after," said Duncan.

"Amen," said Cheever. He took a solitary sip, then put the glass aside and took his first look at Stella in the flesh.

Eleanor was standing in the living room with an arm around her daughter; already the two of them looked inseparable. In fact, it almost looked as if they were about to participate in a three-legged race. Talking to them was a fortyish woman who Cheever assumed, from the black bag and stethoscope, was a doctor. Duncan led Cheever forward by the arm.

"Stella," said Duncan, "I'd like you to meet Detective Cheever. For seven years he's been looking for you."

"I can't tell you how glad I am to finally meet you," he said, his smile so wide his facial muscles actually ached.

The detective found it hard to take his eyes off the girl. Stella had retained the whitish-blonde hair she'd had as a child. She took a step forward to shake Cheever's hand, and seemed to glide more than walk. He cupped his big hand around her graceful, artistic digits.

"So this is what a miracle feels like," he said.

Everyone around them laughed; only Cheever knew his words were serious.

Her hand was thin, but her grip was firm. Her skin was milk white, and her complexion was almost opaque. She was tall and thin, and reminded Cheever of a plant that had shot upward, reaching for the sky. Stella didn't seem delicate exactly, but there was a fragile quality to her, or maybe it was just that she somehow seemed out of place. Like a snowball in summer, he thought, looking at her white skin.

She smiled, but spoke carefully, as if having to consider every word: "I am sorry that I put you to such effort."

"This happy ending makes it all worthwhile. I'm just glad you're all right. There's no place like home, right?"

Stella smiled, but didn't answer.

Cheever found himself thinking about Diane. He wondered what she would have looked like all grown up, and wished he'd had the chance to see.

"And this is Dr. Jamie Schmitt," said Duncan, introducing him to the woman with the stethoscope. "She used to be Stella's pediatrician, and was kind enough to agree to do a house-call checkup on Stella."

Cheever shook hands with her. The cop in him already wanted answers. "Have you had time to do Stella's physical?"

"Not yet," she said. "I think all of us have been too busy hugging."

"As part of your physical," he said, "will you be taking DNA swabs?"

Duncan laughed and said to the doctor, "Once a cop, always a cop."

Then the congressman quoted from the Bible the story of Doubting Thomas the Apostle: "Except I shall see in his hands the print of the nails, and put my finger into the print of the nails, and thrust my hand into his side, I will not believe."

"Guilty as charged," said Cheever.

Dr. Schmitt inquired of Duncan with her eyes if it was okay for her to talk freely.

"Please answer any questions Detective Cheever has," he said. And then he added with a laugh, "And I'm sure he will have a lot."

Dr. Schmitt turned to Cheever and said, "Even though I understand SDPD already confirmed Stella's identity through her fingerprints, I will be taking DNA swabs, footprints, fingerprints, blood, and urine. Lab work will include a CBC and lipid panel. I will also be taking DNA swabs from Mrs. Pierce and the congressman. The Pierce family has authorized me to release all my findings to SDPD."

"Sufficient?" asked Duncan.

Cheever nodded.

"When Eleanor called me with the news," admitted Duncan, "I was more than skeptical. I wasn't as smart as Copper here. I'm told all it took for him was one sniff to know it was Stella."

The old golden had found a place on the floor right next to Stella. Every half minute or so, the girl reached down to scratch the dog's ear.

"So where was she?" Cheever asked, speaking so that only Duncan could hear.

"Where was she what?" asked Duncan. He looked confused for a moment before realizing what Cheever was asking. "I guess that should have been the obvious first question, but with everything going on, I don't think Eleanor or I have gotten around to asking it."

Cheever wondered whether the omission was purposeful. There was some news you didn't want to hear. Denial was what got lots of people through the day. But it was time to face up to the five-ton elephant in the room.

"Sweetie," said Duncan, speaking as gently as he could to Stella, "in all the excitement, I never asked you where you've been these seven years."

Cheever watched as Stella reached out with her thin right hand and touched her father's shoulder. It looked as if she were the one trying to reassure him.

"I was with the Travelers, Daddy," Stella said.

Cheever had once worked a case involving a group of Gypsies. Early on he learned they preferred to be called Roma, or Travelers. "Are you talking about Gypsies?" he asked.

"No," said Stella. "Travelers aren't of this earth."

The adults were uncomfortably silent for a moment. Cheever could see no one knew quite what to say. In his job he was used to dealing with the mentally ill. When people said crazy things, his colleagues often said of them that they were "gone with the fairies." Cheever did his best to speak softly. "Then what are they?"

"They are beings that travel the cosmos."

"Are you saying the Travelers are extraterrestrials?"

"Yes," said Stella.

"And these aliens took you with them?" asked Cheever.

"They invited me to join them," said Stella.

"And you traveled around the universe with them?"

"The universe is too broad of a statement," Stella said, as if this were the most ordinary conversation in the world. She didn't seem the least bit fazed by his questions. "I will say in my short time of traveling with them, I took part in their pilgrimage to places and planets."

"Then the Travelers are some kind of religious group?"

"They see holiness in many places, and in many things. They are caretakers of sorts, and teachers."

Cheever watched unease flicker across the faces of the adults. No one knew how to reply. They were spared from answering when the front door was thrown open, and Michael stomped inside.

"What the hell are all those reporters doing outside?" he asked.

Michael suddenly noticed his father was in the room. Wasn't he supposed to be on his way back to DC? Maybe that explained all the texts and phone calls from his mother. He hadn't bothered to read or listen to any of them. The smallest thing put his mother in a tizzy.

For a moment Michael thought about offering up the excuse that his phone had run out of juice, but since being accepted into the Air

Force Academy, he'd been trying to live by their cadet creed: *We will not lie, steal, or cheat, nor tolerate among us anyone who does.*

"Sorry I didn't respond to your calls and texts, Mom."

Michael took notice of the others in the room, nodding at Cheever, looking at Dr. Schmitt with surprise, and then trying to identify the girl his mom was clinging to. He felt his expression shift from incomprehension to disbelief to denial that he could be seeing what he thought he was. And finally to an incredulity that yielded to shocked certainty.

"No fucking way," said Michael.

For once his mother didn't lecture him on cursing.

He started walking toward Stella; she met him halfway and threw her arms around him.

"Stella?" he said. "Stella?"

"I am so glad to see you, Michael."

◆ ◆ ◆

Like most pediatricians, Dr. Schmitt seemed to have a talent for putting people at ease. She was obviously used to working with the toughest critics of them all—the young. After all the extraordinary announcements and reunions, the doctor showed the good sense to let everyone take a breath.

"I'm afraid the clock is ticking, Michael," she said after the siblings had embraced for a good long while. "Do you mind if I take Stella away for a few minutes so that I can conduct a physical?"

"Sure," said Michael, awkwardly releasing his sister and stepping back. He still looked as if he was in a state of shock.

"Is it all right if I sit in on your physical?" Eleanor asked Stella.

The girl nodded, then extended her hand to her mother. It was hard to tell if she needed reassurance, or was giving it, or both.

The women went upstairs to Stella's room; the men adjourned to the living room. Because of the detective's frequent visits over the years, Michael sometimes jokingly called him "Uncle Cheever."

"Hey, big guy." Cheever squeezed Michael's arm. "Are you still driving all the girls crazy?"

"Just most of them," said Michael, still looking in the direction Stella had gone.

"It's not fair," Cheever said to Duncan. "When I was in high school, I was fighting off acne, not girls. What's this guy got that I don't have, besides good looks and smarts?"

Cheever stopped talking for a moment, making sure the women were out of hearing range. Then he turned to Michael and said, "Just before you stepped through the door, Stella made the rather startling announcement that for the last seven years she's been traveling around space with extraterrestrials."

Michael looked from Cheever's face to his father's. "You're kidding."

"He's not," said Duncan.

"That's crazy," said Michael, shaking his head.

He might as well have been saying, "She's crazy." That's what his body language was saying.

"You ever hear anyone refer to *coping mechanisms* or *defensive mechanisms*?" Cheever asked.

Michael nodded. "Yeah," he said. "That's like how people deal with things like stress. Some people might exercise; others might go to a movie or have a drink. They try to find some way to cope."

"That's right," said Cheever. "And in some instances they have to do a lot more than that. In order to survive something bad, people have been known to trick their own minds. Sometimes they even supply themselves with a different reality and alternate history just so they don't have to deal with what happened to them. I suspect your sister did that. I think it's likely your sister's alien story is a coping mechanism."

"You think bad things happened to Stella?" asked the boy.

"I wouldn't rule it out," said Cheever. "Unfortunately, when children are abducted, that's generally the case. She might not want to think about what happened to her. Of course I might be all wrong about that.

There could be other reasons for Stella concocting a story. It's possible she wants to protect her abductors."

"Why would she do that?" asked Duncan.

"Have either of you ever heard of Stockholm syndrome?" asked the cop.

Both father and son shook their heads.

"Long story short," said Cheever, "half a century ago there was an attempted bank robbery in Stockholm. During the six-day standoff, the robbers and their hostages got friendly with one another to the point where the hostages sympathized with their captors. Since that time there have been a number of other abduction/hostage relationships where the same thing happened."

Duncan frowned. "So you think Stella came to sympathize with her captors?"

"It's a possibility."

"Then I guess it's good we have a mental health professional on his way over here. I had my office arrange for that even before Stella started telling her little-green-men story."

"Did she really say there were little green men?" asked Michael.

"No, she didn't," said Duncan. "That was your father using humor as a defense mechanism. Stella didn't describe her aliens other than to call them Travelers."

"If anyone had kidnapped me," Michael said, "I'd want to see them nailed."

"Given a little time, that might be what Stella wants as well," said Cheever, "but in the meantime, I'd ask that you be supportive, especially because it's likely your sister will have a tough time adjusting."

"Why?" asked Michael. "She's home now."

"You would think that would solve everything," said Cheever, "but that hasn't been the case."

His grim expression was noticed by both father and son.

"What aren't you telling us?" asked Duncan.

"I've always held out hope that Stella would one day return," Cheever said. "Because of that, I've done a lot of reading on victims who survived their abductions. There's no single profile. But when you've been to hell and back—and that's what happened to too many of these individuals—it's not easy adjusting."

Cheever stopped talking. He thought about those who'd been abducted, and later had turned up alive. None were unscathed; all of them were damaged in one way or another.

"Anyway, I don't mean to be a buzzkill here," he said, "especially given the circumstances. After seven years, Stella has returned, and that's a cause for celebration. Time will sort out her stories. Right now she might not be ready to deal with what happened to her; she might not be ready to even admit it to herself."

The detective let his words sink in. He wanted the Pierce family to realize how psychologically fragile Stella might be.

"Today I'm not planning on questioning Stella for very long," said Cheever. "My goal is to try and establish a rapport with her, and show her that I am on her side. I'm not going to challenge her alien story, especially if it's her security blanket. The human mind finds a lot of ways to cope. I expect Stella's aliens will vanish over time, and the truth will surface, but right now that version of events might be what's keeping her . . . intact."

Duncan and Michael both nodded.

They heard voices and footsteps coming down the stairs. All three women were laughing and talking.

"Who's ready for cocoa?" asked Eleanor.

"I am!" said Stella.

Cheever caught sight of Stella's smile. The cop couldn't help but remember how his own little girl had loved cocoa. Her time on the planet had been short, but Diane loomed large in his memories.

Since her death, he wondered, have I had hot chocolate? He didn't think so. Drinking cocoa was an activity he had done just with his daughter. It wasn't something he had ever wanted to do by himself, but the prospect suddenly appealed to him. Apparently he wasn't alone. Everyone seemed to want some.

"Who wants marshmallows?" asked Eleanor.

"I do," said Stella. She turned and noticed Cheever's eyes on her.

"Cocoa is really good that way, Detective Cheever," she said.

Diane had liked it with marshmallows, too, he remembered.

"Marshmallows sound good to me," he said.

CHAPTER SEVENTEEN

Cheever took stock of all that was going on. Eleanor was in the kitchen. She'd gone from making cocoa to making macaroni and cheese; apparently it had been Stella's favorite dish when she was a girl.

Duncan collected the empty cocoa cups and joined Eleanor in the kitchen, where she was humming happily. Cheever watched Duncan looking at his wife and smiling while she hummed and whistled. Her back was turned to him, but she must have sensed his presence because she turned around. She smiled, and as Duncan put the used cups on the counter, she surprised him with a kiss.

Stella isn't the only one who's returned, thought Cheever.

Michael and Stella were talking with Dr. Schmitt. Anyone looking at the siblings would never know they'd been apart for seven years. Stella seemed as comfortable around her family as if she'd never left. Cheever caught Michael's eye and gave him a nod. Michael responded to the prearranged signal and said to Stella, "It's been a long time since I beat you in Ping-Pong. Want to play?"

Cheever suspected the girl knew she was being herded away so the adults could talk, though she smilingly followed her brother out of the living room.

Duncan came out of the kitchen and looked at Dr. Schmitt expectantly. "How is my daughter doing?" he asked.

"Physically, Stella appears very healthy," she said. "Given the circumstances, I know you must be concerned as to whether there was sexual trauma; in my examination I didn't find any sign of that."

"Thank God," said Duncan.

The doctor continued, "I asked Stella whether she'd ever had any sexual partners, and she told me that she hadn't."

"Did you need to qualify, or explain, your inquiries?" asked Cheever.

"No. Stella seemed acquainted with human biology."

Dr. Schmitt continued with her rundown. "Stella's vision and hearing are exceptional, and her pulse and blood pressure are both good. Her height seems to be following the expected curve. She's on the thin side, but seems quite fit. When I get to the office, I'll have her blood work and urine samples processed, but I expect everything will be fine."

"Her physical didn't reveal any surprises?" asked Cheever.

Dr. Schmitt shrugged. "Pending lab results and further tests, Stella appears to be a healthy young woman. In terms of statistical norms, she exhibits a few slight deviations, but nothing too out of the ordinary."

"Can you offer specifics?"

"Stella hasn't begun menses yet, whereas most girls her age have. Her extreme paleness is also something I want to monitor. Of course it could simply be explained by her having spent very little time in the sun."

"If that's so, it suggests she was confined," said Cheever.

"That's one possibility, but there are many others. In a winter climate with little sun, many people are pale. Or individuals who are bedridden for as little as a week frequently lose their color."

"You heard what Stella had to say about the Travelers," said Duncan.

She nodded.

"What are your thoughts on that?"

"I am not a mental health professional," said Dr. Schmitt, "and don't feel that I am qualified to comment other than to say patients make up stories for any number of reasons."

"Can we count on doctor/client privilege that you will not divulge what you heard?"

"Duncan," said Eleanor, but Dr. Schmitt held up a hand and smiled to show she was fine with the inquiry.

"You can count on my discretion, Congressman."

"It's just that I have to deal with the media," he explained, "and I think it is best not to mention extraterrestrials, especially because I'm the vice chair of the Science, Space, and Technology Committee."

Duncan noticed the blank looks and added, "We're the committee that has jurisdiction over NASA, among other departments."

That was a strange coincidence, thought Cheever.

"We're so grateful for your visit," said Eleanor, giving the doctor a hug. "We can't tell you how appreciative we are."

"It's truly been my pleasure," said Dr. Schmitt. "I can still remember how saddened I was—how saddened everyone in the practice was—when Stella disappeared."

"Let me walk you out," said Duncan. "I'll divert the media while you make your getaway."

◆ ◆ ◆

The press started peppering Duncan with questions the moment he opened the front door, and continued shouting questions while he made his way down the walkway. With all eyes on him, Dr. Schmitt was able to get to her car with a minimum of pursuit.

Duncan remembered the same media throng seven years ago. Facing the cameras hadn't scared him at the time. It was having a missing daughter that had terrified him, and he'd been willing to do anything to try and get her back.

He motioned for silence, and the media reluctantly complied. The lights from the cameras were shining in his eyes. During his time in

Washington, Duncan had learned how to appear comfortable in front of the camera and personalize his address.

Making eye contact with the cameras, he said, "Today I am the luckiest man alive. My daughter, Stella, has come home."

Duncan ignored the flurry of questions shouted at him, again holding up his hands for silence.

"I hope you can understand that right now, the only thing I want to do is spend time with my daughter and my family, and because of that, your questions must wait for another time. For seven long years we've prayed for my daughter's return, and we thank God that our prayers were answered."

He offered a wave and a smile. As he began walking back to the house, the media clamor rose to a fevered pitch, but he didn't turn around to their plaintive cries. For once he wasn't a politician. He was just a dad who wanted to spend time with his daughter.

◆ ◆ ◆

The plaintive cries weren't reserved only for the media. There were plenty of cries coming from the playroom.

"Michael is a tad competitive," Duncan acknowledged.

"I wonder where he got that from," said Eleanor.

Her comment elicited a kiss from Duncan.

"Isn't that enough PDA?" asked Cheever.

"No," said Duncan, kissing his wife again.

"Did you ever look at our garage after we converted it into a playroom?" asked Eleanor.

"I don't think so," Cheever replied.

"There's everything out there kids might like," she said, "including the Ping-Pong table, a pool table, pinball machines, electronics, free weights, and a big-screen TV with stereo speakers. I'm afraid it was a shameless attempt to keep Michael and his friends close to home."

They heard Michael shouting, "I can't believe how lucky you are!"

"It sounds like Stella's table-tennis game has improved," said Duncan.

"I wonder if she plays a mean pinball," said Cheever.

◆ ◆ ◆

Michael paused before serving. "It is sort of strange having you back," he said.

"It is sort of strange being back," said Stella.

"I never thought I'd see Mom all smiley again. I don't think she's had a good night's sleep since you were gone. And for once, Dad was here—I mean, really here. After you left, he sort of got obsessed with one thing and another, and that was even before he was back east most of the time."

"What about you?" she asked.

"I kind of went my own way," he said. "I guess we all did. I missed you, of course. But I was also pissed at you."

"Missed and pissed," mused Stella.

"Yeah, I mean I was sad you were gone, but always being in your shadow got old real quick."

"My shadow?" she asked.

He nodded. "In case you didn't know, you were the perfect child, and you never did anything wrong. Mom *worshipped* your memory, and Dad was always doing something or other to *honor* your memory. How'd you like to grow up in that shadow?"

"It must have been hard," she said, "but now that I'm back, they'll see how imperfect I am."

"I hope so. I'm tired of being the only black sheep in the family."

Then, without warning, he served the ball, catching Stella unaware.

"My point," he said.

"You jackass," she said.

"Jackass?" said Michael. "I haven't heard that . . . since we were kids. I better help you update your insult vocabulary, *loser*, or else no one will even know you're *dissing* them."

◆ ◆ ◆

Duncan looked at his watch. "That shrink should be arriving any minute now," he said.

"In that case I'd better have my talk with Stella now," Cheever said, "assuming it's all right with both of you."

When neither parent voiced an objection, Cheever went to the garage to get Stella. From the doorway he watched the game in process. Michael was clearly a good athlete, able to hit the ball where and how he wanted it. He could spin, slice, and put topspin on the ball, but despite his skill, Stella was able to keep the ball in play. In fact, it was Michael who was red-faced and sweating; Stella calmly returned his ball time and again with what looked like a minimum of effort. For Michael, it must have felt like hitting to a backboard. Finally, though, he snuck a shot by Stella.

"Good shot, Michael," she said.

Cheever wondered if Stella had purposely given him the point.

"Sorry to interrupt the game," said Cheever, "but I'm afraid it's nosy-cop time, which means I need to borrow Stella for a few minutes."

◆ ◆ ◆

Cheever and Stella weren't the only ones who went up to her room. Copper followed the two of them and joined Stella atop her twin bed. The golden retriever looked like he was smiling and kept extending his paw to Stella.

"He's glad to see you back," said Cheever.

"He went crazy when he saw me," said Stella.

"He should have been named Argos."

Stella looked to him for an explanation.

"One day you might read about Argos in *The Odyssey*," he said. "Argos was a loyal dog who waited twenty years for the return of his master, Odysseus. When Odysseus finally arrived at his home in Ithaca, no one recognized him save for Argos, who gave him a rousing welcome. Right afterward, Argos died. He'd fulfilled his last duty."

The girl gave Copper a kiss and said, "I'm glad you didn't die after you welcomed me home."

Cheever smiled at them. He had probably been in Stella's room more than a hundred times over the years. All of its contents were in a file; all of its contents were in his brain. A few years back, Eleanor Pierce had reluctantly given most of her daughter's clothing to Goodwill, but just about everything else remained as it had been.

During many of his visits to the home, Cheever had prowled around the room by himself. On one occasion he remembered getting down on his knees and walking around in the hopes of having Stella's vantage point. It hadn't helped. But now here he was, back where he'd started.

He thought back to the time Linda Fabian had walked around Stella's room. The psychic had been confused. She had said Stella was alive, but that she was far away.

Far, far away, she had said.

Cheever took a seat on the edge of the bed, careful not to disrupt Stella and Copper.

"You've grown so tall," he said. "I'm afraid your parents are going to have to get you a new bed."

Stella smoothed the bedcover and shook her head. "I like this one."

"I'm curious about a picture that we couldn't account for, Stella," said Cheever. "There was a family photo taken in Big Sur that your mother remembered being in your room. After you went missing, your mom couldn't find that picture."

"I took it," she said in a soft voice.

She reached inside the pocket of her pants and withdrew a folded and well-worn picture.

"You've had that all these years?"

She nodded.

Cheever felt his pulse quicken. When he'd worked the case, there had been so little to go on; they hadn't been sure evidence like the missing photo could even be considered evidence. "Why did you take it?"

"I wanted a picture of my family."

"So you took it with the knowledge that you were going away?"

Stella nodded.

"Did you know how much you'd be missed?"

"I probably should have, but I didn't. My only excuse is that I was seven. I guess I was so excited that I didn't think about it at the time."

"You weren't scared by the prospect of going off with strangers?"

"I was more excited than anything," she said. "For the first time it felt as if the stars were within my reach."

"So the Travelers asked if you wanted to come with them."

"The Travelers don't speak like we're doing right now, but I understood their invitation."

"How did you communicate with them?"

"Through mindspeak," she said. "If it seems that I am having trouble talking to you and the others, it's because I am out of practice."

Cheever tried to hide his surprise. He had noticed Stella's sometimes halting speech, and had wondered at it.

He asked another seemingly random question. "What do the Travelers look like?"

"Their appearance changed depending on where we were and what we were doing."

"You make them sound like shape-shifters."

"I don't know that word. The first Traveler I encountered, I thought was an angel."

"Why did you think that?"

"She came to me in the form of light."

"And you understood her thoughts?"

"That's right."

"Why did you return home at this time, Stella?"

She thought about that before answering. "The disharmony was growing perilous."

"Disharmony?" asked Cheever.

Stella nodded, and then said, "I think you should talk with my mother."

Cheever made a mental note to do that. "Were you glad to come back home?"

"I'm not sure if I am home."

"What do you mean?"

"Who is to say if my stay here is temporary or permanent?"

"I imagine you are."

"That decision might, or might not, be my own. Time will tell."

"So for the last seven years you've been traveling around the universe?"

"Space has been one of my travels."

"Aren't there laws of physics that say that faster-than-light travel isn't possible?"

"I don't know about those laws."

"For years I've been trying to figure out how you disappeared seemingly without a trace. Tell me how the Travelers were able to take you away."

"I don't know," she said.

"Why don't you know?"

"I don't remember what happened after I agreed to go with them. When I awakened, I was on the ship."

"How much time passed between your being taken and your awakening?"

"I have no idea," she said. "Time is different out there."

The detective mixed up his questions again, jumping from subject to subject. "Where did you get the clothes you're wearing?"

"They were provided for me."

"Did you pick them up at the Gap?"

That made Stella smile. "It's been a long time since I've been to the Gap."

"Do you know what kind of fabric your blouse is made of?"

She shook her head, but then added, "I know it's not made from animal products."

"How do you know that?"

"The Travelers don't believe in killing animals for food or materials."

She reached over to her nightstand and opened a drawer. Inside, everything was as she had left it. There were colored pens, some jacks, and a deck of cards. Stella reached for the cards and smiled.

"Do you like to play cards?" asked Cheever.

"I haven't played since I left," she said, "but I remember I used to love playing Go Fish with anyone who would play with me."

"It's been years since I've played that game." Diane had liked playing it as well, he remembered. It had been a way of passing the time during her stays in hospitals.

"How about I'll be the dealer?" said Cheever.

Stella handed him the deck, and Cheever dealt each of them seven cards. She studied her hand and then appeared to take a read of Cheever.

"Do you have queens?" she asked.

"Apparently I'm playing with a cardsharp," said Cheever, passing over a queen.

CHAPTER EIGHTEEN

Dr. Benjamin Froke sat in the center of the living room. He'd been told when he arrived that some cop was questioning Stella. Froke didn't like the idea of having to cool his heels, but there had been work to do in the meantime. Ostensibly he was taking down a family history, but what he was really doing was following a script established by the man who had hired him, or, more likely, the organization the man represented. If he was working for the devil, at least the devil was making it look as if he was very well prepared.

Froke's acting talents were called upon for much of the interview. He feigned surprise when the parents offered up Stella's background and where she claimed to have been during her time away. All of that had already been spelled out in the paperwork Froke had been given.

The psychiatrist paused between asking questions of the family, acting as if he was considering what was being said, and then responding after additional thought. Froke often liked to wing his sessions. Most of his patients didn't care as long as he filled their prescriptions. His job was to bill and pill. He'd been tempted to end more than one session by asking, "You want fries with that?"

He briefly glanced at his script. "As a child, did Stella have any imaginary friends?"

"Yes," Eleanor said. "What was that name?"

"Fuzzy," said Duncan.

"No," said Michael. "Fizzies."

"Was Fizzies male or female?" asked Froke.

"Male," said Eleanor. "I think."

"How long did this imaginary friend persist?"

The Pierce family exchanged glances.

"About a year," Duncan answered.

"How old was Stella then?"

"Three or four," said Eleanor.

Froke wrote the answers down. "Would you say Stella has a very active imagination?"

"What do you mean?" asked the congressman, his tone defensive.

"For example, as a girl did she enjoy telling, or acting out, fantastic stories?"

"To some extent," said Eleanor. "I remember on several occasions she played the role of a fairy princess with a magic wand."

"Do you know if she ever saw the movie *E.T.*?"

Michael chimed in: "We watched it together. I remember she cried."

"What about any of the Star Wars films?"

"I think she saw most of them," said Michael.

"So, even as a child, she would have been familiar with the concept of aliens?"

The heads nodded.

"Did she ever threaten to run away?"

"No," said Duncan. His tone was flat and final.

"Would you describe her as a happy child?"

"Very," said Duncan.

"Did Stella have any particular fears or phobias?"

"She didn't like the dark when she was a child," said Eleanor. "That's why her drapes were always open. She liked the light from the night sky, and the moon, and enjoyed looking out to the stars."

"Stars," said Froke, repeating back what Eleanor had said. That was about as much improvising as the script allowed for.

"She didn't like spiders either," said Duncan. "I imagine she still doesn't."

"That's right," said Eleanor, remembering. "She was afraid of spiders."

"Do you remember Stella ever voicing a desire to travel?"

Husband and wife conferred with their eyes before Duncan answered, "Almost every night I used to read her stories. She was curious about different places and customs."

"You read her adventure stories? Places with foreign settings?"

Duncan thought about it. "From what I remember, many of the books were set in foreign lands, or even different worlds."

"Tell me some of the stories you read."

Duncan thought for another moment. "*Ali Baba and the 40 Thieves. Aesop's Fables. The Hobbit. Black Beauty. Mary Poppins. Little House on the Prairie. The Borrowers. Charlotte's Web. Peter Pan. Sinbad. Cinderella. Snow White and the Seven Dwarfs.* Lots of others."

"She liked stories with exotic locales?"

"She liked stories, period," said Duncan.

Footsteps coming down the stairway announced the arrival of Stella and the cop. The adults stopped talking while Froke got to his feet and studied his new patient.

"Cheever," said the man, stepping in front of Stella and offering his hand.

Froke grasped Cheever's hand and said, "I'm Dr. Benjamin Froke."

Even though Froke released his grip, the detective held on for a second longer and said, "Stella's tired, Dr. Froke. For her sake, I'd make your session with her a short one."

Keeping his voice carefully neutral and trying not to show his immediate dislike for the man, Froke said, "It would be helpful for me to know what the two of you discussed."

"Oh, I doubt if it would be very helpful," said Cheever, his tone light and playful. Stella was smiling at him. "We talked about favorite foods, and played a few games of cards."

"I won!" said Stella.

"I demand a rematch," said Cheever.

And this is what I waited for, thought Froke. He tried to maintain a pleasant expression on his face. "Perhaps you'll teach me how to play," he said to Stella, extending his hand in greeting. "It's nice to meet you, Stella. I am Dr. Froke."

It had been a long time since Froke had felt any true excitement at the onset of a session. But this time he felt butterflies. Whatever was going on seemed big. And the riddle of Stella Pierce's missing seven years intrigued him.

"How are you feeling, Stella?" Froke asked.

"Fine," she said, "but tired."

"It's been a big day for you, hasn't it?"

She nodded.

◆ ◆ ◆

Cheever waited with the Pierce family for Stella's session to finish. He looked at the time again. The shrink's session with her was now pushing an hour.

Even though he'd only met the other man for a minute, there was something about Froke that got under Cheever's skin. It was probably his supercilious attitude. There had been a time when Cheever hadn't thought much of mental health professionals, but that was before he'd fallen in love with one. Rachel Stern had taught him more about disorders and phobias and behavioral science than he ever knew existed, and he had come to realize the importance of these practitioners.

Eleanor yawned, but apologized with a smile on her face. Her daughter was home. Duncan had also had a long day, but you wouldn't know it by how he was acting. He kept patting Cheever's and Michael's shoulders and hugging Eleanor. The Pierces, thought Cheever, were behaving like professional athletes in the aftermath of winning the championship game; the hooting and hollering was done, and they didn't quite know what to do with all their happiness.

More than anything, he suspected, they just wanted to hug their daughter.

"If you want," said Cheever, "I could go tell him enough is enough."

Eleanor looked more than ready to take him up on his offer, but Duncan spoke for the couple: "We'd better give him a few more minutes."

Five minutes later the shrink trudged down the stairs to the living room. From the gravity of Froke's bearing and expression, he looked like a surgeon who'd performed a life-or-death operation and was ready to deliver news of the outcome.

"Stella and I had a good talk," he said. "Now she needs to unwind, and sleep."

Cheever bit his lip to keep from telling Froke he'd said the same thing an hour earlier.

Eleanor said, "Michael, can you go upstairs right now and sit with your sister? Tell her I'll be up in a little while."

Froke turned to Cheever. "I am afraid what I have to say is for the family only, Detective."

"We'll waive your confidentiality concerns," said Duncan. "We want Detective Cheever to hear everything you have to say."

Froke shrugged and said, "As you wish." He took out some paperwork and his notepad, consulting both before speaking.

"In therapy, the notion of a breakthrough is frequently misunderstood," Froke said. "Most individuals have this mistaken idea that there comes this grand moment when the therapist yells, 'Eureka.'"

Froke's preamble, thought Cheever, didn't sound original.

"The real breakthroughs," continued Froke, "are rarely even noticed. They are accomplished through small, incremental steps, with each session building upon the last. It would be unrealistic to expect immediate results. Still, Stella and I had a very fruitful session tonight.

"As you are aware, Stella says she has been with the Travelers, a name she says that the extraterrestrials call themselves. As you were also told, Stella says these aliens go around traveling the universe.

"The more Stella talked, the clearer it became that her Travelers story is an elaborate avoidance mechanism. It might even be a metaphor for the way she has lived these last seven years, always traveling from place to place. Or it might be that she's dissociated to avoid very painful memories.

"Based on my initial session with her, it's clear that Stella will need intensive therapy. Given the circumstances, I'm sure you don't find that surprising. My recommendation is for both individual and group sessions. Stella's readjustment is likely to be very painful, both to her and the ones who love her. Everyone here needs to remember that Stella is not the same little girl who left. Half of her life has been lived away from home, and we don't yet know what her experiences have been during her time away. After the initial euphoria of her return diminishes, conflicts will certainly arise."

The shrink again referred to his notes, and then continued. "In pioneer days, there were instances of white children being taken in raids and raised by Native Americans. Years later, when those children were returned to their families, there were usually terrible problems. The children had been raised in another culture, with different ways. For them, acclimation was not easy. Blood was not thicker than culture and experience. Sometimes love alone could not surmount these barriers.

"Judging by Stella's tale, in her own mind she compares herself with those displaced pioneer children, although it wasn't Indians who raised her, but aliens. That's her way of telling us how different she now is. I would take it as a warning as well. Stella feels displaced. In order to ameliorate her readjustment to the family, you will need to offer her unconditional love. The more comfortable she feels, the faster she will heal."

Froke looked around the room after he finished his summation. From the way he was preening, thought Cheever, the shrink seemed to think applause was in order.

In a little voice, Eleanor said, "She still seems like our Stella."

"There is a part of her that is," said Froke. "But you will have to be accepting of the part that isn't."

"How long do you think she'll be holding on to this Travelers story of hers?" Duncan asked.

Froke shrugged. "It would be impossible to guess. She has obviously constructed an elaborate paradigm, and I find it unlikely that she'd give up such a deep-rooted defense mechanism easily. Among severely abused children, these types of imaginative scenarios are not uncommon."

"Dr. Schmitt didn't find any evidence of physical abuse," said Cheever.

"I'm sure, Detective, that you've seen examples of mental abuse that were as debilitating as physical abuse."

"I know this sounds selfish as hell," said Duncan, "but would it be wrong if for now I asked Stella to keep her little green men story to herself?"

Froke stroked his chin. He was glad the congressman had made this request. If he hadn't, Froke's handlers had instructed him to make it. "I don't see a problem with that. Not everything has to be public. You and Stella can choose what to divulge and what to keep private."

Duncan turned to Cheever. "Do you have any problem with that, Detective?"

Cheever shook his head. "Not on my end."

"In that case, when I talk to the media tomorrow, I'll say Stella's under a doctor's care and that I can't offer any particulars of her time away because that might impact the police investigation. Does that work for both of you?" Duncan asked.

Froke and Cheever nodded.

"Did Stella talk to you about being taken by the Travelers, Doctor?" asked Cheever.

"She called it an *invitation*," said Froke. "She said the Travelers invited her to be a part of their incredible journey. When they first communicated with her, Stella said she thought they were angels. In hindsight, I am sure that's how she justified her going off with strangers."

"Are you saying Stella knew she was doing something wrong?" asked Cheever.

"I wouldn't categorize it in the rubric of *right* or *wrong*. Individuals justify their actions through a variety of means."

Froke took note of the cop's skeptical expression. It was hard for him not to. "Is something bothering you, Detective?"

"Yes, Doctor. The facts as I know them."

"And what facts are those?"

"The sins of omission," said Cheever. "And there are plenty of those: seven years' worth, in fact."

"What do you mean?"

"In the little time I had with Stella, I found it interesting that she didn't know the name of the president. I also brought up a lot of recent kid-favorite music and movies, as well as entertainers and celebrities who have become famous during the last seven years. Time and again Stella had no idea *what* I was talking about or *who* I was talking about. It was the same thing with major world events. She drew a blank. As for language, my work keeps me up on current slang. Words and phrases that every American teenager knows were lost on Stella."

The longer Cheever spoke, the more strained Froke's smile appeared. When the detective finished, Froke shook his head. "So what are you suggesting, Detective Cheever? Are you implying that for the last seven years, Stella has been off traveling the cosmos with aliens?"

"That wouldn't be my first guess," said Cheever.

"What would?"

"I don't usually engage in guessing games."

"Perhaps you will humor me."

Cheever shrugged. "My best guess is that Stella was held captive in a remote location where she was denied access to television, radio, and magazines."

"And given such a sterile environment, do you find it surprising that Stella constructed an alternate universe?"

"No, that wouldn't surprise me," said Cheever. "What does surprise me is Stella's returning from that kind of captivity and still appearing to be the happy, gregarious girl that she apparently is."

"Or that she's trying to appear to be. I don't think it's too surprising that today, of all days, Stella is overjoyed to be home."

Froke let the Pierces absorb the full impact of his little smile. "I am glad to hear, though, that you won't be spending time investigating aliens."

Cheever offered up the smile of the unamused. "Actually, I always like to find whatever facts I can, and let them guide me. Facts are very stubborn things. They tell a story whether you like it or not."

CHAPTER NINETEEN

Froke opened the door to his Solana Beach condominium. He was a renter, but he told the women who visited him there that the ocean-view dwelling was his. The reality was that it would be a long time, if ever, before he could afford to buy a place like this. His medical-school debt was daunting, even though the windfall he'd received earlier in the day would help with that. He'd actually hidden the $25,000 in the laundry hamper, waiting until he figured out the best way to spend it.

Maybe he could milk this thing for a lot more money. Whoever wanted him to treat Stella Pierce had deep pockets and resources. They'd swung him the referral and provided him with a detailed guide to treating her.

He wondered if her disappearance had something to do with her father being a congressman. It was possible, he supposed, but the time frame made it unlikely. The girl had gone missing before Pierce had been elected. And the congressman seemed to be as much in the dark about what had happened to his daughter as everyone else in his family.

They weren't the only ones in the dark, thought Froke. He was supposed to be the Pierce family's answer man, but he couldn't make sense of the situation either. The girl had gone missing for seven years and then come back with a story about being away with aliens. That was crazy enough, but what was even crazier was his being paid big bucks to discredit her story with the family, and control the girl through supposed therapeutic sessions. It wasn't as if anyone was going to believe what she was saying anyway.

Froke approached his wet bar and decided to go old school, making himself a gin and tonic. He had waited all day for his chaser, and went to the kitchen cabinet and pulled down a vitamin bottle. It was time to get his daily dose of Cotton, one of the street names for OxyContin. He swallowed the pill and knew in a few minutes he'd be feeling much better.

With his drink in his hand, Froke opened the living room curtains. It was too dark to see the ocean very well, but he could hear it. The waves were loud, making their form of tubular thunder. He liked it when the big drums came out; it stirred in him the notion to invite over some company. But even booty calls had their price. He'd have to listen to some woman blathering, and at the moment he felt blathered out. Froke took a sip of his drink, then loudly chewed on a piece of ice as he considered the pros and cons of tendering such an invitation.

His musings were interrupted by the sound of loud organ music. Froke reached for his pocket. He had set his phone on mute so he wouldn't be disturbed by incoming calls or messages. But it wasn't his phone that was ringing. It was the cell phone Scarecrow had given him. The phone's ringtone was Bach's Toccata and Fugue in D Minor. Froke delayed a moment, not wanting to answer it, but then did.

"It used to be thought that those who chewed on ice were sexually frustrated."

Froke jumped back, swallowing the ice. He heard the sound coming from two places—the receiver and the living room. His hands, one holding the glass and one the phone, rose in fright—or perhaps surrender. In the shadows of the living room, sitting in his easy chair, was Scarecrow.

Scarecrow must have disconnected the call; now his voice was coming only from the living room: "But now they say that those who frequently chew on ice might be suffering from anemia. Do you have an iron deficiency, Dr. Froke?"

"What the hell are you doing here?" Froke said, pocketing the phone.

"I am here to expound upon our last conversation. And I am here to discuss today's session with Stella and her family. Are you lucid enough to converse with me on those subjects, or has your chill pill already addled your thinking?"

Froke took another step backward. "I'm not impaired," he said.

"That better be the case," said Scarecrow. "We expect you to be mindful of your drug use. And consider this fair warning: if you ever use before one of your sessions with Stella, within twenty-four hours the California Medical Board will be notified of your many violations of the Hippocratic Oath, as well as state laws."

"I never use when I'm working . . . ," began Froke.

One of Scarecrow's eyes emerged from the shadows, and the scrutiny unnerved him. Of late, there had been a few occasions when he had used during his workday. Somehow Scarecrow knew that. Somehow *they* knew that.

"I'll make sure never to do that," Froke promised.

The flinty eye nodded, then disappeared once more into the shadows.

"I thought today's session went well," said Froke. "I took a family history and—"

"There is no need to recapitulate what was said. I know what was said."

"You were . . . listening?"

"You were being monitored."

The tone of Scarecrow's voice, and the word he used, suggested something more insidious than electronic eavesdropping. By now the Cotton should have been making Froke feel better, but he was feeling anything but.

"I did as you instructed," said Froke.

"When you followed the script, you did well."

"You didn't prepare me for the cop. When he started talking about 'sins of omission,' I wasn't sure where to go."

"It was clever of the detective to take a read on Stella's knowledge of popular culture in the last decade," said Scarecrow. "That wasn't foreseen, and it should have been. But you won't need to worry about the cop in the future. Within the week he will be satisfied as to Stella's whereabouts during much of the seven years in question."

"It's difficult to treat someone," said Froke, treading carefully over what he perceived as thin ice, "when you don't know the full story."

"You are not treating Stella. You are managing her. And you will proceed on a need-to-know basis."

Scarecrow produced his phone again, and stabbed the screen a few times with his index finger. "There," he said. "We have laid out tomorrow's session for you in the e-mail that you just received."

Froke heard the sound of a doorbell ringing. He opened his phone's e-mail app and saw that a file had been sent to him. Judging by the sender, Froke had sent the file to himself.

"Any file we send to you has a life span of two hours," said Scarecrow. "The file can only be opened by your phone or by your laptop. It can't be copied, forwarded, or printed."

"Two hours?" asked Froke.

"Minus the minute we've been chatting."

Froke started scanning the e-mail. It was detailed, which probably shouldn't have surprised him. There was a critique of how he'd handled that day's session, and questions and topics he was supposed to cover with Stella and her family during their next session.

"And the file disappears?"

"Into thin air," said Scarecrow.

"How am I supposed to remember everything that's here?"

"I suggest you read, study, and take notes."

"That will take hours."

"You have one hour and fifty-eight minutes."

Froke finished reading a paragraph that suggested ways he could best manipulate Eleanor, Duncan, and Michael. It crossed his mind that Scarecrow most certainly would have been advised on the best ways to manipulate *him*.

"What if I need more time?"

Scarecrow shook his head.

"What's the harm in giving me a copy of what I'm supposed to discuss, just like you did today?"

"We don't like paper trails," said Scarecrow. "We don't like *any* trails."

Froke scrolled further into the file. There were tests he was supposed to administer to Stella starting tomorrow. The results of those tests would show Stella needed socializing, with the strong recommendation that she be mainstreamed into high school as soon as possible.

"I'll do my best to comply," said Froke, "but I hope you realize what a difficult position this puts me in. I'm being asked to proceed, while at the same time not knowing what all of this is about. That's like an actor being told to play a role, but not being given a complete script."

"It worked on *Casablanca*."

"What worked?"

"The actors were operating on the fly. They didn't know the ending. And in your case, I'd consider it well advised not to want to know anything more than necessary."

Scarecrow's tone didn't change, but the threat was still unmistakable. Froke took a deep, steadying breath, cleared his throat, and nodded. Scarecrow said nothing, but there was a reason for that. He was gone. He had vanished like a ghost—or a CIA spook. So why was it that his threat seemed to linger?

After making sure there was no one in his condo, Froke sat down at his writing desk; in what felt like a defiant gesture, he gulped down his gin and tonic. Then he began reading the file and taking notes. Now that he knew his session with Stella had been monitored, Froke couldn't help but wonder if someone was watching him now.

This feels like an episode from *Mission Impossible*, he thought, with the secretary of state ready to disavow everything. He wondered if his message would go up in a puff of smoke, and on an impulse he got up and went to his briefcase. Inside, he looked for the paperwork Scarecrow had given him, but there was nothing there. Froke had gone directly from the Pierce house to his Solana Beach condo, but somewhere along the way all his paperwork had disappeared.

He returned to his desk. He was even more aware of the time than before, and managed to get to the end of the file before the two hours concluded. Finishing the work, though, didn't make him feel any better. Scarecrow, and whatever he represented, cast a long shadow. Froke wondered if he'd been right about the actors not knowing how *Casablanca* was going to end. He had sounded very sure of himself, but he sounded sure about everything he said.

Froke looked at his phone's display. There was nothing there. Then he looked at his e-mail. As Scarecrow had promised, the file had vanished.

CHAPTER TWENTY

After the death of his daughter and the disintegration of his marriage, Cheever had never expected to fall in love again. His relationships had become few and far between, and he had assumed he was so habituated to being single that no person or thing would ever change that. Being in his fifties, he had thought the doors to his heart couldn't be breached. Passion, he was sure, was a thing of the past. All that had changed when he'd worked on what had up to then been the strangest case of his life. Holly "Helen" Troy had been a witness to a homicide, or perhaps had committed the homicide. Cheever had never dealt with a witness like Holly. Because she was diagnosed with dissociative identity disorder—once known as multiple personality disorder—she offered up the perspectives of multiple, and sometimes contradictory, witnesses. In navigating the riddles of that case, Cheever had consulted with her therapist, Rachel Stern, to try and understand what Holly had seen and experienced.

Initially Cheever had been skeptical of the doctor. At the time he viewed psychiatry as being akin to quackery. But Cheever soon discovered Rachel's intelligence and humanity. Like him, she hadn't been expecting love to come into her life. Cheever thought himself lucky that as accomplished and smart as Rachel was, she had chosen him to be what she called her "special someone." The detective was more informal, referring to the psychiatrist as "my gal."

Rachel had made a late dinner so that the two of them could dine together at her Point Loma home. Usually they ate outside on the porch to take advantage of her ocean view, but because of the late hour and the evening chill, they had decided to sit at the dining-room table. Rachel made pasta primavera, and brought out a bottle of Robert Mondavi Reserve Cabernet Sauvignon for their celebration of the return of Stella Pierce. In the time she and Cheever had been together, the psychiatrist had become well acquainted with the name Stella Pierce. She had seen how the case still haunted Cheever, and could always tell when he was ruminating about Stella's disappearance. Cheever's faraway look, furrowed brow, and frown lines told her what he was thinking about, and how it still bothered him that he couldn't make sense of what had happened to Stella.

"When the Falcon called me with the news that Stella was back," Cheever said, "I pulled the car over to the side of the road because I felt so overwhelmed. And then after our conversation, I began crying."

"Seven years of bottled emotions needed a release," Rachel said.

"I can't even remember the last time I cried."

"One day I hope to understand the male aversion to tears," she said.

"They were happy tears," Cheever admitted.

"I would hope so."

They smiled at each other. Rachel extended her hand, and Cheever grasped her fingers in his own.

"I'm wondering if the doctor has time for a consultation," said Cheever.

"Can you afford my fee?" she asked, squeezing his hand.

"I look forward to it," he said.

Rachel reached for her glasses and put them on. Cheever wondered whether she was aware of her "tell." Whenever she put on her glasses, it was time to work. She wore them for her clients and for business. Rachel ran a hand through her salt-and-pepper hair, pushing it away from her eyes.

Cheever justified his talking to Rachel as "patient-client privilege. In this case she was also his "consultant." That allowed him to speak freely to her. "At the onset I should say that prior to my talking to Stella, she was seen by a medical doctor," said Cheever. "Although the doctor's prognosis was qualified and she wants to do further tests, it's her belief that in Stella's time away, she did not suffer physical or sexual abuse."

"What wonderful news," Rachel said.

"That wasn't the only surprise," said Cheever. "When asked where she was for the last seven years, Stella said she was with a group she called the Travelers. According to Stella, the Travelers are not from Earth. They're aliens."

Cheever was watching Rachel's face. When he'd heard about aliens, he'd been incredulous; Rachel's features indicated only interest.

"Go on," she said.

"When the two of us talked, I didn't press Stella for too many details about the Travelers. I thought it better to go easy with her at first. I was thinking she was protecting someone, and that her story might be a result of Stockholm syndrome, so I did my avuncular thing with her, talking about everything and anything. That's when I discovered her seven-year blank. From what I could determine, Stella has no knowledge of world events during her time away. Even more striking for someone her age is her lack of familiarity with pop-culture figures. She seemed not to know any films, music, or TV shows from the last seven years, and judging by her answers, she was totally out of touch with current events."

"Interesting," said Rachel.

"Despite that, what I think I found most surprising was how well adjusted she seemed to be."

"Why did that surprise you?"

"From what I know and what I've read, in the aftermath of being released from captivity, victims usually exhibit a host of symptoms, including anxiety, suspicion, depression, mood swings, and PTSD. But Stella doesn't seem to be experiencing any of those things."

"She didn't act like someone who'd been a prisoner for seven years?"

Cheever shook his head. "And my gut tells me it wasn't an act. She came across as both an innocent and a wise old soul."

"So what's your explanation?"

"I'm working on that. You've taught me not to jump to conclusions."

"And who says an old dog can't learn new tricks?"

"They brought in a therapist," said Cheever, "a young-gun children's psychiatrist named Benjamin Froke. Do you know him?"

Rachel raised her head and pursed her lips, something she often did when searching her memory. Finally she shook her head and said, "He's no one I've met or that I've heard of."

"Good," said Cheever. "In that case I can bad-mouth him."

"He wasn't to your taste?"

"He struck me more as an actor than a shrink."

Rachel's nod encouraged him to continue.

"Maybe I'm just used to the way you work," he said. "You listen carefully, and then ask pertinent questions. Before making any pronouncements, you analyze everything, and even then you don't speak in absolutes. That wasn't his way. Froke acted as if he was Moses coming down from Mount Sinai bringing with him the word of God."

"So if I'm to judge from what you're saying, you thought Dr. Froke was full of himself."

"Young men shouldn't be that smug."

"Could your disliking him be a case of two alpha males actively marking their territory?"

Cheever shrugged. "There might have been a little of that going on."

"Tell me about Dr. Froke's pronouncements."

"He said that Stella had created her story of the Travelers as an 'elaborate paradigm' of avoidance so she wouldn't have to deal with what really happened to her. Froke is convinced the whole Travelers thing is a defense mechanism, and given time and therapy, she'll one day abandon the story and be able to tell what really happened."

"And you didn't agree with his take on the situation?"

"I am not certain of it one way or another. What I didn't like was how definitive he was. I am a great believer in gut instinct, but I know better than to think my hunches are infallible. I try and let the facts guide me. Froke acts like he already has all the answers."

"It's possible he was trying to reassure Stella's parents with his observations, as well as offer them a suggested course of action. For the sake of the parents, he would have wanted to appear confident and not have them overreact, especially to her story of the Travelers. His offering up potential explanations for the Travelers probably reassured the parents and gave them some guidance on how to deal with the situation."

Cheever thought about that and slowly nodded. "He did caution the Pierce family about their need to be patient with Stella, and used the example of settler children being abducted by Native Americans and then raised in their ways. Froke said when those children were returned to their biological families, they had a terrible time readjusting."

Rachel nodded without commenting.

"If you had been brought in as a consultant," asked Cheever, "what would you have told Stella's family?"

"Please don't ask me to second-guess a colleague," she said.

"I don't want you to do that. But I do want your take on the situation. And I want your advice to help me going forward."

"Okay. Well, you might be surprised to learn that I've had clients who have also been convinced that they were abducted, or perhaps, more accurately, had dealings with aliens."

"Really?" said Cheever.

Rachel nodded and considered her words. She'd never violated doctor-patient confidentiality, even with her special someone, and wasn't about to start now. But there was plenty of background she could offer Cheever. "The belief in having experienced alien contact is not as rare as you might think. It's estimated that three million Americans—or roughly one in one hundred adults—believe they have had an encounter with aliens. That doesn't mean that all those individuals are claiming to have been abducted, but it does mean they are certain they have had contact with aliens in one form or another.

"Some of the stories are quite graphic, and could be labeled surreal. There are women who believe their eggs have been harvested, and men who claim the same of their sperm. Other accounts sound less bizarre, although the majority of those interviewed said they remembered feeling paralyzed while being examined naked by the aliens. You would think you could discount those kinds of claims by saying that most of these individuals are mentally ill or psychotic. For the vast majority, though, that simply isn't the case. These are individuals who tested out as being mentally competent."

"If they aren't crazy," said Cheever, "then what are they?"

"It depends on who you're asking," she said. "The majority of doctors and mental health professionals suspect the claimants have experienced a form of sleep paralysis. I don't know if you've ever awakened before your body has, or fallen asleep and found yourself unable to move. Sleep paralysis occurs when your brain and your body aren't in sync. That might not sound scary, but imagine being awake and being unable to move or to speak. Even if this paralysis doesn't last long, because the individuals have no control of their bodies, they often feel panic and fright. To use a horror-film analogy, they've experienced the invasion of a body snatcher. Maybe that's why many who experience sleep paralysis feel an insidious unseen presence nearby. Some report a weight on their chest, as if from being pinned down. It's possible that the notion of a succubus or incubus came as a result of sleep paralysis. And that invasive feeling isn't only confined to Western culture. Eastern cultures have their own words and traditions describing this phenomenon. The Japanese call it *kanashibari*, which translates to 'being bound hand and foot with an iron rope,' and the belief is that a devil is perched atop a sleeper's chest; in China the notion of nocturnal suffocation is referred to as *bei gui ya*, which translates to 'held by a ghost.'"

"So if I understand you," said Cheever, "you're suggesting that in modern times, extraterrestrials have supplanted ghosts and devils."

"That might or might not be the case," she said. "What can't be argued is that sleep paralysis often produces vivid hallucinations that seem absolutely real to the individual affected. Some say this interruption of the REM cycle can produce what's called the 'hag phenomenon'—during the limbo between sleeping and waking, you are at the mercy of a ghost, or a demon, or yes, an alien. This REM interruption might explain the bright lights reported by many of those who believe they've had an alien encounter."

"When I sleep, I probably snore so loudly that I scare off ghosts, demons, and aliens."

"I never had any idea your snoring was protecting me."

"No need for thanks," Cheever said.

"My sawing-wood hero," she said.

Cheever gave a half bow, then picked up his wineglass and took an appreciative sip.

"In all of this," he said, "the most important thing I need to remember is that Stella is back safe and sound."

"Amen."

"But that doesn't mean her case is closed. Care to offer up any other insights?"

Rachel thought for a moment. "I've always found it interesting that most of those who believe they've been abducted by aliens feel special, and are glad they were abducted."

"They like to think they were chosen?"

"Yes," said Rachel. "And reports of alien abduction are commonplace enough that mental health professionals have a name and an abbreviation for it: Alien Abduction Experiences, or AAE."

"It sounds like a sorority: alpha, alpha, epsilon."

"Maybe it is. Some in the mental health field also call it 'Close Encounters of the Fourth Kind.'"

Cheever took another sip of wine and thought about what Rachel had said. "There is still one significant difference between Stella and those who claim to have undergone AAE."

"And what's that?"

"Those people were not missing persons, and their supposed encounters didn't last for very long. Stella's situation is different. She claims she was with the Travelers for seven years."

Rachel nodded. "I believe it was Obi-Wan who said, 'Many of the truths we cling to depend greatly on our own point of view.'"

"And that's what makes you so exceptional," said Cheever. "Any shrink can quote Freud. But how many of them can quote Yoda?"

"It's not something I typically advertise," she said. "Implanting false memories is far easier to do than you might think—especially with an impressionable young child. There have been many studies showing this, with the bottom line being that the individual with false memories is absolutely sure that what they are saying really happened, even though it never did."

"Let's assume Stella's Travelers are a false memory. How did it come about? And *why* did it come about?"

"Those are good questions," said Rachel, taking off her glasses. "And I'm afraid *you'll* have to find the answers."

CHAPTER TWENTY-ONE

Stella greeted Cheever at the front door. Her pale face looked that much more ghostlike because it was sprinkled with flour.

"We're making chocolate chip cookies!" she said. "Do you want some?"

Cheever sniffed the air. "My sense of smell says I want a dozen, but I think I'll listen to another sense and only have one or two."

"What other sense?" she asked.

"Common sense," he said.

Duncan rose from his chair in the living room and came to shake Cheever's hand. "Let's see if your willpower equals your common sense," he said. "Mine surrendered many cookies ago."

"You better quit before you begin looking like a fat-cat politician," said Eleanor, emerging from the kitchen.

As she gave Cheever a hug, the detective tried to hide his surprise. Eleanor looked like a different woman, young and vibrant. The couple put their arms around each other's waists. They were more animated than Cheever had ever seen them.

Stella returned from the kitchen and extended two warm cookies toward Cheever.

"You're not trying to bribe a police officer, are you?" he asked.

The girl looked to her parents, and Eleanor said, "He's only kidding."

Cheever thanked Stella for the cookies, then took a bite of one. As he chewed, he began nodding appreciatively. "These are"—he paused and reconsidered before saying *out of this world*—"really good."

Eleanor turned to Stella. "I promised Detective Cheever that he could chat with you before dinner. Why don't I take out that last batch while you and the detective have a talk?"

"Don't let Daddy have any more," said Stella. "He's eaten a lot, and we need to have some for Michael and Luke."

"How sharper than a serpent's tooth it is to have a thankless child!" moaned Duncan.

The Shakespeare reference was probably lost on Stella, but not the fact that her father was joking. Both of them made faces at each other and laughed.

◆ ◆ ◆

Stella picked up a cell phone and some earbuds from a chair in her room, then cleared a space on the chest for Cheever to sit.

"Here you're back for only a day and you already have a cell phone?" asked Cheever.

"It's Michael's old phone," she explained, "which he only uses to listen to music. He has like two thousand songs in the cloud. I've already listened to about a hundred of them."

"You must like music," said Cheever.

"I do," she said, "but I'm not sure about Michael's taste in music."

Stella took a seat in her old desk chair. It was too small for her, but somehow she still looked comfortable.

"That's a nice outfit you're wearing," said Cheever. "Is it new?"

Stella nodded, running her hand along the arm of her blouse. "I went shopping with Mom and Dad this morning. And then we went and saw Dr. Schmitt in her office. She did more tests on me."

"Did you get a clean bill of health?"

"She said I was as healthy as a horse."

"I'm sure that made your parents very happy."

"Dr. Schmitt also said I was a lot stronger than I looked."

"I better not arm-wrestle you, then."

"You better not!"

"So how do you explain this strength of yours?"

"What do you mean?"

"Without the pull of gravity, astronauts lose significant body mass, especially when they're in space for extended periods of time. How is it that you weren't similarly affected?"

"I wasn't always in space. And when I was—or I should clarify by saying when I was more like myself physically—I followed diet and exercise protocols."

Protocols, thought Cheever. It was an interesting word for a fourteen-year-old to be using.

"Did the Travelers follow those same protocols?"

Judging by her smile, the question apparently amused her. "They had no need."

"Why not?"

"The Travelers aren't corporeal unless they choose to have a form."

Corporeal. He added another unique vocabulary word to the Stella list. "They don't have bodies?" asked Cheever.

Stella appeared unsure how to answer. "They have a *presence*," she finally said.

"But this presence doesn't take a physical form?"

"Yes and no," she said. "You know when a Traveler is in your proximity."

"I hope you don't mind my asking you these questions, Stella," he said. "I worked your case for so long it became a big part of my life, and even with you now back, I need to know what happened to you during the seven years you were gone."

She nodded to show she understood.

"Have you ever heard the expression *false memories*?" he asked.

"It seems like that's all I heard today," she said.

"What do you mean?"

"After I saw Dr. Schmitt, I had an afternoon session with Dr. Froke. He had a *lot* to say about false memories."

"If you don't mind, I'd like you to synopsize for me what he had to say."

"I don't mind," she said. "He told me and my parents that my time with the Travelers was likely a false memory."

"How did you respond to that?"

"He didn't give me much of a chance to respond. And Mom and Dad seemed to prefer Dr. Froke's explanation to mine. They go silent whenever I talk about anything that has to do with the Travelers."

"I'm told therapy won't do you any good if you're not being truthful."

"If Dr. Froke asks me a question, I will answer it honestly, even though I don't think he's interested in the truth."

"What do you think he's interested in?"

"I'd say he wants to establish a plausible explanation for my disappearance that doesn't involve the Travelers."

"And why would he want to do that?"

"I'm not sure. I only know that I don't hear Dr. Froke's voice in his questions or comments."

"How could you not hear his voice if he's the one doing the talking?"

Again she seemed to have to search for the right phrasing. "I listen beyond words," she said.

"Are you saying you're a mind reader?"

She shook her head. "It's more that I pick up impressions, especially when they're louder than words. Because I'm used to mindspeak, reverting back to talking feels painfully slow. It would be like your having to forsake the power of speech and communicate instead through writing."

"So you're saying mindspeak is a form of thought communication?"

Stella nodded. "I'm sure that's why my speech seems halting to you. I've been away from it for so long it feels cumbersome."

"If you're not in the habit of speaking," said Cheever, "how is it that you know a word like *cumbersome*?"

"My vocabulary was . . . imparted . . . through mindspeak. Incorporating the right word into speech is easy, at least when compared to utilizing the many facial accompaniments that are used with speech."

She punctuated what she was saying with a nod and a smile. "I'm doing my best with nonverbal communication, such as nodding and smiling and frowning. But there's so much more to show, just like your face is expressing right now. Even without the benefit of mindspeak, your furrowed brows, pursed lips, and narrowed eyes express your disbelief of what I'm saying more than any words could."

"And here I thought I had a poker face."

Stella smiled. Cheever wondered whether it came naturally. "I can also read your concern for me," she said, her voice soft. "It makes me feel cared for."

"I'm glad," he said. "And in case you can't divine it from my facial expressions, being a professional skeptic is part of who I am."

He gave her a playful wink, which she returned uncertainly. Her awkward attempt made Cheever laugh, and Stella joined in.

"I'm sorry I can't conduct this interview with mindspeak," he said. "Is that how you always communicated with the Travelers?"

"That's how everyone communicated."

"Were there others besides the Travelers?"

"There were twelve of us. We came from all over Earth."

Cheever made a surprised sound. "Tell me about them."

"What would you like to know?"

"Let's start with their names and where they came from."

After a moment's pause, she said, "That's difficult."

"What's so difficult about providing me with names?"

Stella replied as if measuring each word: "You need to understand that mindspeak makes names irrelevant."

On the job, Cheever often spoke to individuals whose native tongue wasn't English. It was frequently a struggle for them to be understood. Finding the right words was a torture of sorts. Stella seemed to be experiencing that.

"Explain that," said Cheever. "I'm used to everyone having a name."

"When you mindspeak with someone, you know their . . . *essence.* That makes names superfluous. From your life experience, you are used to faces being substantial and thoughts being invisible, whereas I see the substance of thoughts. You identify an individual by a name, or by looking at a face, or by hearing a particular voice. All of that seems insubstantial to me."

"So you can't provide me with a single name from those dozen people?"

"I wish I could share their essences with you. In that way you would know them."

"You said these dozen individuals came from around the world. Did anyone else in your group come from this country?"

She thought about that and finally said, "One of them did."

"What can you tell me about this individual?"

"I wish I could imbue you with his spirit, Detective. That's how I know him and see him. But that is not the tangible you want. You ask for the one-dimensional. He is about my age, but then so was everyone I traveled with. We are close to the same height, but he is heavier than I am. And his skin color is much darker than mine."

"Do you know what part of the country he came from?"

She shook her head. "He arrived a few days after I did. We all came together within a month's time. But it seems to me that at first he missed eating fish. That was his favorite food. And for the first few days he missed the water."

Thinking about that seemed to jar a memory. "He said his family was destined to be on the water because of their name."

She stretched out a hand, as if trying to grasp the thought.

"So it's likely his last name is water related," said Cheever. He began thinking of possibilities. "Could it have been Fisher or Brooks?"

"No and no," said Stella.

"How about Lake?" tried Cheever? "Or Wade or Bay?"

"I don't think so."

"Flood, Rain, or Falls," said Cheever.

"Those don't *feel* right," she said.

Anyone else probably would have said that they didn't *sound* right, he thought.

"I'll look into it further," the detective promised. "You said everyone in your group was about the same age. Was there a reason for that?"

"We were a class of sorts," Stella said. "I know one of the reasons we were selected is because we were predisposed to mindspeak."

"What does that mean?"

"Each of us heard the Travelers calling to us. They were testing our receptivity to mindspeak."

What she said reminded Cheever of the movie *Close Encounters of the Third Kind*, but he didn't mention that.

"So the rest of your original group is still with the Travelers?"

"Would an angel willingly depart heaven?"

"You returned."

"I had my reasons."

Cheever remembered how Stella said she came back because she perceived a growing disharmony. When questioned, Stella had referred Cheever to her mother. He still hadn't asked Eleanor about that.

"So how is your reentry to Earth going?" He didn't hide either his smile or his kidding tone.

"I think it's a little early to tell, isn't it? But Dr. Froke, for one, believes I'm ready to return to school."

"So soon?" said Cheever.

"Dr. Froke has told my parents that peer interaction is necessary to develop my socialization skills. He also says the sooner I get back into the mainstream, the better it will be for me."

"What do you think about that?"

Stella shrugged, but it seemed to Cheever that there was a slight time delay, and he wondered if she had to think about shrugging before doing it. "It doesn't seem that long ago when I went to kindergarten, and I was equal parts excited and scared. But I'm glad my parents are so happy about the prospect of my returning to school. They want everything to be like it used to be. They want their little girl back, and would prefer the Travelers never be mentioned again."

"They said that to you?"

"They didn't need to. It was clear they agreed with Dr. Froke that I should avoid commenting on the last seven years. According to the doctor, we need to *sort everything out* before I talk about my time away."

"It might not seem like it, but your parents are looking out for you."

"I know."

"So, when will you start school?"

"It might even be this week."

Cheever whistled. "That's fast."

"Dr. Froke had me take a test. Apparently the results confirmed my 'intellectual readiness' to rejoin my class."

"How did he explain that?"

"He said it's clear I've had schooling, but that for the time being, I'm repressing its true source with the fiction of the Travelers."

"He said that in front of you?"

"He offered that explanation to my parents. He also said he believes it's likely my false memories are based on my favorite childhood stories."

Cheever moved his eyes from Stella to the bookcase, which was still overflowing with books.

"Did Dr. Froke ask you about any of your favorite stories?"

"He asked my parents. He feels my story about the Travelers has several obvious roots. For example, on the night I went missing, my mother told him how I recited 'Twinkle, Twinkle, Little Star.' The poem's final lyric mentions a traveler."

"I don't think I know the last lyric."

Stella recited it for him:

"As your bright and tiny spark,
Lights the traveler in the dark,
Though I know not what you are,
Twinkle, twinkle, little star."

"Lights the traveler," said Cheever. That *might* explain how Stella had come up with the name Travelers. He was actually surprised Froke had picked up on that potentially telling passage.

"Dr. Froke also says my story might be drawn from the *Pied Piper of Hamelin*. He emphasized how the Pied Piper was this alien figure, and then he quoted from Browning about how there was no guessing his 'kith or kin.' This Piper offered a wonderland to the children, Dr. Froke said, just like the Travelers offered me the universe."

"And here I always thought the Pied Piper was a cautionary tale of what happens if you go back on your word," said Cheever.

"And I always thought it was just a story," said Stella.

Cheever heard her plaintive note. Stella had an analytical mind and an adult's vocabulary, but the girl that she was sometimes came out as well.

The thought of Diane came to the detective's mind. His little girl had been forced to be an adult long before her time; his little girl had died so young. Had he read the story of the *Pied Piper* to her? Cheever couldn't remember whether he had or not. That was unusual for him;

normally he remembered everything. Maybe it was a blessing to forget some things, or at least to have the balm of distance to lessen the hurt.

Cheever awoke from his reverie, trying to remember what he and Stella had last said.

"I'm sorry," whispered Stella.

"Sorry?" Cheever didn't understand.

"You should know, Detective Cheever, that your daughter was and is a beautiful"—it took her a moment to find the word—"spirit."

Cheever didn't know what to say. He stammered in search of the right word or sound, but couldn't find anything. Both of them suddenly heard male voices coming from downstairs.

"Michael's home," said Stella.

"Then we'd better go down," said Cheever, glad for the reprieve.

CHAPTER TWENTY-TWO

With his mind reeling, Cheever followed Stella downstairs. How had she known about his daughter? Eleanor must have said something to her. That had to be it.

The last time he had been this disoriented was when he'd worked the case of Holly Troy. Most of Holly's multiple personalities weren't human; they were goddesses straight out of Greek mythology. At least in this case he wasn't dealing with goddesses, although extraterrestrials seemed to be just as troublesome.

Stella reached the landing and came to a stop. From his vantage point on the stairs, the detective followed her gaze. Luke Hart must have felt their eyes on him; the kid looked their way. *Her* way—Cheever doubted whether he even registered in the young man's consciousness. He heard Stella's intake of breath and realized that the boy wasn't the only one affected. Both tried to not overtly stare, but they kept being drawn back to each other's eyes.

Cheever wondered if he was witnessing love at first sight. He'd always been skeptical if there really was such a thing, but seeing this kind of current made him think it just might be possible. It was odd, he thought, that no one else seemed to be noticing what was going on between them.

"Mrs. Brock isn't an English teacher," Michael was saying to his parents. "She's a slave driver."

Michael suddenly became aware of his sister and Cheever. "Hey, Stella," he said. "Hey, Detective Cheever."

At the sound of her brother's voice, Stella resumed moving toward them. Michael turned to his friend. "Do you remember my goofy little sister, Luke?"

"I—yes," Luke managed to say.

And then the two of them were standing awkwardly in each other's presence, too shy to extend a hand or offer a hug. Cheever decided to spare them their uncertainty and put a friendly hand on the young man's shoulder.

"It's good to see you again, Luke."

"You, too, Detective."

Cheever looked around, pausing on Stella. "The first time I talked to Luke, he was afraid I was going to arrest him."

"Is that true?" asked Eleanor.

Luke looked at Stella and smiled. "I'm afraid so. Two days after you went missing, Detective Cheever came over to our house and started asking me questions. It felt like he was giving me the third degree."

"What's the third degree?" asked Stella.

"It's an expression," said Luke, "that kind of implies . . ."

He seemed to lose his answer somewhere in Stella's eyes.

"It means Luke felt like he was being tortured," Duncan explained.

"A lot of people seem to think spending time with me is a form of torture," said Cheever.

Everyone shared a laugh, but Luke was quick to say, "It wasn't your fault. It was my guilty conscience."

"What could have possibly made you feel guilty?" asked Eleanor.

Cheever was the only person who knew about the valentine card Stella had left for Luke. Seven years ago the boy had made a tearstained confession.

I'll bet he still has that card, thought Cheever.

"I was worried that I had withheld potential evidence relating to your disappearance," said Luke. "Detective Cheever was nice enough to say that I didn't do anything wrong, and that I needn't have worried."

Cheever was the only one watching Stella. He saw a smile come to her face and wondered if she remembered leaving the card.

"What's that I smell?" said Michael, sniffing the air.

"We made cookies for you and Luke." Stella's words were for both of them; her eyes were for Luke.

"Cookies!" said Michael, heading for the kitchen.

"Don't spoil your appetites," warned Eleanor. "We'll be serving dinner within the hour. And I'm hoping both of you gentlemen will be dining with us."

"Luke's no gentleman," said Michael.

"Thank you for your offer, Mrs. Pierce," said Luke, as if to show he was a gentleman. "I gladly accept."

Michael coughed the words *kiss ass* into his hand.

◆ ◆ ◆

Eleanor set up a buffet-style tostada bar, with a choice of black or pinto beans, shredded cheese, tomatoes, avocado, lettuce, sprouts, sour cream, and two kinds of salsa.

Everyone sat down at the dining room table. Cheever was guessing the table hadn't been used in more than seven years. The detective found himself being more of an observer than a participant in the conversations. He watched Stella and Luke trying to unsuccessfully avoid each other's eyes. Luke had the quintessential look of a SoCal surfer, with broad shoulders and sun-bleached hair. His tanned face hid his blushing; Stella didn't have that camouflage.

There came the point in the meal where the adults were all holding their stomachs and proclaiming they'd eaten too much. The young people, who had eaten twice as much, amazingly still had room for more.

"Who's up for fro-yo?" asked Michael.

Stella and Luke both said, "I am," in unison.

Eleanor started shaking her head. "Why don't you stay home with us, Stella? Your brother will bring you some."

You didn't need to practice mindspeak, thought Cheever, to sense the girl's disappointment. But Duncan picked up on his daughter's unhappiness as well.

"You can't watch over Stella every minute," said Duncan. "I think it will be okay to let her go with the boys. Her big brother will watch out for her."

Michael flexed his arm for the table, and Luke tried to punch him on his muscle.

"Missed," said Michael.

"That's because the target was so small," said Luke.

"Am I supposed to be reassured by that behavior?" asked Eleanor.

"I'll be fine, Mom," said Stella.

Relenting, Eleanor sighed and said, "Okay, you can go for frozen yogurt. But I don't want you to make any other stops, Michael. And know that I'll be worrying every minute all of you are away."

"Thanks, Mom," said Stella.

"And one more thing," said Eleanor. "I'd like a salted-caramel yogurt with toppings of peanuts and hot fudge."

◆ ◆ ◆

Cheever couldn't be talked into a frozen yogurt; Duncan ordered a "red, white, and blue," which was vanilla yogurt with raspberries and blueberries and a granola topping.

Eleanor walked her children to the door. "Promise me you'll be back soon," she said.

Michael raised his right hand and said, "I promise."

The problem with his promise was that he was clearly crossing his index and middle fingers.

"Don't worry, Mom," said Stella. "We'll be back soon."

Eleanor hugged her daughter and whispered, "You better be."

"We'll be back before your yogurt melts," promised Luke.

"It's a good thing I've always had Luke to count on," Eleanor said.

As the children closed the door behind them, Duncan said, "You need to sit down with our guest and have a cup of coffee."

"And what will you be doing?" she asked.

"I'll be doing the dishes."

Eleanor let herself be led to the sofa. Duncan delivered two cups of coffee, then returned to the kitchen.

"That's how it used to be," said Eleanor. "I'd cook, and Duncan would do the dishes. You never realize how wonderful normalcy and routines are until they get removed from your life."

Although her children had only been gone for five minutes, Cheever could see Eleanor was already getting edgy. As they sipped their coffee and more time passed, her uneasiness grew. Every half minute or so, her eyes turned toward the front door, looking expectantly for a child who wasn't there.

"A watched pot never boils," said Cheever.

"My main goal in life is to be nothing more than an overprotective parent," she said.

"There are worse things," he said.

Cheever tried to take her mind off the ticking clock. "I've been meaning to ask you something," he said. "Twice I've interviewed Stella and asked her if there was a reason why she returned when she did. And both times she wouldn't answer, but instead deferred to you."

Eleanor looked surprised. "I wonder why that is."

"She told me your disharmony was growing perilous. Her emphasis was on the word *perilous*, but she wouldn't clarify. It was almost like she was protecting a confidence."

"And she said you should ask me?"

Cheever nodded. This time Eleanor's glance wasn't toward the front door, but to the kitchen, where her husband was doing the dishes. Despite his being out of earshot, she still seemed reluctant to speak.

"Stella also made me believe that she returned out of obligation and love," said Cheever, "and said that it wasn't easy for her to return. She likened it to the reluctance an angel might have departing heaven."

"She said that?" whispered Eleanor, then began nervously stroking her neck before adding, "But she couldn't have known."

"Known what?"

Eleanor shook her head, and once more cast a glance toward the kitchen. Then, in a voice that was little more than a whisper, she confessed: "I was in the process of taking my life when Stella showed up at the front gate. I was one-third of the way there, and just about ready to take my second dose of pills. I had it all planned to make it look like an accidental overdose."

Cheever nodded. Over the years he'd seen how much pain Eleanor was in. He wasn't surprised that she had decided to end her life. In the back of his mind, he'd always feared she would. That was one of the reasons he visited the Pierce house as often as he did; he hadn't wanted Eleanor to lose hope.

"But how could she have known?" said Eleanor. "No one knew."

She looks like a deer caught in the headlights, thought Cheever. It was probably how *he'd* looked when Stella brought up the subject of his daughter.

CHAPTER TWENTY-THREE

Three kids in a car, doing what kids do, cranking up the tunes and singing along.

Luke was in the passenger seat, his left shoulder angled so that he could look at both Stella and Michael. Even though the music had to be new to Stella, she seemed to intuit the words, and her singing was good enough to tone down the sharp edges of the discordant male notes.

Angelic, Luke thought. That's how Stella's voice sounded.

They played some Macklemore & Ryan Lewis, then a little from Drake, before all of them teamed up with Rihanna and Eminem to sing "The Monster." Everyone had their own groove. Michael and Luke were doing the Eminem rap lyrics, while Stella was channeling Rihanna's voice.

She looked at Luke and sang the words, "You think I'm crazy."

Just looking at her made Luke short of breath, and forced him to play catch-up with Michael's rhyming and rapping.

And then the song was over, but none of them wanted that moment to stop. "Again," said Michael, tapping "Replay" on the touch screen.

His visible wince was noticed by Luke and Stella.

"You okay, bro?" asked Luke.

Stella said nothing, but reached out and put her hand on Michael's shoulder. The sound of her gasp surprised everyone.

"What's wrong?" said Michael.

"Your arm," she said.

"It's nothing," said Michael.

The music had started, and Rihanna was singing about getting along with the voices in her head.

"Never do that again, Michael," she said.

"Do what?"

"You could have died."

Luke responded to Michael's hard glance, lifting up his right arm. "I swear to God, I didn't say a thing."

"That would have killed Mom," said Stella.

"You're one to talk," said Michael. "For seven years Mom has been dying one day at a time because of you."

"Let's all chill," said Luke.

"And you know what your disappearing act did to me?" said Michael. "Mom smothered me. She was always hovering over me. It was a big joke among all my friends. 'Cray Mrs. Pierce,' they'd always say."

"I'm sorry," whispered Stella.

And all the while, Rihanna sang about being friends with the monster under her bed.

Luke turned off the music and watched as Michael let out some air and seemed to deflate.

"I'm not telling you what to do, Michael," Stella said in a soft voice, "but I hope if you ever make that kind of leap again that you do it for the right reasons. At least Luke did it out of love."

"More like stupidity," said Luke.

"I won't argue that," said Stella.

Michael laughed and said, "Burn!"

Not burn, thought Luke, but fever. He couldn't stop looking at Stella.

◆ ◆ ◆

Tiffany Milton's BMW 340i, with its personalized license plate of PURRRR, was parked in front of Yo, Fro, Yo!

"Did you know the Y-Girls were going to be here?" Luke asked.

"Courtney mentioned something about them maybe stopping by," Michael said.

"Great," said Luke, then turned to Stella. "I'm not a fan of your brother's sometimes girlfriend."

"What about Courtney's BFF, Tiffany?" Michael asked. "Are you more of a fan of hers?"

"After listening to them cheering for you to jump," said Luke, "I can do without any of the Y-Girls. How about we go to Seaside Yogurt instead?"

"Girls were cheering for Michael to jump from that cliff?" asked Stella.

Luke still wondered how Stella knew about Michael's plunge. He thought about deflecting her question by asking one of his own, but instead found himself nodding.

From inside of Yo, Fro, Yo, a young blonde woman began waving at Michael.

"We can't take off now," said Michael. "Courtney spotted me."

Luke looked at Stella and said, "You can avoid the drama if you want by staying in the car. I would."

"I'll be fine," she said.

◆ ◆ ◆

Luke held open the door to the frozen yogurt shop for Stella. He wasn't doing the door-holding to be polite; he *wanted* to do it. Since first seeing Stella, Luke had felt all stirred up inside. He had always been self-reliant, had always structured his world around the ocean, but now it seemed there was an even bigger world out there.

As Stella entered the store, lots of inquisitive eyes looked her way, but then the attention turned to Michael and Luke, and many of those there began to clap and cheer. All seven of the "first team" Y-Girls were there, along with at least two dozen of their friends from Torrey Pines Academy.

Courtney came up and kissed Michael. "Since yesterday there have been almost a hundred thousand YouTube views of you leaping off Dead Man's Cliff. The footage has gone viral!"

Tiffany wasn't about to be outdone. She extended a long red fingernail, running it up and down Luke's sternum. "There have been all sorts of comments from girls who wanted to know about 'the sexy guy' who jumped in after his friend."

Luke cast a side-glance at Stella. Michael was also nodding knowingly. That explained how Stella had known about their cliff jumping. But Stella didn't meet Luke's eyes. Her attention was on the movements of Tiffany's nail along his chest.

"I guess you two haven't met," said Luke, taking a step back and out of nail range. "Tiffany, this is Stella. She's Michael's sister."

"Really?" said Tiffany. "You're *that* Stella Pierce?"

Stella nodded.

"You're like the Boogey Girl, did you know that?"

"I am not sure what the Boogey Girl is," said Stella.

"Everyone who grew up around here knows your name," said Tiffany. "You're like this huge cautionary tale of stranger danger and how you always have to be careful. All the parents were afraid their kid might end up as the next Stella Pierce."

Courtney and Michael came over and joined them. "You mean this is your sister, Michael!" screeched Courtney. "I heard about her on the news. What's your name, Michael's sister?"

"I'm Stella."

"And you're like fifteen, aren't you?"

"In a few months," said Stella.

"Will you be going to TPA?"

When Stella nodded, Courtney said, "We could call you Elly."

Luke wondered who looked less enthused at that prospect—Tiffany or Stella.

"We're kind of in a rush," said Luke. "We promised Mr. and Mrs. Pierce we wouldn't be long."

"But you just got here," said Tiffany. "We've all been waiting for you."

"I didn't know everyone was going to be here," he said. "And I have a ton of homework."

"There's such a thing as putting it off until tomorrow morning," she said, "but let me guess: you have a date with a mermaid?"

"Midtide's at six," he said, "so dawn patrol starts early. The waves are supposed to be cranking."

"If I were you, the wave I'd be concerned about getting is a good-bye wave," said Tiffany. She turned to Stella. "What about you? Do you surf?"

"I never have, but it looks fun."

"Looks are always so deceiving, though, aren't they?" said Tiffany.

"I'm not sure I understand."

Tiffany answered by offering up a not-altogether-pleasant smile. "So what happened to you all those years ago?" she asked.

"I went away," said Stella.

Michael stepped forward, partially blocking Stella from Tiffany. "Let's go put our order in," he said.

"You're so pale that wherever you went, there must not have been much sun," said Tiffany.

"You're right about that," said Stella, and then she let her brother lead her away to the counter.

"Really?" said Luke, but whatever else he might have said to Tiffany was swallowed by the approach of others.

"Dude," said Joey Gold, taking off his trademark fedora and waving it in homage to Luke, "you were awesome!"

"I don't think I would have made that jump," said Nick Watson, "even if it was Bella Thorne in the water calling for help!"

Nick's parents owned a beachfront home in Del Mar; it was a frequent setting for the Y-Girl parties.

"That was one great tape," said Joey.

"I haven't seen it," said Luke.

"Your jump was way cool," said Joey, "but the ladies liked what came afterward even more. When you guys got up on the rocks, Tiffany zoomed in on you bare-chested, squeezing water out of your shirt."

"That's why it's getting so many likes," said Nick.

By then the other Y-Girls were surrounding Tiffany and Courtney. Luke heard Tiffany say, "I'll bet she orders *vanilla*," which was enough for him to roll his eyes and shake his head.

"Later," he told his friends, then walked over to join Michael and Stella.

Luke listened to his best friend order for his parents, then put in his usual of Cookies on Cookies, which was cookie-dough frozen yogurt topped with crushed Oreos. Stella carefully considered her selection before announcing she wanted S'mores, which was frozen yogurt with marshmallow sauce, chocolate chips, and crushed graham crackers.

"It's been a long time since I've had S'mores," she said in a voice that sounded nostalgic.

"I'm going with a Blue Greek," said Luke, which was frozen Greek yogurt with blueberries and granola.

As they waited for their orders, Stella asked, "What's the dawn patrol?"

"It's what I practice and your brother doesn't," said Luke.

"I need my beauty sleep," said Michael.

"No argument there," said Luke. Then he offered a better explanation for Stella: "When you're a member of the dawn patrol, you're usually out in the water before first light."

"And what is midtide?"

"Sometimes, but not always, it's that sweet spot between low tide and high tide where there's a lot of wave action."

"Do you surf every day?" she asked.

"Most days," he said, "but I usually pass on ankle-buster days."

At her questioning look, Luke explained, "Small waves."

Their to-go order was handed to them, but it took them another two minutes to pass through the gauntlet of friends and well-wishers.

When they left, Tiffany pretended not to notice that Luke held the door open for Stella.

◆ ◆ ◆

"The Y-Girls," said Michael. "You gotta love 'em." In an aside meant only for Luke, he added, "And if you do, you better glove 'em."

"Why are they called the Y-Girls?" asked Stella.

"Why, oh why," said Michael.

"It's a group of seven girls that hang around together," said Luke, "and all of their names happen to end with a *y*."

"So they're kind of like the Seven Dwarfs," said Stella.

Both Luke and Michael started laughing, and the more Stella tried explaining her reasoning to them, the harder they laughed.

"You said there were seven of them," she said. "And their names end in a *y*. That's how it is with the Seven Dwarfs except for Doc and Bashful, and since another word for *bashful* is *shy*, which ends in a *y*, you could pretty much call them the Y-Dwarfs."

"Courtney is definitely Dopey," said Luke.

"Who is Tiffany?"

"She's not one of the Seven Dwarfs. She's the Evil Queen."

"What about Kimberly?"

"Grumpy, for sure," said Luke.

"Cassidy?" asked Michael, but then answered his question at the same time as Luke: "Sleepy."

"And no doubt about Brittany," said Michael.

Luke nodded, and they both said, "Happy."

"We got to get the word out," said Michael. "Match the seven Y-Girls with the Seven Dwarfs."

"Maybe we can put up a poster of Snow White and the Seven Dwarfs, and people can fill in names."

"That would be classic!" said Michael.

In fits and starts, the two of them continued to laugh, but Luke wasn't laughing when he turned to Stella and said, "You're Snow White."

She frowned. "I guess I had better watch out for poisoned apples, then."

◆ ◆ ◆

Eleanor was watching for the return of her son's car, and was there to greet everyone at the door.

"Stella is fine, Mom," said Michael. "You can relax. And your first-born is okay as well."

Eleanor still felt the need to give her daughter a hug. "Tomorrow we'll go and pick out a cell phone for you," she said.

"Another one of your Big Brother phones?" asked Michael.

"It *will* have a GPS tracking app," admitted Eleanor.

Michael turned to Stella. "I had to wear this horrible-looking GPS watch until I was twelve, and then Mom gave me a cell phone with a GPS tracker. What I didn't know was that the phone did more than monitor my location. Mom was also able to read all my texts and listen to all my calls. It took me a few years to figure out she wasn't psychic."

"I was just being protective," said Eleanor.

"That's one word for it," said Michael. "Another might be pathologically paranoid."

"Let's eat our yogurt before it melts," said Luke.

"Blessed are the peacemakers," laughed Duncan.

◆ ◆ ◆

Spoons scraped the bottoms of the bowls, searching in vain for one last bite of goodness.

"Yum," said Stella. "That really tasted like s'mores, but without Michael's pyromania. Do you still do that?"

Her brother nodded. "It's the only way to roast a marshmallow."

Stella rolled her eyes—or tried to. Luke thought her attempt looked funny, although he said nothing.

"In seven years you haven't changed at all, have you?" she asked.

"Why change when you're already perfect?" said Michael.

This time Stella's eye-rolling looked more polished. But she followed up her pretend contempt by hugging her brother.

"Don't ever change," she said.

"Remember when they used to fight like cats and dogs?" said Eleanor.

"I should be going," announced Luke.

Stella smiled and said, "Have fun with dawn patrol and midtide."

"You should go surfing with me sometime. I'll bet you'd be a natural."

"I'd love that," said Stella.

"I wouldn't love it," said her mother. "When was the last time you went swimming in the ocean?"

"It's been a while," admitted Stella, "but you used to call me a fish."

Eleanor shook her head and said, "I'm not sure I like the idea of you surfing."

"Maybe you could put some water wings on her, Mom," said Michael.

"Do you still want him to never change?" asked Duncan.

"We could start with a boogie board, Mrs. Pierce," said Luke, "and go out on a small wave day."

"I suppose," said an unsure Eleanor.

Luke's and Stella's eyes met for a triumphant instant, and then each looked away.

◆ ◆ ◆

Michael accompanied Luke outside, ostensibly to get the backpack he'd left in the car, but when they were only a few steps away from the house, his real purpose was revealed.

"What's with you and my sister?" he asked.

"What do you mean?"

"I mean, I don't know which of the two of you was flirting more."

Instead of denying it, Luke said, "Remember I used to tell you about my dreams?"

"You mean you and the mermaid?"

"She wasn't a mermaid. She was sort of this vision."

Michael nodded. He'd teased his friend about the girl of his dreams for years.

"There's something about Stella that's just like my vision."

"Dude," said Michael, "my sister's not right for you." In a voice not much more than a whisper, he added, "The truth is that she's kind of messed up right now."

"What do you mean?"

Michael sighed. "You got to keep this between us, bro."

"You know I will."

"You can't tell your parents or anyone."

"I promise I won't tell anyone."

Michael scraped the sidewalk with his shoe, almost like he was trying to rid himself of some sticky gum. "Stella's explanation for being gone these last seven years is that she was off with aliens, and I'm not talking the illegal kind. I'm talking E.T."

It took Luke a moment to absorb what his friend was saying. "She said she was with extraterrestrials?"

Michael nodded. "She's seeing a shrink. He thinks she's got this thing called Stockholm syndrome, and because of that, she's protecting whoever abducted her."

"Wow," said Luke, not knowing quite what to say.

"My parents are making me talk to the shrink, too," said Michael. "It's the pits, let me tell you. The shrink says Stella's story about aliens is a defense mechanism. He also says Stella is probably clinging to it because it allows her to avoid thinking about what really happened to her. What it boils down to, he's pretty sure, is that Stella is repressing a lot of bad crap."

"That sucks," said Luke.

"Yeah," Michael agreed, and scraped his shoe some more. "But I thought you better know, especially with the way you guys were eyeing each other. So what I'm trying to say is . . ."

He searched for the words, but Luke found them first: "Stella is vulnerable, and she's already been through a lot, and she doesn't need some guy making her more messed up than she already is."

"That about covers it," said Michael.

"Okay," said Luke.

They took their usual leave of each other, pretending all was normal.

"See you later, masturbator," said Michael.

"In a while, pedophile," said Luke.

Luke went through the security gate and trudged down the street to his house, taking no notice of the two sedans parked on the street.

◆ ◆ ◆

"Play it back," said Scarecrow. "And allow Henry and Em to hear it as well."

Henry and Em were in the other sedan. Those weren't their real names, but were in keeping with their assignment of monitoring Dorothy.

Tin Man did as told, allowing the others to listen in on a private channel. Scarecrow hadn't assigned the names haphazardly. In *The Wizard of Oz,* the Tin Man had no heart; neither did *this* Tin Man. The difference between them was that this Tin Man enjoyed being heartless.

It was the Guardian of the Gates who had assigned Scarecrow and his subordinates to monitor Dorothy. Like Dorothy, Stella had gone away. And there were those who were interested in hearing about Stella's Oz. Still, the primary job of Scarecrow and his crew was to control Stella. They needed to rein her in and play on her doubts.

Scarecrow didn't know the full story. He wasn't sure if he even wanted to know the full story. But he had been waiting for someone like Stella to come along. He had been preparing. That's how he and his crew had been able to act right away. They'd had a shrink picked out and a backstory in place. Around the world other potential targets had been identified, with other go teams at the ready.

The other members of Scarecrow's team listened to the conversation between Michael and Luke. At its conclusion, Scarecrow said, "The toothpaste is working its way out of the tube. We knew that would happen over time, and we knew it would be fruitless to try to get it back in. The Guardian of the Gates believes by exposing Dorothy now, she will be easier to control. He suggests we let Dorothy's peers circulate her narrative, allowing us to stay in the deep background. That way we can hope for a more malleable Dorothy."

The Tin Man stuck his head out the window and looked around.

"What are you doing?" asked Scarecrow.

"I'm looking for falling houses," he said.

◆ ◆ ◆

Tiffany glanced at the display on her cell phone. She hadn't heard it ring, but could see someone had left her a message. The caller, she was pleased to see, was Luke Hart. Maybe he had come to the correct conclusion that surfing shouldn't be his first priority.

She listened to the message, and at first didn't follow what she was hearing. Michael Pierce was saying, *"Dude, my sister's not right for you. The truth is that she's kind of messed up right now."*

It's a butt-dial, she realized. Tiffany listened closely and heard Michael say: *"You got to keep this between us, bro."*

"You know I will."

"You can't tell your parents or anyone."

"I promise I won't tell anyone."

"Stella's explanation for being gone these last seven years is that she was off with aliens, and I'm not talking the illegal kind. I'm talking E.T."

Oh my God, thought Tiffany. This was better than she could have imagined. For a few seconds she couldn't hear what Michael and Luke were saying, but then the sound improved.

"The shrink says Stella's story about aliens is a defense mechanism," said Michael. "He also says Stella is probably clinging to it because it allows her to avoid thinking about what really happened to her. What it boils down to, he's pretty sure, is that Stella is repressing a lot of bad crap."

"That sucks," said Luke.

Then the message was over. Tiffany played back the recording.

Wait until the Y-Girls hear this, she thought.

CHAPTER TWENTY-FOUR

Two days after his last visit to the Pierces' home, Eleanor opened the front door for Detective Cheever and said, "Good or bad?"

"Good or bad what?" he asked.

"You said you were coming over to deliver some news," she said, "but you didn't specify whether the news was good or bad."

"What if it's neither?"

Eleanor shook her head. "News is either good or bad, even though you might not know which it is when you first hear it."

"My wife is becoming a philosopher," said Duncan, who came over and shook Cheever's hand.

"I wouldn't want to take your job," she said.

"I'm a member of Congress. That makes me the opposite of a philosopher."

"Are you headed back to DC?" asked Cheever, taking note of the luggage in the living room.

Duncan nodded. "I'll be flying out this afternoon. There are some important votes I really can't miss."

"I told him I'd write the Speaker a note excusing his absence," said Eleanor, "but he declined my offer."

"I'll be back in four days," said Duncan, "and I'll be open to all offers at that time."

Husband and wife looked at Cheever expectantly.

"Guy Wilkerson was released from prison this morning," he said.

"Shit," said Duncan.

Eleanor's face turned white. After visiting Wilkerson in prison, Eleanor had come back changed. Whatever he had said or done to her had cut deep.

"I think Stella needs to hear the news," said Cheever.

"She's only a child," said Eleanor. "I wish she didn't have to hear such filth."

"Stella!" yelled Duncan. "Please come downstairs."

From upstairs they heard a "Coming!" Moments later Stella appeared. Her head was slightly bobbing, and the strains of rock music could be heard. Duncan motioned for her to lose the earbuds, and she stopped playing the song.

"When you went missing, Stella," said Cheever, "we ended up arresting a man named Guy Wilkerson. My investigation proved that Wilkerson had been stalking you for weeks, if not longer."

"Bastard," hissed Eleanor.

Cheever knew she wasn't given to such outbursts; just the thought of Wilkerson could still push her buttons.

"I'm surprised he was able to get released so soon," said Duncan.

"The State was afraid to keep him any longer," said Cheever, "especially knowing his lawyer is in the process of preparing a multimillion-dollar suit alleging false arrest and a host of other charges. I'm sure we'll both be deposed in the near future on those matters, Congressman."

Duncan shook his head. "Wilkerson was in possession of stolen property in the form of Mr. Sparkles, was found with child pornography, groped two of the children he was supposed to be tutoring, and clearly violated terms of his parole by being within a hundred feet of Stella's elementary school when he took pictures of her."

"His lawyers will still try and make it look like we had a vendetta against him," said Cheever.

"If they want to start throwing mud, they're going to quickly find that a lot more of it is going to stick to their client than to his accusers," said Duncan. "Everyone is going to see that Wilkerson is a pervert with a capital *P*, and while he might not have abducted Stella, he's guilty of plenty else."

"So this man was imprisoned because people thought he kidnapped me?" asked Stella.

"That's his claim," said Cheever, "but that's not why he was sentenced. Years before you went missing, Wilkerson had already been arrested and convicted as a sexual predator. And although he was a person of interest in your disappearance, he was convicted on several counts unrelated to that."

Stella still didn't look convinced. "But if I hadn't gone away, would he have been arrested?"

Cheever shrugged. "We'll never know. But what can't be disputed is his guilt. He went back to prison because he broke multiple laws."

"Getting Wilkerson off the streets was our gift to the community," Duncan told his daughter. "I don't want you feeling guilty because this creep spent time in jail. He got what he deserved."

Cheever began passing around pictures. "These are some recent photos of Guy Wilkerson," he said.

"He's aged," said Eleanor.

"It's been seven years since you saw him," said Duncan.

"Take a good look at those pictures, Stella," said Cheever. "If you ever think you see this man, I want you to call me on my cell phone right away."

"Maybe we should get a restraining order," said Eleanor.

"Maybe we should stock up on ammunition," said Duncan.

"Has he directed any threats toward our family?" Eleanor asked.

"Wilkerson is too smart to make overt threats," Cheever said, "even though he's on record as saying Duncan railroaded him into prison and used the power of his office to keep him there."

Duncan put a hand on Eleanor's shoulder. "He's not a threat. He's just a sick little man who's trying to extort some money out of us."

"That's my take on it as well," said Cheever, "but I still want everyone to be on the lookout for him."

The detective turned toward Stella. He thought it important for her to understand what kind of a person Wilkerson was.

"There is no sugarcoating this," he said. "Guy Wilkerson was fixated on you. He knew where you lived, and where you went to school. Wilkerson took hundreds of pictures of you, but you were a girl then, and now you're a young woman. It's likely with the passage of time he's no longer as interested in you, but I still want you to be on the lookout for him."

Stella nodded to show she understood.

"Can't we petition the court to keep Wilkerson out of San Diego County?" asked Eleanor.

Cheever shook his head and said, "I don't think any judge would grant that request, especially in light of what some might view as Wilkerson's having gotten a raw deal."

Eleanor sighed, then turned to her husband. "Are you sure you have to fly out today?"

"I promised the leadership that I would," said Duncan.

"Then before you leave, I want you to take the handgun out of the gun locker so that I can carry it in my purse."

◆ ◆ ◆

Guy Wilkerson had a seat to himself on the Greyhound bus going to Oceanside, courtesy of the California taxpayers. He'd also gotten $200 in gate money. His attorney had advanced him another $800. The lawyer was confident that the two of them would be receiving a nice payday in the near future.

Wilkerson looked out the window, soaking in the sights. For seven years he'd been living in protective custody, afraid to venture outside his cell. The much-publicized disappearance of Stella Pierce had convinced him to stay clear of the general prison population. That had made doing time all the harder.

His complexion reflected prison pallor. Soon he'd be soaking in the rays. And just the thought of a carne asada burrito was making him salivate. In less than an hour he'd be biting into one.

That was one itch he needed to scratch. But there were plenty of others he'd be scratching as well. As a free man, Wilkerson wanted to walk under the light of the moon. And he couldn't wait to lie down on some park grass and look up at the sky. He'd watch the clouds, and imagine what forms they took. And when he'd had his fill of lolling about, he'd take a little walk. There were streets in Oceanside full of citrus trees. He'd get his fill of oranges and tangerines, and spit out the seeds as he walked.

Tonight, Wilkerson decided, he'd splurge. He'd find lodging that offered a thick, plush mattress. For too many years he'd been sleeping on a thin, hard bed that felt like the rack. He couldn't wait to spend a night on a comfortable mattress. How could he not have sweet dreams?

Those were his minor itches. They would be easily tended to. After that he'd begin thinking on how to best relieve some of his major itches.

In the morning he'd stake out a spot at the beach. While working on his tan, he'd take in the scenery. The kiddies loved going to the ocean. And he loved the kiddies.

Wilkerson had first seen Stella Pierce at the beach. Right away he'd noticed her bright eyes. They'd drawn him in. He hadn't been carrying his camera when she appeared in front of him, because a few days earlier he'd had a close call and was afraid the police might be on the lookout for a man with his description carrying a camera. But even without pictures, he remembered everything about her. When her mother had gathered her up, Wilkerson had followed the two of them home. The family lived a few streets over from Del Mar Heights. It had been easy to figure out which elementary school the girl went to, and then gradually he'd learned her name. Bit by bit, he had come to know everything about Stella. He was like a patient spider, most of the time just sitting there waiting in his web. He had done his spinning, confident his patience would ultimately be rewarded.

And then someone had beaten Wilkerson to his prey. Someone else must have noticed how special she was. Someone else must have seen that glow in her eyes. When Stella turned up missing, Wilkerson had grieved. Then he was betrayed: the cops had made everything look worse than it was. They set things up to make it look like he was the one who had taken her.

For all this time, Wilkerson had continued thinking about her. Soon they would meet again. Stella was older now, but that wouldn't deter him. He wanted to see if she still had that special glow in her eyes. They would have their face-to-face soon. Wilkerson wasn't sure what would happen then. But there were plenty of scenarios he could imagine.

Tomorrow he'd buy a moped or electric bicycle. He could put either one on the Coaster commuter train or the bus, and take the twenty-mile ride from Oceanside to Del Mar. Or he could forgo the bus and drive himself.

It was time to renew an old friendship.

CHAPTER TWENTY-FIVE

Since Stella's return, Cheever had expected to make more headway in determining where she had been. Her case had generated plenty of publicity, but few clues as to her whereabouts. Cheever had kept going back to the source, gently questioning Stella, but she had continued to cling to her story of the Travelers. Yesterday, though, Cheever had gotten a call from a man who claimed to know where Stella had lived during her lost years. What he'd related to Cheever sounded plausible. That was why Cheever had left his home at eight in the morning for an eleven o'clock meeting. The witness had agreed to meet him at a restaurant located on the Salton Sea.

Most of San Diego County's population lives along the coast. The farther east Cheever drove, the less traffic there was. He gave up on listening to the radio on the outskirts of San Diego County, when his selections were limited to Spanish-speaking stations playing romantic ballads. Hearing Spanish wasn't surprising; the drive along Interstate 8 paralleled the border of Mexico, and from the freeway there was nothing to distinguish where one country ended and the other began.

There was little traffic along the hundred-mile stretch between El Cajon and El Centro. Most of the people Cheever passed were "Zonies"—Arizonans who beat the heat by spending time in San Diego. He turned north on State Highway 111. Even though it was the main artery into the Coachella Valley, the route was mostly deserted save for the agricultural trucks coming from Mexicali and Calexico. The road took Cheever past small agricultural communities that had never known anything but hardscrabble existences. The area wasn't a dust bowl, but did look more in keeping with *Grapes of Wrath* Oklahoma than modern-day California. Old date and citrus groves could be seen along the roadside. Some were being worked; some were abandoned and showed the skeletal remains of trees.

It had been at least twenty years since Cheever had last visited the Salton Sea. There had been nothing compelling him to return until now. Everyone agreed the Salton Sea was dying, but no one knew how long its death throes would continue. The lake was now 50 percent saltier than the ocean. Some tilapia and desert pupfish continued to live in its waters, a testament to the miracle of survival.

For more than half a century, there had been talk about how to save the Salton Sea. The latest incarnation of the lake was an accident; in 1905 massive flooding caused diversion canals along the Colorado River to overrun, and for eighteen months the river flowed into the spot with the lowest elevation in the desert, an area below sea level. That's how the largest lake in California had been formed in the middle of the Sonoran Desert. For a time the Salton Sea had been a tourist spot known for its fishing and sailing. It drew such luminaries as Frank Sinatra, Jerry Lewis, and the Beach Boys. In the fifties and sixties, the roar of speedboats filled the air. There was building along its shores, and there were plans for future developments. But then the area began to dry up, both literally and metaphorically.

As bad as the dying lake was, those in the know said the real concern would be its moldering corpse. Many decades of agricultural runoff had left behind arsenic, selenium, and DDT. For now this potential Love Canal was contained by the water, but lurking beneath was the waiting monster. When California let Owens Lake dry up, the state hadn't realized it was creating the number one source of dust in the country. If the Salton Sea dried up, it might become an even worse environmental hazard, unleashing a torrent of toxic particulates in its desiccated wake.

Cheever's meeting was still an hour off; he'd purposely left time for detours. His first stop was Slab City. Residents of "the Slabs" liked to claim it was the last free place in America. The area got its name from the slabs of concrete left behind from an abandoned marine barracks. Every winter there is an influx of snowbirds into Slab City. Because there is no charge for parking, campers fill up the area. Of course there is a price for not paying a price. There is no electricity, running water, or sewers, nor is there trash pickup. Squatters live in the midst of what many view as a dump site. But in the middle of all the trash, Cheever could see some homesteads that displayed a semblance of habitability. There were no white-picket fences or welcome mats, but attempts had been made to clear away the trash and make the surrounding area appear livable. Some of the "choicest" spots in Slab City—campers ensconced by the slab bunkers—looked almost homey in a Mad Max kind of way.

Cheever studied the Slabs like he would a crime scene. He categorized what was there and what wasn't. This was the fringe of society, and its inhabitants had more than their share of personal demons. The few residents who could be seen didn't make eye contact. It didn't matter what their mental state was; they knew he was a cop, and that was enough for them to avoid engaging with him. Cheever's work often brought him in contact with the mentally ill. He always felt sorriest for their children. When crazy was your normal, stability was a rare commodity. Had Stella spent time in the Slabs? If so, out of necessity had she imagined a place other than this world of garbage?

Feral-looking cats roamed the grounds, while feral-looking people sat in front of their ramshackle campers in old, worn sofas and chairs. If this was the last free place in America, thought Cheever, then freedom was greatly overrated.

There were two more stops he wanted to make before his meeting, so he put Slab City in his rearview mirror and continued along Beal Road until he reached the three-story structure known as Salvation Mountain. He'd read up on this unlikely roadside attraction. The colorful adobe, clay, and straw structure had been built by Leonard Knight, who had died a few years before. At the centerpiece of the mountain was the red-and-hot-pink message GOD IS LOVE. Biblical passages adorned the mountain. The thousands of gallons of paint that had gone into painting the surreal mountain had all been donated. After Knight's death, volunteer artists had continued working to keep his mountain standing and his legacy alive.

What was it about deserts, Cheever wondered, that brought out fanatics as well as the true believers? Jesus and John the Baptist came to the desert; so did the devil and Charlie Manson. Saints and sinners claimed to have visions among the dunes. In such a locale, Cheever almost expected to see penitents wearing camel-hair garments and leather loincloths.

In the unforgiving desert, Knight had painted a tree springing from his mountain. Upon its branches were written such virtues as *goodness*, *faith*, *joy*, *peace*, and *gentleness*. Next to the tree was the reminder of John 3:16 *For God so loved the world that he gave his only son.* All the vivid colors of Salvation Mountain made it stand out in the drab monochrome of the desert. Knight's imagination had taken him to heaven. Had visions like his inspired a girl to travel the universe?

Cheever drove to his last stop, the art collective known as East Jesus. Despite its name, East Jesus wasn't a religious refuge; the name referred to its being out in the middle of nowhere, about a mile from Salvation Mountain. As remote as the area was, East Jesus still had Wi-Fi, through which the art community managed to maintain a website. Cheever had perused that website the day before. Seeing pictures of its artwork had convinced him he should see the site firsthand.

He parked on the outskirts of the complex. Visitors seemed to be neither encouraged nor discouraged, but judging from the signage, the cacti in the area weren't the only thorny inhabitants. There were people living and working in this colorful Petri dish, and the handiwork of various artists could be seen in walls of old bottles, sculpture gardens, and the reuse of trash.

Cheever began his tour. Op art seemed to be making a comeback among the repurposed junkyard art. Housing ranged from campers, to tents, to a dome. Abandoned vehicles had been turned into art, as well as living spaces.

"What's up, Dick Tracy?"

Cheever turned. Standing at the doorway of a vintage Winnebago was a petite thirtyish woman with mostly green hair. Her dye job matched her green Girl Scout outfit. She was also wearing a black sash with what appeared to be merit badges. Her bare arms showed lots of ink, and she had a nose ring.

"Selling cookies?" Cheever asked.

"Not me," she said. "Haven't you heard sugar's a gateway drug?"

"If that's the case, I better warn my doughnut-eating colleagues," he said.

"I thought when you got a badge, there was a law that you had to lose your sense of humor."

"I must have missed that memo, Scout."

"Gaea," she said, correcting him.

"Mother Earth," said Cheever. "And if I remember my mythology, Gaea was also the daughter of Chaos."

Gaea did a double take. "You remember right, Dick Tracy."

"I'm Detective Cheever, Gaea," he said, "and what I'm attempting to do is make sense out of chaos. Do you mind my looking around here?"

"That depends. What are you looking for?"

"I'm trying to find out if a formerly missing girl spent time in these parts."

Cheever reached inside his pocket, pulled out his phone, then showed Gaea a picture of Stella.

"You said she was formerly missing?"

"That's right."

"But she's not missing now?"

Cheever nodded. "The girl went missing for a number of years. I'm trying to figure out where she was during that time."

"Where does she say she was?" asked Gaea.

"She claims she was traveling through space with extraterrestrials."

Gaea didn't even appear surprised. "Was she astral projecting, or was she in an actual spacecraft?"

"She said she was in the company of others, so I assume it was a kind of spacecraft."

Gaea nodded. "I've always wanted to go on a cosmic journey myself," she said, "but without the anal probes. What is it with aliens and anal probes?"

"I couldn't tell you."

She extended her hand for Cheever's phone and took a close look at Stella's picture before shaking her head. "I've never seen her."

"How long have you lived here?"

"Almost nine months," said Gaea. "How old is the kid?"

"She's fourteen now, but she was seven when she went missing."

"We discourage kids from hanging around here," she said. "When it gets hot, most of us aren't much for clothes. We're also not into censorship of any kind, so this place is meant for mature audiences only. But that doesn't mean kids don't troop through here. On occasion they do."

Gaea was close enough to Cheever that he could better see her merit badges. Apparently they had been earned through sex, drugs, and rock and roll. The badges depicted empty liquor bottles, a cannabis leaf, a Les Paul electric guitar, and a tribute to "Sweet, Sweet Connie." There was also a depiction of a woman baring her breasts, along with another badge showing an extended middle finger.

Noticing Cheever's scrutiny, she said, "I call them demerit badges."

"I assume you earned them."

"Every one," she said, "and a lot more besides that aren't on my sash. I didn't want the sash to look like the bragging rights you see on those five-star generals with all their hardware."

"Seeing as you can't earn a demerit badge by helping me cross the street," said Cheever, "what do you say you earn one by giving me a tour of this place?"

"Any chance you're going to tip your tour guide?" she asked. "We're trying to earn enough money to buy this place before some developer does. That's why East Jesus is now officially a nonprofit, tax-exempt charity."

"I'll keep that in mind," said Cheever.

"Follow me," she said.

The two toured the compound. Gaea took her guide duties seriously, offering up a history of the place. She also supplied the names and the stories behind the sculptural art currently on exhibit. There were television sets with messages (among them "Blah," "Blah," and "Blah"), and a lizard monster. Of the burned-out remains of a car, Gaea said, "That was our Car-B-Cue." There was a rusted-out swing set, and windmills. Cheever paused longest at the art she identified as *Terminator*, the *Time Travel Machine*, and the *Tower of Barbarella*.

"Are you looking for anything in particular?" asked Gaea.

"I'm looking for a passport to the universe," he said.

"Art takes you on a journey," she said. "Your spaceship might or might not be here, because this is an ever-changing exhibit. It's Dada that way. Here today, gone tomorrow."

Cheever nodded. "Thanks for the tour," he said, and reached for his wallet, fishing out a twenty-dollar bill. "Do I get a receipt for my taxes?"

"You do," she said, taking the twenty. "We're registered as a 501(c)(3) tax-exempt charity duly noted by the state of California."

She reached under her sash and revealed a hidden sheath. From it she pulled out a small knife that still managed to look exceptionally deadly. The blade appeared to have been honed to razor sharpness.

"Official Girl Scout accessory?" asked Cheever.

"Be prepared," she said.

With the pointed tip of her knife, she sliced free one of her badges. Then she produced a small red Sharpie, and on the back of the badge she wrote, *$20 donated.*

"There's your receipt," she said. "You can give that to the IRS."

The badge she'd selected and signed showed an extended middle finger.

"You must want me to get audited," said Cheever.

◆ ◆ ◆

Cheever drove back in the direction he'd come from. From what he'd been told, the Ski Inn was the only restaurant and bar in a twenty-mile radius. Despite his stops, he was still a few minutes early.

Rather than wait inside, he decided to take another walk. He was at the Salton Sea, so he might as well see it up close. From a distance the body of water beguiled, but the mirage vanished as he drew closer. The lake was bubbling in spots, producing a rotten-egg smell. There was also the stench that came from the skeletal remains of piscine corpses and decomposing algae.

Still, Cheever wasn't deterred, continuing his walk toward the shoreline. The ground beneath his feet was crusty, and it cracked under his footfalls to reveal a lurking sludge. Birds hadn't yet gotten the memo on the sorry state of the lake. A variety of species were floating on the water and walking the shoreline. Environmentalists stressed the importance of the lake, saying it was an important stop for many species that migrated along the Pacific Flyway, but birds didn't vote, and that made it easy for politicians to ignore their plight.

Even in the lake's failing state, though, Cheever could see why it was such a popular spot for photographers. Everywhere he turned there were otherworldly vistas. Just as ghost towns were popular motifs for shutterbugs, this was a ghost lake, with the same kinds of attractions. Crumbling edifices spoke to better days. If you had to pick a spot for the zombie apocalypse to start, it would be hard to do better.

Cheever cupped his hand over his eyes and looked into the distance. Most of the lake was devoid of human presence or activity. What might a little girl with an active imagination think of this alien landscape? For a minute he stood on the shore of the dying lake, considering that.

Then Cheever sensed something. He turned toward the direction from where he had come. His reptilian brain always seemed to be on the job; the eye in the back of his head was always alert to being observed. Staring at him was a middle-aged Hispanic man wearing a baseball cap and dark sunglasses. He raised a hand to acknowledge Cheever, who lifted his hand in turn and then began walking back to the Ski Inn.

As Cheever drew close, he asked, "Mr. Diaz?"

"Call me Beto," said the man.

Beto was a common nickname for Latino men whose first names ended in "-berto."

"I'm Cheever."

The two men shook hands. Cheever wasn't surprised to see the fading prison ink on the man's hands. He had already made Beto for someone who had spent time in the stir.

"So you're the Good Samaritan?" asked Cheever.

Beto shrugged. "That girl's turning up seems to be big news, and when I saw her face on the news, the first thing I thought was, 'I know that kid.' Either that or she's a dead ringer for Elle."

"Elle?"

"That's what Dickie Rath called his niece. Sometimes he called her Double L."

The name was not too dissimilar from *Stella*, thought Cheever. He gestured toward the restaurant and said, "Why don't we talk inside?"

"Fine by me," said Beto.

The sign at the door read **CASH ONLY**. As they stepped inside, Cheever was surprised to see that most of the seats at the bar were already taken. Everyone seated looked to be having a liquid lunch; everyone seated was also north of eighty years old. Ben Franklin was right, thought Cheever. There were a lot more old drunks than old doctors.

On prominent display at the bar was a pile of cans for sale. According to the labels, the cans contained fish assholes. The bartender, who was about as old as his clientele, seemed to know Beto and acknowledged him with a smile and wave.

The two men took seats at a table. "You live around here?" asked Cheever.

"Brawley," Beto said, "but I'm always coming through here on business."

"What business is that?"

"I drive a rig. And I've got some rentals here and there."

"What originally brought you to this area?"

"I can credit the state of California."

"Calipatria?" asked Cheever.

Beto nodded. Calipatria was a state prison.

"What for?"

"Grand theft auto and possession of a controlled substance."

"Most former cons don't extend a helping hand to the police. Why did you?"

"I figured I better get ahead of the shitstorm."

"What shitstorm is that?"

"The shitstorm that's sure to happen when a congressman's daughter turns up after being missing for years. I want to go on record right now as saying I didn't know the girl was kidnapped."

Cheever nodded. Self-preservation was a great motivator.

From behind the bar the bartender called out to them: "You two eating? Cookie just showed up."

"His wife's the cook," said Beto. "From experience I'd go with the patty melt or the cheeseburger."

"I'll have the patty melt with onion rings and a Coke," Cheever said.

Beto called to the bartender, and as he spoke, he signaled with his fingers, almost like a baseball catcher. "Two patty melts, two onion rings, one Coke, and one Bud," he yelled.

The bartender relayed the order to the unseen "Cookie," then turned back to Beto and asked, "No pickle juice?"

"Not this time," said Beto.

Cheever's upturned eyebrows asked the question.

"It's a great hangover cure," explained Beto.

"Better than fish assholes?"

That got a smirk out of Beto. "You see all those dollars hanging up on the wall behind the bar?"

Cheever nodded. He had wondered about the hundreds and hundreds of dollars that lined the wall.

"Tourists think it's good luck to write their name and where they're from on a dollar bill, and then have it tacked up on the wall."

"This doesn't exactly look like a tourist spot."

"Maybe that's why it is," said Beto. "This place draws tourists from around the world."

"What's the attraction?"

"Where else can you get a buzz a couple of hundred feet below sea level? How low can you go? This is it."

"And what better way to remember that experience than by buying a can of fish assholes?"

"Every man cave should have one for a conversation piece."

"If you say so," said Cheever.

One of the drinkers at the bar left his drink long enough to drop some change into the jukebox, and Patsy Cline began singing "Crazy." Cheever thought it was an appropriate song and sentiment for his investigation.

"Tell me about Dickie Rath," he said, "and about Elle."

"I can't tell you much, because I don't know much. In fact, I'd be surprised if anyone around here could tell you much about him. He was a desert rat who kept to himself. Rath said he needed the quiet to hear God talking. I think he fancied himself a prophet."

"And what was it he prophesized?"

"He said the Second Coming of Christ would reveal that he was an alien, just as were all the spirit beings mentioned in the Bible. He also said that heaven could be found in space. I think that's the main reason he chose to live here. From what he said, on most nights he was out stargazing."

Cheever had camped in the desert on several occasions. What he remembered most was the night sky, and how the stars had seemed so vibrant and close. It was almost like you could reach out and touch them.

Had Stella spent years looking at the stars? Had she been taught that Christ was an alien, as were the angels?

Diaz leaned in a little closer, and then spoke in a low voice to make sure he wasn't overheard. "One time Rath was a little less tight-lipped with me than usual, and he quoted Jesus, saying, 'Did not Christ say, if your right eye offends you, then pluck it out?' From what I could gather, he apparently took those words to heart."

"He plucked out his eye?"

Diaz whispered, "It wasn't his eye that offended him. It was his impure thoughts. So he cut open his nut sack and removed one of his balls."

Cheever flinched. "It sounds like he was mentally ill."

"You think?" said Diaz, not hiding his smirk.

"You haven't told me how you came to know Rath."

Diaz shifted a little in his seat. "We had an arrangement," he said. "I own some undeveloped land a few miles from here. It's a spot about a mile from the main road. I allowed Rath to camp there."

"He was your tenant?"

"Not in the legal sense," said Diaz. "Every year Rath gave me what we called a 'love offering.'"

"And how much was this 'love offering'?"

"This last year it was eighteen hundred dollars."

"And what did Rath get for that?"

"As much silence as he wanted."

"Does your camp come with electricity or water?"

"There are no connections for any of that, but Rath didn't seem to notice. He set up some solar panels, and ran his lighting off those. And he had this solar cooker he seemed proud of. He said when the sun was shining he could boil water in ten minutes."

"Where did he get the water?"

"There's a hot spring on the land. The spring isn't very big—you can't bathe in it or anything—but it supplied him with enough water for his needs. He even set up one of those solar showers."

"When did Rath first settle here?"

Diaz thought about that. "It was around six or seven years ago."

"Was Elle with him then?"

He shook his head. "She turned up later. Rath said she was his niece."

"No one questioned him?"

"Like I said, he kept to himself and was pretty self-contained. There probably weren't even a handful of people who knew about the girl."

"Elle didn't go to school?"

"Rath homeschooled her, or that's what he said. I only saw the girl a few times, but whenever I did, her nose was always in some book."

"Describe her," said Cheever.

Diaz's description sounded enough like Stella that Cheever pulled out his phone. "Is this the girl?" he asked.

After a few seconds of staring at the picture, Diaz nodded. "That's Elle," he said.

"No question in your mind?"

"None," he said.

Their beverages were delivered to their table. Diaz took a big pull from his beer and wiped away a frothy mustache.

"When was the last time you saw Rath and the girl?" asked Cheever.

"It was three or four months ago."

"When did you notice they were gone?"

"It was just a few weeks back," he said. "His love offering for the year was overdue. That's when I found the Airstream was gone."

"Describe the Airstream."

"It was one of those older, shiny ones that look like a spaceship."

Cheever felt a prickle along his spine at the mention of a spaceship. Could the Airstream have been Stella's spaceship? Had she hidden away from the sun during the day, and then emerged in the evening to look out at the heavens? Did that explain her pallor?

"So, six or seven years ago, Rath shows up here, and then he lives under the radar all that time. And sometime during his stay, his niece came to live with him?"

"He's the one who said she was his niece."

"And Rath had no friends or family in the area?"

"None I knew about."

"How did he support himself?"

"I think he got a monthly check from the government, but I don't know the details."

"What kind of vehicle did he drive?"

"His fifth wheeler died not long after he settled in with the Airstream," said Diaz. "He was always working to get it running again. I guess he finally did. But on those rare occasions when he left his homestead, he drove a dirt bike."

Their burgers and onion rings were brought to the table, and both men began eating. Cheever thought about what he'd been told, and between bites asked, "Who else around here would know Rath?"

"You got the mini-mart next door to here," said Diaz. "I imagine he had to have made himself known there. But for most services like getting gas or doing any banking, he would have gone to Brawley or Salton City."

The detective thought about Rath's life. It didn't sound like an easy existence. He'd lived in a camper in a spot that was harsh and inhospitable and secluded, all so that he might hear God. And God had told him to emasculate himself.

"Hard work being a prophet," said Cheever.

Diaz agreed. "It's not for pussies."

CHAPTER TWENTY-SIX

"The Airstream was right about here."

Diaz indicated a spot that was somewhat sheltered by an outcropping of rocks. Cheever examined the sandy dirt. The ground showed indentations from something heavy.

"You never took any pictures?" asked Cheever.

"I never saw the need. And I'm sure Rath wouldn't have liked it if I had."

"Where's the hot spring?"

Diaz pointed. "It's about a hundred yards that way."

Cheever began walking in that direction, his eyes moving right to left, searching the ground. There were some partial shoe prints, and Cheever took a few pictures, but he knew that even if he put a request for a criminalist through the proper channels, it was unlikely he could get the Imperial County authorities to send out someone to gather trace evidence. This wasn't a crime scene. This was more like the case of a cop with a wild hair trying to get answers to something that didn't mean anything to anyone except him.

The hot spring proved to be more of a seep than a desert oasis, with a trickle of water leaching out into a depression in the ravine.

"Rath had some special pots he used," said Diaz, "and a makeshift filtration system. He said on a good day he could get as much as five gallons."

Cheever nodded, but his attention was on the surrounding area. There was a trail along the ravine that he was guessing human feet had helped to form. Cheever followed the wash, then scrambled up to a ridge. The elevation wasn't very high, but in a flat desert, the slight rise stood out, and afforded the best view in the area.

A big rock was positioned in the middle of the rise. Someone had to have brought the stone there. It was the right size to sit on. Not far from the seat was another human-made formation. Someone had been particular about gathering rocks and placing them in a very specific sequence. It took Cheever a few seconds to realize he was looking at a depiction of the solar system. The colors and sizes of the rocks represented the sun and the eight planets. Pluto hadn't made the cut. Cheever took some more pictures. While he was clicking away, from the corner of his eye he saw a glint in the sky. He shaded his eyes with his hand and looked upward, trying to make out whatever had caught his attention, but didn't see anything.

"What are you looking for?" asked Diaz.

"A UFO," said Cheever.

CHAPTER TWENTY-SEVEN

Froke had always hoped a high-profile client would land in his lap. Even though he was only a few years into his job, he was already tired of being little more than a highly paid pharmacist, writing out scripts for depression and anxiety. Managed care wanted Band-Aids, not insights, dispensed. But now he wondered if Stella Pierce was a case of beware of what you wish for.

Few people knew he was treating the congressman's daughter, and maybe that was a good thing. During his internship, Froke had worked with psychopathic murderers who hadn't scared him as much as Scarecrow did.

At that moment, Froke assumed Scarecrow was listening in on his session with Stella. He couldn't go anyplace these days without wondering if he was being monitored.

"So tomorrow's the big day," said Froke.

"I suppose so," said Stella.

He pretended to write down something; what he was really doing was checking his notes from the night before. Froke had to make sure he covered the curriculum that had been given to him. One of the talking points was Stella's going back to school.

"It's normal to be anxious," he said.

Stella nodded. She wasn't much of a talker, even though Froke had her parents convinced that she opened up to him during their sessions.

"That's why I think it makes sense for you to start on a regimen of antianxiety and antidepression medication," he said.

Scarecrow and company wanted Froke to convince Stella to start taking meds. What he wasn't telling her was that in addition to anti-anxiety medication and antidepressants, his overseers wanted him to prescribe antipsychotics as well. None of those meds were called for—in fact, they were contraindicated—but Froke was doing his best to be a good salesman even though Stella had so far resisted his pitch.

"My parents tell me you've been trying to convince them of the same thing," she said.

"I believe your situation will improve with some prescribed medications."

"What *situation* is that?" she asked.

"I suspect you're depressed but not even conscious of that," he said. "I don't want you falling down into a deep, dark hole, so I'm looking to have you get ahead of that."

"If I fall down that hole," said Stella, "I can understand your wanting to put me on medication, but not before."

Froke didn't like a kid challenging his prognosis, even though she was absolutely right. "That isn't the only reason for the meds. You need to understand that you are presenting with a delusional disorder."

"How is it you are so certain of that?" she asked.

He pretended exasperation as he pointed to the sky. "Some astronomers believe there are one hundred billion galaxies in the universe," he said. "That means there are ten billion galaxies in the observable universe. The key word there is *observable*. That's the universe we've been able to see. And in each of those galaxies there are about one hundred billion stars. In the Milky Way alone there are one hundred billion planets. That makes our own little planet insignificant, doesn't it?"

Stella knew what was coming next: Froke would ask her why she imagined that of the billions of people on the planet, she had been singled out. But she tried to derail his train of thought.

"Earth is not insignificant," she said. "It's special."

"Why is it special?"

"If you saw it from out there, you would know."

"You mean if I was in some spacecraft looking at it, as opposed to some other planet?"

"Yes."

Froke shook his head. "That sounds rather simplistic. If I had a magical spacecraft and could go anywhere in the universe I wanted, it stands to reason that I would encounter planets of unsurpassed beauty and see sights I couldn't even imagine."

"Yes," Stella said, suddenly enthused.

"Well, if that's the case, why is this planet special?"

"Of all the planets that have been seeded, none has the potential to be so great, and none has the potential to be so terrible."

The words didn't sound like those of a kid. Froke wondered whether the speech had been rehearsed. "That's quite the sentiment," he said.

"That is what the Travelers believe," she admitted.

"Explain to me about this notion of seeding," he said.

"Long, long ago the Travelers facilitated conditions on the planet to make an abundance of life possible."

"So the Travelers are our ancestors?"

"Not really."

"But I thought they *seeded* the planet."

"They did, but not in their image. They offered ingredients appropriate to this planet that helped foster life."

"And have they done this with other planets?"

"Yes."

"How many?"

"I don't know."

"If the Travelers did this thing so long ago, then they would have to be an incredibly advanced race."

"They are."

"They must be like gods."

"No."

"No? But in the time since they first seeded Earth, their technology must have progressed to an almost unimaginable degree."

"While they have advanced technologically, their journey has been more of an inward one."

"If their journey has been an inward one," he said, "then what are they doing traveling around space?"

"That is what Travelers do."

"Do the Travelers have a home planet?"

"They did at one time. Now space is their home."

"And what they essentially do is go around checking on the planets they seeded?"

"That is only one aspect of their travels."

"What else do they do?"

"They study and explore and visit."

"Visit?"

"They have favorite spots to visit."

"So what you're saying is that they sightsee for pleasure?"

Stella shrugged. "I wouldn't call it that. I would say it's more of a pilgrimage."

"And you were part of that pilgrimage?"

"I was allowed a hint of it."

Froke stifled a sigh. At least he'd managed to cover most of the bullet points his handlers had wanted him to bring up. Even though Stella seemed interested in this topic, it wasn't part of *the agenda* they were supposed to be discussing.

"Our time is almost up, Stella. I hope you'll reconsider the issue of medication, especially with your starting classes at high school. The pills would help with your anxiety."

Stella tilted her head, as if thinking about something. "Why do *they* want me to take pills?" she asked.

Froke tried to make his alarm look and sound like confusion. *"They?"* he asked. "Who are *they*?"

Stella didn't answer. But neither did she hide the disappointment in her eyes. Not for the first time, Froke felt like a fraud. When he'd entered med school, he hadn't wanted to go into psychiatry. It had just sort of happened.

He stood up. It was time this house call came to an end. He wondered what Scarecrow would have to say about this session.

"It's not your fault you're not good with pain or blood, Dr. Froke," Stella said.

Was she hinting at suicide? he wondered.

But then she continued. "Your body betrayed you. Your hands used to tremble when you tried to treat patients. Your peers called you Shake 'n Bake."

Froke's face reddened. "Where did you hear that?" he demanded.

"It still plays heavily on your mind," Stella said. "When you broadcast your pain so loudly, I can't help but hear it."

Just hearing the nickname conjured up bad memories. Froke remembered the time he had wet his pants when paramedics had brought in a patient whose wife had slashed his genitals. The man's injury wasn't life threatening and didn't even prove to be that serious, but Froke had still voided his bladder when confronted with the sight. Even the patient had thought that was funny, laughing along with everybody else in the ER.

For a moment, Froke wanted to admit his deception. He wanted to beg Stella's forgiveness. But he was afraid of what Scarecrow might do to him. Yes, he was scared of blood, especially the spilling of his own.

"I won't dignify your imagination with a response," he said, "but I will say that the difference between us is that I have tried to address my deficiencies and surmount my problems. I accepted the realities, and I coped. You would be wise to do the same thing."

With as much dignity as he could muster, Froke departed Stella's room.

CHAPTER TWENTY-EIGHT

Cheever called Eleanor Pierce from the road, and asked if Stella would be free to talk in half an hour's time.

"That should work out fine," she said. "Stella's session with Dr. Froke is just ending now."

"How's Stella doing?" Cheever asked.

"She seems happy, and tomorrow she starts school. I'm pretty sure I'm more nervous than she is, maybe because I know how cliquey kids can be."

"It's a parent's job to worry."

"I grieved for seven years. It's a relief to be able to worry instead."

◆ ◆ ◆

Cheever found Stella sitting at a table in the backyard. She was busy removing the peel from an orange, and greeted him with a smile.

"Would you like a section, Detective?" she asked. "Or would you like your own orange instead? There are so many, they're falling off the tree."

"I'll take a section if you don't mind," he said.

She separated a piece and handed it to him. Cheever thanked her, then popped it into his mouth. The orange was both sweet and sour to the taste, and he appreciated its tartness. Still, the last note was a bit sour, and he cringed. That seemed to amuse Stella.

"I saw Dr. Froke driving away," said Cheever, "and I think he had that same sour expression."

"He stayed over to talk with my mom. Part of it was arranging our new schedule, where we'll be going to his office twice a week. But most of their conversation was about his being disappointed with me."

"Why is that?"

"I haven't been agreeing with him or going along with his agenda."

"That explains it," said Cheever. "I knew Froke's sour look was familiar, because I've been causing those kinds of looks all my life. What did you do to upset him?"

"He wants me to start on medication that I don't want to take."

"What kind of medication?"

"Pills for anxiety and depression," she said. "Why does he want me to take medication I don't need?"

"I'm sure he would say you do need it."

"He knows that I don't."

"How can you be so certain?"

She shrugged and said, "He was broadcasting his doubts."

"Are you talking about mindspeak?"

"Yes and no," she said. "A few of his thoughts came in and out, and I got this impression that he was pushing the pills because he was being told to."

Cheever considered her words. "Maybe he was being cautious. Maybe the Big Brother you were hearing was just his medical training coming through. Doctors sometimes aren't sure of the best course of treatment for their patients. Maybe Dr. Froke thinks the default protocol for a patient like you is to start them on medication."

Stella shrugged, clearly unconvinced.

"Okay," said Cheever, "why would Dr. Froke—or anyone else—want you taking unnecessary medications?"

"Wouldn't that be a good way of showing that I'm not right in the head?"

"And I thought I was a suspicious old cop," said Cheever.

Stella took a self-satisfied bite from a section of the orange.

"The reason I'm here today," said Cheever, "is because *I am* a suspicious old cop. A witness came forward who says you lived with a man who claimed to be your uncle in a remote desert setting a few hours from here."

Cheever studied Stella's reaction. You can't be a cop for more than thirty years without being good at reading people. He didn't have Stella's purported ability to mindspeak, but he knew body language and had learned to trust his eyes and instincts far more than a lie detector.

Stella stared at him blankly before saying, "He's wrong."

"I showed him your picture. He says you're older now, but he's positive you're the girl."

"Do you want me to act outraged?" asked Stella. "Do you want me to get angry? Is that what I'm supposed to be showing on my face now? I'm sorry, but those types of responses no longer come naturally to me. I think I'm getting better at smiling and responding happily, but I'm not good with my negative emotions yet. They're being developed, though."

"You never lived in a silver Airstream trailer near the Salton Sea?"

Stella shook her head. "I've never heard of the Salton Sea, and I don't know what an Airstream is."

"I took some pictures at an art community called East Jesus," he said. "Have you ever heard that name?"

"No," she said.

Cheever turned his phone toward her. "I'd like you to take a look at these photos and tell me if anything you see looks familiar to you."

With his blocky forefinger, he tried to access the pictures, but Stella shook him off and reached for his phone. When she was finished scrolling through the photos, she handed back his phone and said, "I've never seen that artwork before, or that place."

"And yet I found there was something alien about many of those pieces. And I can see how an active imagination could picture the Airstream as a spaceship."

"How do you even know what a spaceship looks like?" she asked.

"I don't. I suppose my ideas are based on what I've seen in movies."

"I was never with that man, or in that place, or in that trailer," she said.

"You know I'm going to be trying to find other Salton Sea witnesses?" said Cheever. "You know I've worked your case so long that I have to see it through to the end?"

"I'm glad of that. Your involvement makes me feel like I have a guardian angel. I would guess my being identified by your witness is a case of mistaken identity. But let's say it wasn't. What reason would he have to identify me?"

It was sort of like her pill question, Cheever thought. And once again, he didn't have a good answer.

"Like most cops, I hate working a case and coming up short on answers. That's why I keep digging and digging."

"I'm sorry I haven't made your job easier."

"No one likes an easily solved puzzle," said Cheever, "but now at least I can be curious and not anxious."

"You were anxious?"

"Maybe that's not the right word. When you first went missing, I barely slept. My fear was that I'd overlooked something, and I was afraid whatever it was could be a matter of life or death. As time passed, other worries surfaced. I didn't want your abductor getting away with the crime. In my mind I kept reworking the crime, trying to think what I could do, or what I should have done. I guess you could say I was obsessive."

"I'm sorry."

"My girlfriend actually encouraged me to have a special remembrance of you. She said that would help me say good-bye and put the case behind me."

"And did you do that?"

"I suppose I did. It wasn't elaborate. It wasn't like the celebration of life that your family had in your honor. There were no pictures or speakers recalling favorite memories. Six months ago I looked out at the ocean at Torrey Pines Reserve, and silently read a passage from *Charlotte's Web*."

"What passage?"

He thought for a moment. "It was where one of Charlotte's children was explaining to Wilbur that it was his time to be floating off into the air, and Wilbur was pressing him on where he would go."

"And he said, 'Wherever the wind takes us,' didn't he?"

"He did," said Cheever. "And before floating away he said, 'We take to the breeze, we go as we please.'"

"You picked the right passage," said Stella.

"It seems like a silly exercise now."

"I hope not," she said.

"Speaking of passages, your mom tells me that you're going to school tomorrow. Are you excited?"

"I am," she said, "even though I'm not sure what to expect."

CHAPTER TWENTY-NINE

Guy Wilkerson was out stretching on the corner of the residential street. It was a little before seven in the morning. Those who drove by gave him no notice; walkers and joggers were a common sight. After being confined for seven years, having the opportunity to exercise where and when he chose was nice, but it was secondary to his purpose. He was on the hunt and had methodically identified the spoor of his prey. He knew the makes and models of all the cars in the Pierce family, as well as those of their family friends. In fact, he had chosen to do his exercises at the entrance to their cul-de-sac.

He finished his warm-up and started jogging. Slow but steady wins the race; it was just a matter of getting to his final destination.

Although he'd spent hours learning familial routines, Wilkerson wasn't even sure if that was necessary. Whenever Stella was near, he could *feel* her. Something in his being was attuned to her. When she was close, his spine tingled; it was almost like his vertebrae turned into a vibrating fork.

He kept jogging. In a few minutes he'd circle back, then run right up to the Pierce house. Just outside the security gate he would pause, stopping to tie an imaginary loose shoelace. But now it was a little early for that. It would be at least half an hour before Stella's brother, Michael, set out for school. So why was his body beginning to feel like a tuning fork?

Behind him he could hear a car coming up the street. He didn't even have to turn to know she was there. But he couldn't help himself. His head turned as the car passed, and there she was, sitting in the passenger seat. Their eyes met, and Wilkerson saw the girl's surprise. She knew who he was. She knew what he was. Although they'd been apart for years, he could still detect her special glow.

He continued jogging. Part of him hoped the mother would stop the car and confront him. That would allow him to be close to Stella. And he'd stare at the girl the entire time he was telling Ma Pierce it was a free country, and he had every right to be where he was. He'd make her freak out as he had when she'd visited him in prison. Then he'd tell the bitch that unless she wanted another zero or two added to his lawsuit, she'd better shut the hell up and leave him alone. And as he finished talking, he'd look at Stella and lick his lips.

The car didn't stop, though. That meant the girl had chosen not to say anything to her mother. Wilkerson liked that. He watched the vehicle make a left. That was the way you'd go if your destination was the high school.

He kept jogging.

◆ ◆ ◆

Looking into Wilkerson's eyes—looking into his soul—switched something on in Stella. It was more than just going on alert or feeling the need for flight or preparing for a fight. A hyperawareness came over her. She looked at her mother and felt her thoughts in her head.

Maybe we should have talked about homeschooling Stella. Why didn't we ever discuss that? I'm a teacher. Wasn't that once my calling?

Never before had Stella picked up entire sentences or even words. Since her return there had been occasions when she had tapped into the emotional currents that came with a recurring thought or a memory that couldn't be put aside. But now everything was not only amplified, but more specific.

Maybe she should tell her mother about Guy Wilkerson. Hadn't Detective Cheever made it clear that he wanted to be contacted right away if Wilkerson ever turned up? But Stella maintained her silence. She feared the consequences of speaking more than not speaking. If she told her mother about Wilkerson, Stella knew she would be confined to the house. Her mother probably wouldn't even let Luke Hart take her out for surfing lessons. And it would be the excuse her mother needed to homeschool her. Although Stella had mixed feelings about going to school, she knew it was time to go out into the world.

At the moment, though, it was a noisy world. Her mother's thoughts continued their intrusion. Stella had this feeling that seeing Wilkerson had switched on some kind of defensive mechanism in her brain she wasn't even aware she had.

Playground politics can be so mean. And there are so many cliques at the Torrey Pines Academy. Stella won't know how to navigate them.

She tried to shut out her mother's worries and thoughts, but had only limited success. It wasn't like she could put her hands over her ears. Luckily, the high school was only a five-minute drive away.

◆ ◆ ◆

"It's nice to meet you," said Rosa Hernandez, shaking Stella's hand.

I guess the congressman's not going to be here. He's probably sleeping in. I wish I could have slept in.

Hernandez was the high school's freshman counselor. She motioned for Stella and her mother to be seated.

The counselor reached for her to-go container of coffee, and took a big gulp. "Thank heavens for vitamin C," she said.

Come on, caffeine, kick in.

Hernandez started talking about the high school. It was a speech she'd given many times, and she was able to recite the pertinent facts without even thinking about them.

"We're proud of the fact that the Torrey Pines Academy is ranked fifth in the state academically, and that's out of almost five thousand high schools. So, yes, our students are smart and motivated."

Hernandez took another long pull of her coffee.

And a lot of those same students are spoiled, overprivileged brats.

"But I wouldn't worry about this school being too much for you academically, Stella," she said. "The numbers from your entrance exam were very impressive, especially in science and math. And if you have any questions about your course work or need help, we offer after-school tutoring every day in the library."

The counselor turned a page. She had never before encountered a transcript as barren as Stella's. There were no middle-school records whatsoever.

The supervisor said I shouldn't ask about the gap in her records. Supposedly it's being worked out on the district level. I guess if you're the daughter of a congressman, you can just waltz in here.

Stella tried to shut down the intrusive thoughts, focusing her attention on the framed pictures of Mrs. Hernandez's two girls. Pictures of those same girls could be seen on the walls. Judging by their most recent photos, the girls were a few years younger than Stella.

"Are those your daughters?" asked Stella. "They're beautiful."

"Sylvia and Laura," Mrs. Hernandez said, and Stella felt her happiness. "They're eleven and ten, going on eighteen and twenty-one."

The counselor turned to Eleanor. "They grow up too fast, don't they?"

That was something Stella's mom could wholeheartedly agree with: "Oh yes."

The mothers shared a smile. Then Mrs. Hernandez reviewed Stella's course schedule.

"The first few days are probably going to feel overwhelming," she said. "Getting familiar with a new school is always difficult, but I want you to know that my door is always open to you."

"Her brother, Michael, is a senior here," said Eleanor. "He's supposed to be looking out for Stella."

Isn't he the boy who jumped from the cliff? All the kids have been watching that video. But does Mom even know? Better not to say anything, I guess.

"I'm sure he will," said Mrs. Hernandez.

The counselor looked at the wall clock, then turned her gaze back to Stella. "First period starts in ten minutes. Do you want to have a student escort you to class?"

"I thought I could do that," said Eleanor.

Michael had warned Stella not to let their mother be a 'helicopter mom.' "If you don't set boundaries," he'd said, "she'll hover over you and smother you."

"Since Mrs. Hernandez gave me a map of the school," said Stella, "I might as well use it and walk to class on my own."

Her mother said, "Wouldn't it be easier . . ."

Stella shook her head. "I'm okay, Mom."

"It sounds as if your little one is ready to fly the nest," said the counselor.

Eleanor opened her mouth to object. The words didn't come out, but her thoughts did.

For seven years I've been separated from my daughter. Even if she thinks it's time to fly on her own, I am not ready to let her do that. I should have proposed homeschooling with Duncan and Dr. Froke. But the reason he wanted her back in school so soon was that he thought she was in need of socialization. He probably wouldn't have liked the idea of homeschooling. But I still should have pushed for it.

Stella tried to not be drawn in by her mother's heartbreak. She rose to her feet, and was followed by the counselor, and finally her reluctant mother. Mrs. Hernandez shook Stella's hand and said, "Good luck." Then she shook Eleanor's hand and said, "She'll do great; you'll see."

Nice girl was the last thought Stella heard.

Mother and daughter walked out of the counselor's office, and then Eleanor took Stella in her arms. "Call me if you have any problems at all."

"Okay, Mom."

Her mother's tears moistened her face, and she could feel her mom's emotional roller coaster. It was enough to roil Stella's stomach. The two disengaged, and her mother tried wiping away her tears, but then gave up. "I love you," she said.

"I love you, too, Mom."

"Your brother said he would give you a ride home. And he promised to be there if you need any help. I'll text him and remind him of that."

"It will be okay, Mom. I'll be okay."

"I'll be texting you as well. Please text me back. But you had better hurry to class. You don't want to be late on your first day."

Eleanor started to walk off, but then she came back and gave her daughter one more hug.

I'll be waiting for her at home, just like I have for so long.

◆ ◆ ◆

As Stella exited the administrative offices, she left the relative quiet behind and entered the tumult of two thousand teenagers making their way to classes. The noise reverberated throughout the quad, and almost stopped Stella in her tracks. It wasn't only the conversations she had to contend with; it was all the thoughts. The encompassing chaos had a roller-coaster effect on her, making it difficult to focus on her map. With unsteady steps she continued walking toward her geometry classroom.

Bodies careened toward her, veering off at the last moment. Hundreds of conversations overlapped. Most hands were wrapped around phones. She heard music, and discussions being carried out over speakerphones. Faces came in and out of view, and with them Stella heard voices, some aloud and some only in her head.

"Damn, that girl's putting off so much glow I need my sunglasses!"

Stella tried to identify the mind behind the words, but there were too many probing eyes. And then there was a female thought aimed at her.

"She's probably anorexic and bulimic. Real girls have curves."

Stella stepped away from a heavy girl about her age giving her the evil eye.

"Goldilocks, Goldilocks, why don't you try my porridge? Trust me, it will be just right. You'll want to slurp it down."

She met the eyes of a boy fixated on her flaxen hair, and turned away from his hungry stare. His smile belied the anger Stella sensed, but then she heard, *"Stuck-up ho. What do you call a blonde with half a brain? Gifted."*

His mean laughter followed her, but Stella knew she was the only who could hear it.

"That's the chica in the news, the congressman's kid that came back."

A brown-complexioned boy studied her. He had a full, dark mustache, which he stroked with his thumb and forefinger. And then the voice in her head changed again, becoming female this time.

"Isn't that the girl Tiffany was talking about? Yeah, that's got to be her. Tiffany called her Rip Van Vanilla. I'll have to tell her about Rip's being here. She'll want to know."

Her glee was unmistakable. There was something else she was broadcasting, something mean, but Stella tried to block that out. She needed to keep moving. The different buildings all had numbered classrooms, and she finally found the room she was looking for. As she stepped through the door, most of the tumult was left behind her. Her hands were actually trembling, and she took several deep, steadying breaths. "Mad World," she thought. It was a song on Michael's playlist whose haunting lyrics had prompted her to play it over and over again.

"Mad World" was what she was experiencing.

There was an adult seated behind a desk at the front of the room. Stella approached the man and waited for him to look up.

Finally he did, and she said, "Mr. Rankin?"

He nodded, and she said, "I'm Stella Pierce," then handed him one of the forms given to her by Mrs. Hernandez.

"That's right," he said. "You're the new student."

She's the congressman's kid. I voted against him, but she doesn't need to know that. God, she's probably another stuck-up prima donna. That's all I need.

◆ ◆ ◆

The static, as Stella thought of it, cleared up as the day went on. She suspected the adrenaline rush brought on by Wilkerson and the start of school had triggered the way her mind heard things. At the advent of the threat, her awareness had escalated, but as the hours had passed, the static had gradually turned into background noise. That was a good thing. It was hard to endure all the voices in her head.

For lunch Stella bought the vegan selection, a pita plate with hummus and salad. Instead of sitting down at one of the indoor tables, she walked outside and followed a pathway, then found a seat atop a retaining wall. The cafeteria was near enough that she could hear its din; it was far enough away to not be intrusive.

The sun felt pleasant on her face, and for a few seconds Stella closed her eyes. Then she felt the vibration of her phone and reached for it. Luke Hart had texted her.

Where r u?

Stella thought about his question, then texted him her GPS coordinates.

Luke texted back: How about in English?

It took her a moment to understand that he was making a joke of what she'd written, and that GPS coordinates weren't the location he wanted. Stella tapped a new answer: Roughly 120 meters southwest of the cafeteria.

Is that near Performing Arts?

She looked over at the nearest building. Sandwiched between two huge decorative masks—one frowning and the other smiling—were the words *Performing Arts.*

Yes, she typed.

C U in 5.

While Stella ate her hummus and salad, it almost felt like she was being observed by the two masks. Her eyes were more drawn to the frowning face. Had some tragedy befallen him, or was it a series of sad tidings?

In the midst of her musings, a slightly breathless Luke showed up. "Hey," he said.

She matched his word and smile: "Hey."

"Michael's driving off campus for lunch. I'm supposed to text him if you want anything."

"I already grabbed lunch," she said, showing him the remains of her plate.

"Okay," Luke said skeptically. "But if you want some real food, Michael's getting takeout pizza."

"That was always his favorite."

Luke motioned next to where Stella was sitting. "Do you mind?"

"Of course not," she said. "I'd welcome your company."

He vaulted up next to her, made himself comfortable, and said, "It must suck to be the new kid at school. Because of that, I brought you a present."

Luke handed her an apple.

"Thank you," she said. "Where's your lunch?"

"Michael's getting me a calzone," he said.

"Is he bribing you to babysit me?"

Luke shook his head. "It was my idea."

"Let's share the apple," she said, taking a bite and then handing it to him. "My mom used to always say, 'An apple a day keeps the doctor away.'"

Luke took a bite. "My mom's family came from Ohio, and she says we're related to Johnny Appleseed."

"I don't know who Johnny Appleseed is."

Luke passed back the apple. "He's this guy who traveled around the American frontier planting apple seeds and growing orchards. His real name was John Chapman, but everyone called him Johnny Appleseed. He wore this tin hat that he also used as his cooking pot. If you believe the old stories, he was a gentle soul who didn't hurt anything, not even insects."

"He sounds like he was a good man," said Stella. "And I wouldn't be surprised if you were related to him."

Luke looked pleased at that. "I do like apples," he admitted.

Voices rang out from the front of the Performing Arts Building. Half a dozen students, some in costume, were shouting. Standing in the middle of a circle of young men was a young woman.

"What!" she called. "Must I burn again? Are none of you ready to receive me?"

The young man nearest to her showed his upturned hands. "The heretic is always better dead," he said. "And mortal eyes cannot distinguish the saint from the heretic. Spare them."

The girl raised her eyes, looking right at where Stella was seated, and beyond her. "O God that madest this beautiful earth, when will it be ready to receive Thy saints? How long, O Lord, how long?"

Stella turned to Luke, her eyes asking for an answer to what they were seeing. "Sometimes the drama students like to do their practicing outside," he said. "They're getting ready for the play *Saint Joan*."

"What's it about?" asked Stella.

"There was this girl called Joan of Arc," he said. "She said God told her to lead the French army into battle and drive the English out of the country."

"And what happened?"

"I think she succeeded, or at least she did for a time, but in the end she was burned at the stake."

Stella shuddered. "Really?"

Luke nodded. "They accused her of being a heretic and a witch."

"When in doubt," Stella said, "blame the witches."

This time it was Luke's eyes asking for an explanation.

"I just came from Mrs. Baum's class," said Stella. "We were reading from *The Crucible*."

"Been there and done that," said Luke. "That was one strange play."

"Mrs. Baum pointed out some of the metaphors going on in the play. She said every generation has its witchcraft trials."

"You'd think once would have been enough."

"You would think," said Stella.

◆ ◆ ◆

Stella's last class of the day was biology. As the students were being dismissed for the day, Dr. Rommel growled, "We have frog day tomorrow." Stella wondered what he meant, but didn't ask. Like everyone else, she was glad the school day was over. Besides, it was clear Dr. Rommel did not encourage class participation. In fact, he had the ability to freeze any unwanted conversations by turning his thick lenses in the direction of the offenders.

Michael had texted Stella to say she should walk past the front entrance of the school toward the western parking lot, and that he and Luke would be looking for her. As she walked in that direction, Stella heard the laughter of girls, but took no notice beyond that until a familiar voice said, "There she is!"

Tiffany was pointing a finger at her. Standing around Tiffany were the giggling Y-Girls.

Several individuals started running her way. A man with a shoulder-mounted camera moved to intercept Stella, but a woman with a hand-held microphone was the first to reach her side. In close pursuit was a second man, who was also holding a microphone.

"Stella Pierce?" asked the woman.

"Yes?" said Stella.

"I'm Delaney Lee from NBC9 San Diego. Do you mind talking with me for a minute?"

"Talk?" asked Stella.

The second reporter joined them, and Stella found another microphone shoved her way.

Delaney Lee asked, "You are the daughter of Congressman Duncan Pierce?"

"Yes," she said.

"And for seven years you've been missing?" asked the reporter.

"I've been away," said Stella.

"As I understand it," the woman said, "you are on record as saying that during that time you were with the Travelers. Is that right?"

Before Stella had a chance to answer, the male reporter began talking. "I'm Guillermo Aleman, Stella," he said, "from San Diego News Three. You say these so-called Travelers are extraterrestrials, isn't that right?"

Stella opened her mouth to answer, but then decided to say nothing. This wasn't Delaney Lee's first go-around with ambush journalism, however.

"The Travelers abducted you, didn't they?" she asked.

"No," said Stella.

"They stole you from your parents when you were a little girl."

"They didn't steal me," she said. "They invited me to join them."

The competing male reporter followed Lee's lead. "You deny that they enticed you with candy and promises to get you to go along with them?"

"They never did anything like that," said Stella, "and they never would."

"So you went off with them willingly?" asked Lee.

"Yes," said Stella.

"You're saying for the last seven years you haven't been a prisoner?" asked Aleman.

"I was never a prisoner."

It was Lee's turn to ask a question: "But you were going around the universe with these Travelers?"

She opened her mouth to answer, but was interrupted by Michael's voice screaming, "Stella!"

She looked around for him and was surprised to see dozens of students clustered around her, including Tiffany and some of the Y-Girls.

"Stella!" Michael yelled once more.

This time she was able to follow her brother's angry voice. Half his body was hanging out the driver's-side window of his car, and he was wildly gesturing to her.

"Why did the Travelers want you to accompany them?" asked Aleman.

"What did your father say when you told him where you'd been all these years?" asked Lee.

The crowd drew in closer to hear her answers, and Stella felt penned in.

"Coming through," said a loud voice that she was overjoyed to hear.

Luke Hart pushed his way through the circle, and she hid her face in his protective arm.

"Let's pull a ghost," he whispered into her ear.

With Luke leading interference, they began walking in the direction of Michael's car.

"Bye-bye, Space Girl," said Tiffany, offering up mock-concern.

The Y-Girls echoed her words: "Bye-bye, Space Girl."

CHAPTER THIRTY

Even before Luke and Stella could put on their seat belts, Michael said, "What the hell happened?"

"They were asking me about the Travelers," said Stella.

"How could the media have known about the Travelers?" asked Michael.

He hit the accelerator. Luke knew that when his friend was upset, he drove fast. Michael turned to Luke, challenging him to say anything.

"Why is it you keep thinking I'm the one who's talking?" said Luke. "I didn't say anything to anyone. I swear it."

"Someone had to have tipped them off," said Michael. "Only our family knew, and Detective Cheever, and Stella's shrink."

"The Y-Girls somehow knew," said Luke.

"And you didn't say something to Tiffany?"

Luke shook his head. "Not a word."

"Why are you the one who's acting so angry, Michael?" asked Stella.

"Because you know talking about the Travelers is going to make you look crazy, don't you?"

"Isn't that *my* problem?" said Stella.

"You're not the only one involved. You're making our family a laughingstock."

"Would you rather that I lied?"

"I'd rather that you weren't so messed up," he said.

"That's enough," said Luke.

"Don't tell me what's enough. Our family has been treating Stella with kid gloves. We should have told her that her Travelers story was bullshit. Instead, we've been dancing around the elephant in the room."

"That's right," said Stella. "You didn't want to talk about the Travelers. No one in our family did."

"You want a conversation nonstarter?" asked Michael. "Tell someone you went off into space with extraterrestrials. What do you say to that?"

"I can think of lots of things," said Stella. "For example, you could have asked, 'Where did you go?' and 'What did you see?'"

"You're my sister, Stella, and I love you, but I am not going to feed into your delusion. Mom and Dad say you have refused to take meds that might help you think straight. It's time you reconsidered that."

Stella turned her head, looked out the window, and let out an almost imperceptible sigh.

"It's not fair to blame Stella for being caught off guard," said Luke.

Even though she knew Luke was trying to help, Stella said, "What's not fair is my having to worry about what I should say or what I shouldn't say, instead of just being able to tell the truth."

"I'm going to call Courtney," said Michael, "and find out what happened."

No one responded; no one in the car was feeling very good about themselves.

"Next time people ask you questions," said Michael, "don't feel like you have to answer."

"Including you?" Stella asked softly.

Michael pressed down on the accelerator by way of answering. The three of them drove the rest of the way home in silence. As the car turned onto their cul-de-sac, Stella saw a familiar-looking face standing at the corner. Guy Wilkerson smiled at her. Stella didn't alert the others.

◆ ◆ ◆

Dr. Froke took the call on the cell phone that had been provided for him. He knew who would be on the other end of the line even though the phone's readout said *Unknown Caller.*

"You will soon be getting calls from the media," said Scarecrow. "They might even camp out at your workplace or on your doorstep. They will want to know if you are treating Stella Pierce. You will neither confirm nor deny this. You will merely cite doctor-patient confidentiality.

"There will be pictures surfacing that show you going to the Pierce home, as well as Stella being escorted into your practice. When shown these pictures, you are to reply, 'No comment.' Is that understood?"

"Yes," said Froke.

"In the coming days you'll likely hear some inaccurate news reports," said Scarecrow. "But you will do nothing to disabuse anyone of the notion that Stella is taking antipsychotic drugs or has severe mental health issues. Is that clear?"

"Yes," said Froke.

It was also now clear to Froke why Scarecrow had been pushing him hard to get Stella to take meds. His handler wanted it to look as if she was certifiably crazy.

"If you perform as I have directed," said Scarecrow, "you can expect to be rewarded."

"Thank you," said Froke.

When Scarecrow had first given the psychiatrist the money, he had thought it was manna from heaven. Since that time he'd learned thirty pieces don't come without a price.

The dial tone told Froke the conversation was over.

◆ ◆ ◆

From inside the vehicle, Scarecrow made a second call. "Status?" he asked.

On the speakerphone he heard Uncle Henry say, "Shaggy is buying a used electric bike."

When Wilkerson had first shown himself, Scarecrow had given him the nickname Shaggy Man, one of L. Frank Baum's *Oz* characters. His crew had quickly shortened it to Shaggy.

Auntie Em added, "Supposedly this bike will be able to go ninety miles on a single charge."

"That's going to make Shaggy a lot more mobile," said Henry.

"I guess he's had enough of jogging," said Scarecrow.

"Now he's going to be able to do a much better job of stalking her," said Em.

"Continue to monitor Dorothy. Don't intervene unless it appears Shaggy is in danger of physically threatening her."

"Understood," the two said.

◆ ◆ ◆

It was an afternoon of surreptitious conversations. First it was Michael and their mom talking behind a closed door, after which their mother made two or three private phone calls. When Eleanor finally emerged, Stella was expecting to be asked questions, but those never materialized.

Normally Eleanor watched the five o'clock local news. When she didn't turn on the television, Stella said, "Don't keep the TV off for my sake."

"I don't want anything upsetting you," she said.

"I was there, Mom. I know what happened."

Despite her mother's objections, Stella turned on the television. It was ten minutes into the broadcast before the anchor said, "Last week Congressman Duncan Pierce's fourteen-year-old daughter, Stella, returned to their home after a seven-year absence. Up until now, no one has commented as to where she might have been. We have more from our reporter Delaney Lee."

Stella listened to a recap of her disappearance, along with old footage, and then watched the replay of the journalistic ambush at school. At its conclusion she heard Tiffany and the Y-Girls saying, "Bye-bye, Space Girl." There were also clips of both Detective Cheever and Dr. Froke being asked for their comments: Cheever said he was engaged in an ongoing investigation and had nothing to say; Froke was even more succinct and said, "No comment."

Her father, as the vice chair of the Science, Space, and Technology Committee, could not avoid comment.

"As everyone is aware," the congressman said, "my daughter disappeared seven years ago. During her time away, it's clear she experienced some hardships. Since her return she has been under treatment, and we would ask everyone to respect her privacy."

Her mother used the remote to turn off the TV. "Your father was put into a position where he had to say something, Stella."

"I understand."

"He's a public servant, and a public figure."

"I'm okay, Mom. I'll be upstairs studying."

"We love you, Stella."

Stella smiled and nodded, but in her head she could still hear the Y-Girls chanting, "Bye-bye, Space Girl."

CHAPTER THIRTY-ONE

Just a few minutes after Stella settled into her room, her cell phone rang, and she saw her father was calling.

"I hope you're not too mad to talk with your old man," said Duncan.

"Of course not, Dad," said Stella.

"Your mom says you saw me talking about you on TV."

She didn't answer, but instead let her father keep talking.

"I'm sure that was upsetting. If your own family doesn't have your back, who does? But there were reasons I said what I did. I could tell you I have a constituency and I have to be accountable to them, but that's only part of the answer. What you don't know is that I also made that statement for your own sake."

"You told people I was crazy for my sake?"

"I know that's hard to believe, but I said it so that no one will view you as a threat."

"Why would anyone think I'm a threat?"

"I don't want to go into details, but suffice it to say there is an unacknowledged war that's currently going on. Information is the world currency. Countries and corporations are seeking any technological advance that might give them an edge. That's why I don't want anyone thinking there might be something to your story. It's better that you stay under the radar."

"Has something happened to make you cautious?" she asked.

Her father sighed. "What I know is sketchy, and came to me through roundabout channels, but I'm still proceeding under the assumption that where there is smoke there is fire. That's why I'm being protective of you. And more than anything, I want you to know I love you."

"I love you, too."

"I wish I was there in person," he said. "I wish I could tuck you into bed like I used to, and tell you a silly rhyme."

"I'm not too old to hear silly rhymes," said Stella.

"And I'll never be too old to tell you a silly rhyme." He thought for a moment and remembered one of the old rhymes he used to tell her:

"Good night, sleep tight,
Don't let the bedbugs bite.
But if they do, take your shoe,
And squash them until they're goo."

◆ ◆ ◆

It was almost an hour after her father's call when Stella heard the sound of a chime. She reached for her phone and saw that Luke had texted her.

Hey?

Hi, typed Stella.

U studying?

I was.

For a minute Luke didn't respond, but finally his words came up on the display: R u ok?

My dad called and made me feel better. Right now I think Michael's more upset than I am. He wants to protect me, but doesn't know how.

He still thinks you're seven.

Do you?

NO WAY!

Good.

But if you need a bodyguard at school tomorrow, just tell me.

I'll be okay. Mom called the school to complain about the reporters bothering me, and they told her the media wasn't supposed to be on school grounds without their permission. The principal said she would make sure it didn't happen again.

You're a celebrity, he wrote.

Yeah, sure, she wrote back, and then added: Would you mind if we talked on the phone?

I'll call you right now.

Stella's phone rang a few moments later. "This is better," she said.

"I agree. It's girls who usually love to text."

"It's cumbersome. And it's so easy to misinterpret what's being written."

"You won't get an argument from me."

"Then again," said Stella, "I'm not a big fan of talking either."

"That doesn't leave too many communicating options."

"That's what I'm finding out. And that's probably why I'm frustrated. When those reporters were asking me questions, I wanted to show them, instead of tell them."

With an innocent voice, Stella asked: "Do you think I satisfied their curiosity?"

Luke struggled to find the right answer, but in the midst of his dilemma, he heard Stella laughing.

"Did you just pull one on me?" Luke asked.

"I'm still getting the hang of humor. Did it work?"

"It worked. I was trying to figure out how to gently say that what you said to the reporters was kind of like throwing fuel on the fire."

"I set myself up to be Joan of Arc?"

"Let's hope not. Besides, you're not a saint, are you?"

"Mortal eyes cannot distinguish the saint from the heretic."

"Wasn't that one of the actor's lines we heard?"

"It was."

"How could you possibly remember that?"

"Space girls are good at things like that."

This time it was Luke who found himself laughing. "You're getting pretty good at this humor thing," he said. "As for what the Y-Girls called you, they're just jealous. Tiffany contacted the media to try and make you look bad."

"Maybe Tiffany did me a favor."

"How so?"

"It felt wrong not being able to talk about my life. It was like I had some awful secret that I was embarrassed by. Tiffany freed me."

"She would hate thinking she did that. Tiff's not exactly an altruistic sort."

"Why does she want to show me up?"

"She thinks you're a threat to her. In Tiffany's world she's the queen. She holds court with the Y-Girls and the wannabe Y-Girls. And she doesn't like anyone challenging that order."

"But I have no interest in Tiffany and her court."

"And I'm sure that bothers her as much as anything. You won't play her game. And there's also me."

"What about you?"

"The two of us have a little bit of a past, and Tiffany acts the same way my dog, Andre, does when it comes to his toys. Just as soon as the novelty of a new toy wears off, Andre loses all interest in it. The only thing that rekindles his interest is when anyone pretends to be interested in one of his discarded toys. As soon as that happens, that's the toy Andre wants to play with."

"So you're the discarded toy she's suddenly rediscovered?"

"That's my take on it."

"Was Tiffany your girlfriend?"

"We went out a few times, but we were always with a group. She didn't like it that I surfed and that I made it a priority in my life. Tiffany needs to be priority number one. So when I continued to surf, that was the end of our story."

"When are you going to give me my surf lesson?"

"What are you doing tomorrow morning?"

CHAPTER THIRTY-TWO

In the darkness that just preceded dawn, Luke and Stella stood on the beach looking at the ocean.

"I like to study the water and the waves before I go out," said Luke. "You see lots of surfers doing that. There's a rule of thumb that the bigger the waves are, the more time you should spend watching them. You want to take a reading of the waves and gauge how they're rolling in. You also need to be aware of the wind and swell. Beginners especially need to know about rip currents. Do you know what those are?"

"My mother used to warn me about them," said Stella. "It's a current that can carry you away from the shore."

Luke nodded. "You don't have to worry about rip currents as long as you remember they're confined to a narrow channel. If you find yourself being dragged out to the ocean, just swim parallel to the current."

"Got it," said Stella.

"Looking out at the ocean right now, I can see a rip current." Luke pointed, and Stella's eyes followed the direction of his finger. "See the break in the incoming waves? That chop is a giveaway. You can also see the water color is different from what's around it. And see how that foam is going out to sea? The rip current is taking it away."

"I see," said Stella, and she did.

"It's something to be aware of," said Luke, "but today you don't have to worry because we're going to be spending our time in the white water, where the waves have pretty much already broken."

Stella looked at the white, frothy water near to the shore. She was warm, despite the sea breeze. Luke had found an old wet suit that fit her perfectly.

"Everyone thinks of surfing as catching a wave," said Luke. "But the reality is that you spend a lot more time paddling than you do riding waves."

He put a toe on the foam board he'd brought for Stella. "This beginner board is really buoyant, as you'll see. It's also real forgiving when it comes to balancing.

"Now before we start working on your pop-up technique," said Luke, "let's find out if you're natural or goofy."

"We're going to find out what?" said Stella.

"Imagine that there's a patch of ice in front of you," said Luke, "and you want to step on that ice and slide on it. Which foot would you put forward first to do that?"

Without thinking about it, Stella extended her right foot.

"Really?" asked Luke.

"Is that wrong?"

"It's goofy," he said, "but not wrong. The vast majority of surfers are what's called natural surfers. You're that rarity who's a goofy."

"I'm not sure about that name, but my feet do feel right this way."

"That's all that matters. Now before we start working on your pop-up, let's do some stretches."

Stella followed Luke's lead, doing the stretches as he directed.

"You're a lot more limber than I am," he said. "Do you do yoga?"

"Not yoga exactly," she said, "but something that's not too dissimilar."

"That should help you with your pop-ups," he said. "It's important to be able to pop up from your board quickly in order to catch the wave you want."

Luke directed Stella to lie down on the surfboard. At his command of "Go," she popped up on the board, positioning her feet and body as if she were catching a wave.

"You don't want to look like a kook," said Luke.

Perplexed, she said, "I don't want to look crazy?"

"You don't want to look or act like a wannabe surfer. So I'm going to make you feel as if you know what you're doing out there."

Stella followed his instructions. She bent her knees (so she didn't look like a kook), positioned her legs to parallel her shoulders, and balanced her arms.

She didn't only do the pop-ups on land. Luke had her sit atop her board. "Visualize being out in the ocean," he said, "with a wave coming your way."

Stella closed her eyes. It was almost as if she could feel the motion of the ocean.

"Go," said Luke, and she popped up on her board. In her mind she was dancing with the ocean and gliding atop the water.

Luke must have liked what he was seeing. "Let's go get wet," he said.

◆ ◆ ◆

The reality exceeded her imagination. Stella laughed at the joy of being carried along by the water. When her ride came to an end, she turned her board around and began paddling back to where Luke was waiting.

She's glowing, thought Luke. Her wide smile told him how much she was enjoying herself. She was even better in the water than she'd been on land.

"We have to think about leaving," said Luke. "I promised your mother we wouldn't be late for school."

"Just a few more," said Stella. "I haven't felt this good since returning home."

"Tell you what," he said. "Let's paddle out to the break, such as it is. The good news is that only a few surfers are out there so they won't be all territorial about the waves. The bad news is that the waves are almost nonexistent. But you might get lucky and find something to ride."

"What are we waiting for?" she asked.

◆ ◆ ◆

Where the hell was she?

Guy Wilkerson had positioned himself to watch the comings and goings at the Pierce house. Not content to only watch from the street, he had spent part of the morning finding a vantage point from which he could see into the back of their house. He knew which room was Stella's. Even though her curtains were usually shut, he could sometimes make out the moving silhouette of her young body. But today the room had remained dark.

During his surveillance Wilkerson had caught a few glimpses of the mother and the brother, but not Stella. That meant she was either still sleeping, or she'd left the house prior to his arrival at dawn.

She's not home, he thought. He could feel her absence. It left him with a hollowness inside, almost as if he was hungry.

That other boy must have picked her up, that surfer kid with his sun-bleached locks. Wilkerson knew Luke's routine. He'd tried to find out whatever he could about everyone in Stella's life using the computers at the library. Through social media he'd been able to track down Surfer Boy. The stupid kid liked to advertise his favorite haunts. Wilkerson knew where he ate, where he hung out, and where he surfed . . .

That was it. The kid had picked up Stella early and taken her to one of his surfing spots. At that very moment, he was showing off for her. Shredding. That's what surfers called it when they took waves aggressively, cutting in and out of them.

Surfer Boy wasn't the only one who could show Stella shredding.

Wilkerson took off at a run. He had stowed his electric bike in the bushes. The vehicle didn't look like much, but it had been modified to go almost thirty-five miles per hour, far faster than was street legal. And right now he was ready to push the bike to its limits. He had to get to the beach. There was shredding to do.

◆ ◆ ◆

As they paddled out to the lineup, Luke offered Stella nonstop surf advice. "Normally we'd paddle around the break to get out," he said. "That's surfer etiquette. You don't want to interfere with someone's ride. But today, deserted like it is, we don't have to worry about that. And right now, even though the incoming waves aren't much, I still want you to try a turtle roll."

They'd gone over a turtle roll onshore. Luke hung back while Stella paddled toward the swell. He watched as she flipped over on her board and cut into the wave upside down. Since he was on a shortboard, Luke's maneuver was different. He took the wave by diving under it, and came up next to Stella.

"Good job," he said. "When you take out a shortboard like mine, you'll be doing duck dives like I just did," he said. "But here comes a wave. I want you to do another turtle roll."

Stella rolled over, and as the wave passed, she rolled over again. When Luke joined her, she was laughing. For the moment, gravity was no longer weighing her down.

◆ ◆ ◆

Wilkerson looked to his right, then to his left. The beach was uncrowded, with most of the activity being generated by joggers and strollers. There were only a few surfers out in the water.

He stood on the sand debating his next move. Surfer Boy had a few other spots where he liked to catch waves. Wilkerson was pretty sure he hadn't gone to Black's Beach; that would have required a long hike down the cliffs that would take too much time on a school day. But maybe he was at Tabletops or Cardiff Reef or Swami's. There were all sorts of surf spots up and down the coast, each with its own name.

But Wilkerson was feeling something. It was that sensation he had when she was near.

He looked up and down the long shoreline again, but didn't see anyone who resembled Stella. Then his eyes settled on the scattered figures in the water. One of the dark-suited bodies caught his eye.

There she was, bobbing in the waves like some exotic bird.

◆ ◆ ◆

"The lineup is the area where the waves are forming," Luke said. "It's there the surfers are waiting to pounce. Before you try and take your first wave, you need to know the rules. The first thing to remember is that the surfer closest to the curl has the right-of-way. What you never want to do is drop in on another surfer. That's a real kook move.

"And you don't take waves you can't handle. You have to surf within your ability. At the same time, when you commit to a wave, you need to go all in. And don't ever be a snake. Nobody likes a snake."

"What's a snake?"

"A snake is a cheat. You can wait a long time to get your chance at a good set. A snake tries to claim a wave that's yours by paddling in front of you to be closer to the curl."

"I'll try to never be a snake," promised Stella.

"You could never be a snake," he said.

Each looked at the other; Luke was the first to glance away. He was afraid of falling into her eyes and not being able to get out.

"Ready to take on an ankle snapper?" he asked.

"Ready," she said.

"I'll try and find you a ride even in these conditions," he said.

The two of them sat bobbing in the water. Luke kept vigil. A minute passed, then another, and just when Stella feared they'd have to leave without her getting a ride, Luke yelled, "Go!"

Her pop-up was perfect, and Stella balanced herself atop the board. A moment later a wave carried her away.

◆ ◆ ◆

Wilkerson watched from the shore. He wished he had his camera, wished he could have caught the moment. It looked as if Stella was floating on water, or walking on it. She was this sea nymph, a goddess with winged sandals. She wasn't surfing; it looked as if she was moving between two worlds.

The small wave was breaking left to right, and Wilkerson was able to watch her ride it almost all the way to shore. When she finished, she raised up both of her arms. Or were they wings she lifted? That's what they looked like to Wilkerson.

He almost covered his ears at the shouting that followed. Surfer Boy whooped it up, splashing the sides of his board like some two-year-old in a kiddie pool. Then he began paddling toward her with strong, sure strokes.

The two boards came together in the shallows; Stella's tip was pointed out, his was pointed in. There was no distance between the boards; their bodies pressed against each other. Luke extended a congratulatory hand, and Stella pressed her flesh against his. The moment turned from celebratory to something else. He leaned into her, and she leaned into him, and then the two of them kissed.

No one was close enough to hear Wilkerson's wail.

◆ ◆ ◆

In less than a second, Luke's world completely changed. Stella's kiss took him to a different place. There was nothing to explain it; there was nothing to liken it to.

It was vertigo; it was like falling into a wormhole. But he wasn't landing in one spot. It seemed as if a million worlds were opening up to him. He went through hyperspace, but wasn't sure if he came out on the other side.

The ocean had been his mistress. He had thought no vastness could surpass her. But now he saw the ocean as only the beginning. There was more, and more.

Then and now, thought Luke. There had been his life before the kiss, and now his life after. It was not the same, would never be the same.

"Thank you," he whispered to Stella.

◆ ◆ ◆

The two of them walked back to shore. Luke had volunteered to carry both boards, but Stella had insisted on carrying her own.

Neither of them said much. For his own part, Luke was feeling the aftereffects of what had felt like an out-of-body experience.

He snuck a peek at her, but she sensed his scrutiny, and their eyes met. Both of them smiled.

"If I hadn't promised your mom that I'd get you to school on time," Luke said, "I'd take you to breakfast or somewhere."

"Let's do that another morning," she said.

He felt the need to tell her more; he wanted to share.

"You made me feel part of," and then he stopped to think before adding, "the infinite."

"You are part of the infinite."

He let out some pent-up air and nodded. "I might have been afraid of being lost, except you were there with me."

"I was there," she said.

"You really did go off with the Travelers, didn't you?" he asked.

"I did."

They came upon their towels and the piles of clothing they'd left on the beach.

"What the hell?" Luke said.

He dropped down to his knees and held up a T-shirt that was in tatters. Someone had cut it up.

Stella lifted up her blouse. The fabric hadn't been gashed repeatedly as had Luke's shirt, but it had been slashed in one spot.

She pressed the blouse against her chest. The slasher had plunged his knife into the spot where her heart was.

CHAPTER THIRTY-THREE

From outside the door, Luke called, "Everything okay in there?"

"I'm fine," Stella said. "I'll be out in a second."

She finished putting on a floral halter sundress and slipped on some sandals. It was lucky that both of them had left their school clothes in the car. She was changing inside the women's bathroom off the beach boardwalk. Luke had insisted upon standing guard while she did so.

Stella exited the bathroom, and Luke said, "You really did only take a second, and you really do look great."

"I'll take that as a compliment."

"It was meant as one," he said. "I know girls who take hours to get the same look you achieved in seconds."

"You changed as well," said a surprised Stella.

"Surfers only need a towel to change in public," he said. "But usually I don't use a towel that's been slashed into tatters."

Both of them set off at a jog. Luke had parked on the street two blocks from the beach. "As soon as we get to the car, you're going to have to call your mom," he said. "She'll need to contact the attendance office so that you can get a late pass for first period."

"That's not going to make her happy."

"Lucky for you, Michael isn't the most punctual person in the world. Your mom is used to doing it for him."

"That's a relief," said Stella. "I'll tell her that time got away from us. That's true enough."

"I hope she doesn't get too upset with your slashed clothing."

"I think I'll avoid that discussion by throwing my blouse away."

There was something in Stella's words that didn't sound right to Luke. "Is there a reason you don't want to tell your mom what happened?"

"I don't want her to be worried," Stella said. "And . . ."

"And?"

"Seven years ago the police arrested a man named Guy Wilkerson. They were sure he was involved in my disappearance, but because it turned out he wasn't, they released him from prison. That doesn't mean Wilkerson isn't a threat to me, though."

"Do you think he's the one who cut up our clothes?"

"I'm sure of it." Stella remembered the combination of desire and hatred she'd felt through the tattered fabric. Wilkerson had left his mark like an animal might leave its scent. But instead of trying to explain what she'd sensed and how she had experienced it, Stella offered an easier explanation: "I saw him lingering near my house."

"Did you tell your parents or the police?"

"It happened yesterday. I know I should have said something to my mom, but if I had, she wouldn't have let us go surfing or spend time together. And I was afraid she'd get it into her head to confine me to the house and homeschool me. That's not something I want."

"That's not something I want either," said Luke, "but you should have said something, especially since this guy is dangerous. And I wish you'd warned me so that I could have been watching out for this creep."

"You're right," said Stella.

"If you see this guy again, you need to tell your parents, and you need to call the cops."

"That sounds like the sensible thing to do," said Stella, but she made no promise that she would.

As they approached Luke's car, he unlocked the doors with his remote. Then he scanned the area protectively before lifting the boards up to the roof rack.

"What if I don't see Wilkerson today?" asked Stella. "Does that mean you'll give me another surfing lesson tomorrow?"

She sounded excited at the prospect, which made Luke very, very happy. "You better believe it," he said.

◆ ◆ ◆

As soon as Stella entered Mr. Rankin's algebra class, all the students began talking. Her media interview had gone viral; everyone in school knew about "Space Girl."

"Thank you, Stella," Mr. Rankin said, taking her pass. "Please have a seat."

In a louder voice, he added, "And unless the rest of you want an impromptu quiz, settle down."

Voices lowered, and conversations came to a stop. All eyes followed Stella.

It was less than five minutes later when she received her first note. The wadded piece of paper skidded off her desk and landed on the floor. She reached down and scooped it up, then unfolded it. In block writing the sender had written: *Is it true that once you've had an alien, there is no going back?*

Stella heard several boys snickering, but she didn't turn to look at them. She put the note in her purse, but as soon as Mr. Rankin's back was turned, two more notes landed on her desk. One of them was written in a feminine hand and read, *E.T., call home!* She opened the second note: *How about showing me Ur-anus?*

The tittering in the classroom prompted Mr. Rankin to turn away from the equation he was writing on his whiteboard. He stared at his students and said, "Anyone care to tell me what's so funny?"

There were a few scattered laughs, but the teacher's hard glance made quick work of those. Under his baleful gaze, all the noise stopped. He went back to his whiteboard. With Mr. Rankin occupied, the boy sitting behind Stella tapped her shoulder. She half turned her head, and the boy whispered, "Note from Lance." Stella reached down with her hand and received the note. When she looked back to identify the note's sender, a boy sitting in the row to the right and two seats back waved to her. Then Lance began moving his eyebrows up and down. She wasn't sure what that meant, even though those around him seemed to find it funny.

Stella considered putting the note away unread. Maybe her disinterest would discourage others from sending her notes. But as Lance continued his eyebrow gyrations, she decided to see what he'd written. Stella opened the note and tried to make sense of it: *Are you a member of the million-mile-high club?*

She mulled over the words. Her apparent confusion resulted in a new outbreak of laughter. Most in the classroom were apparently privy to the contents of the note; those who weren't were quickly apprised. Ugly laughter filled the room, making her feel dirty.

◆ ◆ ◆

For the second day in a row, Luke and Stella met at the same secluded lunch spot. Stella had grabbed a pasta primavera salad to go; Luke had brought a peanut butter-and-banana sandwich and some oatmeal cookies from home.

"Why don't we share our food?" suggested Stella.

Luke looked at her lunch, made a little face, and said, "My agreeing means I must really like you."

He took a tentative forkful of her salad and looked pleasantly surprised. Stella bit into his sandwich and happily sighed.

"I forgot how good peanut butter is," she said.

"I practically live on it," said Luke. "It's what I eat most days for breakfast and lunch. But I don't just go the PB-and-J route. Usually I add some kind of fruit. Maybe tomorrow I'll bring you a peanut butter-and-apple sandwich."

"That sounds good."

"I use tart apples, like Granny Smiths. We've got a lime tree in our backyard, so I usually squeeze some on the apples. And sometimes I put some strawberry jam on the slices as well. I like getting the taste of peanuts along with the sweet and sour."

Stella took another appreciative bite of Luke's sandwich and then handed it back to him. Her gaze drifted over to the Performing Arts Building. Luke noticed where she was looking.

"Hoping for more of *Saint Joan*?" he asked.

"I enjoyed what we saw yesterday," said Stella. "It actually inspired me to go learn more about her. Did you know Joan carried a banner into battle, not a sword?"

He shook his head. Normally it wouldn't have been a subject that interested him, but Stella's enthusiasm was contagious. It was also atypical of the girls her age that Luke knew, most of whom liked to act world-weary.

"Joan wasn't educated," she said. "She could neither read nor write. But when she was put on trial for heresy, she managed to make her prosecutors look silly."

"But wasn't she found guilty?"

"It wasn't an impartial verdict," said Stella. "Because of that, at the age of nineteen, she was burned at the stake. Afterward, her executor admitted that he feared being damned for his role."

"Nowadays everyone would have just thought she was crazy," said Luke.

"I suppose you're right. But doesn't everyone in this school think I'm crazy?"

"They don't know you."

"Joan said she began having her visions when she was thirteen. I'm not much older than that. I wonder if my visions are that much different from hers. She had her God; I have my universe. She thought she was a messenger of God."

"You don't think that."

"Don't I? I *am* a messenger."

"My mom is always saying, 'Don't blame the messenger.'"

"That sounds like good advice."

"Then you won't blame me for what I saw on the way over here?"

"I won't blame you, even though you've made me curious."

"First," he said, "I need to know something. You're not performing at tomorrow night's high school talent show, are you?"

"I'm not even sure what a talent show is."

"It's a showcase for students to perform their act. It draws dancers, singers, and musicians—people like that."

"That sounds like fun. But why did you ask me if I'd be performing?"

"Because as I was walking over here, I saw talent-show posters being put up, and on them they're advertising a 'Special Performance by Space Girl.'"

"I don't know anything about that," said Stella.

"That's what I figured. It's a joke, even if it's not a very funny one. I'm sure the Y-Girls are behind it. That sounds like their kind of bullshit. After lunch I'll go to the office and ask to have the posters taken down."

Stella thought about that but then shook her head. "There's no need," she said.

◆ ◆ ◆

As Stella entered Dr. Rommel's biology class, she was met by an acrid, chemical smell that seemed to be coming from everywhere. Then she saw the trays set upon each desk. In the center of each of the trays was a still, spotted frog.

She started toward her desk to get a better look, but a boy stretched out his arm and blocked her path. In his hand was one of the frogs.

"Froggie went a courtin'," he sang, and then made it look like the frog was dancing. On an invisible dance floor of air, the frog hopped from one webbed foot to another.

Stella backed up, but didn't get far. A second boy held his frog as if it was a microphone and sang, "It's not easy being green."

Turning to a girl who had mostly purple hair, Stella asked, "What's going on?"

The girl shrugged and said, "We're dissecting frogs today."

"What?"

"I know," said the girl. "Gross, right? Payton says he'll give ten bucks to any girl who kisses her frog. He says it's our chance to find a prince."

The boy using his frog as a microphone began crooning, "Someday my prince will come."

Stella looked again to the purple-haired girl for answers. "What prince?"

"You never read *The Frog Prince*?"

Stella shook her head.

"It's a story about a witch who casts a spell on a prince and transforms him into a frog. And the witch says the spell can only be broken if a princess kisses the frog."

The boy who'd originally impeded her way raised his frog up to her lip level and said, "Pucker up."

At that moment Dr. Rommel stepped into the classroom. His eyes swept across the classroom; all the talking stopped; all the frogs were suddenly returned to their trays.

"I will offer you my first and last warning," he said. "The frogs are a learning tool, and will be treated as such. If I catch anyone using them for any other purpose than their dissection, you will fail this course. Now everyone sit down."

The class did as he instructed, including Stella. As she sat, she was confronted by the eyes of the lifeless frog staring at her.

Dr. Rommel took a seat at the front of the class. While wiping clean his thick glasses, he said, "On your tray you will find a scalpel, scissors, and forceps. These instruments are not toys. They can cut, and they can hurt. They are only to be used for the dissection of the frog, and must be handled with caution. Failure to do so will result in your being sent to the assistant principal, as well as failing this class. Is that understood?"

He finished cleaning his glasses, put them on, and stared around the classroom. *"Entendido?"* he asked a Hispanic boy.

"Like I don't speak English," the young man muttered, but then in a loud, sarcastic voice, he said, *"Sí, señor."*

"Everyone will be expected to make precise laboratory notes," said Rommel. "I will be grading those notes. I will also be grading the precision with which you do your dissection. I do not expect you to be cutting willy-nilly. I want to see careful, well-thought-out incisions. I want to see a complete frog heart, and that includes its three chambers, which means there had better be two atria and a single ventricle. There is a list of body parts identified on your work sheet. I suggest you carefully study all the diagrams before you begin your scalpel work. Remember: a stitch in time saves nine. And for your edification, I am not referring to sewing, but the notion of wisely expending time on properly dealing with a present problem so as to spare you from being beset by future problems. The first on-the-job rule an apprentice carpenter learns is to measure twice, so as to only have to cut once. You will spend two laboratory days doing this dissection, and at its conclusion, I don't want your frog to look as if you've put it through a blender. Does everyone understand?"

Heads nodded.

The teacher turned to an Asian girl. *"Wakarimasu ka?"* he asked.

"Whatever language that is," she said, "I don't speak it."

Rommel continued to look at her.

"Yeah, whatever," she said.

The teacher looked around the class. "Any questions?" he asked.

His tone and body language were meant to discourage any questions, but that didn't stop Stella from slowly raising her arm.

"What?" he asked.

"May I be excused from this assignment?"

"For what reason?"

Stella considered how to answer before saying, "I would prefer not to."

Rommel's pasty face changed colors, turning a purplish red. "I didn't know we had in our presence Bartleby, the Scrivener."

Stella didn't know how to respond; Rommel didn't give her a chance to say anything anyway.

"I would prefer not to," he said mockingly. "*I would prefer not* having to teach indulged rich kids. *I would prefer not* having to drive a ten-year-old Dodge when half of you in this class have new Beemers. *I would prefer not* having children take issue with my curriculum. And *I would prefer not to* respect your wishes.

"Do you have any idea how important it is to have a working knowledge of anatomy? Do you want to be operated on by a doctor devoid of flesh-and-blood experience? This exercise is designed as an introduction to anatomy. The same things that make a frog tick make us tick."

Rommel stared at Stella. Normally students didn't meet his eyes, but Stella did. He tried to wait her out. Students invariably squirmed and turned away when he stared them down, but she didn't. Normally his glasses acted as a shield, pushing back all gapers, but not this time. Something about her calm manner got to him.

"If you don't want to be here," he said, "by all means get out. Maybe the bleeding hearts in administration will let you get away with doing a virtual dissection, despite my objections that it's a pale imitation of the real thing. You and your ilk want to avoid real life by leading a virtual life, in a virtual world, in a virtual universe. That's the problem with this generation."

He waved his hand in her direction. "Go," he said, "go."

As Stella gathered up her belongings, Dr. Rommel said, "The leopard frogs we are dissecting are not endangered amphibians. They were bred in laboratories for this purpose, not hustled away from an idyllic setting of lily pads."

One of the male students called out, "Ribbit," and eyes turned away from Rommel and Stella to the frog impressionist. No one saw Stella take her index finger and press it to her lips; no one was witness to her placing that same finger on the mouth of her frog.

She got up from her seat and walked toward the door.

"And no one has ever accused frogs of being very bright. If you put a frog in a pot and heat up the water gradually, he'll happily stay put until he's boiled alive."

As Stella stepped through the door, Mr. Rommel said, "Bye-bye." When she didn't respond, he said, "She must have a frog in her throat."

The class began laughing. It was the purple-haired girl who happened to glance over to Stella's empty desk, or what should have been an empty desk. She opened her mouth and screamed.

That's when everyone saw the frog. But this frog wasn't dead. It was sitting up in the middle of the tray. Its eyes were open; it didn't have to move its head from side to side to see. It was a frog, after all.

A boy extended his hand toward the frog. It was no illusion, no trick of lighting; the frog was alive. The creature leaped, vaulting over the human head in front of it. Screaming and shouting and bedlam broke out.

The frog hopped right, then left. Most of the students shrank away, afraid of contact. Maybe they believed they'd contract warts. Maybe they were just scared. A few of the students tried to rein in the frog. Their efforts failed. The frog jumped out an open window.

The purple-haired girl found her voice. "It had on lipstick!" she said. "Did anyone else see that?"

CHAPTER THIRTY-FOUR

Cheever approached Mary Beth Carey's cubicle, keeping something hidden behind his back. Even though she couldn't see what he was holding, Mary Beth sniffed the air and asked, "Is that my favorite perfume I smell?"

"The nose knows," he said. "This morning I stopped at VG's just as they were bringing out doughnuts from the oven. It was just me and the surfers waiting in line."

"You didn't bring me a surfer as well?" she asked.

"I didn't want to distract you from work."

"Beware of cops who bring gifts," she said.

"Isn't that the truth? By the way, I brought you your two favorites: a maple bar and a raised glaze."

"So much for my diet," she said. "Now who is it you want me to kill?"

"The maple bar is for all the work you've done on Salton Sea, and for your continuing help in finding out what happened to Dickie Rath."

"And the raised glaze?"

"That's my bribe for getting your help in a new search," he said. "To quote John Keats, I need you to find someone whose name was writ in water."

"I'll say this for you: you've managed to pique my interest *and* my appetite."

"I'm not giving you much to go on," said Cheever. "Stella Pierce told me she wasn't alone in space. According to her, there were about a dozen other kids, a UN of schoolchildren who were around her age."

"Space school," said Mary Beth, lifting her right hand up and pretending she was reading from a title. "That sounds like a bad Hollywood plot. Was their spaceship painted yellow, and did it have flashing lights?"

"Since when did you get so cynical?"

"Since I started working here," she said. "You might remember that I was with you seven years ago at the beginning of this case. You had me help Eleanor Pierce input Stella into every missing-child registry in this country. After that we set up pages for her on every social media site so that we could get Stella's face and story out there. Of course at the time I didn't know she'd gone off with aliens."

"You saw yesterday's news?"

Mary Beth nodded. "And this morning I was flipping through the radio channels and hearing all the shock jocks making their jokes about it."

"Forget what you saw and heard," said Cheever. "In person Stella comes across as an innocent, while at the same time wise beyond her years."

"Maybe Yoda was one of her teachers," she said.

"Comedian you are," said Cheever, doing a Yoda imitation. "Anyway, it's not a teacher I'm interested in; it's a student. Stella said one of her fellow voyagers was an American. She described him as dark-skinned, about her height and age, but heavier. Early on this kid talked about missing his home on the water. Unfortunately, Stella couldn't narrow down where he lived, but she seemed to remember his surname was water related."

"Plummer?" Mary Beth suggested.

"No cracks," Cheever said. "And I don't mean water related as in a septic system. Stella thought his last name was related to a physical body of water."

Mary Beth jotted down the information. "Did she specify whether this kid was black or Hispanic or another ethnicity?"

"She wasn't sure."

"Needle in a haystack," she said with a sigh.

"It wouldn't be a challenge for you otherwise."

"You don't really think Water Boy is anything other than a figment of Stella's imagination, do you?"

"As a matter of fact, I bet he's real," Cheever said. "My take is that she crossed paths with him. Maybe he was part of some child-abduction ring. Maybe they were transported together. Right now I'll take any piece in the puzzle of Stella's past, and that includes your taking another run at Dickie Rath."

Rath was the mystery man from the Salton Sea area that Beto Diaz claimed had identified himself as Stella's uncle. So far Mary Beth hadn't been able to find a person by that name in the system.

"I'm thinking Rath might have shortened his surname, so today I'll be inputting such possibilities as Rathbone, Rathburn, and Rather. He also could have lost the first syllable, and been born Konrath or Kornrath or Conrath. Or maybe it's a variation of a name, like Rathke or Raith."

"Happy hunting," said Cheever, "and happy eating."

"You never told me what you thought of Alberto Diaz," she said.

"No, I didn't," he said. "I didn't want to prejudice you beforehand."

"Everything he told you has checked out," she said.

"I know."

"You still don't sound convinced."

"Maybe it's a vocational failing from being a cop for too long," he said, "but I couldn't help but think that everything he said was convenient. It even sounded rehearsed. You ever hear of George Van Tassel or the Integratron?"

Mary Beth thought about it, then shook her head.

"Van Tassel was an aeronautical engineer," Cheever said. "By all accounts a brilliant guy. For the last twenty years of his life, he lived in Joshua Tree, and spent much of his time constructing this incredible building. He said it was based on Moses's Tabernacle. Van Tassel was also busy building an electrostatic generator. He claimed to have had help with these projects from Nikola Tesla, as well as extraterrestrials.

Van Tassel believed he was channeling their thoughts. And, yes, he claimed he visited the mother ship and talked to the aliens. Van Tassel was convinced his generator could rejuvenate human beings, as well as work as a time-travel machine."

"Did Diaz bring this up?" asked Mary Beth.

"No," said Cheever, "that would have been too obvious. But seeing as my investigation involved extraterrestrials, and Van Tassel's tabernacle is only thirty miles away from where Stella and Rath were supposedly living, I'm pretty sure Diaz—or whoever set him up—knew I'd connect the two."

"What does Diaz have to gain from this?"

"On the surface, nothing."

"So you think someone is pulling his strings and feeding him what to tell you?"

"I'm not usually one for conspiracy theories. But how many former cons go out of their way to help the police?"

"Did you press him on that?"

Cheever nodded. "He claimed that he was covering his ass and getting ahead of the inevitable investigation that would be coming down the pike because of Stella's being a congressman's daughter."

"Strange," said Mary Beth.

"What?"

"You're suspicious of an utterly plausible story, and yet you have me doing a search on what sounds like an absolutely unbelievable story."

"I'll tell that to Marvin the Martian," he said.

As Cheever began walking away, Mary Beth made sounds approximating the opening theme from "The Twilight Zone."

"Cute," said Cheever.

"It's a cookbook!" she shouted.

CHAPTER THIRTY-FIVE

As mother and daughter got into the car after Stella's meeting with Dr. Froke, Eleanor asked, "How was your session?"

"I don't think it was very fruitful," said Stella.

Eleanor offered a knowing nod. "Finally you and Dr. Froke seem to be in agreement on something."

After Stella's session, her mother had met privately with Dr. Froke for half an hour.

"I make Dr. Froke nervous," said Stella.

"Why do you think that?"

"He sweats a lot, especially when I don't go along with his agenda."

"He says you're still resisting taking medication."

Stella nodded. "I am."

Eleanor started the car, and measured her words before responding, "What I'd like you to remember is that Dr. Froke is the professional here."

"Does that mean we should automatically go along with what he says?"

"No, but it doesn't mean we should automatically oppose it either."

"I am not schizophrenic, Mom, and I don't have bipolar disorder, and I'm not psychotic. The medications Dr. Froke wants to prescribe me are for people with those diagnoses, and yet my only *symptom* is a story he wants me to renounce."

"He says you're exhibiting signs of paranoia."

"That's because I wondered aloud if my treatment was being managed by someone other than him."

"That would sound paranoid to me as well."

"It's hard to defend not being paranoid," said Stella, "without sounding paranoid."

Stella knew better than to say anything about her ability to occasionally pick up a thought or a memory. That would only make her parents think she'd lost her hold on reality. It was easier to just be silent. She turned her head and looked out the passenger window. They were passing by one of the wetlands bordering Interstate 5. A large white bird was fishing, completely unmindful of all the traffic going by. Luke had given her a crash course on the shorebirds. She had loved the way the sanderlings ran in and out of the surf, staying just ahead of the waves. There were terns and gulls and willets. And in the estuaries running into the ocean, she'd seen herons and egrets. Snowy egret, she remembered. That was the name of the beautiful white bird that was fishing.

"Please don't shut me out, Stella," Eleanor said. "You know I love you, sweetie."

Stella turned back toward her mother. "And I love you, Mom."

"You know I'm trying to do what's best for you?"

"I know."

"Dr. Froke said he brought up the subject of electroconvulsive therapy with you, but that you weren't receptive to the idea of it."

"I was more than unreceptive," Stella said.

"A few years back, I had it done to me," Eleanor admitted. "The hope was that it would help me get over my depression."

"Did it?" asked Stella.

Her mother shook her head. "But it might work out better for you. The procedure is considered only mildly invasive."

"Having electric currents passing through my brain so as to trigger seizures does not sound mild."

"The currents are small, as are the seizures."

"Is that supposed to reassure me?"

"Dr. Froke thinks it might be beneficial for you. He believes it will stimulate the neurons and the chemicals in your brain."

"My neurons and chemicals are just fine, thank you. Just because you were depressed for so long doesn't mean I'm suffering like you were, Mom."

Eleanor took a few seconds to respond: "Why is it that you returned when you did?"

"I felt your pain, Mom. I tried to direct healing thoughts your way, but they didn't bring you peace. I hoped time would help, but it didn't. I sensed when things got worse."

Eleanor half whistled, half blew out air. Her mouth opened, but the words were slow to come.

"Detective Cheever said you told him you came back because of me," she said. "The two of us have never talked about that. I admitted to Detective Cheever that on the day you returned, I was in the process of ending my life. But how could you possibly have known that?"

"You're my mother," Stella said simply.

◆ ◆ ◆

As they pulled into the driveway, Stella wished the afternoon shadows weren't already encroaching. There would only be another hour of sunlight. She had hated being cooped up at Dr. Froke's office, and had even suggested moving her session outdoors. Dr. Froke had rejected the idea, of course.

Maybe she could ask Michael to join her for a run on the beach or a walk in the Torrey Pines Reserve. As she entered their home, though, her brother's greeting made it clear an outing wasn't in the offing.

He glowered at her and said, "Great job."

"What?" she asked.

"Don't play innocent," he said. "What happened to you in biology class today?"

As Eleanor entered the house, she saw her children staring each other down.

"What did you hear happened?" said Stella.

"I heard you refused to dissect a frog. I heard Dr. Rommel was upset and ordered you to go to the office."

"That's true."

"But you didn't go quietly," said Michael.

"I said nothing as I left the classroom."

"You didn't need to say anything. Did you have this frog thing all planned out in advance?"

"What are you talking about, Michael?" asked Eleanor.

"I gave you a ride home," Michael said to Stella, "and you never mentioned what happened."

"I didn't think you'd be interested."

"How could I not be interested when everyone in school is talking about it?"

"Can someone tell me what happened?" said Eleanor.

Keeping his eyes locked on his sister, Michael said, "Stella decided to be clever and pull a switcheroo with a dead laboratory frog and a real frog. I guess she thought it would add to the legend of Space Girl."

"That's not what I did."

"As Stella was leaving the classroom," Michael said, "a frog started hopping around the room. And it just so happened that the frog she was supposed to be dissecting suddenly went missing."

Eleanor turned to her daughter. "Is that what happened?"

Stella thought about it and said, "More or less."

"Ever since you came home, everything has been crazy," said Michael. "I'm supposed to be looking after you. When you came back, it was like a redo for me, you know. But you're not making anything easy."

"I'm sorry you're upset, Michael. But my going away wasn't your fault. It was no one's fault. You can blame me or you can blame it on the stars, but don't blame yourself. And the last thing I want is you thinking in terms of a redo, or having you think that you have to watch out for me."

"That's enough!"

Eleanor's shrill command got the attention of both children.

"Do you know how ridiculous this squabble is? I'm hearing both of you talk about a redo. What we have right now is our redo. We're a family again. Let's not squander the miracle that we've all been given."

"Mom's right," said Stella. She looked at Michael: "Truce?"

"Truce," said Michael. "But the next time you're planning on pulling one on Old Man Rommel, you better tell me about it in advance. I just wish I'd been there to see him running around trying to catch that frog. Everyone said the more he exerted himself, the more his glasses fogged up. And when he thought he had the frog cornered, and made this sudden move to catch him, the only thing he managed to do was split his pants."

"I wasn't around to see that either," said Stella.

"A few kids caught it on video," said Michael, "but it's not something I think you should watch."

"Why not?" asked Stella.

"Because when Rommel split his pants, it wasn't a pretty sight. Apparently he was going commando. Talk about disgusting."

◆ ◆ ◆

Michael raced through his dinner, explaining that he had a lot of homework to get to. Stella wasn't sure, though, if his speed-eating might not have something to do with their tiff earlier. It didn't take much, she thought, for him to get mad at her.

After she and her mother finished eating, Stella made some buttered popcorn and brought a tub of it upstairs. She knocked lightly on Michael's door and heard him say, "Come in."

Since returning home, she hadn't really spent any time in her brother's room. That's how Michael seemed to want it. She opened the door and said, "I thought you might like some popcorn."

"Did you put lots of butter on it?" he asked.

"Gobs," she said.

"Then you may enter."

If he was as swamped with studies as he'd indicated, she didn't see any sign of opened books or lesson plans. Instead, he seemed to be listening to music. Stella handed him the tub of popcorn, and without asking, she took a seat and began looking around the room.

There were a lot of posters taped up on the walls and even the ceiling. Michael's interests could be seen in the pictures. There were athletes Stella didn't know, mostly football players, and glam shots of young actresses, along with musical paraphernalia of bands he followed. Michael's love of aircraft and flying were everywhere; there were posters showing the US Air Force Thunderbirds in flight, as well as some of the US Navy's Blue Angels. The jets were in tight formation; one of the shots showed a Thunderbird flying upside down right above another flying right side up.

Taking up one wall were framed pictures of Michael soaring in a glider, and a shot of him in a single-engine plane that was captioned FIRST SOLO FLIGHT! He had even managed to get his picture taken while sitting in the cockpit of a Thunderbird. There were family and personal pictures as well: in one, he and Luke were kayaking through churning white water; another showed the two of them carrying surfboards. His high school history was documented with a shot of him making a tackle during a game, and a picture of him in a tux with his arm around Courtney, his junior prom date.

There was a picture of their father standing with the president, and a shot of their mom helping a young Michael at the beach. She had been remembered as well. There was a picture of her holding up six fingers and smiling. In the shot, she had a missing front tooth, and a second tooth that was only halfway in.

Caught in time, thought Stella. She smiled at the memory, but at the same time felt bittersweet sadness.

Michael watched her as he crunched on his popcorn. "I'm your little sister," she finally said. "That means you have to forgive me for everything."

"Who made that law?"

"The universe and our birth order," she said.

"Well, with all deference to the universe and our birth order, screw that."

"Younger sisters are supposed to be pests, aren't they?"

"I could deal with a pest," he said, "but not a martyr."

"I don't want to be your martyr, or anyone's."

"Thus spake Space Girl. Did you know that before you showed up, a few people at school were actually calling me Spaceman? I kind of liked it, too. And I earned the nickname. I'm the one who's going to the Air Force Academy. Me. And it wasn't like Dad pulled strings to get me in. I applied to the Academy without even letting Mom and Dad know. That was my secret plan throughout high school. That was my motivation to study and do all the extracurricular stuff. I'm going to be the one majoring in astronautical engineering. I'm the one who's going to be working on the Falcon Satellite Program. I'm the one who's going to be right in the thick of space technology and aerospace avionics. But you show up, and voilà! You're Space Girl."

"That name's not exactly a compliment, you know."

"So says Saint Stella," he said. "Ever since you did your vanishing act, I've had to grow up with Saint Stella. This house was our shrine to Saint Stella. And for a long time I bought into that. You probably don't remember this, but the night before you disappeared, you asked if we'd miss you if you were gone. You have no idea how much I regretted saying that I wouldn't. Every time I thought about it, my stomach hurt. I was afraid you went into this darkness not knowing I loved you, not knowing how much I really missed you. I kept wishing I could take back those words. That's why I went along with Mom's program for years. I was carrying so much shame I couldn't refuse.

"You want to know why I jumped off that cliff? You do those kinds of things when you have a perfect sister. That's what you were. Forever perfect. How could I compete with that? I couldn't. But I could drive fast, and do stupid things, and convince myself that I was my own person and no one was pulling my strings. That was how I got out from under your shadow. Or at least that seemed to work until you returned. And now I have to deal with the second coming of Saint Stella."

"Given a choice, I think I prefer Space Girl."

Michael tried not to smile, but he did. Then he shook his head. "In less than a week's time, you've managed to be on the national news, get everyone in school talking about you, make my best friend fall for you, and return the old mom to me who hasn't been there for seven years. What are you going to do for an encore?"

"I didn't plan any of this," she said. "Everything just sort of happened. And I never wanted to get between you and Luke."

Michael waved her last comment away with a sweep of his hand. "I'm glad he's happy. I never saw him like this before. I didn't even think he was capable of falling hard for anyone. I guess we can chalk up another miracle to you."

"I'm no miracle worker."

"You promise?"

"Scout's honor," she said.

"I thought you only went as far as being a Brownie."

"Don't tell anyone."

"Were you really in space?" he asked.

"If you believe what everyone else says, that's impossible."

"I'm asking you."

"Yes," she said.

"Was it as fucking awesome as I think it would be?"

"It was that awesome and more."

"Maybe you really are my sister."

"Maybe?"

"Maybe I'm glad you're home."

"I love you, Michael."

He tried to hide the tears forming in his eyes. "Thanks for the popcorn," he said.

◆ ◆ ◆

From her bed, Stella stared out at the stars. The view of the night sky was her favorite thing about her room. At night she liked to listen to music while looking out the window. The last time her mother had checked in on her had been an hour ago. Her mother was still looking in on her a few times each night.

It was to be expected, thought Stella. And at least it gave Michael some breathing room.

Stella felt the vibration of her phone, and saw that Luke was calling.

"You're not canceling for the morning, are you?" she asked.

"No way," he said. "I just wanted to hear your voice."

"I made you call," she said, "because I wanted to hear yours."

"I almost believe that," said Luke.

"I am afraid it's true."

"Did you bewitch me?"

"You called, didn't you?"

"Sorceress."

"Michael and I talked earlier," she said. "I think he's okay with us now."

"For real?" he said, sounding relieved.

"For real," she said.

"That's good to hear. I hated feeling like I was sneaking around with you."

"We'll sneak no more. Michael and I hashed a lot of things out."

"Sounds like you had a constructive evening."

"I even had time to research frogs just in case Rommel throws a surprise quiz my way. I memorized everything there is to know about a frog's anatomy, which is a lot more than I would have learned by dissecting one."

"So you're the one I call with all things frog?"

"I am," she said. "Did you know that frogs don't drink with their mouths? They actually drink through their skin."

"That's something I didn't know," he said. "But did you know that frogs get to eat what bugs them?"

Stella groaned.

"On a more serious vein," said Luke, "I'm really looking forward to tomorrow. This morning was . . ."

He sought out the words, but couldn't find them. Apparently he didn't have to.

"It was," she said.

"I saw and felt things I didn't even know existed."

"Yes," she said.

"Did you feel the same?"

"I did."

"It's almost like I'm hearing everything that's unsaid between us inside my head."

"Maybe you are."

"Did you clear it with your mom for us to get an early start?"

"Yes, but she said I better not be late to class again."

"I'll make sure of that."

Luke paused before voicing a concern. "You didn't see your stalker today, did you?"

"No, I didn't see him," she said.

Stella wondered if she should say anything else. Earlier she'd had this sense that Guy Wilkerson wasn't very far from her house. Because of that she'd stayed away from her window. From her bed she could look out and see the stars, and yet not be seen from the outside.

Luke didn't question her further, though, which spared her from having to say anything.

"I'll see you in my dreams," he said.

"It's a date," she said.

CHAPTER THIRTY-SIX

During her time at Torrey Pines Academy, Tiffany Milton had worked hard to have everything just so. She had played the game better than anyone, and as a result, she and her chosen Y-Girls pretty much controlled the social scene. Everyone in the school who counted wanted to be part of what they had. But now there was a threat to that order.

The way everyone in school was talking, it was like Space Girl had kissed that frog and turned it into a prince. Stella Vanilla Winkle had gone away for seven years, come back with a fanciful story of little green men, and then pulled some sleight of hand with a little green frog. Because of that, everyone was acting like she was the Homecoming Queen. Well, she wasn't.

Space Girl wasn't the only one who was good with tricks. That's why Tiffany was up and about early that morning. It was time for her to help Space Girl get her comeuppance.

It was time, Tiffany thought, to bring her down to earth.

◆ ◆ ◆

Cheever picked up his office phone and heard Mary Beth Carey ask, "You got a minute?"

"There are physicists who would tell you time is an illusion," he said.

"If time is an illusion, why am I always fighting my supervisor for the overtime that's owed me?" she asked.

"Maybe the two of you were meant to be locked into that timeless struggle. Or maybe Thoreau was right when he said, 'Time is but a stream I go fishing in.'"

"Stay at your desk," she said. "If you've got the time, I've got a fish."

Homicide was located on the fourth floor of San Diego's downtown headquarters on Broadway. Mary Beth would be coming from the Forensic Science Laboratory, so Cheever knew it would take her a few minutes.

He wondered what fish Mary Beth had caught. Then he made a mental note to himself: stop on the way home and get some tuna fish for Gumshoe.

His calico had changed Cheever's mind about cats. Until he had taken in the waif, he had always thought he was a dog person. The cat had come to him under awful circumstances. She had been the only survivor of a home invasion that had ended with the murder of a mother and daughter and the two family dogs. What had started as a burglary had turned into a double homicide (or quadruple murders if you included the dogs). The murderer had tried to cover up what he'd done by setting a fire. Somehow in the midst of the inferno, the cat had been able to escape.

In the days that followed the murders and the fire, Cheever had been witness to the cat's comings and goings from the rubble. To his eye it seemed like the feline was looking for her former life. Cheever had been moved by the plight of the creature. He'd brought her food and water, and the cat had warmed up to him, coming over every time he visited the crime scene. In those early days, she'd smelled of smoke. It so pervaded her fur that whenever Cheever scratched the cat, his hands came away smelling smoky.

During the course of his investigation, he learned the cat was named Gummy Bear. When no one else came forward to adopt the cat,

Cheever took her home. He'd renamed her Gumshoe, which seemed fine with her. In the end, Cheever had honored the victims in the only way he could: he'd nailed the murderer. It wasn't enough, of course—it never was. But after the murderer was sentenced to death, Cheever had spent a few minutes telling Gumshoe the outcome of the case. It was certainly his imagination, but the cat had seemed to purr louder than he'd ever heard her.

As Cheever often said, the cat was the only good thing to come out of a terrible situation. During their years together, Gumshoe had mellowed the detective, and his shrink girlfriend had mellowed him a little more. He wasn't quite as prickly, or obsessive, as he'd been as a younger detective.

And the Stella Pierce case had taught him patience, if nothing else.

A figure turned the corner, and Mary Beth came into view. She was carrying a folder, and there was a bounce in her step.

Stopping just short of Cheever's desk, she said, "I'd like to acquaint you with LeRon Rivers, or as he was called when he was a kid before he went missing, Rolling Rivers."

She handed Cheever the paperwork she'd printed out. The detective started sifting through old police reports, newspaper articles, and pictures. He looked at the big, smiling face of a seven-year-old boy with a large gap between his two front teeth. It was an image that made you smile. The boy had lived in an outlying area of Atlanta along the Chattahoochee River. By all accounts, Rolling was always playing on the banks of the river, and sometimes beyond. He loved to fish, and often waded in the water.

On the day Rolling went missing, his family assumed he had gotten up early to fish before school. The police had never been able to confirm this. They had also not been able to determine whether the Rivers family was missing a fishing pole. As for LeRon's footprints along the bank of the Chattahoochee, forensics couldn't conclude if they'd been made the morning or the night before.

There was no sign of Rolling having been abducted, and no one reported seeing anything unusual. They did question one suspect at length, a man with a criminal background that included statutory rape, who a witness said had been talking with Rolling a few days earlier. The man had an alibi, though, which seemed to correspond with the time Rivers went missing. Although the boy's body never turned up, it was ultimately presumed that he'd drowned. The "Hooch," as locals called it, was a big body of water that ran for 430 miles. The police had dragged sections of the river between Buford Dam and Peachtree Creek, but found nothing. Still, the search team said the boy's body could easily have snagged on one of the many underwater trees lurking in the water's murky depths.

In one of the reports, an investigator had noted: *Some big catfish and largemouth bass in that stretch where the body probably ended up.* The unsaid conclusion was that Rolling had likely fed the fish he was hoping to catch.

"I've included the up-to-date contacts for you," said Mary Beth.

"Great job," said Cheever. "You're worth your weight in gold."

"I'll settle for doughnuts," she said.

◆ ◆ ◆

All through elementary and middle school, Victoria Amberger had resisted shortening her name to Vicky. It was only as a freshman at TPA that she began encouraging others to call her Vicky. She hoped the nickname would put her in good stead with the Y-Girls.

Normally Tiffany wouldn't have given Vicky the time of day, as she was chunkier and shorter than the usual Y-Girl. But as it happened, Vicky had the same sixth-period biology class that Stella did.

Before the start of school, Tiffany invited Vicky to join her at a nearby park, saying they needed to meet in private.

"Your hair looks great," said Tiffany, touching the smaller girl's blonde locks. "Is that a new style?"

"I had it layered more," Vicky said, delighted to know that Tiffany had taken notice of her before.

"It's really you," said Tiffany. "We're going to have to find you the right boyfriend to go with the hairdo."

A smile overtook most of Vicky's face.

"You know who I think would be perfect for you? Do you know Andrew Brady? He and Lily broke up. We're having a party Saturday, and I know he's coming. If you can make it to the party, I'll personally play matchmaker."

"That sounds great," said Vicky.

Tiffany nodded encouragingly. Andrew was a hunk, but dumb as a rock. That's why he was taking freshman biology again.

"Do you have any classes with Andrew?" asked Tiffany.

Vicky nodded. "We have sixth-period biology with Mr. Rommel."

Tiffany furrowed her eyebrows. "Isn't that the class where something strange happened yesterday?"

◆ ◆ ◆

Halfway through her second-period class, Stella was summoned to Mr. Harnett's office. Harnett was the assistant principal of the school. Because he was the "enforcer" at TPA and because of his temper, students referred to him as "Mr. Hornet."

As Stella was shown into his office, Mr. Harnett got to his feet and extended his hand in introduction. Then he directed her to the one open chair in his office. "Please take a seat," he said.

Already seated were Dr. Rommel and a blonde girl Stella recognized from class.

"I'm conducting an inquiry into what happened in yesterday afternoon's biology class," said Mr. Harnett. "Dr. Rommel reported a strange incident involving a frog. He suspected you were involved in what he describes as a 'spectacle.' Since he came to me, I have been trying to find out what occurred. I told Dr. Rommel that I would be talking to you today, as well as questioning other students from your biology class. I was assisted in my investigation by a student who came to me of her own volition to report what you'd done."

Harnett turned to that student and said, "Why don't you tell us what you saw, Vicky?"

Keeping her head down, not meeting any eyes, Vicky said, "Before I went into our biology class, I saw Stella looking into her purse. I just happened to come up alongside her, which gave me a perfect vantage point."

"And what did you see?" asked Mr. Harnett.

"There was a frog in Stella's purse. It was alive."

"And how are you so sure of this?"

"I heard it croak. That's when Stella shushed it, and then closed her purse."

"Thank you, Vicky," said Mr. Harnett. He turned to Stella and said, "What do you have to say about this?"

"I did not bring a frog to class," said Stella.

Mr. Harnett's white skin reddened. He tapped his fingertips together and scowled. "I can guarantee you one thing, Stella, which is that lying will compound your problems."

"I'm not lying."

"Let's look at the situation, shall we?" he said. "You and each of your classmates had a preserved frog specimen set out on a tray on your desk. These specimen frogs are chemically preserved. They are as dead as a proverbial doornail. But when you left class, your preserved specimen was no longer on your desk. Instead, a frog began hopping around the classroom. I suppose you want me to believe it's a coincidence that a living frog was spotted in your purse just before the start of class."

The assistant principal scowled at her, but not as fiercely as Dr. Rommel did. Rommel had been teaching at the school for a quarter of a century. During that time he'd ruled by intimidation. That had all changed overnight. Today the students weren't calling him Dr. Rommel. They were calling him *Commandant Commando Rommel.* It was this girl's fault. Revenge would be his.

"You might as well admit your guilt," said Dr. Rommel. "There's a witness."

"I am not guilty of what you say," said Stella.

"You sound like a lawyer," the teacher said, then added with a sneer, "or a politician. Vicky has no reason to make up a story."

"Are you *sure*?" asked Stella.

She tried to meet Vicky's eyes, but the girl didn't engage with her.

"What I am *sure* of is that you're a troublemaker," said the teacher.

The assistant principal held up a hand to Dr. Rommel and said, "I am the one conducting this interview." Then he turned to Stella and said, "I'm going to ask you to write up your account of what occurred in biology class yesterday. When you finish, I will review your statement. I encourage you to be truthful. If you admit fault and apologize, I will have more latitude to go easy on you. To quote from Proverbs: 'A gentle answer turns away wrath.'"

"I can't apologize for something I didn't do," said Stella.

"That's your choice. I am not going to tell you what you should write or what you should say. But unless other compelling evidence comes forward, I'll have to suspend you for the rest of the week."

"That's not even a slap on the wrist," protested Dr. Rommel. "That's a vacation."

◆ ◆ ◆

Cheever called Eleanor Pierce. He was hoping to schedule a time to talk to Stella about LeRon Rivers that afternoon, but she cut him off.

"I'm on my way to the high school," she said, sounding flustered. "Stella is being suspended."

"For doing what?"

"The assistant principal says she let a frog loose in biology class and was a disruptive influence."

Cheever couldn't imagine Stella acting like some juvenile delinquent. He knew Duncan was out of town, and didn't like how overwrought Eleanor sounded.

"Sounds like Stella could use a character witness," he said. "How about I meet up with you at the high school?"

"That would be too much of an inconvenience . . ."

"It's not a bother. Let's meet in front of the school in half an hour."

"You're a godsend."

◆ ◆ ◆

When Cheever and Eleanor were shown in to the assistant principal's office, the cop couldn't help but remember those occasions in high school when he'd been singled out for misbehavior. In retrospect, what he'd done didn't seem so terrible—there had been a food fight his sophomore year, and two years later he'd organized senior ditch day—but even so, he recalled that getting called to the administrative offices had been a nerve-racking experience. Of course Cheever wasn't worried so much about what the school would dole out in the way of punishment; it was his father's retribution he feared. His dad hadn't been a spare-the-rod kind of parent.

When Eleanor introduced the detective to the assistant principal, Cheever could see the administrator's surprised face.

"I'm a friend of the family," Cheever explained, "and was invited to sit in on this proceeding."

Cheever didn't try and hide his wink to Stella, who was clearly glad to see him. That made the assistant principal's face even redder.

"It's not really a proceeding," said Harnett. "The administration of TPA has a zero-tolerance policy when it comes to certain violations or disruptions. It's because of that, I am suspending Stella."

"Where's Stella's accuser?" asked Cheever.

"The *witness*," Harnett said, "has returned to class."

"Did you interview her?" asked the cop.

"I took down her statement, if that's what you mean."

"That's not what I mean," said Cheever. "From what I understand, you're taking the word of one student over another."

"There was also a teacher involved. It was out of concern for that teacher that Vicky—the witness—came forward. After hearing what Vicky had to say, I was satisfied with her story and confident that it explained what subsequently occurred in the classroom."

"What happened?" asked Cheever, looking to Stella for an explanation. But Harnett answered before she could.

"The witness saw Stella looking inside her purse right before class," he said. "That's when she heard a croaking sound, and saw the frog in Stella's purse."

"There was no frog in my purse," said Stella. "And there was no croaking. There couldn't have been croaking."

The assistant principal covered up a yawn. They'd gone over this before. He opened his mouth to speak, but Cheever spoke first. Something Stella had said intrigued him.

"What did you mean when you said there couldn't have been croaking?"

"Only male frogs make those kinds of sounds," said Stella.

"And?" said Cheever.

"The frog I was supposed to dissect was female."

"How do you know this?" asked Cheever.

"When I was doing my virtual dissection of a frog, I learned that one way of distinguishing female frogs from male frogs is by the relative size of their eyes and ear circles. My frog's ear circles were smaller than its eyes; it was female."

"Were all the frogs being dissected in your class female?" asked Cheever.

Stella thought about this and finally said, "I'm pretty sure they were."

"And female frogs don't croak?"

Stella nodded.

Cheever turned to Harnett. "You need to determine if all the frogs being dissected in Stella's class were female. And you need to see if the jailbreak frog made any croaking sounds during its great escape. I'm sure there are videos of the event. And finally, I want to talk to Stella's accuser, who supposedly saw and heard the frog in her purse."

"You will not be talking with one of our students," said the assistant principal, "unless her parents agree to it."

"You need to follow school procedures, of course," said Cheever, "but might I suggest before calling the parents that you talk to your witness and tell her an SDPD detective would like to question her. My guess is that will send her running for the hills."

CHAPTER THIRTY-SEVEN

Cheever proved to be psychic. When Vicky Amberger heard a policeman wanted to talk to her, she suddenly came down with blue flu. She reported to the school nurse, told her she wasn't feeling well, and asked to go home. Before leaving for the day, Vicky changed her statement, saying she was no longer sure she had either seen or heard a frog in Stella's purse.

Given Vicky's change of heart, Mr. Harnett told Stella she would not be suspended and not subject to any discipline "at this time."

He declared sternly, "The frog situation has still not been resolved to my satisfaction, and I will continue my investigation into it."

"Good luck with that," said Detective Cheever with a straight face. "If you need any help, just give me a call."

Hornet flushed red, quickly scratched out a late pass for Stella, then brusquely dismissed everyone. Once Cheever, Stella, and Eleanor were outside the administrative offices, they began to talk among themselves. For having prevailed, Stella looked and acted rather somber.

"I don't know why that girl made up a story," said Eleanor. "Do you have any idea why she would have done that, Stella?"

With downcast eyes, Stella said, "I'd rather not talk about it now, Mom."

Cheever didn't think he'd ever seen Stella look and sound quite so pensive. Eleanor also seemed to recognize the sadness in her daughter.

She hugged Stella and whispered, "I love you. And I'm sorry if others haven't been welcoming to you."

"It's okay, Mom."

"I know you have to get back to class," Cheever said. "Can we talk after school?"

"That's fine," said Stella.

"I want to discuss LeRon Rivers," he said. "We got a bingo on a boy your age who went missing near the Chattahoochee River in Georgia at around the same time you did."

Stella didn't react other than to nod. Cheever had thought his news might have the effect of cheering her up; after all, she had mentioned that the boy in question had a "water name" and that he was dark skinned. But being right didn't seem to bring Stella any satisfaction. Cheever realized it had to be disheartening to never be believed.

"I'll see you around four o'clock," he said.

Stella nodded, offered Cheever and her mother a muttered, "Bye," and then walked off.

◆ ◆ ◆

From inside the sedan, Scarecrow carried out a conversation with the Guardian of the Gates. Somewhere above the Guardian, Scarecrow was sure, was the Wizard. He wondered if the Wizard had all the answers to the Stella Pierce situation.

"Any indication we're on Jinnicky's radar?" asked Scarecrow.

Jinnicky the Red Jinn was the code for the Chinese. There had been one or two peeps from Operations that the name Jinnicky wasn't exactly politically correct, but to date it hadn't been replaced. Scarecrow had been warned to watch out for any indication that "Jinnicky" was on the scene. By controlling Dorothy, they would keep her from attracting the interest of Chinese intelligence.

"From our end we haven't seen anything to indicate that Jinnicky is interested in Dorothy," said the Guardian. "But Sir Hocus has been making inquiries in a number of sensitive areas."

That wasn't good, thought Scarecrow. Sir Hocus was Congressman Pierce.

"He's not the only one digging," said Scarecrow. "Colonel Plum has been active. It wasn't enough for him to be told about the niece in her uncle's Airstream, nor was he satisfied that an eyewitness made a positive ID on Dorothy. His continued digging unearthed LeRon Rivers."

"Unearthed," mused the Guardian, seeming to enjoy the implications of the word. Then he added, "The solution to pollution is dilution."

"What's that mean?" asked Scarecrow.

"We'll come up with more and more angles for Colonel Plum to work. And all those angles will lead him to dead ends. We'll also try and forestall Sir Hocus. Let's just hope the flags he's raising don't alert Jinnicky. In the meantime, continue doing what you're doing."

"Dorothy knows she's not in Kansas anymore," Scarecrow said. "What she did with the frog tells me she is beginning to come into her own."

"That's one way of looking at it," said the Guardian. "But I could just as easily say that gravity is reasserting itself on our Dorothy. Doubts are now weighing her down. This afternoon you will hear me conversing with her. I am confident our talk will weigh her down further. Dorothy's universe is about to shrink when I tell her that her time in Oz was just a dream."

"There's no place like home," said Scarecrow.

◆ ◆ ◆

Stella's phone started ringing just moments after she sat down in the passenger seat of Michael's car. Her phone display didn't reveal the caller. It read: *No Caller ID.* Stella answered it anyway.

"Good afternoon, Stella."

"Who is this?"

"My name doesn't matter, as we have never been formally introduced. But since I have been closely monitoring you for these last seven years, I feel that I know you very well. What I am about to tell you, I am sure on some level you already know. Your first impulse will be to disregard everything I say. But the more you consider my words, the more you will realize that they make sense.

"There was no spaceship. There was no journey with the Travelers. That was something that others wanted you to believe. That was something they needed you to believe."

"You're saying I imagined the last seven years?"

"No," he said. "You have been one of the pioneers in what is known as the transhuman evolution. The word *transhuman* was coined by Julian Huxley. Ironically, Julian was the brother of Aldous, who wrote *Brave New World*, a book that despaired of the future of our species. Transhumanism is the next stage in what *Homo sapiens* can become. Huxley envisioned using technology to overcome the limitations of our bodies and brains. He predicted that future. Others are working to make it a reality."

"Are you one of those others?" she asked.

"I represent an interested party who realizes the great potential benefits of the transhuman evolution. At the same time, we are aware of its dangers should certain foreign powers get their hands on these technological breakthroughs.

"Our hope is that you'll cooperate with us so as to fulfill your potential, as well as the potential of humanity. We know about the special hardware that was inserted into your cerebral cortex. Without it, mindspeak wouldn't have been possible. Essentially, you were hardwired to download and upload information."

Stella felt the pounding of her heart. When she spoke, though, she tried not to show her uncertainty.

"If any special hardware really was inserted," she said, "then it was the Travelers who were responsible, not you."

"The Travelers were responsible," he said, "in that the Transhuman Project borrowed from their science. The spaceship you were on was also a by-product of their science, although to date it has never left Earth."

"I don't know what your game is—"

"No game," he said. "You and your peers were carefully selected. All of you had certain inherent gifts. The mind uploading that you underwent—also known as whole-brain emulation—has given you a breadth and depth of knowledge unheard of."

"The Travelers—"

He interrupted her: "Long ago, the Travelers helped our race, and then they moved on, leaving us the tools to help ourselves evolve. You can assist us in unlocking many of the secrets of the Travelers."

"I don't believe you."

"I think you do. And the more you consider what I've said, the more you'll perceive that I'm telling you the truth. For now, all I ask is that you reflect on our conversation. That's all. In a few days, you'll hear from me again. I will have some proposals that should be of interest to you."

"Don't bother to call," she said.

Stella clicked off and put her phone into her purse.

"What was that all about?" asked Michael.

"I'm not sure," she said.

"If some guy is threatening you, I want to know about it."

Stella reached out, touched Michael's arm, and said, "I'm okay. But I'm sure glad I have an older brother."

He looked both proud and embarrassed. "Mom told me about what went on with Hornet today. That must have sucked."

"Yeah," she said, "it kind of did."

"One day there will be a bullshit machine," he said, "and anytime anyone tells a lie, the machine will say, 'Bullshit.'"

Stella laughed. She didn't tell him that in the world she came from, there hadn't been any lying.

Unbidden, the thought came to her: unless it had *all* been a lie.

◆ ◆ ◆

They listened to music on the drive home. Michael played Mike Posner's "I Took a Pill in Ibiza," and Stella found herself singing the chorus along with Posner: "All I know are sad songs."

Then she suddenly went silent and thought: Are there any other kind?

At that moment she felt a chill. She turned away from the radio and sought out its source. Guy Wilkerson was on the corner. He waved to her.

Stella fought the instinct to wave back.

◆ ◆ ◆

From the entrance to Stella's room, Cheever said, "Your mother told me she thought you were tired, and it looks like she's right. You want me to come back another day?"

Stella was under her bedcovers; the bed that had seemed far too small no longer felt that way.

"I told her I wanted to close my eyes for a few minutes," admitted Stella, "but not because I'm tired. I've been thinking. Come on in. There's even an adult-size chair for you. I found it in the garage."

"Thanks," Cheever said, taking a seat in the chair. "So what is it you were thinking about?"

"I got a call on the way home," she said. "The caller knew a lot of things about me and my situation. It seemed he knew some things that I didn't even know. He tried to tell me I was never in space, and said I was part of a transhuman program, which he claimed was the next step in the evolution of *Homo sapiens.* He also said my brain, as well as those of the others in my class, had been enhanced so as to allow for mindspeak."

"Human evolution," mused Cheever. "That's the same thing Dr. Frankenstein was working on."

That got a little smile from Stella.

The cop grew serious: "Did your caller specifically identify mind-speak by name?"

"He did. And he also knew that was how we started communicating early in our voyage. I think he's telling the truth about the hardware in our brains, except in his scenario, it wasn't the Travelers who did that to us, but something he called the Transhuman Project."

"You once told me that you sometimes picked up words or memories or sensations. What was your read on the caller?"

Stella shook her head. "I couldn't pick up anything beyond his words. That was kind of surprising because lately there have been times when I've heard the complete thoughts of others in my head. Of course I would never tell Dr. Froke that. He would say I was schizophrenic."

"You once told me that I no longer needed to worry about my daughter," said Cheever. "You said she was a beautiful spirit." He tried to keep his voice from cracking. "Were you hearing my thoughts then?"

"It was more like I was feeling your pain."

"How would you know my daughter is a beautiful spirit?"

"In my journey with the Travelers, I became acquainted with death. It is not the closed door that most believe it to be."

"Why couldn't you tell me much about LeRon Rivers or the other students?"

"I could tell you countless things," she said, "but just not the answers to the questions you asked me."

"Is it really that hard to describe what someone looks like?"

The question seemed to amuse Stella. "Most of the places we went," she said, "our bodies couldn't go."

"What do you mean?"

"The universe is almost as large as imagination itself. When you travel such distances, bodies become an impossible hindrance. That's why for most of the last seven years, I've been what you might call a spirit."

"What does that mean?"

"The corporeal doesn't work in the vastness of space. For most of our journey, I was out of body."

"I still don't understand."

"My mind went where my body couldn't."

"How does that work?"

"The mind goes on a journey while the body is left behind. As I understand it, many other people have done this, even without the help of the Travelers."

Cheever thought about her claim. He had heard of individuals—shamans and the like—who *claimed* to have done what she said.

"A lot of those making such claims," said Cheever, "were out of their minds on drugs."

"I didn't take drugs," said Stella.

"You didn't take them knowingly. But what if your mysterious caller was right? What if the Travelers didn't take you on a journey around the universe?"

"How would such a ruse benefit anyone or anything?"

Cheever shrugged. "That's the great unanswered question, isn't it? Perhaps, as he alluded, you're the key to opening a treasure trove of technology left behind by the Travelers. Or it could be the caller is fronting for a group that wants to control you. There are a lot of vested interests that wouldn't want your story to gain traction. But then again, I am just one of the six blind men."

"What six blind men?"

Cheever cleared his throat and said:

"It was six men of Indostan
To learning such inclined
Who went to see the Elephant
(Though all of them were blind)
That each by observation
Might satisfy his mind."

Stella was smiling. "I never heard that poem," she said, "but I remember that story. My father read it to me. It was about six blind men touching different parts of an elephant, and each being convinced that what they were describing was correct, and that what their neighbors were describing was wrong."

"That's right," said Cheever. "The man touching the leg thought the elephant was a pillar; the man touching a tusk thought it was a pipe."

"And one man had the trunk and said an elephant was like a tree branch!" said Stella.

"And another had his ear and said it was a great fan," said Cheever. "I always remember that story when it comes to my own work. I have to tell myself that one piece of information, or one clue by itself, usually doesn't tell the whole picture. As the poem concluded:

'And so these men of Indostan
Disputed loud and long,
Each in his own opinion
Exceeding stiff and strong,
Though each was partly in the right
And all were in the wrong!'"

"All were in the wrong," mused Stella.

CHAPTER THIRTY-EIGHT

That night the full moon began to show itself at about the same time Luke arrived at Stella's house. The two of them walked out to Luke's car, and he opened the passenger door for Stella to get in. There were two surfboards on his roof rack: his sleek shortboard and Stella's bulkier practice board. After she was seated, he sat down in the driver's seat.

"Are you sure about this?" asked Luke. "We can have them make an announcement at the show that there was a mistake and that you never signed up to perform."

"I imagine that would disappoint a lot of people, wouldn't it?"

"The truth is what the truth is."

"Since when has that made a difference?"

Luke looked at Stella. "That doesn't sound like you."

She was quiet for a moment before saying, "You're right. Today has been kind of challenging."

"I figured as much," he said. "That's why I brought you something."

He handed Stella a small box. As she cupped the box in her hand, he said, "Today I was looking at that valentine card you made for me so long ago. Since I'm not very artistic, I decided to let nature do the talking for me. I went beachcombing this afternoon, hoping for the perfect find."

Stella lifted off the top of the box, revealing a small, egg-shaped white stone. She took the stone out of the box and held it up. It was silver white on its exterior, but within its hard surface was a translucence from which a glow seemed to emanate.

"It's beautiful," she said.

"It's a moonstone," he said. "I went to Moonlight Beach looking for it. They always seem to have the best moonstones there."

"Thank you," she said, cradling it.

"In ancient times," said Luke, afraid to meet her eyes, "moonstones were supposed to symbolize true love."

"In that case," she said, "I'll need to find the perfect moonstone for you."

"Tonight should be perfect for that with the full moon," Luke said. "We could go to Moonlight Beach if you want. Moonlight brings out a special shimmer in the moonstones."

"Yes, I very much want to do that."

"If you like," he said, "we could get an early start."

"You're talking about my skipping the talent show?" she said.

He nodded.

"It sounds like you don't want me to perform."

"I don't want you to get hurt," he said. "I don't trust Tiffany and the Y-Girls."

"Your concern will be my armor," said Stella. "And I'm not going to let them interfere with either my performance or our moonstone hunting."

Luke nodded. "I had a feeling that would be your choice, so I made a special mix for our drive."

Before the music started, he warned her, "These are oldies. I heard someone in drama class say they were using Joan Osborne's 'One of Us' in the production of *Saint Joan*, and I thought you might like it."

The song might have been old, but it was new to Stella. She tried not to tear up at the song's refrain, but didn't quite succeed.

"Trying to make his way home," she whispered. All this time, that's what she'd been doing—trying to make her way home.

Then the second song started up. "Lightning Crashes" by Live was also new to her, but Stella could understand why Luke had selected it.

He turned his eyes momentarily from the road and smiled at her reassuringly. Stella didn't know if Luke thought she was the angel in the song, or the newborn, or the dying woman. But the song and Luke certainly understood the forces pulling at her from the center of the earth.

The song ended as they entered the high school parking lot. More than half the spaces were already taken. By all indications, the talent show was going to be playing to a full house.

"What are you singing tonight?" Luke asked.

"I'm not yet sure," she said.

"Will it be a cappella?"

"Not quite," said Stella.

CHAPTER THIRTY-NINE

Cheever poured Rachel a glass of wine. Because Homicide Team IV was up on the rotation, he wasn't drinking. That was also the reason the two of them were at Cheever's Leucadia home and not her Point Loma house. Given that most homicides occurred in the middle of the night, and also in the middle of REM sleep, it was easier for Cheever to act on autopilot from his own home while waking up.

They sat in Cheever's small backyard. He had bought a fixer bungalow in the coastal town back when fixer bungalows were to be had in the six, not seven, figures. His home had always been a work in progress. The first time Rachel had come over, she had charitably commented, "It has good bones," with "lots of potential." What it had was location. The bungalow was only a few blocks from Ponto Beach.

As Cheever handed Rachel her glass, he asked, "Sure you don't want a piece of cheesecake while I'm up?"

"I'll take in the calories I really can't afford in liquid increments," she said.

Cheever made a disparaging sound. "You look great," he said.

"Please don't get an eye exam anytime soon," she said.

The glow from the moon made the diamond studs in Rachel's ears sparkle. He reached gently for one of her lobes and said, "Moonlight becomes you."

"Sweet talk becomes you," she said, taking his hand in hers. When they'd first started dating, everyone had thought they were an odd couple. Psychiatrists usually marry other doctors. Ask cops if they marry from any typical profession, and you'll likely hear the answer, "Starter wife, current wife, or future wife?"

Odd couple or not, Cheever and Rachel were profoundly happy with each other. She was the only person outside the force he'd ever felt free to discuss his cases with.

"Are you going to make me beg?" she said. "Before attending to my wine, you were in the middle of telling me Stella's reveal."

"How could it be a reveal if I couldn't understand half the things she was telling me?"

"Tell me anyway."

"I'd need the kind of brain augmentation Stella believes she had in order to understand what she was trying to tell me. The logistics of death flights was only the start. Stella said she really isn't special, but believes her imagination and cognition have become accelerated because the circuits in her brain were essentially reprogrammed."

"Go on."

"That's easier said than done; the circuits in my brain weren't reprogrammed. In fact, my circuits barely work. Stella tried to take on the blame for my not understanding all she was telling me by saying our communicating would be much easier with mindspeak. Apparently you can pass not only thoughts, but insights, from one person to another person. She also tried to make me feel better by telling me that nowadays English is essentially her third language."

"Third?"

"She thinks of mindspeak as her first language, followed by mathematics, but not the math we know. As Stella explains it, mathematics is this never-ending symphony. I didn't tell her I got a D in algebra when I was a kid. It was obvious, though, I was missing most of the notes of her symphony. You know how cutting-edge technology makes our generation feel antiquated? If I'm to believe what Stella says, the digital revolution hasn't even started yet."

"Did she explain the frog?"

"She only said that there is a thin line between existence and non-existence, and that those boundaries are constantly in flux. What could I say to that?"

"I don't know. What did you say?"

"I'm a cop. In my line of work, I've always counted on Occam's razor. It's been my experience that the simplest explanation is invariably the correct explanation. I work with the template of the Seven Deadly Sins, and I look at a crime scene and say, 'Who did this, and why did they do it?'

"But every time I try to apply Occam's razor to Stella, a new wrinkle appears. This afternoon she was bothered by a call she got from an unknown caller who claimed to be privy to what had gone on in her life during the last seven years. This caller challenged Stella's story of going off into space with the Travelers. He said she was part of a special program designed for the evolution of our species."

"That sounds like classic paranoia," said Rachel, "with the government or some secret society being involved in a covert program for nefarious purposes."

"But it wasn't Stella making this claim. She said the caller was putting forth an alternate reality. At this time it's not a story she's embracing, but she seems to believe the caller might have been interspersing some truths in the midst of his lies."

"So where has Occam's razor gotten you?" asked Rachel. "What's the simplest explanation?"

"Stella was abducted," Cheever said, "by an unknown party for unknown purposes."

"And is that also what your gut says?"

"My gut isn't talking except to give me indigestion."

CHAPTER FORTY

Luke and Stella were handed programs as they entered the auditorium. There were a dozen acts scheduled, with Stella listed as the last performer. According to the program, she was supposed to be playing music from *Star Trek*.

"Real funny," said Luke.

Instead of commenting, Stella said, "Why don't we sit down and watch the other acts?"

Luke nodded, and offered her his arm. She took it, and the two of them started down the left aisle looking for seats. Around the auditorium there was a stir at Stella's appearance, and dozens of hushed conversations began taking place. The stage curtains opened enough for a few heads to pop out.

"She's here," one of the observers could be heard saying. Then the heads disappeared and the curtains closed.

"It looks as if no one was sure you'd really show up," whispered Luke.

"Since I didn't sign up in the first place," she said, "they would have good reason to wonder."

"Are you worried?"

"Should I be?" she asked.

"You have a great voice," said Luke.

"You're not exactly impartial."

"Even when I sing in the shower," he said, "I don't sound good. Every time I've heard you sing along with a song, you've somehow managed to improve it. I've never heard anyone else do that."

A girl with pink hair and large black-framed glasses came down the stage stairs and made directly for them. She had eschewed a clipboard in favor of a tablet and was looking very officious. The girl came to a stop in front of Stella.

"I'm Amanda," she said. "I'm the director. You're Stella Pierce?"

Stella nodded.

"You haven't been to any of our rehearsals," Amanda said with an accusing voice.

"I wasn't told about the rehearsals," said Stella.

Amanda sighed. "I was beginning to doubt you'd even be performing. Did you bring your *Star Trek* music for us to plug in to the sound system?"

"I only brought my voice."

"No accompaniment? You'll only need a microphone?"

"That's right."

"At least that makes it easy," she said. "We'll need you backstage before your act is due to go on. We can mike you up then."

"Thank you."

"Any idea how long your set will go?"

"I imagine no more than ten minutes."

"That's perfect. We've asked all the performers to not go any longer than that."

"I promise I won't."

Amanda tapped a few entries into her tablet. "Good," she said. "See you in about and a half."

Stella thanked her, and Amanda went running off, disappearing behind the stage curtains.

Most of the aisle seats were taken, and Luke and Stella had to settle down only three rows back from the stage. From their seats they heard the sights and sounds of the controlled chaos leading to the start of the show. During one sound check, the curtain was left partially open. The Y-Girls were apparently helping out with the production, and they saw Tiffany look their way before turning her back and not acknowledging them.

"I wonder if Tiffany knew that you'd rise to her challenge," said Luke.

"I wonder."

The stage lights were turned low, and a spotlight shone down to the center of the stage. Courtney Crane came out wearing a low-cut, red-sequined dress. She pretended to take umbrage at the wolf whistles directed her way, putting her hands on her hips and mock-glaring at a few of the boys who were making noise, but it was clear she relished the attention.

"Good evening, TPA!" she said. "And welcome to the thirty-second annual Torrey Pines Academy Talent Show."

Loud applause met her announcement, and Courtney added, "Go, Evergreens!"

When the cheers died down, Courtney said, "I'm Courtney Crane, and I will be the first presenter tonight. We have a great show in store for you."

Courtney referred to an index card, and then carefully—albeit haltingly—read, "Our first performer is sophomore Emma Wong. She is a classically trained pianist who will be playing Claude Debussy's *Clair de Lune*. She says this piece was taken from Debussy's Suite Bergamasque. Emily thought that *Clair de Lune*, which means 'light of the moon,' was perfect for tonight's full moon."

The spotlight faded from center stage, with softer lights shining down upon a young woman sitting on a piano bench. Her fingers moved up and down the keyboards, and from the first moments, her soft and beautiful music enthralled the audience. For more than five enchanting minutes, the young pianist played. When she finished, enthusiastic applause rewarded her efforts. As Emma rose from the piano bench, Courtney emerged from backstage, holding an opened florist's box with a dozen long-stem roses. Emma took the flowers, hugged them tight to her chest, and then waved to the audience and hurried backstage.

When the applause subsided, Courtney introduced the next act. "I think we all know Will the Thrill Ravines, Jake the Snake Keating, Isaac I. Sack Fuller, and Gabriel Go Gomez from their exploits on the football field," she said, "but now we get to see them in a whole new light with their quartet called Styling."

Four boys bounded out to the stage looking like the quintessential barbershop quartet. All of them sported white linen blazers and pants, along with red, white, and blue straw boater hats. Their faces were half-covered by the props of fake handlebar mustaches that each of them made a point of stroking.

Will called the quartet to order by blowing on a pitch pipe, and the foursome displayed their harmonizing with the lead, bass, tenor, and baritone. That led them into "My Darling Clementine." They were midway through the song when everything changed. The quartet tossed aside their hats, ripped off their mustaches, and showed their Chippendale moves upon stripping off their coats. Their careful harmonies were suddenly reconstructed into the rants and riffs of rapping. From the audience, students began hooting and dancing in their seats while listening to the vocal editorials being rapped over a throbbing bass and loud drums. As the rapping ran its course, the background instrumentals grew softer. The audience began to applaud, assuming the performance was over, but Will once again produced his pitch pipe, and the quartet managed to segue into the song "Shine On Silver Moon."

When Styling finished singing, there was a long and loud ovation. The foursome tossed their straw boater hats Frisbee-like into the audience; then each of them gave Courtney an enthusiastic hug as they gathered their boxes of chocolates.

"Life is like a box of chocolates," shouted Jake Keating as he left the stage with his chocolates held aloft.

The next act was introduced by Kimberly, and as the show continued, different Y-Girls came out to introduce each new act. Luke and Stella watched troupes of dancers, a yo-yo performer, gymnasts, a comedian, and singers and musicians. Everyone got roses or chocolates, depending on their sex.

"I guess it's time," Stella whispered to Luke as the tenth act was leaving the stage.

"Do you want me to come with you?" he asked.

She shook her head. He touched his index and middle finger to his lips, blew a kiss her way, and said, "Break a leg."

At Stella's look of confusion, he said, "It means good luck."

She departed with a smile on her face.

Luke watched her walk up the aisle. The moment she disappeared from sight, he began to second-guess his decision not to go backstage with her. I'm just overreacting, he tried to tell himself. But he grew even more uneasy when he saw that Tiffany was to be the closing presenter for the evening. As she emerged onto the stage, it was clear the queen bee wasn't about to be upstaged by anyone. Tiffany was wearing a half-red, half-silver costume. The red half made her look like a devil, including one horn; the silver half made her look like an angel, complete with half a halo. Her wig of long hair was similarly divided between red and silver. The red side of her dress was short to the point of being risqué; the silver side was below the knee. Half her blouse was see-through; the other half was modest. She was wearing black fishnet stockings and red stiletto heels.

"Devil?" she asked the audience, pointing to her red side. "Or angel?"

The boys in the crowd reacted predictably, screaming for the devil to come out.

Tiffany pretended she couldn't hear. The second time around, she pointed to her angel side, then pointed to the devil. She accentuated the devil side with a bump and grind, which landed her another ovation.

Luke hoped that Tiffany had gotten her fill of attention, but he doubted it was enough. It never was. She'd probably still take some kind of shot at Stella. He tried to think what she might have planned, and found himself looking up in the rafters to see if there was a hanging bucket. The week before, he'd seen the movie *Carrie* playing on the TCM channel. He remembered how a bucket of pig's blood had been positioned over the stage, and just as Carrie's Cinderella moment arrived and she was pronounced prom queen, the bucket of blood was dumped on her.

Luckily, thought Luke, Tiffany didn't seem to have watched the movie or read Stephen King's book. There was no bucket of blood to be seen. But the uneasy feeling in his gut wouldn't go away. He knew Tiffany. She didn't need Stephen King to tell her how to target someone.

◆ ◆ ◆

Backstage, Amanda finished testing Stella's microphone. "One more time," she said.

"Testing one, two, three," said Stella.

"That's perfect," said Amanda.

"One of the lights isn't activating," Amanda's assistant yelled, and the director hurried away to help, leaving Stella standing by herself. From her vantage point of stage right, Stella watched Tiffany talking to the audience and acting out her dilemma of being an angel or devil. The other Y-Girls were also watching Tiffany from backstage, but they were positioned stage left. The Y-Girls acted delighted with their friend's performance.

Finally, Tiffany got around to introducing the next performer, a junior juggler named Evan Rosenbluth.

"I've always admired men who know how to throw their balls in the air," said Tiffany.

When the groundlings responded, she said, "What? What?" Then she added with a wink, "The devil made me do it!"

Stella was having trouble listening, and not just because of Tiffany's pandering. She was distracted by something that *felt* ugly. Its presence came at her like a bad smell, although there was no odor attached to it. She took a few breaths, opening her mind to what was out there. Then she identified its source, or part of it at least. Guy Wilkerson was in the audience. She was certain of that, even without seeing him. His ugly intentions couldn't be contained within his body. His foulness was seeping out, a toxicity that felt poisonous to her.

Once again, Stella's awareness heightened. Like it or not, voices raised themselves in her head. It wasn't only Wilkerson's ugliness; there was this miasma of malice weighing upon her spirit. Again, she tried to open her mind to find its source. That's when Courtney glanced at her for a moment, only to look away guiltily. But Stella clearly heard the other girl's thoughts: *Wait until Tiffany gives her the box.*

The flower box, thought Stella. Her eyes settled on the remaining box of flowers. The box was closed, but the evil intentions surrounding it could not be contained.

"Tonight Evan will be doing his juggling to the music of Gilbert and Sullivan's *Modern Major-General,*" Tiffany said.

As Tiffany concluded her introduction, the Gilbert and Sullivan music began to play, and the juggling act commenced. Everyone was looking at the stage except for Stella. She was staring at the florist's box. Opening it would give her no pleasure, she knew, but it would be better to deal with what was inside of it on her own terms.

As Tiffany rejoined the Y-Girls and accepted all their praise, Stella walked toward the card table that was now empty save for one box of chocolates and one florist's box. There was no mistaking what was meant for her. Her name had been printed on the florist's box with a silver Sharpie. As she reached for it, Stella felt a venomous thought hurling her way: *Bitch!*

The surge of ill will was now accompanied by a voice: "What are you doing?"

Stella wasn't deterred. She ignored Tiffany's question and opened the box. Inside were twelve rose stems to be sure, but they seemed to have been selected only for their abundance of thorns. There were no flowers. Hanging on the thorns were impaled frogs. The still creatures stared at Stella; she looked back in pity.

The up-tempo music of Gilbert and Sullivan continued, and with it the pace of the juggling. There was a backstage monitor showing what was happening onstage. So many balls in the air, thought Stella. She was grateful for the music. It helped drown out the toxic chorus of Y-Girl thoughts.

> I can tell undoubted Raphaels from Gerard Dows
> and Zoffanies,
> I know the croaking chorus from the Frogs of
> Aristophanes!
> Then I can hum a fugue of which I've heard the
> music's din afore,
> And whistle all the airs from that infernal non-
> sense Pinafore.

Stella closed the box. She shook her head, then turned toward the Y-Girls. Her look didn't accuse; it pitied. Most of the group turned away from her glance, but not Tiffany. There was no way she was going to let Space Girl look at her dismissively.

Tiffany crossed the divide between them, closing the distance until she stood in front of Stella.

For a moment the Y-Girls hesitated to follow her, but then Courtney said, "Let's go," and Kimberly, Brittany, Emily, Cassidy, and Sherry all closed ranks. As they gathered behind Tiffany, the closing lyrics of a "Modern Major-General" played.

> For my military knowledge, though I'm plucky
> and adventury,
> Has only been brought down to the beginning of
> the century;
> But still in matters vegetable, animal, and mineral,
> I am the very model of a modern Major-General.

Tiffany seemed to unconsciously pick up the cadence of the song, offering up a staccato rant directly in Stella's face.

"You think your Princess Leia act makes you special, don't you?" said Tiffany. "But it's not working, and you know why? It's because you're crazy. Shouldn't you be going back to the asylum you came from?"

"I'm afraid you are right about that," said Stella, and then handed her the rose box. "This is yours," she said. "You need to own it."

Tiffany automatically took the box, but then dropped it on the table, acting like she'd been burned.

"I don't believe in your space voodoo," said Tiffany. But then she was clearly distracted. "What's all that croaking?"

"Maybe it's the frogs of Aristophanes," whispered Stella.

"What?" Tiffany could barely hear over the croaking sounds, which seemed to be springing up from everywhere.

"Tiffany!" hissed Amanda, waving at her and gesturing to the stage. "Get out there now!"

The juggler had long finished, and the audience was beginning to stir. Tiffany reached for her hair, making sure it was in place, and smoothed her outfit. As she started toward the stage, Tiffany abruptly jumped to the side, as if reacting to the warning rattle of a rattlesnake. She landed awkwardly on her stiletto heels, snapping one of them off. Cursing, she wobbled out to the stage on unsteady legs.

Tiffany pretended not to hear the laughter at her drunken gait. In an overloud voice that had the audience covering their ears, she said, "Let's give another big hand to Evan."

As the audience applauded, Tiffany's head jerked from side to side.

"Frogs," she said.

A few in the audience tittered, wondering if Tiffany had lost it. She was looking to her right and left and covering her ears.

Then she shouted, "Can you hear me?"

The audience response of "Yes" was sustained and substantial, even though Tiffany seemed to have trouble hearing it.

"We have one final performer," she said, and then began speaking louder again, as if trying to drown out some sound.

"If you think this last performer is out of this world," Tiffany said, "then she'd tell you there's a good reason for that. Singing for you is Stella Pierce, who has been lost in space for the last seven years."

Tiffany gave Stella a wide berth as she hobbled offstage. She kept looking around, apparently distracted by something.

As Stella positioned herself in the middle of the stage, she acknowledged the uncertain applause. Her presence was still, contained, and her clothes were understated. She had on a batik blouse, jeans, and high-top cloth sneakers. Her long blonde hair was contained in a single braid.

In a soft voice, she said, "I would like to say that I haven't been lost in space. As for whether I've been found, I guess the jury is still out."

Some clapping followed her response, and Stella looked out over the audience. There were a lot of cameras taking in her every move. She caught Luke's eye, and smiled for him. Then she looked to the very back of the audience. Guy Wilkerson was in the shadows, but he was not hidden from her.

Stella decided on her swan song. It was a late choice, but she thought it was the right choice. When she left the stage, it would be for good. She would return to the universe one way or another.

In the stillness, she raised her right hand, lifting it high, as if reaching for the sky, and then both of her hands began to move, almost as if she was weaving something. Music seemingly emerged from her fingertips, an eerie sound that carried throughout the auditorium. The music didn't seem to be coming from the speakers. Some in the audience tried muting the sound by lifting their hands to their ears, but that didn't shut out the notes. The music was in their heads.

From backstage, Tiffany screamed, "Get out!" But she couldn't get rid of her demon that way. Tiffany ran over to the pink-haired director. "Cut the witch's mike! Cut it!"

Amanda tried to lower the volume on her soundboard, but that wasn't good enough for Tiffany. She pulled the plug on Stella, shutting down all sound from the speakers. But that didn't stop the music.

"Is she playing a theremin?" asked a grandmother who had come to see her granddaughter dance.

"What's a theremin?" asked the student sitting next to her.

But the old woman didn't have the words to respond; tears were falling down her cheeks as she imagined she was hearing the chorales of angels.

And then words came out of Stella's mouth; some recognized the lyrics to the song "Mad World," but no one in the audience had ever heard a song sung like this one. The barriers and laws of time and space and gravity no longer existed. It wasn't enough for the audience to walk in Stella's shoes; she took them with her on her journey.

Down, down the rabbit hole they went. The mad world opened up to them, and they fell in. They saw the universe around them as she had, felt as she had, felt as she did.

The words came, and with them, images—haunted and gaunt faces, so many faces, and all of them tired and worn from a senseless grind.

"Going nowhere," sang Stella, "going nowhere."

The figures were in a hurry, but none knew where they were going. There was only the milling of the directionless.

"No tomorrow," sang Stella, "no tomorrow."

It was a dream; it was reality. It was alien; it was the state of humanity. Everyone wanted something greater, but they were tethered to fathomless despair. The listeners were forced to hear beyond the words. They were not allowed to be passive. Some reached for the light; some were too afraid and sobbed into their hands. The song was about them; the song was *in* them.

And then Stella sang of dreaming and offered her confession, telling them the dreams in which she was dying were the best she'd ever had. And with her words she took them into her dreams, and into her dying, and into the death flights she had experienced.

She offered the universe but demanded mortal payment; she showed them that death was but another journey. Some were terrified of dying, or of her; some wanted nothing more than to board the flight to the beyond. For those who could think outside their soon-to-be-cast-off shells, the universe opened, and they saw a distant port, and one beyond that, and another.

And in the audience, the listeners cried not so much at the thought of death, but at Stella's bringing them back to the life they knew, and to their mad world.

Stella experienced her first day of school, as did they. Her insecurities were displayed and felt and sung, but it wasn't only Stella's song; it was everyone's song and everyone's loneliness.

"Hello teacher, tell me what's my lesson?" sang Stella.

Dr. Rommel stared at Stella through his thick lenses; Dr. Rommel stared at all of them. They were on the viewing end of his microscope but still not seen. The teacher was looking right through them. Did they even exist? Were they the frogs on the trays being dissected in a glance?

And then, once more, Stella sang of her dreams of dying, but most in the audience now understood her exultation that came with such a dream: there were some places bodies could not go and were not meant to go. Those seeking incredible journeys needed to shed their baggage.

And to do this they needed to aspire beyond a world gone mad, a world they reentered as Stella's song came to an end.

The music was done. The Piper's tune was finished. For a long moment, the auditorium was silent, as if everyone inside it needed to take in a deep breath.

And then all hell broke loose.

CHAPTER FORTY-ONE

A young man called to the passersby, doing his best to explain. "I know it sounded like me," he yelled, "but that was the Mr. Hyde in my thoughts. And that's where he stays, just in my thoughts. I'll bet he's in you, too. Yeah, I thought some things when she walked by. But they say guys my age think about sex every seven seconds. So what I was thinking was normal. How was I to know she was listening?"

A different kind of awakening had been felt by another student; her soliloquy was offered more to herself than to those nearby.

"I wanted to dance onstage tonight," said the girl, "but I was afraid I would be laughed at. I was afraid of being judged by others and found wanting. But now I dance to the moon." And around the school grounds, moving to the music she heard, she began to dance. No one laughed at her, and some even applauded. But she did not dance for others; she danced for herself.

Near the auditorium steps, a young woman called out to everyone, and no one: "I didn't actually say anything to her, not aloud, that is. Mental body shaming is different, isn't it? Besides, the person I was really shaming was me. On that day I had bad cramps and felt bloated. When I get that way, I want to eat carbs, but I was on this diet. I hate diets. I hate having to try and fit into this school's impossible body standards."

Her confession prompted another: "The emperor isn't wearing any clothes!" screamed a wild-eyed boy. "The emperor isn't wearing any clothes!"

And then there was a third voice in the chorus: "You're right! We think our secrets clothe us, but they don't. I'm gay! You hear that? I'm gay!"

Some did not need to shout. A girl marveled at the changes she felt. "My demons seemed so large," she said softly, "but now I can see they're small. They're manageable. In the space of a single song, I have grown, and they have shrunk. I don't know how that's possible, but it is."

Peace for one, turmoil for another: "When is that song going to leave my head?" asked a girl. "What it says to me is 'J'accuse! J'accuse! J'accuse!' And my answer? 'Guilty! Guilty! Guilty!' But I would change my answer. Help me to change my answer."

"I didn't want her song to end," said a boy, speaking to a girl he'd always wanted to talk to but had never gotten up the nerve. "I wanted to beg her to keep playing. I wanted to get down on my knees and worship her. But I knew that wasn't what she wanted. What I need to do is put that kind of love out to the world, even if it's mad."

And the girl spoke to him, spoke to the boy she'd noticed, but never dared to say anything to. "And I am part of that mad world. I play my role in the grand illusion. I'm trying to get the perfect grades so I can get into the perfect school and lead the perfect life. But we're all imperfect. Look at me. I have everything going for me, right? I'm almost seventeen, and I've never been kissed. I'm not looking for a perfect kiss, but someone who wants to kiss me."

"I want to kiss you," said the boy.

As close as they were, the space still seemed far. But each of their gravities brought the other in closer, and he extended his fingertips and orbited around her until their faces came together.

◆ ◆ ◆

This wasn't Scarecrow's first rodeo, but it felt like it. From the beginning, everything had been so nebulous. That was the exact right word.

Things were cloudy, unclear. The root of *nebulous* was *nebula*, a far-off galaxy. That's how the first Star Wars movie had opened: *A long time ago in a galaxy far, far away.* But this wasn't supposed to be some space opera. Or was it? That was the problem. Scarecrow had never been told what Dorothy really was or how she should be dealt with. He had more background than the rest of his go team, but was still kept on a need-to-know basis.

And Dorothy, it seemed, was one of those damn Russian nesting dolls. You kept opening one doll after another, and the surprises never seemed to end. This, what they were dealing with now, was the aftermath of just one song. How was it that a single song could result in so much chaos? The shit had hit the fan big-time.

His phone rang, as he'd known it would. "How bad are things?" asked the Guardian of the Gates.

"Dorothy's song caused a near riot," said Scarecrow in a tone that was in no way apologetic. They certainly hadn't been warned that her singing a song might be problematic. "You'll need to do all sorts of damage control from your end."

"Where is Dorothy now?"

"Auntie Em and Uncle Henry were in the audience monitoring her, but they were part of the fallout. When both of them became disoriented, Dorothy disappeared. We're tracking her cell phone now. It shows she's still in the immediate area. We're trying to reach her through that, and we've also got ears on the boyfriend, who is trying to track her down. The two of them came to the show together, so it's likely she'll be contacting him."

"Call me when you have her in sight," he said. "There is a new development from our end. Because Sir Hocus was making noise, we were afraid his inquiries might alert Jinnicky. That's why we decided to bring him in. The Wizard will be talking with him shortly."

Sir Hocus, Scarecrow reminded himself, was Congressman Pierce. It was getting so you needed a goddamn program. Scarecrow was sick of all the Oz names. He was beginning to feel like he was in fucking Oz. Any minute now he'd see flying monkeys.

"It's essential we get Dorothy in our sights posthaste and make sure of her safety."

"I understand," said Scarecrow. "But you should know one more thing. Shaggy was in the audience. Her song apparently set him off big-time."

"Shit," said the Guardian. "Could he be with Dorothy?"

"No," said Scarecrow. "Reports are that he's still on the high school grounds."

"Find her! Find out what she's up to. And call me as soon as you have her in your sights."

The line went dead.

◆ ◆ ◆

Stella emerged from behind a eucalyptus tree. She had used evasive tactics to distance herself from Guy Wilkerson. After her song she had heard his howling. He'd been like a wild animal baying at the moon. She'd thought she could escape the auditorium unseen, but he'd come running after her. Stella had gone in and out of buildings, and then doubled back. As an extra precaution ,she'd run from one eucalyptus tree to another, hiding in the shadows of the trees and making sure she wasn't being followed.

"Excuse me," Stella said, interrupting a young man opening his car door.

When he saw who had called to him, the boy gaped. "It's you," he said.

"I'm Stella," she said.

"I know. I'm Brad. Brad Pickering. I was there. I saw you."

"I'm wondering if you can give me a ride, Brad."

He nodded enthusiastically, his head bobbing up and down. "Oh yes," he said. "I'd be honored."

Brad ran around to the passenger side and opened the door for her. After Stella sat down, he closed the door behind her.

When he sat down in the driver's seat, Brad said, "Wow. I can't believe it's you." Then he shook his head and showed her his trembling hands. "I'm feeling kind of overwhelmed by your presence. Having you here is, like, mind-blowing."

"What year are you in school?" asked Stella.

"I'm a senior," he said. "I know your brother, but we're not friends or anything. I mean, we run in different circles. I'm kind of in the nerd group."

"That's kind of where I am, too," said Stella.

Brad started laughing.

"What?" she asked.

"Nerd group?" he said. "You're in a league of your own. Your song was like nothing I've ever experienced. I saw. I felt. It was mind-altering. It was mind-expanding. You know what I was wondering while walking to my car? I was thinking you might be God."

"I am no more God than you are."

Brad started his car and turned to Stella, but he couldn't quite meet her eyes.

"You gave me the stars," he said. "Where can I take you?"

◆ ◆ ◆

Luke tried to fight down his panic as he did another loop around the auditorium. Where was Stella? Had that stalker gotten to her? Or had she decided to go away on her own?

Stella's song had been a revelation to Luke, and he was pretty sure he knew her better than anyone. With her words, he had felt so many things weighing on her. She had returned home a stranger, and instead of home sweet home, she had been a stranger in a strange land.

He looked at his phone. She still hadn't responded to his texts and phone messages. He wondered whether he should leave another.

Luke thought about going over to the parking lot again. He'd been there five minutes ago, looking to see if she was waiting there for him. Of course he wasn't the only one at loose ends. Everything and everyone had gone crazy after Stella's song. Even now, people were acting as if they didn't quite know what to do. Some in the audience had cheered until their voices gave out; others had sat contemplatively; some looked lost; some acted hypnotized. No one left the performance untouched. The audience was still milling around. Everyone seemed to have the need to talk about what they'd seen.

Something caught Luke's eye. There was a crowd gathered around two policemen. His first thought was that something had happened to Stella, but that was before he saw Tiffany talking to the cops.

"I think she must have used some kind of aerosol drug on all of us," Tiffany told them.

She turned her head, looking for support from the Y-Girls, but none of the others said anything. They all looked dazed; they were certainly not alone in that.

"I thought you claimed that this Stella Pierce was involved in an assault and battery," said the officer with the notepad and pen.

"She threatened me backstage," said Tiffany. Once more she looked for backing from the Y-Girls, but they remained silent. "And if you look around, you can see lots of people are still tripping out. There's no way that could have happened if she hadn't drugged everyone. I think it must have been LSD or something like that."

Luke thought about stepping in, but judging from the skeptical cops, he didn't see the need. It was clear they thought they were wasting their time.

He moved away from the circle of onlookers. He thought about calling Michael or Mrs. Pierce. Stella had asked Michael to do her a favor and stay home with their mother while she performed at the talent show—she hadn't wanted her mother to feel she had to protect her. As far as Eleanor Pierce knew, Stella was at a school function with Luke. That was true enough. But it was also a lie, Luke knew, enough for Mrs. Pierce to freak out if she knew Stella was missing.

His phone chimed, signaling an incoming text. Luke's heart skipped a beat when he saw Stella was the sender. He read her text and then looked at its accompanying picture.

> I love you, Luke. You will always have my heart. I know it would not be fair to ask you to go with me, so I will not be selfish. Leaving you breaks my heart. I wish our circumstances were different, and that we were not star-crossed.

Star-crossed, thought Luke. Wasn't that some *Romeo and Juliet* kind of crap? It meant destiny, or the stars, were conspiring against you. It meant their relationship was doomed. Bullshit. He wasn't going to accept that. Her heart wasn't enough. He needed her.

I love you, he texted, and the stars have nothing to do with us. Where are you?

As he awaited her response, he studied the picture she'd sent. The image showed white stones formed into a heart.

Moonstones, Luke realized. And then he knew where she was. And he was also afraid Stella wasn't going to text back. She had offered him a final farewell.

He began to run toward the parking lot. Moonlight Beach was about a fifteen-minute drive away. But he needed to be there sooner than that. A thought came to him, perhaps inspired by the cops he'd seen. He slowed down to a walk and flipped through his phone contacts, hoping the contact number he'd been given as a kid, and had kept over the years, still worked.

Luke found the contact's name and hit "Dial." The call went through; the number seemed good.

"Pick up, pick up," he said.

Luke's wish was answered: "Cheever."

"Hi, this is Luke Hart. I'm—"

"I know who you are, Luke."

"It's Stella," he said. "Something happened tonight, and she took off. I think I know where she is, though. We were supposed to go to Moonlight Beach tonight. I'm on my way there now, but I remember you once told me you lived in Leucadia—"

"I'm five minutes from Moonlight," said Cheever. "I'll go look for her now."

CHAPTER FORTY-TWO

It was a good thing he'd spotted Surfer Boy and followed him. If he hadn't, Stella might have slipped through his grasp. But she wasn't going to get away from him again, thought Wilkerson.

After Stella gave him the slip, he'd noticed Surfer Boy and managed to stay close to him. Wilkerson had thought she might contact him. And she had. Then Wilkerson had heard the kid call some friend and give up her location. That's all he needed.

Wilkerson's electric bike didn't have the speed of a car, but it was a lot more mobile, and he didn't have to worry about red lights or stop signs. He pushed the bike to its limits, traveling from the side streets to the Coast Highway and back. With all the stops and starts on the 101, it was possible he might even beat Surfer Boy to Moonlight Beach.

And even if he didn't, wasn't it the case that sometimes it was the last mouse that got the cheese? Wilkerson had no doubt he'd find Stella. They had their special connection, after all.

He went shooting by the Self-Realization Center. It was a large compound full of gardens, compounds, and meditation centers. All the locals called it Swami's. The monks there taught yoga and meditation, and followed the teachings of some guru. Wilkerson wasn't interested in the koan *What is the sound of one hand clapping?* No, tonight what interested him more was the sound of one hand killing.

◆ ◆ ◆

Cheever cruised through Moonlight Beach's upper parking lot. There were only a few cars there, and Stella wasn't to be seen. The cop knew the parking lot had a ten o'clock curfew, but the beach itself only officially closed between 2:00 a.m. and 4:00 a.m. to discourage transients from sleeping there.

He drove toward the sand and parked at the end of B Street. After Luke's call, he'd jumped in his car, not even bothering to change, barely pausing long enough to get Rachel's kiss and blessing. His penny loafers weren't exactly beachwear. Cheever thought about taking off his shoes and rolling up his khaki pants, but then decided to hell with it. The boy had made it sound like every second counted.

The beach facilities were all but deserted. There was no one on the playground or the three volleyball courts. The snack shack had been closed for hours, and the barbecues and fire pits were deserted, save for a few distant stragglers who were warming their hands over a fire. Cheever thought about going over to question them, then thought better of it. Stella would either be at the beach or not.

He jogged down to the sand, and looked first to the south, and then to the north. The moonlight offered good visibility; he could see the lights of Del Mar on the point to the south, and the Carlsbad power plant to the north. No people were nearby; both stretches of beach looked equally deserted.

North or south? Cheever wondered.

He had been told that a century ago, people had waited for low tide and then driven their Model T automobiles north from Moonlight Beach to Oceanside, a distance of some fifteen miles. Cheever decided to follow the path of those old cars. It was low tide now; he didn't have to worry about the waves. All he had to do was find Stella.

◆ ◆ ◆

Stella took a deep breath and then spoke into the phone: "Hi, Mom."

"I was just about to call you, Stella," said Eleanor. "Isn't it time you and Luke came home?"

"I did come home, Mom. I came home mostly for you."

"What I meant—"

"I know what you meant. But what if I hadn't come home?"

In a low voice, Eleanor said, "What are you trying to say?"

"Do you remember that ghost story Candy Stewart told on the beach?"

"I think I remember everything about that night," said Eleanor, "because that was the last night I thought I'd ever have with you."

"And do you remember what Jason said to his mother when he returned?"

"He told his mother that having a picture of him shouldn't have been necessary. He said that he'd always been and always would be in her heart, and that she needed to look no further than that."

"That's right."

"That's easy to say," Eleanor said, her voice rising in panic, "but it's not so easy to live. It's well and good to say your memories should sustain you and that love is eternal, but that doesn't take into account the relentless pain of absence."

"There is no future if you only look backward, Mom."

"I know that now."

"Do you?"

"I do, sweetie. Why are you saying all of this?"

"Because sometimes things happen that you don't want to happen. Because nothing is constant. Because you have to accept the blessing of those people who are a part of your life and who make your life special, just as you have to accept their absence. In the end there is always the hope that you will meet up in some way and at some time in the future. And it might not be in a way that you imagine or hope, but it will most assuredly be a grand reunion. I'll see you again, Mommy."

"What are you saying, Stella?"

"I'm saying I love you."

Stella ended their conversation. She stared out at the ocean and saw the long and attenuated reflection of the moon on the water. There was a shimmering silver bridge without an end in front of her. All she had to do was follow it.

She removed her clothing.

◆ ◆ ◆

Luke parked at the end of the turnaround on C Street. During his breakneck drive, he'd snuck a few glimpses at the picture Stella had sent. In the center of the shot were all the moonstones formed into a heart, but there were a few other details that made Luke believe he knew right where she'd snapped the picture.

He ran down the incline, churning up the sand. The moonlight played on the ocean, giving it an iridescent glow. He ran south, and it seemed to him that moonstones had been placed as tiny markers to lead him to the treasure.

There, Luke thought, there was his moonstone heart. He dropped to his knees, staring at the message she'd left him. But there was no sign of Stella.

His cell phone rang; the readout told him the detective was calling.

"Where are you?" asked Cheever.

"I'm about one hundred and fifty yards south of the lifeguard tower," said Luke. "Stella was definitely here, but I don't see her now."

"I went north," said Cheever. "I'll turn around and jog your way. If I see her, I'll call."

The moon provided good visibility, but the cool night had kept people away from the beach. There was no one around to ask if they'd seen Stella.

Think, Luke told himself. She was here. Where could she have gone? He studied the moonstone heart she'd made for him. Then he gently stretched his hand over the rocks, touching them with his fingertips and with his being. She'd managed to gather at least twenty moonstones. That meant she'd scoured the area for them.

There were footprints going to and from the moonstones. He looked at the impressions. Stella must have been walking around barefoot. Had she put her shoes back on, or was she still barefoot? He followed the footprints in the sand with his eyes. He was no tracker, but he couldn't see any shoe prints in the vicinity of the heart.

He turned around, scanning the area for anything unusual. That's when he saw the clothing hidden among the seaweed. He ran to the clothes. Stella's high-top cloth sneakers were there, as were her jeans and batik blouse. He checked her pants and found her cell phone. What did that mean?

Without considering his movements, Luke turned his head west, and his eyes followed the silver trail of moonlight extending into the horizon. Way out there, far beyond the breakers, he thought he saw something. Was it a dolphin? No, if that was the case, he'd be seeing more than one fin gliding through the waves. Dolphins traveled in pods.

It was Stella. She was swimming away from him. She was swimming away from the world.

Luke ran to the shoreline. "Stella!" he screamed.

He jumped up and down and kept screaming her name. But the swimmer didn't stop. She was too far away to be able to hear him.

Swim after her, he thought. But she was already dangerously far out there. By the time he caught up with her, she would probably be exhausted and maybe even hypothermic; she might not even have the strength to get back to shore.

Luke turned around and began sprinting toward his car. He'd grab his surfboard and paddle out. There was no way Stella was leaving this earthly plane without him.

◆ ◆ ◆

Wilkerson tried to blend in with the shadows as Surfer Boy ran past him, but there was no need. Romeo wasn't seeing anything except his damsel in distress. Wilkerson had watched him screaming from the shore, trying to get her attention. She was too far away to hear him, though.

But now the boy had a plan. Wilkerson watched as he pulled down his surfboard.

Wilkerson had a plan, too.

◆ ◆ ◆

Surfer Boy slowed at the water's edge as Wilkerson had counted on him doing. There was no way he was going to race into the surf with his clothes on. He ripped off his shirt and kicked off his shoes. Then he started pulling down his jeans. Of course he didn't notice Wilkerson's approach. His eyes were fixated on her distant figure.

Wilkerson had selected the perfect beach stone. It was a cobblestone as big as his fist, and he swung it at Surfer Boy's temple.

The kid dropped. He never even screamed. As he flopped around on the beach, his blood colored the sand red. The blow caused his body to spasm. Surfer Boy wasn't going to be getting up anytime soon; Surfer Boy might never be getting up. But he was alive for the moment, and that suited Wilkerson's purposes. He shook his fist and the bloody rock that was in it toward the faraway figure in the water. She would sense him, he knew. She would hear him.

"I'll crush his skull unless you come back!" he screamed. "I swear to God I'll kill him!"

Wilkerson strained to see the far-off figure. Was she still swimming away from shore? Even with the moonlight it was hard to see.

"If you leave us, he dies!" screamed Wilkerson.

And then he felt like doing a little jig. Stella had definitely changed her course. She was now swimming toward shore.

"Drop your weapon!" a voice commanded.

Wilkerson knew the voice of his old nemesis. For seven years the cop had been asking him questions. He had been unrelenting and unforgiving, judging Wilkerson even for the crimes he hadn't committed.

"Surfer Boy attacked me," said Wilkerson. "I was just protecting myself."

Once more Cheever said, "Drop your weapon!"

"You were always wrong about me. But you could never admit it. You owe me a long-overdue apology."

"Drop it!"

"You spilled that pizza on me, and then you paraded me in front of the press, making me look like a lowlife."

"Step away from that boy, drop the stone, drop to your knees, and cuff your fingers behind your head."

"Do you believe in God?" asked Wilkerson.

"Yes," said Cheever.

"And do you think all of us are a reflection of God?"

"We're supposed to be."

"Then why did God make me like I am? I'm twisted. Isn't that what you always told me?"

"I provoked you to try and find out what happened to Stella."

"Stella, Stella, Stella. The first time I saw her, I was almost blinded by her light. I was drawn to her, of course. Do moths get blamed for being attracted to the light? It's their nature. But what about *my* nature? I felt almost cleansed in her light. But then she went away."

"She came back."

"And now her light is even brighter. She knows what I want. It's what I've always wanted. But I was interrupted. Seven years ago she was meant to die by my hands. I kept getting closer to doing the deed. I was circling her like a shark. Every day I would make sure I got a glimpse of her, and at night I would kill her in my thoughts, and in my dreams.

"Can you imagine what I felt when I heard she was gone? It was hell. I was more jealous and angry than you could imagine. Someone else had gotten my prize. Someone else had her."

"That's why you should take her deliverance as a sign. God gave you another chance."

"Is that the same God who made me? Do you know how much I hate love stories? They mock me, because I always knew I would never have a love story of my own."

Cheever didn't like Wilkerson's vibe. He seemed to have come to a decision, and not a good one.

"Put down the stone. This is your last warning."

"Why? Surfer Boy isn't going to make it anyway."

Wilkerson snuck a quick glance at Luke. The boy didn't look good; his breathing was loud and erratic. Still, the kid was young and strong.

"But I could be wrong. As long as his heart's beating, I know he won't give up. Her love sustains him even now, and I can't have that."

With a sudden motion, Wilkerson lunged toward the downed figure. The rock, clenched in Wilkerson's hands, was meant to cave in the boy's head. But the stone never reached its target. The sound of gunfire wasn't loud on the beach; it was mostly swallowed by the surf. But the shot tore through Wilkerson's chest.

It was a fatal wound, but for a few seconds, Wilkerson was able to ignore it. He turned his head, and his eyes followed the trail of moonlight, looking for the brightest light of all at the end of it.

CHAPTER FORTY-THREE

Cheever fought through his shock, and tried to save the boy's life. He did chest compressions as he spoke.

"You'll be all right, Luke," said Cheever. "Help is on the way."

He was pretty sure the kid couldn't hear what he was saying. Cheever suspected Luke had a fractured skull. He was no doctor, but it wouldn't have surprised him if the kid also had a cerebral hemorrhage.

The cop continued to do chest compressions through the kid's shaking, spasms, and rattling teeth. It was hopeless, he knew, but he wouldn't give up.

"Luke!"

The cry could be heard over the breaking waves. That's when Cheever turned and saw her emerging from the surf. He thought of Botticelli's *Birth of Venus*; she was that beautiful and more.

"Luke!" she called again.

There was something commanding about Stella's voice. Cheever could feel it down to his toes. It was a summons not easily ignored.

Stella ran to Luke. Later, in his report, Cheever would say that she applied mouth-to-mouth resuscitation. But it wasn't that. At first she cradled his damaged head to her breast; then she kissed him.

"I'm here, Luke," she said. "Follow my voice back home."

And then she kissed him again, and this time in a whisper repeated, "I'm here, Luke."

Cheever took off his blazer and draped it over Stella's back. The shooting, and everything else, had taken its toll on the cop, and at first he didn't believe what he was seeing. Luke's breathing wasn't as labored, and his face had color. Even the swelling in his head had gone down, and the bleeding had all but stopped.

It was impossible, of course. So much of this was impossible.

Cheever went and stood over Wilkerson. Thirty years on the force, and he'd never had to draw his gun. Not once. He got a case of the shivers, and then the dry heaves.

"I'm sorry," Stella said, touching him with her hand. Her voice, her words, made him feel a little better.

"It's not as if I can exactly see the future," she said, "but now I can better see the past. And I now know one of the reasons I was selected. Seven years ago Wilkerson was going to kill me. Had he chosen another path since then, Wilkerson could have lived, but he did not. You shot him, but you were not his executioner. His fate was decided long ago."

Cheever continued to shiver, despite Stella's comforting words, despite her saying Wilkerson's fate was decided long ago. It didn't feel like long ago.

"That's how it must have been with all the others," said Stella. "I am sure we would have all died—or maybe we did die—without that second chance."

It was a convenient explanation for what the Travelers had supposedly done, thought Cheever. Or maybe, he thought, it was a convenient explanation for what *he* had done.

"Thank you for saving Luke," she said.

Cheever shook his head. "You saved Luke. You came back. But how did you know he was hurt?"

"I heard him calling."

"You were halfway to Japan. There's no way you could have heard anyone on the shore shouting."

"I have heard from much farther distances than that."

"You told Luke to follow your voice back home."

"There are times when we need someone to show us the way."

They heard sirens in the distance. Police and paramedics were on the way.

"Stella . . ."

Both of them heard Luke's whisper.

Stella dropped down to her knees. "I'm here, Luke."

His soft words seemed to come with shadows: "I was afraid you'd drown."

"Mermaids don't drown. And neither do Space Girls."

"That's good to know," he whispered.

"An ambulance is coming for you," said Stella. "Do you hear the siren?"

"I do," he said. "Will you stay with me?"

"We're valentines, aren't we?" she said.

CHAPTER FORTY-FOUR

In the immediate aftermath of the shooting, Cheever was put on administrative leave. There was nothing to suggest the shooting wasn't justified, but he still found himself undergoing one round of questions after another.

His story was simple: he'd come upon Wilkerson moments after he'd attacked Luke Hart. After multiple warnings, he'd shot Wilkerson when he again tried to attack Hart with a cobblestone. Shortly after that, Stella Pierce had returned from her swim and begun mouth-to-mouth resuscitation on Luke.

Cheever had been told that Luke's and Stella's stories confirmed his own.

All of them had told the truth, thought Cheever, even though none of them had told anything resembling the full story. He wasn't even sure what the full story was.

His account of what happened didn't include his own investigation into Stella's missing seven years. There was no mention of Dickie Rath and his mysterious niece, Elle, or Beto Diaz. He didn't discuss the missing photograph of Stella and her family that she had produced after a seven-year absence. Mindspeak hadn't been brought up, nor had the Travelers. There was no place in his report to talk about LeRon Rivers or the other "students" supposedly voyaging with Stella. And he couldn't muddy up the investigative waters by talking about Stella's intuitive side, which seemed to divine so many secrets, including some of his own. Cheever had known better than to write about the frog. And during his interrogation, he kept hearing about some mysterious song that Stella had sung at a talent show. That was yet another omission.

In the end, his report was simple and factual. It was also a crock.

UFO stories and extraterrestrials seemed to go hand in hand with San Diego and Southern California. George Van Tassel and the Integration was only the start of it. Space cults had long made the area their home. One group had been around San Diego for decades doing its waiting-for-Alien Godot routine. And the Heaven's Gate cult had made quite a local splash when thirty-nine of its members had committed mass suicide in Rancho Santa Fe. Their leader, Marshall Applewhite, told his followers that the approaching Hale-Bopp Comet was being accompanied by a UFO. He said their souls would be carried by this spaceship to another planet, and there, be reincarnated.

None of that had gone into Cheever's report either, although he wondered if it should have.

After two days of grilling Cheever, SDPD decided they'd asked enough questions, and Cheever decided he'd jumped through enough hoops. Supposedly it was all over. Cheever suspected it would never be over.

There were explanations for everything that had occurred. Cheever wasn't one for the inexplicable. So he'd found reasons to explain everything from the frog (suspended animation) to Stella's song (mass hysteria) to her mind reading (if her brain had been enhanced with hardware, then she could use deductive language along with the interpreting of body language to gauge what others were thinking) to her supposed healing of others (hypnosis). But when Cheever put all of his explanations together, they seemed to be more of a stretch than everything Stella had actually done.

He drove home to Leucadia. Gumshoe greeted him at the door and insisted upon some purr time. Cheever didn't object.

Rachel would be over later. She was supposed to be bringing takeout. That was as much of an agenda as Cheever wanted. But it wasn't to be. Although he hadn't expected any visitors, he got one.

"I'm thinking you must be Greek," said Cheever.

Congressman Duncan Pierce was standing on his doorstep bearing gifts. His arms were laden with food and drink.

"You're probably right," he said. "But if Eleanor had her way, I'd be even more Greek. She wanted me to bring you everything but the kitchen sink, but I told her I wasn't going to deliver any more than I could carry."

"Shall we lighten your load," said Cheever, "and open one of those bottles of wine?"

"By all means," said Duncan.

It looked as if Eleanor had been cooking for days. Duncan filled Cheever's table with casseroles, appetizers, homemade bread, and desserts.

"Rachel is coming over later," said Cheever. "I better call and tell her not to bring any food."

"I'll open the wine," said Duncan. "Any preference?"

"Only that it be either red or white," he said.

Cheever made his call, talked briefly with Rachel, and then found that Duncan had poured some merlot in his absence. The two men raised their glasses, and Duncan said, "To what Edgar Mitchell wanted to say to all politicians when he walked on the moon in 1974."

"And what did he want to say?"

"He said he wanted to grab us by the scruff of our necks, force us to look at the earth from the vantage point of a quarter of a million miles away, and tell us, 'Look at that, you son of a bitch.'"

"So the toast is 'Look at that, you son of a bitch'?"

"It is."

"I can drink to that," said Cheever, and the two men clinked glasses.

"Anyone who has seen that view," said Duncan, "has said it's life changing. That perspective, I am told, puts everything in perspective."

The men sipped their wine thoughtfully.

"In 1962, President Kennedy challenged our country in his 'We choose to go to the moon' speech," said Duncan. "Like Kennedy said, we made that choice not because it was easy, but because it was hard.

"Back then our country had a purpose; we had a goal that united us. Nowadays, more than at any other time in history, I'm convinced the world also needs a goal that unites every race, creed, and color. We need another great dream. The human race needs a reason to look up instead of down. I decided that's my mission, and what I'll work to try and bring about."

"The stars are ours?"

"They're something to aim for."

"Big target," said Cheever.

"None bigger," said Duncan. "I came here to tell you that, and a few more things besides. Can we talk freely, with everything off the record?"

"Let's adjourn to the living room," said Cheever. "It can serve as the confessional."

Duncan followed Cheever; both took seats in easy chairs that were comfortable, if mismatched.

"Here's the catch-22 of what I'm about to tell you," said Duncan. "It's top secret, and yet it's unofficial. I'm told it's true, and yet I can't corroborate it. And even though I am telling you this, I have to qualify every word so that you can't say you heard it from me."

"Is this the part where one of us turns into a cockroach?" said Cheever.

"I'm a lawyer," said Duncan. "There are those who would say that already happened to me. And yet I'd like to hide behind the shield of my profession and make this conversation between us privileged."

"You mean this nonconversation that didn't take place?" asked Cheever.

"That very one."

"That's fine by me."

Duncan swirled his wine around in the glass, looking at it and thinking how to begin. Finally, he said, "When Stella was caught on camera telling the world about the Travelers, I found myself in a very difficult position. My inclination was to defend my daughter, but that was before certain individuals convinced me it would be in her best interests, as well as the country's, to imply that she was unbalanced. That was also the best way, I was told, to keep her off the Chinese intelligence radar.

"My reaction to hearing that, I am sure, was the same as yours. Why in the hell would Chinese intelligence be interested in my daughter? That's when I was told the story of a Chinese youth named Li Jie Zhang. Seven years ago Zhang disappeared in circumstances similar to Stella's. Zhang, however, only went missing for one year. He returned to his home in China, where he found his mother on her deathbed."

Cheever tried to keep his expression neutral, but he couldn't help but remember how Stella had come to the conclusion that all the children who went with the Travelers would have otherwise been doomed to die an early death. There had even been a suspect in LeRon Rivers's death—a con with a record who had been seen talking with him the day before he died.

The congressman continued his story. "After his mother died, Zhang was sent to an orphanage. There was no family to take Zhang in. His father had died when he was a baby, and there were no close relatives to adopt him.

"Zhang didn't much like being in the orphanage, and those running it were apparently not enamored with him. The staff was of the opinion that Zhang was mentally ill because of all the strange stories he told. Among those stories was that during his year away, he had been traveling with extraterrestrials.

"The background I have is sketchy here, but apparently American intelligence was on the lookout for anyone with a profile like Zhang's. Why that is, I don't know, but I can say that surreptitious arrangements were made for Zhang to be adopted in the United States.

"During his almost five years here, Zhang has thrived, although he goes by a different name now. Chronologically, he is a youth; in the field of theoretical physics, he is a giant."

"Have you talked with him?" asked Cheever.

Duncan shook his head. "His adoptive parents are trying to help him lead a normal life."

"Am I to infer from your story that American intelligence believes that seven years ago, a number of children were taken from this planet by extraterrestrials known as the Travelers?"

"I wish it was as easy as that," said Duncan. "Intelligence confirms what they call a *Pied Piper effect.* They say over a short period of time, at least a dozen children from around the planet vanished, and to date, two of those children have returned.

"You would think a congressman would be able to learn more than that, but that's as much as I can vouch for. There is plenty in the way of speculation as to why and where they went, but there seems to be more disinformation than there are facts. Under any microscope, truth and fiction blur."

"That sounds convenient," said Cheever.

"I suppose it does."

"And I'm just supposed to accept it?"

"I'm sure that's what the very few people in our intelligence community who know about Zhang would prefer. As for me, I'm glad you won't accept it."

"What does Stella say about all this?" asked Cheever. "Does she want to talk to Zhang?"

"She hasn't expressed any interest in doing that," said Duncan, "but I have this sneaking feeling that they've already been in communication."

"I want to question her," said Cheever, "before she decides to swim off."

"You don't have to worry about that. She told me that even had Wilkerson not attacked Luke, she would have turned back. The farther from shore she swam, the more convinced she was that she was making a mistake."

"Why?" asked Cheever.

"Don't you want to hear that answer from her?"

Cheever thought about it. "I suppose so," he said.

But he knew what had brought Stella back. Love had prevented her from leaving. Even the lure of the universe hadn't changed her mind.

"Is she at Luke's side now?" he asked.

"That was the only thing that kept her from joining me here," said Duncan. "She's stayed with him all this time. The doctors are talking about discharging Luke as soon as the day after tomorrow. They say his recovery is miraculous."

"In my line of work, we're not quick to credit miracles," said Cheever, "but I'm beginning to think Einstein had it right when he said, 'The most beautiful thing we can experience is the mysterious.'"

Cheever saw his unexpected guest to his car. He waved to Duncan as he drove off.

Rachel would be along any minute now. She was the one who had clued him into what Einstein had said. He was glad she'd offered him the dispensation that not everything needed an answer. Sometimes, he was coming to believe, it was enough to take part in the ride and marvel.

Cheever looked up to the moon. The full moon was past, but the satellite still loomed large in the night. He knew the moon was almost a quarter of a million miles away, but tonight it felt as close as it had ever been.

Tonight it almost felt within reach.

AUTHOR'S NOTE

It has been about fifteen years since I first came up with the idea for *The Homecoming*. Long ago I wrote up an outline and a few chapters, and then I let the idea gestate. Now and again I went on some event or trip in hopes of jump-starting the book. I visited the Salton Sea, and participated in a naval homecoming that took place in Coronado. I thought about my characters and fleshed out the book.

The more I thought about the appropriate devil's advocate for this novel, the more I began to consider bringing back Detective Orson Cheever. I first introduced Cheever in my novel *Multiple Wounds*. To date, I believe *Multiple Wounds* is the most ambitious of all my novels. It's a psychological thriller that incorporates mythology, murder, and mayhem, and in the center of that storm is Cheever. Because I was allowed to work with San Diego Police Department's Homicide Team IV, my Cheever character became a special creation, and *The Homecoming* allowed me the opportunity to reintroduce him. In the first book, Cheever had to deal with goddesses (or at least the manifestation of them); in this book, he is confronting the notion of extraterrestrials. I never make it easy on the poor guy, but he is a cop who loves the challenge.

I suppose I am the same way. *The Homecoming* was not an easy book to write. I have written classic whodunits, with carefully placed red herrings and the mystery neatly tied up in the end. This wasn't one of those books. I know some readers might not like certain ambiguities in this novel, but I would say that there are some cases, just like life itself, that defy easy explanation.

The mystery genre is broad and encompasses many subgenres. Still, even within the genre, typically you are dealing with murder or multiple murders. I am fortunate that my publisher, Thomas & Mercer, and my editors there, have never required me to have a murder in my mysteries. To my thinking, you can have an intriguing mystery without a body. After all, a mystery is an investigation into something. In my novels *St. Nick* and *The Homecoming*, I eschewed murder as the focal point of the books, and am appreciative my publisher allowed me that latitude.

I was a boy when Neil Armstrong walked on the moon on July 20, 1969. It was well past my bedtime when I watched Armstrong take his "giant leap for mankind" along with the rest of my family. I have had many wonderful experiences in my lifetime, but nothing has ever grabbed me like Armstrong's moon walk. In the years since, I can't think of how many times I have looked up at the moon and thought with incredulity: *We have walked there.*

Despite all the technological advances over the last fifty years, there is nothing that tells the universe that "we have arrived" more than humanity's footprints on the moon. Is it any wonder that I wanted to write a mystery and sprinkle it with a pinch or two of stardust?

Thank you for taking the journey with me.

—Alan Russell

June 14, 2017

ACKNOWLEDGMENTS

When you write about cops, it's always nice to have friends in law enforcement looking over your shoulder, making sure you get it right. Dave Putnam was a deputy sheriff in Southern California for thirty years and was kind enough to answer all my questions. These days, Dave has hung up his badge and has become an accomplished writer. Luckily, he still carves out time to answer lots of questions from writers like me.

Once again, the "usual suspects" were there for me, seeing to the many stages of publication that come with the writing of a book: Gracie, Cynthia, and Caitlin. As I wrote this novel, my triumvirate of strong women became a quartet with the addition of Jessica. I look forward to the day when more women get involved in politics and take over the running of this country. If those future leaders are anything like my quartet, the country will be in great hands.

I'd also like to thank my readers. I'm glad you've allowed me to explore so many themes. You've continued to read my novels while I've seemingly run the gamut of crime fiction, PI novels, police procedurals, capers, comedic mysteries, psychological thrillers, and suspense. Your indulgence has enabled me to be a professional writer for the past three decades.

Readers who would like to contact me can go to my website at www.alanrussell.net, "like" me on Facebook at AlanRussellMysteryAuthor, or write to me at alanrussellauthor@gmail.com.

Thank you!

ABOUT THE AUTHOR

Photo ©2012 Stathis Orphanos

Critical acclaim has greeted bestselling author Alan Russell's novels from coast to coast. *Publishers Weekly* calls him "one of the best writers in the mystery field today." The *New York Times* says, "He has a gift for dialogue," while the *Los Angeles Times* calls him a "crime fiction rara avis." Russell's novels have ranged from whodunits to comedic capers to suspense and have been nominated for most of the major awards in crime fiction. He has been awarded a Lefty, a Critics' Choice Award, and the Odin Award for Lifetime Achievement from the San Diego Writers and Editors Guild. A California native, Russell is a former collegiate basketball player who nowadays plays under the rim. The proud father of three children, Russell resides with his wife in Southern California.